DISASTER!

"What's wrong, Zach?"

"I've been looking at the long-term climate trends. You remember, you wanted to get a better fix on the greenhouse effect?"

"I remember asking you about the long-term effects of the greenhouse warming," replied Dan. "If the sea level keeps rising we'll have to build a dike around the launching center at La Guaira."

"If what I've come up with is right, and I think it is, we're in for *big* problems. I mean, major catastrophe."

"We will have to abandon the launch center?"

"It's worse than that, Dan. A whole lot worse. It's not just Astro. It's a cliff. The climate doesn't change gradually, it all of the sudden shifts and *bang!* you've got the glaciers melting down, Greenland and Antarctica melting down, the sea levels going up thirty meters, rainfall patterns *radically* shifting, all the coastlines of Earth inundated—it's a mess, a goddamned catastrophe like out of the Bible!"

"When?" Dan asked. "How soon?"

"Soon. A few decades. Maybe as soon as ten years from now. I think maybe it's already started."

"But there must be *something* we can do about it."

"Learn to swim."

EMPIRE BUILDERS

BEN BOVA

A TOM DOHERTY ASSOCIATES BOOK
NEW YORK

EMPIRE BUILDERS

Copyright © 1993 by Ben Bova

Cover art by Boris Vallejo

A Tor Book
Published by Tom Doherty Associates, Inc.
175 Fifth Avenue
New York, N.Y. 10010

Tor® is a registered trademark of Tom Doherty Associates, Inc.

ISBN: 0-812-51165-4
Library of Congress Catalog Card Number: 93-21613

First edition: September 1993
First mass market edition: March 1995

Printed in the United States of America

0 9 8 7 6 5 4 3 2

To Robin and Mike Putira

ONE

don't want your crappy little company!" said Dan Randolph.

"The hell you don't!" Willard Mitchell snapped.

Dan gave a disgusted snort and leaned back in the stiff unpadded chair. Mitchell glared across the table at him. The two lawyers, seated beside their clients, shifted uneasily in their chairs.

The room was windowless, deep underground, without even a video screen on the wall. Just bare lunar concrete lit by glareless fluorescents set behind the ceiling panels. Technically, the chamber was not a cell or even an interrogation chamber. It was a conference room where defendants could meet in private with their lawyers.

Dan Randolph fished a small oblong plastic box from his inside tunic pocket. About the size of his palm, it was a flat gray color with a single row of tiny winking lights set across its face. All the lights were green.

"No bugs in here," he muttered, adding silently to

himself, At least none that this little snooper can sniff
out.

He slipped the detector back into his pocket and
turned his gaze again to Mitchell, still glaring at him
from across the wobbly conference table. Randolph was
on the small side, but solidly built, a welterweight with
sandy hair that was turning gray at the temples. He had
a pugilist's face: strong square stubborn jaw, a nose that
had been slightly flattened by someone's fist a long time
ago. But his light gray eyes glinted with a secret amuse-
ment, as if he were inwardly laughing at the foolishness
of men, himself included.

Across the table from him Willard Mitchell was scowling grimly. Once he had been lean and athletic, a polo
champion at Princeton, a well-known young yachtsman.
But years of living in the Moon's easy gravity had softened him. Now he appeared older than Randolph, bald
pate gleaming with perspiration, badly overweight and
overwrought. Like Randolph, he was wearing business
clothes: a collarless waist-length tunic and matching
slacks. But where Dan's suit of sky blue looked trim and
new, Mitchell's pearl gray outfit was baggy, wrinkled,
rumpled; stains of sweat darkened his armpits.

"This is all your doing, Randolph," he snarled in a
heavy grating voice. "Don't think I don't know that you
set me up."

Dan raised his eyes to the glowing ceiling panels.
"Lord spare me from my friends," he said to the air. "I
can protect myself from my enemies."

Mitchell's lawyer, a sallow-skinned old man with the
build and demeanor of a cadaver, dressed in a blue so
deep it looked almost black, leaned toward his client and
whispered something that Dan could not hear.

Mitchell scowled at his lawyer, but turned back to Dan
and grumbled, "All right, all right, as long as we're stuck
here—what's your offer?"

Mitchell was on trial before the Global Economic
Council's lunar tribunal for illegally exceeding his allot-

ted quota of lunar ores. He was guilty. He knew it, his lawyers knew it, and the tribunal had the evidence to prove it. The fine that the tribunal was about to assess would bankrupt him.

Dan Randolph leaned both elbows on the rickety table and hunched forward in his chair. "First off," he said, his voice crisp with suppressed anger, "I did not set you up."

"The hell you say."

"Goddammit to hell and back! The day I turn *anybody* over to the GEC will be two weeks after the end of the world. If I wanted to grab your pissant little outfit I would've done it myself. I don't need the double-damned GEC to help me."

Mitchell fumed visibly, but held back from answering.

Randolph's lawyer, a strikingly red-haired young woman new to the Moon, was sitting attentively at her boss's left. She said mildly, "Mr. Mitchell has asked to hear your offer, Dan."

He grinned at her. "Yeah. Right."

"So?" Mitchell growled.

Randolph spread his hands. "I'll buy your stock at the current market price—"

"Which is forty percent below par because of this lawsuit."

"—and pay the fine that the GEC's going to sock you with. You continue to operate the company; you remain CEO and COO. You can buy back your shares at market value whenever you want to."

Mitchell sank back in his chair, the expression on his fleshy face somewhere between suspicion and hope. "Now, wait a minute," he said. "You buy my shares—"

"All your shares," said Randolph. "Sixty-three percent of the total outstanding, so I'm told."

The other man nodded. "You *buy* the shares. You pay the fine. I stay in charge of the company. And then I can buy the shares back?"

Randolph gave him a crooked grin. "The harder you work, the more the shares'll be worth."

"Suppose I let the company go to the dogs and leave you holding the bag?"

Randolph shrugged. "That's the risk I take. But I don't see you shitting on your own baby."

Mitchell glanced at his lawyer, who remained dead-pan, then turned back to Randolph. "I don't get it. What's in it for you?"

Dan's smile turned dazzling. "A chance to shaft Malik and his double-damned GEC. What else?"

TWO

Daniel Hamilton Randolph was the richest human being living off-Earth. While there was no dearth of suspicious souls who were convinced that no one could get that filthy rich while staying entirely within the law, for the most part Dan Randolph had earned his wealth legally.

Once, briefly, he had been accused of piracy. By Vasily Malik, who had then been director of the Russian Federation's space program. Dan had evaded the charges against him, married the Venezuelan woman Malik was engaged to, and personally broken the Russian's jaw, together with a knuckle of his own right hand.

Now, ten years later, Dan's marriage had long since ended in divorce. The woman he had loved, the woman who had thought she loved him, was now Malik's wife. And Malik himself had survived the turmoil and treachery in the Kremlin to become the new Russian Federation's representative on the Global Economic Council.

In the middle of the twenty-first century, space was

becoming vitally important to the Earth's global economy. Even the United States, which had abandoned its space program decades earlier, was now building factories in orbit and allowing its citizens to operate mining facilities on the Moon. Under GEC supervision, of course. The GEC had legal control of all extraterrestrial operations, from the teams of explorers combing the rusted sands of Mars to the hordes of insect-sized probes examining Jupiter and the outer planets; from the factories and laboratories in orbit around the Earth to the mining operations on the Moon that fed them.

Dan Randolph had amassed his fortune from space. When America had floundered and waffled, too preoccupied with earthly problems to move boldly in space, Dan had battled his way to a job with the Japanese building the first solar power satellite. "When the going gets tough," he announced to anyone who would listen, "the tough get going—to where the going's easier."

Not that the going was altogether easy among the Japanese. It was on the Moon, in a brawl with four sneering Japanese mining engineers, that his nose had been broken. But he had won that fight, and won the grudging respect of all his fellow workers. Some of those fellow workers were women, and somehow Dan managed to be highly attractive to them. His rather ordinary features seemed to intrigue them. "Is it my smile?" he once asked a buxom Swedish electronics technician who shared his bed for a while. She considered carefully before she answered, "Your smile, yes. And your eyes. There is the devil in your eyes."

By the time he had returned to Earth he was a moderately wealthy man. He started his own company, Astro Manufacturing, and headquartered it in sprawling Houston, where a handful of entrepreneurs were desperately trying to start a new industrial revolution despite their own government's persistent indifference and occasional outright hostility. Houston, because by then Dan had met Morgan Scanwell, an earnest, incorruptible young politician who had the energy and drive to match Dan's own. Scanwell helped Dan to make the contacts that funded the fledgling Astro Manufacturing. Dan raised money for Scanwell's political campaigns. They joked between themselves that one day Scanwell would be in the White House and Dan would be on Mars.

They made an unlikely duo. Morgan Scanwell was austere, abstemious, a man whose ultimate guide was his deeply held religious faith. Dan Randolph was a hell-raising scoundrel who was out to make as many millions as he could while cutting a swath through the female population of every community in which he lived.

The glue that held the two men together was Morgan's wife, Jane Scanwell: a tall, regal woman with long, flowing copper red hair, alabaster skin, and eyes the color of a green icy fjord. Utterly loyal to her husband, Jane had no other goal in life than to see Morgan Scanwell elected President of the United States.

She was unobtainable. Naturally, Dan fell in love with her. It was impossible; it was sinfully treacherous. But as Morgan Scanwell inevitably abandoned his moral rectitude and succumbed at last to the women who sought to touch his power, Jane came at last to Dan Randolph's bed. To their mutual surprise, she discovered that she had fallen in love with this scoundrel, her husband's best friend.

By the time Scanwell was campaigning for the presidency, Jane had painfully terminated her affair with Dan. She had the strength to end it; the White House was more important to her than romance. "The country needs Morgan, Dan," she said, convincing herself by trying to convince him. "And he needs me. We can't jeopardize his chances by sneaking around behind his back. If anyone found out he'd be finished."

Morgan Scanwell was governor of Texas then. Dan's personal fortune was nearing a billion dollars. He knew that Jane's mind was made up, so he went back to his old ways and became notorious again for his sexual pursuits.

While he was squandering his energies on every woman he desired, Jane allowed a compliant Oklahoma legislature to confer a residency upon her, so she could run for vice-president alongside her husband.

Morgan was elected president, only to face a string of crises that killed him. The Russian Federation emerged from its own desperate internal cataclysms with a new belligerency. After coming so perilously close to dissolution and civil war that the rest of the world expected the tottering new Federation to collapse, the Russians regained control of their sprawling land and peoples. The United States, half disarmed, was suddenly confronted with a resurgent, bellicose Moscow. America had long since lost real interest in space, and had allowed Japan and Europe to take the leadership in space developments. Now the Russians, with the world's most powerful rockets and still armed with thousands of ballistic missiles, quickly took a stranglehold on all space operations—military as well as civilian.

The U.S. economy was foundering. The Russians were making demands on an unprepared America. Congress studied opinion polls that showed the American people were in no mood for a war that would rain hydrogen bombs on their heads.

America bowed. And Morgan Scanwell suffered a fatal stroke. Dan Randolph left Texas when Congress revoked all federal licenses for space operations. Astro Manufacturing moved to Venezuela, and Jane Scanwell became the first woman President of the United States.

She still held a deep passion for Dan Randolph. But now that passion had turned to hatred.

THREE

The Global Economic Council's lunar tribunal was based in Copernicus City. Like all the other centers on the Moon, Copernicus was deep underground, gouged out of lunar rock to protect its human population from the lethal radiation and enormous temperature swings up on the airless surface.

Ostensibly, the GEC was politically neutral. It insisted that all lunar habitats be given geographic names rather than being named after national biases. Thus the Russian penal colony was officially titled Aristarchus Center, even though most lunar residents still called it by its older name: Lunagrad. On all GEC maps, the great Japanese manufacturing center was called Alphonsus City, rather than Yamagata Industries Lunar Operation #1. The place where humans had first set foot on the Moon's dusty surface was still called Tranquillity Base; the American astronauts had, even then, been thinking in non-nationalistic terms.

The lunar tribunal had all the aspects of a court of law.

There was a banc with high-backed seats for three judges, although officially they were titled "conciliators."

But as Dan Randolph took his seat among the rows of benches for onlookers, he thought that the conciliators never really reconciled grievances; all he had ever seen them do was take a man's hard-earned wealth and hand it over to the GEC. He looked with mixed emotions at the sky blue flag of the United Nations standing to one side of the banc. He knew the world could not afford the divisive competition of nationalism, especially when even the smallest nation could manufacture biological weapons that could slaughter millions. But the alternative was a global government to which there was no appeal: a worldwide bureaucracy that was gradually imposing a dictatorship by committee, leveling everything on Earth to the same flat gray dullness. And now they were extending their grip to the Moon.

There was no jury box in this courtroom. The three conciliators listened to the evidence and made their decision. There was no appeal, either.

Mitchell and his zombie of a lawyer entered the tribunal chamber from the side door. The robot recording machine said, "All rise," and the three conciliators trooped in from the door behind the banc. They wore ordinary business clothes rather than robes. Two men and one woman, the chief of the team.

Dan glanced at his own lawyer, sitting beside him. Katherine Williams was a pert, young, ambitious redhead who had swiftly risen to the top of his legal department despite fierce competition. She knew all the tales about Dan Randolph's skirt-chasing. When Dan had first interviewed her for a job, she had firmly announced that she did not sleep with the boss. Not yet, Dan had thought, eying her with approval. Now, several years later, she was his top lawyer, and he wondered what her body looked like underneath the tailored royal blue jacket and fitted gold slacks she was wearing.

"The tribunal is ready to pass sentence," said the

woman occupying the middle chair up on the banc. Her
voice was sharp, cutting. "Does the defendant have anything to say in his own behalf?"

Mitchell's lawyer got to his feet, a tall scarecrow
dressed like a funeral director. With a voice to match, he
intoned sorrowfully, "The defendant deeply regrets the
actions which have led to this proceeding, Your Honors.
He regrets his actions so deeply, in fact, that he has
divested himself of all ownership in the company that he
has founded and directed, Mitchell Mining and Smelting.
His remorse has led him to repudiate the ownership of
his own company; this is similar to renouncing parent-
hood of one's own child. It is a deeply wrenching emo-
tional . . ."

"Counselor," snapped the chief conciliator, "are you
telling us that Mr. Mitchell has sold off his company?"

"Yes, Your Honor. And I respectfully request that this
act of true remorse and regret be considered punishment
enough for his mistaken actions of the past."

The woman snorted disdainfully and glanced at her
two male colleagues. "To whom has he sold his company?" she asked.

"To Astro Manufacturing, Incorporated, Your
Honor."

"I see. Is there a representative of Astro Manufacturing in this chamber?"

Dan got to his feet. "I represent Astro, Your Honor.
My name is Daniel Hamilton Randolph."

All three judges smiled at Dan the way Torquemada
might have smiled at a rabbi. Dan smiled back and said:

"Your Honors, Astro is quite willing to pay the penalty that you have already decided to assess against
Mitchell Mining and Smelting."

Dan knew that the penalty was already recorded in
their computer file of this proceeding. If they changed it
now, because Astro could afford an astronomically
larger fine or because they hated Dan Randolph's guts,
it would give Astro's lawyers a perfect excuse to claim

prejudice and demand a new trial.

The three judges put their heads together and conferred briefly, hands over the tiny microphones imbedded in the desktop before them.

Finally the chief conciliator, her face grim, leveled a hard stare at Dan. "Mr. Randolph, this tribunal cannot help but believe that your acquisition of Mitchell Mining and Smelting is nothing less than an obvious ploy to thwart justice."

Dan put on an expression of injured innocence. "But Your Honor, the truth is exactly the opposite. I'm sure that the fine you've assessed against Mitchell would bankrupt his company and drive him out of business. His assets would become the property of the Global Economic Council. The GEC would have to assume the burden of running the mining and smelting operation—"

"GEC management would see that the operation remained within its allotted quotas," the chief conciliator snapped angrily. "There would be no attempts to illegally increase profits by dumping excess ores on the world market and driving prices down from their mandated levels."

Dan's smile turned slightly impish. "Yes, we all know GEC operations never show any profits. Somehow, when the GEC takes over a company, it always seems to run at a loss."

His lawyer made a polite little cough, a warning to get off that tack. This is no time for sticking the needle into them, she was telling Dan.

Still facing the judges, Dan went on, "However, Astro Manufacturing is quite willing to pay the fine you've assessed. And Astro will manage Mitchell Mining and Smelting at a profit, I'm sure, while staying within the GEC's mandated quotas. That will generate more tax revenues for the GEC. Everybody gains. It's a win-win situation."

"And what of Mr. Mitchell?" the chief conciliator demanded. "What punishment will he receive for his blatant disregard of the law?"

Dan smiled his brightest. "Why, he'll have to work for me. That ought to be punishment enough."

Dan and his lawyer rode alone in his private trolley back to Astro's main base at the great ringed plain of Alphonsus, where Yamagata Industries had set up its first and still largest lunar center.

One of the privileges of great wealth was privacy. Another was convenience. Dan was one of only two men who had a private trolley vehicle on the Moon. The other was Saito Yamagata, once Dan's boss, for many years now his friend and sometime partner.

Like cable cars that climb mountains or cross chasms on Earth, the lunar trolleys were suspended from cables made of lunar aluminum and titanium. Cryogenically cooled, the cables carried electricity at low resistance that powered the trolleys swiftly and smoothly ten meters above the battered lunar terrain.

"You almost blew it, boss," said his lawyer. She was sitting in a softly yielding padded chair, swirling a drink she had fixed for herself at the minibar.

Dan looked up from the display screen built into his desktop. "Close doesn't count, except in horseshoes, Scarlett."

"My *name* is Katherine," she said, with a slight frown. "My friends call me Kate."

"And what should I call you?"

The frown turned into a grin. They had played this little game a thousand times in the years that she had worked for Dan Randolph. "Ms. Williams will do."

"Scarlett," he said. "With that bricktop of yours, your name has to be Scarlett."

She went back to frowning.

"That *is* your natural hair color, isn't it?" Before she could answer, Dan added, "Doesn't matter. It's gorgeous. Never change it."

She cocked an eyebrow as if she were going to retort,

but thought better of it and sipped at her drink. Dan went back to scrolling through the messages that had accumulated during the morning. One of them was from Zachary Freiberg, his chief scientist.

Dan routed all the other messages to the people he hired to get things done. Zach Freiberg he called himself. The scientist's message was marked Urgent and asked Dan to call immediately, regardless of time zones on Earth. Dan called out Freiberg's name to the computer and within seconds his face appeared on the screen.

"What's wrong, Zach?"

Freiberg was obviously in his office in California. Tawny brown hills showed through the window behind him, with palm trees and cypresses framing the view. From the angle of the sun Dan guessed it was midmorning in Pasadena. He registered all this during the couple of seconds it took for his words to reach Earth and Freiberg's reply to return the quarter-million miles to the Moon.

Zachary Freiberg had one of those faces that would look boyish to the day he died: round apple cheeks, round chin, soft features and soft blue eyes. His wiry strawberry-blond hair no longer flopped over his broad forehead, though; in the ten years that Dan had known Zack, the slow recession of his hairline had been the one sign of aging he could see.

Zack looked troubled. "Can we go to security mode?"

"I'm on the trolley, moving too fast for a laser link."

Freiberg bit his lower lip.

"We can scramble," Dan suggested. "Or wait till I'm back in the office and we can use the laser."

"Scramble, then," said Freiberg two and a half seconds later.

Wondering what could be making him so upset, Dan typed in his private security code. The screen flickered briefly, then steadied once again.

"What is it?" he asked.

Unconsciously, Freiberg hunched closer to his screen,

like a man about to whisper a secret in a neighborhood bar.

"I've been looking at the long-term climate trends," he said. "You remember, you wanted to get a better fix on the greenhouse effect?"

Dan nodded, glancing at Kate Williams. She was staring through the window by her seat, watching the pock-marked Mare Cognitum whiz by. How big are her ears? Dan wondered.

"I remember asking you about the long-term effects of the greenhouse warming, yeah," he replied to Freiberg. "If the sea level keeps rising we'll have to build a dike around the launching center at La Guaira."

"Right." Freiberg's round face took on an even more anguished look. "Dan—if what I've come up with is right, and I think it is, we're in for *big* problems. I mean, major catastrophe."

"Will we have to abandon the launch center?"

"It's worse than that, Dan. A whole lot worse. It's not just Astro. It's the whole fucking world!"

Dan had never heard Freiberg use that expletive before. The guy's scared!

Without waiting for Dan to ask, Freiberg went on, "It's a cliff, Dan. The climate doesn't change gradually, it all of a sudden shifts and *bang!* you've got the glaciers melting down, Greenland and Antarctica melting down, the sea levels going up thirty meters, rainfall patterns *radically* shifting, all the coastlines on Earth inundated—it's a mess, a goddamned catastrophe like out of the Bible!"

Dan sank back in his chair. Kate Williams saw the expression on his face and stared at him.

"Nobody's considered the gas hydrates in the deep-sea sediments," Freiberg was almost babbling, "and under the tundra all across the Arctic. They release methane when they're disturbed and the pressure conditions—"

"When?" Dan asked. "How soon?"

"Soon. A few decades. Maybe as soon as ten years

from now." He ran a hand across his forehead. "I think maybe it's already started."

"You're sure? Certain?"

Freiberg nodded unhappily. "I've had half a dozen people check it out. It's real. Floods, killer storms, croplands turned to deserts—the whole thing. All that stuff the environmentalists have been spouting for the past fifty years. It's all going to happen, Dan. And it'll happen so fast there's practically nothing we can do about it."

"We've got ten years?"

"Maybe more. Maybe less."

Dan sucked in a deep breath. He knew he should feel alarmed, frightened. But he did not. He was more annoyed than anything else. His mind accepted what Freiberg was saying; he knew intellectually that this was a real emergency looming, a disaster of incalculable proportions. But deep in his innermost animal being he felt no terror, no panic. The reality of this threat was too remote, too academic, to spark his emotions.

And that's the real danger of it, he told himself. It's too far in the future to stir the guts, even though it's close enough to kill us all.

To Freiberg he said, "Haul your ass up here, Zach. I want to go through this with you inch by inch."

Freiberg nodded glumly. "The numbers aren't going to change, boss."

"Yeah, I know. But there must be *something* we can do about it."

"Learn to swim," said Freiberg.

FOUR

The Global Economic Council was headquartered in Paris, a city just beginning to brighten once again after the turmoil of the past few decades.

Western Europe had found it much more difficult to digest Eastern Europe than even the most pessimistic economic forecaster had predicted. After more than four decades of stagnation and repression, the peoples of Eastern Europe shouted for democracy and freedom. What they really wanted was the economic well-being of their Western neighbors, the higher standard of living that they saw in the capitalist nations.

But the capitalist idea of working hard was foreign to them. At first they demanded bread and meat and milk for their children. And they got it, for it was impossible for the West to deny humanitarian aid to their impoverished brethren. But quickly they began to demand the toys and trinkets of capitalist societies—without working to produce the wealth that could pay for them.

A whole generation simmered in distrust and bitter

animosities as slowly, painfully, the peoples of the formerly socialist world learned that it was the capitalists who truly followed Marx's original dictum: "From each according to his ability; to each according to his work."

At last the Poles and Czechs and Romanians and even the Russians learned to work once again, learned to produce the goods and services that paid for their happiness. The Hungarians reasserted their marketing craft. The centuries-old hatreds between ethnic groups were subdued—but not entirely forgotten—in the new rush to obtain expensive gadgets and personal wealth. Now Paris was a happy city once more.

The economic boom was partially fueled from space.

Much of the wealth that allowed Europe and the rest of the world to prosper came from the energy, the raw materials, the manufactured products produced in space. From the Moon came raw materials for space construction and isotopic fuel for Earth's fusion power generators. From factories in space came new alloys and electronics crystals, medicines and vaccines of incredible purity, solarvoltaic cells cheap and efficient enough to turn a family home's rooftop into a self-sufficient solar energy generator. And hovering in orbit around the Earth, giant solar power satellites converted unfiltered sunlight into electricity and beamed it to energy-hungry cities and factories cleanly, without polluting the atmosphere.

The economic boom that was just getting started was heavily dependent on this new wealth streaming in from space. Five and a half centuries after Europe began the exploitation of the New World, all of Earth was beginning to benefit from the exploitation of cislunar space—a harsh frontier that was rich in real wealth and entirely unpopulated, except for the ten thousand or so men and women of Earth who went there to find their fortunes.

Slowly the Earth was healing from the wounds inflicted by the Industrial Age. Slowly the smokestacks were being replaced by fusion or solar energy. Slowly the petroleum-burning engines were converting to methane or synfuels. Slowly the burgeoning population of Earth was stabilizing at the twelve-billion level.

Too slowly.

Vasily Malik was not concerned, at this precise moment, with these great questions of wealth and the environment. Head of the Russian Federation's delegation to the Global Economic Council, Malik was deep in conversation with the woman who had been the chief conciliator at the trial of Willard Mitchell.

"You have all the necessary documentation?" Malik asked.

He studied the conciliator's face while his words headed toward the Moon at the speed of light. She had a lean, hard face, not easily given to smiling. A spinster's face, Malik thought, knowing that it was chauvinist of him but thinking he was right just the same.

Vasily Malik was handsome enough to be a video star. He was tall for a Russian, brushing six feet; broad-shouldered and heavily muscled, he kept his body in good trim through a rigid schedule of daily exercise. Once he had worn his golden hair modishly long. Now it was trimmed to an almost military burr. His ice blue eyes could sparkle with laughter, but at this moment they were glittering with hope born of a deep and abiding hatred.

"Yes," said the chief conciliator. "He talked Mitchell into selling out to him. If we had known that it would be Randolph we were dealing with we would have tripled the fine. Quadrupled it!"

Malik's broad features eased into a relaxed smile. "You did your best. Randolph is a clever rascal, we must grant him that."

When his words reached her, she nodded bitterly. "It's not fair. Mitchell was guilty. He should have been driven out of business. But now Randolph owns his company and he'll continue to operate."

Malik made a few sympathetic noises and ended the

conversation by asking her to send all the documentation on the trial to him immediately.

Then he leaned back in his imposing leather chair, put his booted feet on his immaculately gleaming desktop, and waited for the fax machine to begin spitting out Dan Randolph's comeuppance. I only wish it were his death sentence, Vasily Malik said to himself.

Nearly three hours later, at eleven o'clock in the morning, Paris time, the weekly meeting of the Global Economic Council's executive committee convened in the small conference room down the corridor from Malik's office.

Muhammed Shariff Sibuti of Malaysia, chairman of the committee for this session, was already seated at the head of the gleaming table when Malik entered the room. A lightweight, in every dimension, thought Malik. Sibuti looked shriveled and old, too small for the chair in which he sat. His starched white high-collared shirt made his wrinkled dark skin look almost as black as the leather of the chair's padding.

"We must begin," Sibuti said, in a voice that sounded like rusty hinges groaning. "We have a very long agenda. A very difficult agenda."

The other committee members were milling around the room, largely ignoring their chairman. Malik saw Jane Scanwell at the long table that had been set out with refreshments and finger foods.

He went to her, under the pretext of pouring himself a glass of hot tea from the silver samovar in the center of the table.

"I have good news from Copernicus," he said softly.

Jane Scanwell glanced up from the coffee cup she had just filled.

The former President of the United States was a handsome woman, nearly as tall as Malik in her heels. She was wearing a skirted suit of forest green over a pale green silk blouse. Her richly auburn hair was neatly coiffed up off her long graceful neck. She surveyed Malik with the cool green eyes of a Norse goddess.

"What did you say?"

"Good news from Copernicus," Malik repeated. "Dan Randolph has made one clever move too many. He has fallen into a trap that I concocted for him."

Jane's sculptured face gave no hint of emotion. She merely said, "You must tell me about it, after the meeting."

"I'll be happy to."

As the meeting droned on, Malik could barely suppress his eager anticipation. Randolph had bested him in so many ways, over the years. It was Randolph who had broken the Russian monopoly on space industry, after Malik had slaved for a decade to drive all competition out of business. Randolph had married the woman Malik had been engaged to, and even though she had divorced the American eventually and had come back to him, there was no real love in their marriage. Both he and his wife were settling for second best.

But Randolph had been in love with Jane Scanwell, once. Perhaps he still was. Perhaps that was what destroyed his marriage, really, and gave the impetus to his philandering ways. How ironic for this womanizer to desire the Ice Queen, the immovable, unobtainable Jane Scanwell! How delicious that Jane Scanwell will be the instrument of Randolph's destruction.

The meeting ended at last and Malik followed Scanwell to her office. It was a spacious corner room with a view of the Eiffel Tower, no less. Fit trappings for a former head of state.

Instead of going to her desk, Jane sat in an armchair next to one of the windows.

"Fix yourself a drink," she said, nodding toward the bar built into the far wall.

Malik said, "Thank you. A good idea after such a long and utterly dry meeting. Can I make something for you?"

"Just a glass of filtered water with a twist of lime, please."

Malik found the bottled water and a dish of fresh limes in the little refrigerator. And vodka in the freezer compartment. When he took the two drinks back toward her, he saw that Jane was eying him carefully, her long legs crossed, the expression on her face unfathomable.

He handed her the water, then touched his glass of vodka to hers. *"Zah vahsheh zdahrovyeh,"* he murmured.

"Here's mud in your eye," Jane replied, with just the ghost of a smile on her lips.

Malik took the armchair on the other side of the window and rolled it next to Jane's.

"Now what were you telling me about cooking Dan Randolph's goose?" she asked.

He grinned at her. "You are full of Americanisms this afternoon."

"I'm an American. What about Randolph?"

"He has just bought out a small competitor of his, a man named Mitchell who owned a mining operation on the Moon."

"What of it?"

"He bought Mitchell's company because Mitchell was about to be hit with a stiff fine by the lunar tribunal for exceeding his allotment of ores."

Jane took another sip of her water, then said, "I see. Dan can afford to pay the fine but Mitchell can't. So Dan buys him out at a bargain-basement price."

"Exactly so."

"So how does that get Dan in trouble?"

Malik's grin spread into a broad happy smile. "We passed a regulation last spring to the effect that any attempt to subvert or avoid the rulings of the GEC is punishable by confiscation."

"We did?" She looked surprised.

Malik made an expansive gesture. "Oh, the wording is rather obscure, something about 'joint and several liability.' The lawyers worked very hard to phrase it so that no one would notice it. And the regulation was buried among several dozens of other minor changes to existing rules. But the regulation was passed; it exists and it is legally binding."

Jane's eyes seemed to focus beyond Malik, as if she were looking at something that was not physically in the room with them.

"Do you mean that you can use that regulation to confiscate Dan's holdings? All of them? All of Astro Manufacturing and everything else he owns?"

Malik nodded. "He stepped into my trap and I intend to snap it shut on him."

"Lots of luck."

"You don't believe I can do it?"

"I believe that Dan is very resourceful, very powerful, and very stubborn. He won't give up easily."

"You can be of great help in this."

"I can?"

"Yes," said Malik, pulling his chair even closer to her. "It will be easier to deal with him here on Earth, rather than on the Moon. He has too many friends there, too many places where he can hide himself away while his lawyers try to find loopholes he can escape through."

"You don't intend to jail him, do you?" For the first time a hint of emotion showed on Jane's face. Malik could not decide whether it was fear or anger. Or something else.

"It would be better," he said slowly, "if he were . . . under protective custody, let us say. Someplace where he can be held incommunicado—only until the confiscation orders have been processed and carried out, of course."

"That's not legal."

"Not in America, I realize that. But the Global Economic Council's regulations do not include a Bill of Rights, you know. And there are many nations on Earth where he could be held indefinitely."

Her face hardened.

"Oh, I don't mean to put him in a dungeon," Malik said, smiling easily. "A small island, perhaps. Some tropical paradise where he can have everything he wants:

wine, women and song."

"Everything except his freedom."

"And his holdings." ·

Jane thought a moment, then smiled back at the Russian. "I know just the place: a coral atoll out in the middle of the Pacific. A very romantic spot, as a matter of fact."

"Excellent!" Malik resisted the urge to rub his hands together gleefully. Instead, he asked, "Is this a place you know from personal experience?"

"My husband and I honeymooned there, a thousand years ago," said Jane.

That took Malik aback. But only for a moment. "I see. Do you think that you could somehow get him to meet you there?"

She nodded. "I'm sure he'd come if I asked him to."

Yes, Malik thought. Dan Randolph would come flying to this woman. What hatred she must have for him! To turn the site of her honeymoon into a prison for her former lover. Ah, women! They are far fiercer than men.

"There is no sense getting angry at me," said Napoleon Bazain, over the muted roar of the plane's engines. "I am merely a messenger. A middleman."

Sergio Alvarez stared down his patrician nose at the Frenchman. "You are a parasite."

Bazain smiled blandly. "No, I work for a parasite."

"It is all the same to me," Alvarez muttered.

The twin-engine plane was cruising high above the Madeira River, an hour out of Manaus. Below them, where there had once been pristine forest there now stretched long ugly brown gashes of bare ground, scars left by the timber companies and the landowners who had chased away the native Indians in the vain hope of turning the area into grazing land for cattle.

Up front in the cockpit sat the pilot and the ecologist, a young university graduate who still had stars in his eyes. Back here, sitting on bare bucket seats amid the big tanks of seed and fertilizer, Alvarez faced reality.

"Why be angry?" asked the Frenchman. His smile was still showing, but his eyes looked uneasy, as if he were worried that this hot-blooded Castilian might toss him out of the plane in a fit of righteous anger.

Bazain was small, light of frame, almost delicate. His face, though, was fleshy with the beginnings of jowls. His thinning hair was slicked back as if he were about to go out on a date. He wore a custom-tailored silk business suit. As far as Alvarez could tell, he was unarmed.

Sergio Alvarez, regional director of the GEC's reforestation program, looked every inch the grandee from Madrid. Thin aristocratic nose, sculpted cheekbones, hair as silver as a newly minted coin. Yet he wore a faded windbreaker and chinos that had lost their crease years ago.

"Listen to reason," Bazain said, almost pleading. "The very fact that I'm on this plane with you proves that we have no intention of doing harm."

"Not yet."

"Not at all—if you simply divert the funds as you've been asked to do."

Alvarez felt his blood seething. "That money is for the reforesting of this jungle! How dare you and your . . . your thugs—how dare you demand extortion money from this program?"

Bazain hunched forward in the bucket seat, rubbing his palms on the knees of his expensive trousers. "It's not me. I only work for them."

"The Mafia." Alvarez spat the word.

"That's an old-time phrase. Nobody uses that term anymore."

"Whoever they are, they are crooks."

"They are businessmen."

"Who want to steal money that is needed to bring this rain forest back to health!"

Bazain sighed deeply. Then, with obviously strained

patience, he explained once again, "What does it matter if we get a share of the program's money? The money comes from the Global Economic Council, doesn't it? And where do they get it? From taxes. They take it from all the national governments in the world, and from the big multinational corporations."

"It doesn't matter where the funding comes from."

"Certainly it matters! They collect billions, hundreds of billions. Every year! So you siphon some of the money they give you to us. All you have to do is go back and tell them that you need more funding. Tell them that the program is more expensive than you had thought it would be. That's what everybody else does."

"I will not!" Alvarez snapped. "Every centavo given to this program will be spent on reforesting the jungle."

Bazain shook his head sadly.

"Don't you understand?" said Alvarez. "The world is being choked to death by the greenhouse effect. The best way to reverse the greenhouse is to plant trees. Billions of trees! Replace what has been cut down and then go on to plant still more. Others are seeding the oceans to grow more algae; they take up carbon dioxide and . . ."

"Spare me!" Bazain raised his hands.

"You don't want to understand, is that it? You don't want to know."

"You must understand something," said Bazain, his voice taking on a hard edge. "Unless we get our share of your money, you will be killed. That is the message I was told to give you. My superiors have been very patient, but their patience is finished. You pay or you die. This plane will be blown out of the air. Your young scientist up there will be killed. Maybe your wife and children, too. They are capable of it."

Alvarez said nothing. He was panting, his nostrils flaring like a thoroughbred racehorse's.

"And if such violence happens," Bazain went on smoothly, "what will come of your precious program then? Even if the GEC presses on with it, it will cost much more, won't it? Dealing with us is far cheaper. And safer."

Alvarez had no answer.

FIVE

Dan Randolph stood at the long, sweeping glassteel observation window that curved across the far end of Alphonsus City's main dome. Away from the GEC tribunal and the need to be dressed respectably, he wore his usual sky blue coveralls, faded from long use, wrinkled and comfortable. No name patch on its breast; merely the sturdy simple logo of Astro Manufacturing. He had no need to be recognized.

"The people who know who I am don't need to be reminded," he often said. "The ones who don't, don't need to know."

The great ringed plain of Alphonsus was so wide that Dan could not see its far side from the observation port where he stood. The Moon's abrupt horizon cut across the tired old ringwall mountains like the brink of eternity, nothing but utterly black sky and solemn unblinking stars hanging beyond its edge.

The floor of the plain was dotted with lunar factories, open to vacuum of course, tended by sterile robots under remote control by sweaty, breathing humans sitting safely underground in their offices inside Alphonsus City. Each factory was protected from the occasional meteoroid by a gracefully curved roof of light honeycomb metal. Most of the roofs bore the flying-heron symbol of Yamagata Industries. A few were marked with the more prosaic ASTRO logo of Dan's company.

On the other side of the ringwall, Dan's company ran a fleet of automated vehicles patiently plying the Mare Nubium, scooping up the top layers of the lunar regolith the way a herd of cows grazes a field. There was oxygen in the powdery upper layers of the lunar soil, and aluminum, titanium, plenty of silicon and even some iron. But the most precious element in the regolith was an isotope of helium—helium-three—born in the Sun and carried across interplanetary space on the solar wind to be imbedded in the porous regolith over long eons.

Helium-three made fusion power practical on Earth. Lunar fuel was beginning to light the overcrowded cities of Earth, cleanly, cheaply, with minuscule pollution and radioactive waste.

It was making Dan Randolph a new fortune.

If he had thought about it, he would have grinned at the cosmic justice of it. Helium-three was created in the Sun by the fusion processes that made Earth's daystar shine. Some of it was wafted off into space; a scant fraction of that found its way to the Moon. Humans mined the stuff and shipped it to their home world, where it was used to power fusion generators: man-made artificial suns that generated the electrical power to run an overpopulated world.

It was elegantly beautiful. And profitable.

But Dan was thinking of other things as he waited for the shuttle to land. In the hip pocket of his coveralls was a message from Jane Scanwell inviting him to meet her at Tetiaroa. No reason given. Just a one-line note, as impersonal as a bill of lading:

IMPERATIVE WE MEET AT TETIAROA AS
SOON AS POSSIBLE.   JANE.

Imperative, Dan repeated to himself. What could be so
imperative? Why Tetiaroa, way out in the middle of the
Pacific? Why won't she answer my calls to her? What's
happening down there that she has to see me as soon as
possible?

A flicker of light caught his eye.

Craning his neck, Dan could just make out the angular
ungainly shape of the shuttle falling like a rock in slow
motion. Another puff of its retros, the cold gas glittering
briefly in the sunlight, and the spraddle-legged vehicle
slowed. It seemed to rock slightly, then squirted several
brief jets of retro fire as it steadied and settled down
softly on the landing pad, a full kilometer out on the floor
of the plain from the edge of the dome where Dan was
standing.

Half an hour later, Zach Freiberg lay sprawled across
the couch in Dan's office, a morose expression on his
boyish face. In the ten years Dan had known Freiberg, it
still surprised him to realize how tall the scientist really
was. Zach gave the impression of being a small, soft
pooh-bear of a guy. But when they stood face-to-face, he
was several inches taller than Dan.

"It's real, boss," he was saying mournfully, his head
resting on one arm of the couch, his booted feet on the
other. "I've had the best people in the business check out
the numbers."

Dan, seated tensely behind his desk, said, "Now let me
get this straight. You're saying that the greenhouse effect
is going to hit suddenly, within ten years. Right?"

Freiberg stared up at the paneled ceiling. "It's already
hitting, Dan. You know that. Droughts in the middle
latitudes; floods in the tropics. Killer storms getting
worse every year."

"Yeah, but you were saying that the ice caps—"

"Will melt suddenly, right. Not gradually. Ten years from now the Antarctic and Greenland caps will start to melt down. Ten years after that, sea levels all around the world will be five-ten meters higher than they are now."

"Fifteen to thirty feet?" Dan's voice sounded hollow, even to himself.

Freiberg nodded.

"What can we do about it?"

"Not a helluva lot," Freiberg said.

"There must be something!"

Freiberg pulled himself up to a sitting position and faced Dan. He had been a planetary geochemist ten years earlier, when Dan had hired him. Since then he had been forced to dabble in so many disciplines that now Dan thought of him as Astro's resident genius: a man who understood what made planets work.

"Dan," he said slowly, "it's taken a couple of hundred years for the greenhouse effect to make itself felt. It's an accelerating phenomenon. Every year it goes faster. It builds and builds. And then it hits a discontinuity. In ten years it'll reach the point where the ice caps start to go."

"But I thought the greenhouse was mostly due to industrial pollution: carbon dioxide and other crap that we pour into the atmosphere."

Freiberg nodded.

"Then, if we stop polluting the atmosphere," Dan said, "won't the greenhouse effect stop, too?"

The nod turned into a weary shake of his head. "Nice try, boss. But there are two problems with it: One, the greenhouse effect is already here. Global temperatures are already high enough to cause disastrous changes in climate, worldwide."

"Yeah, I know," said Dan impatiently. "But if we stop—"

Pulling himself up to a sitting position, Freiberg said, "That's the second problem." His round-cheeked face went tense, grim. "How the fuck are you going to stop

twelve billion people from shitting up the atmosphere? In
ten years or less."

Dan leaned back in his chair, shocked at the younger
man's sudden fury.

"I've done my homework, boss," Freiberg said. "I've
gone through the numbers. You know what we're up
against? We'd have to cut down on the cee-oh-two we put
into the atmosphere by ninety percent. *Ninety percent!*
For starters!"

"Well," Dan said weakly, "I didn't say it would be
easy."

Freiberg's anger dissipated. He went back to being
melancholy. "It can't be done, Dan. There's nothing that
you or I or anybody can do. Mother Nature's going to
solve the problem for us—by killing several billion people."

But Dan said, "Goddammit to hell and back, I'm not
going to sit here and watch the world drown! There must
be *something* we can do!"

"Like what?"

"Shut down all the goddamned factories. Move 'em
into orbit. Stop burning fossil fuels. Convert every motor
on the planet to electricity. Use fusion and solar power.
We've got the technology, for god's sake!"

"How're you going to get the whole flipping world to
change over in ten years?"

"The Global Economic Council," Dan said. Then he
snorted with disdain.

"The GEC? Don't make me laugh."

"They're the only organization in the whole world that
has anywhere near the clout to get the job done. You've
got to show your findings to them."

"I already have."

"Huh? What'd they say?"

"They laughed in my face," Freiberg said.

"What?"

"I said they laughed at me. Their scientists told me I'm
crazy."

Dan felt the breath rush out of him. "Son of a bitch," he said slowly.

Freiberg inhaled. "Maybe they're right. Maybe I am crazy."

Dan shook his head. "If I have to choose between them and you, I'd say they're the ones who're nuts."

"I did have all this checked out by the best people I know," Freiberg said.

Dan rapped nervously on his desktop with his knuckles. "No. If the GEC refuses to listen to you, it's for some reason."

"They can't *want* half the world to drown!"

Dan said nothing; he was thinking furiously.

"Can they?" Freiberg asked plaintively.

"We'll find out," said Dan. Leaning across his desk, he said to his computerized communicator, "Get me on the next flight to Sydney. Book it under the name of Maxwell E. Rutherford."

"Maxwell E. Rutherford?" Freiberg asked.

Dan grinned at him. "Never let the authorities know what you're doing, if you can avoid it. I want to see what's going on down there before I meet with Jane or anybody else."

"Does the 'E' stand for Einstein, maybe?"

"Could be."

Freiberg almost smiled. There's nothing that Dan or anyone else on Earth can do, he realized. But still he felt an illogical glimmer of hope that Dan was gearing up for battle.

SIX

Dan was about to leave his office on the way to the launch facility when his desk phone buzzed. The screen spelled out: URGENT. FROM N. YAMAGATA.

Grumbling slightly, he pulled his personal phone from the breast pocket of his coveralls and flipped it open. As he dashed through his outer office, past his lone human secretary and out to the electric cart waiting to whisk him through the tunnel out to the launch site, he told the phone to pick up Yamagata's call.

Nobuhiko Yamagata's angular, high-cheeked face appeared in the phone's tiny screen. He looked solemn, very unlike his usual cheerful smiling self.

"Nobo, what's wrong?" Dan asked as he clambered aboard the little cart. His single travel bag was already sitting next to the driver, a long-legged mestizo with raven-black hair, beautiful enough to be a video starlet back on Earth. She had been raised on the Moon because her parents had suffered terribly from allergies in the smog and grime of their native Caracas.

"My father," said Nobuhiko gravely. "He is dying."

"What! Sai?"

With a barely perceptible nod, Nobo said, "The cancer has returned. It is spreading through his body. There is no longer any hope."

"Oh for god's sake," Dan muttered. All the medical advances that they've made, he said to himself, and still cancer cuts us down. It's been getting worse, seems like. More people die of it every year.

He asked aloud, "How long . . . ?"

"My father has decided to end it himself. He—" Nobuhiko faltered, swallowed, then went on, "He asks that you assist him."

"Me?"

Nobo nodded, eyes closed.

Saito Yamagata had been Dan's boss, back in those early days on the Moon. Dan had battled for respect from the Japanese, and Sai had rewarded his toughness and drive by protecting him from the chauvinists and sadists who looked on an American as fair game for bullying—and worse. They had become friends, and together built the first of the giant solar power satellites that eventually made Japan independent of Middle Eastern oil. When Dan had gone into business for himself, Sai had backed him with investment capital. Eventually they became more than friends: associates, equals, even business partners on more than one venture.

Dan had known Nobo from the day of his birth in the orbital infirmary attached to their construction center. Nobo—with his father's power behind him—had rescued Dan from certain death at the hands of Vasily Malik, ten years earlier. Saito's political connections and economic strength had helped Dan to break the Russian stranglehold on space industries.

"How soon?" Dan asked the tiny image on the hand-held phone.

"Tomorrow, just after sunset," Nobo replied.

"Where?"

"At the family home in Kyoto."

"I'll be there," Dan said.

There was no need to change his flight to Sydney. Maxwell E. Rutherford would ride the high-boost rocket from Alphonsus to the transfer station in low Earth orbit. There Rutherford would clear customs and immigration, and hop aboard the shuttle to Sydney. Once in Australia he would take a commercial hypersonic transport to Tokyo, where a security team from Yamagata Industries would take him to Saito's estate.

And then Dan Randolph would help his old friend to die.

Hell, thought Dan. Sai's not that much older than I am. He's too young to die.

Jane Scanwell hosted a party that evening. Although her home was still in Texas, as the head of the American delegation to the Global Economic Council she spent so much time in Paris that she had leased an apartment in the embassy district, out past l'Etoile and the Arc de Triomphe, within walking distance of the Bois de Boulogne—for a long-striding Texas woman.

This evening, though, she felt a far distance from Texas. Almost all her life had been spent in politics, and she knew that more could be accomplished at a social gathering than in a committee meeting. But she felt weary of it all: the posturing, the jockeying for position, the constant competition to get your point across, your program adopted, your pork barrel filled.

What have we accomplished? she asked herself as she looked across the roomful of guests. The women wore knee-length frocks decked with jewelry, the men Western business suits no matter what their native tradition. They stood and chatted and laughed, sipped drinks and nibbled canapés.

But what have we accomplished? Jane asked silently once again. I've been to a thousand parties such as this, ten thousand. I've spent my life in politics. So has almost everyone here. Is the world any better off? Are the people happier, healthier, richer?

She shook her head slightly. There are certainly more people than ever before. Twelve billion of them. Maybe we've stabilized population growth. That would be a major accomplishment. Stabilized it at a level where half the world is constantly hungry and the other half resists helping them with every ounce of their strength. At least we've stopped the wars. I suppose that's something to be proud of. We have famines and droughts and floods and millions killed by storms each year—but at least we're not killing each other anymore.

"You seem troubled."

Startled out of her reverie, Jane saw that it was Rafaelo Gaetano who had spoken to her. Young, tall and slim as a cypress tree, darkly handsome, Gaetano was the chief of the Italian delegation to the GEC. The youngest member of the GEC board. And the most ambitious. He was rumored to be strongly linked to the international crime syndicate, especially since his first official act upon joining the GEC board had been to propose that the organization move its headquarters from Paris to Palermo, in Sicily. Since that day, almost everyone in the GEC sniggered that Gaetano was "the Mafia representative."

Whether it was true or not, whether he heard the whispers or not, Gaetano remained a smiling, hardworking, thoroughly charming member of the GEC board.

"A lady as lovely as you, my dear Jane, should never have to frown," he said, handing her a tulip glass of bubbling champagne. His voice was a deep baritone, melodious. "Tell me what dragon is annoying you and I will go forth and slay it."

Despite her cares, Jane Scanwell smiled back at him. "I wish it were that simple, Rafe. I really do."

Gaetano gently took her arm and led her toward the ceiling-high windows of her own living room. "Look," he said softly. Yet his voice penetrated the background babble of the crowd. "All of Paris is out there. You should be enjoying yourself. This is the city of romance, you know."

She arched a brow slightly. "I'm getting a bit too old for romance, Rafe."

"Nonsense! You are in the prime of your life."

"I wish that were so."

"Let me prove it to you," he said, running a finger across his pencil-thin moustache.

She looked at him. Is he serious? she asked herself. He gazed back at her, smiling a smile that might have been amorous, or just friendly. Or perhaps it was the self-confident smile of a healthy young male with a sensitivity for lonely older women.

"There are plenty of younger women here," Jane said at last.

"Yes, that is true," he admitted, somewhat ruefully. Then his grin returned. "But it took you several moments to arrive at that conclusion. I consider that a good sign."

Then he moved away, without another word. Jane stared after him. What's he after? she heard a voice in her mind ask.

And she replied to herself silently, Jane Scanwell, you've been in politics too damned long if you're automatically suspicious of some good-looking young Italian making a pass at you!

Trying to force Gaetano's suggestion to the back of her mind, Jane busied herself attending to her guests. Malik had showed up without his wife, as usual. And, as usual, he was the center of a cluster of admiring women of all ages. Jane made polite conversation, saw that the robots weaving through the crowd with trays of drinks were functioning properly, and tried to avoid whichever part of the big, high-ceilinged room Gaetano happened to be in.

Eventually, inevitably, she slipped out of the crowded living room and strode swiftly down the hall to her cubbyhole of an office. Closing the door firmly behind her, she leaned across her desk and swiveled the phone screen around. She touched a couple of keys and her messages scrolled silently across the screen.

There! Dan's reply to her invitation:

ON MY WAY. YOU-KNOW-WHO.

Jane crossed her arms over her chest and frowned at the screen. Damn you, Dan Randolph. Just like him. "On my way." Doesn't say when he'll arrive. Doesn't even say where he's going, although it's bound to be Tetiaroa. The big oaf wouldn't even sign his name. What's he afraid of?

But then she realized that Dan Randolph had much to be afraid of. She was luring him into a trap, not a romantic rendezvous. She was going to defeat him, crush him, once and for all.

She fought back the tears that were welling in her eyes.

An earthquake shook the Tokyo airport just as Dan was being greeted by the head of the Yamagata security team, a bone-thin man of about fifty, dressed in a severe suit of dead black, who bowed to him and asked:

"Mr. Rutherford-san?"

Dan started to return the bow when the floor beneath him rippled. The crowd streaming past, coming off the plane from Sydney, seemed to freeze and draw in its breath as if preparing to scream. A deep rumble filled the air, like the drawn-out thunder of a dragon lurking beneath the ground. The long decorative streamers hanging from the ceiling high overhead swayed back and forth. Beyond the heads of the people facing him, Dan could see through the big windows on the other side of the terminal that the planes out there seemed to bob up and down, like ships on a choppy sea.

Then it was over. The rumble died away. Before anyone could scream. Before Dan had fully registered that an earthquake was happening. It was over. The floor became solid again. The planes outside were still, as if they had never moved at all. The streamers fluttered only slightly, as if a passing breeze had briefly disturbed them. The crowd flowed back into motion, babbling and chattering.

"Mr. Rutherford-san," the security man repeated, his immobile face showing neither anxiety nor relief, "your transportation is waiting for you."

"Domo arigato," Dan replied. He had not spoken Japanese in years, but he had spent his time on the spacecraft and hypersonic transport from Sydney listening to newscasts from Tokyo to revive his ear for the language.

"You have luggage, sir?" the man asked, switching to Japanese.

"Only this." Dan hefted his soft-sided travel bag. Originally dead black, it looked gray and threadbare from much use.

"This way, please." The security man did not offer to take Dan's bag. He's not a porter and he wants to have both his hands free at all times, Dan told himself.

Glad that he had kept up his daily regimen of exercises while on the Moon, Dan followed after the security man on legs that felt only slightly rubbery in the heavy gravity of Earth. He looked around for the rest of the team. The terminal was crowded, abuzz with hundreds of conversations in a score of different languages. People scurrying everywhere: mothers dragging crying children, red-faced businessmen rushing to their heart attacks, tourists looking sweaty and lost. Half a dozen younger men and women hurrying along the terminal corridor looked as if they might be security types, but it was impossible to single them out from the rest of the crowd.

So far so good, Dan told himself. Nobody but Sai's people knows I'm in Japan. I'll have my Caracas office contact Jane and tell her I'll be a day or two late for Tetiaroa. Give them a bit of time to check out the island, too.

Abruptly the security man opened an unmarked door along the corridor and brusquely gestured Dan to step through. The door snapped shut behind him and four husky young men in coral pink coveralls bearing the flying-heron symbol of Yamagata Industries snapped to spine-popping attention.

Escorted by this new team, Dan followed the black-suited man through another door to the concrete apron outside the terminal. A palpable wall of noise slammed his ears. An executive-style helicopter stood waiting some twenty meters away, its turbine engine whining, its twin rotors already spinning blurrily. Jet airliners screamed and thundered, making the very air quiver as they swooped in for landings or roared up in takeoffs every few seconds. Planes taxied along the concrete guideways, giant, busy, purposeful aluminum ants directed by the traffic controllers at the hub of this vast nest of humans and machines.

The noise actually made Dan tremble. I've been away from all this crap too long, he thought as he clambered up the metal stairs of the copter. It's so peaceful on the Moon, I'd forgotten how raucous things are down here.

He turned as he stepped through the hatch and shouted, "Thank you for your help," to the security man. The man bowed and said something in return, but it was lost in the uproar of the airport.

At least the interior of the chopper was quiet, once the hatch was closed. Good acoustical insulation muffled the helicopter's engines to a soft purr. Dan sank gratefully into a thickly padded seat and automatically buckled his safety belt as the copter lifted quickly into the busy afternoon air.

He was alone inside the luxuriously appointed passenger compartment. The two pilots sat up front, separated by a thick slab of clear plastic. Like a New York taxicab, Dan said to himself. But cabs all over the world now isolated their passengers from their drivers. Violence and crime were no longer confined to one city alone. Even in London the streets were no longer safe after dark.

He took a deep breath, then remembered that he was

rushing to the side of his dearest and most trusted friend in order to help him commit suicide.

Dan shook his head angrily. "The hell I will," he muttered.

SEVEN

"The man is a menace," said Vasily Malik. "He must be brought under control."

Rafaelo Gaetano smiled lazily at the Russian through a haze of cigarette smoke. "Yes, perhaps. But how?"

The two men were sitting on a park bench on the right bank of the Seine, having walked leisurely from the GEC headquarters up the river until they were almost opposite Notre Dame. Without a word of discussion between them, they sat on the bench, overlooked by the towers and flying buttresses and stone gargoyles of the massive cathedral. Gaetano had immediately pulled a silver cigarette case from his inside jacket pocket and offered one to Malik. The Russian had refused with a shake of his head.

"Noncarcinogenic," Gaetano had said. "Guaranteed."

"No, thanks," Malik replied. "I broke that habit once. I have no intention of starting it again."

It was slightly past noon. The sun felt warm, boats slid

by on the ancient river carrying luncheon customers, men and women were picnicking here and there on other benches. The hum of automobile traffic behind them was muted by the thick walls containing the sunken highway, but the stench of petrol fumes fouled the pretty afternoon.

"I have a plan in mind," Malik said.

"About what?"

"Randolph. What else?"

Gaetano had spread his arms along the back of the bench and stretched his legs out so that people walking along the paved path had to detour around his gleaming leather oxfords. He smiled from behind his cigarette at the women who passed by.

Suppressing his annoyance, Malik said, "This is extremely important, you know."

"I know," Gaetano said without taking his eyes off the passing parade. "You hate this man Randolph."

"This is far more important than a personal matter," Malik snapped. To himself he added, I am not some petty Sicilian chieftain pursuing a vendetta.

"Destroying Randolph is of great importance to you," Gaetano said mildly.

"*Stopping* Randolph is of great importance."

"Whichever."

"It should be important to you, too!"

"And why?"

Malik leaned forward, elbows on knees, and forced himself into the Italian's field of vision. "You are the representative of United Europe on the GEC board of directors. What is the most important problem United Europe faces?"

Gaetano turned his head slightly to look at the Russian. "The most important problem? That's easy. We need to lower the taxes the GEC imposes on us."

"Very well." It was not quite the answer Malik had expected, but it was close enough to work with. "How can you expect lower taxes when the Africans and Latin

Americans are starving? Even in India there is renewed threat of famine. To say nothing of Bangladesh."

Gaetano took a deep puff on his cigarette. "Raising taxes on us will only spread the poverty to Europe."

"But we need more money for the poor sections of the world," Malik said. "The southern hemisphere regions are desperate."

Blowing smoke into the air, Gaetano said, "Obviously you have a solution in mind."

"Yes. Increase the taxes paid by the space industrialists."

"Good idea—if you can get away with it."

"They make enormous profits," Malik pointed out eagerly. "Their tax rates are much lower than comparable industries' on Earth."

"The reason they always give is that they take much greater risks, up there on the Moon and in their orbiting factories. And they claim that they plow most of their profits back into expanding their operations."

"Randolph and his ilk live like bloated plutocrats! They think they can hide themselves away from the public eye, living on the Moon or on their enormous private estates, as Yamagata does."

Gaetano flipped his half-smoked cigarette into the river, smiling. "I know you have tried very hard to expose Randolph in the media. Wasn't it you who sent that investigative reporter to the Moon?"

Malik frowned. "The bitch jumped into his bed the instant Randolph crooked his finger at her."

"Now she's a vice-president or something for the Lunar News Corporation, isn't she?"

He's baiting me, Malik realized. This oily Sicilian puppy dog is making jokes at my expense.

The Russian forced himself to an icy calm. "Whatever Randolph has done in the past is of no consequence now. He may have managed to elude justice, but this time I have him where I want him."

"Really?"

"Really. His own greed has tripped him up. He bought out a smaller competitor when the other man was facing bankruptcy over a fine imposed by our lunar tribunal."

Gaetano's eyes narrowed. "That new set of regulations you pushed through last winter . . ."

"Precisely." Malik's appreciation of the Italian went up a notch. Hardly anyone on the board had bothered to read all the fine print in what was supposed to be a dry revision of technical safety specifications.

"How could a man so smart fall prey to such a trick?" Gaetano wondered aloud. "Surely he has lawyers who would protect him."

"Greed," Malik answered. Then, unable to hide his delight, he smiled and added, "And lust."

"Lust?" Gaetano's heavy dark brows rose. "Ah—the lawyer he used was a woman."

"A very clever woman," said Malik, "who will soon be employed by the GEC in San Francisco, which is her hometown, I believe."

Gaetano considered this for a few moments, absently brushing his thin moustache, then said, "So you can confiscate Randolph's entire empire, then. Congratulations, I suppose."

"Not only Randolph's company," Malik said. "Any corporation that is linked to Randolph by partnership agreements is also subject to confiscation."

"Really?"

"The regulations provide so."

"That means that you can start proceedings against Yamagata or anyone else that Randolph has links with."

"Precisely so."

Gaetano gave a low whistle. "I am impressed."

Malik inclined his head in a brief nod of acceptance.

"What more do you need?" Gaetano asked.

He is no fool, Malik conceded. Aloud, he replied, "I

intend to—ah, sequester—Mr. Randolph while we move through the legal procedures of confiscation. Everything will go much more smoothly and quickly if he is not available to interfere."

The Italian said nothing, but his expressive features showed that he was paying full attention.

"It is possible, however, that Randolph's lawyers—"

"His *other* lawyers?"

"Yes." Malik grinned. "His other lawyers may appeal directly to the GEC board on this matter, whether Randolph is available to direct them or not."

"If they make such an appeal, you will need a simple majority of the board to reject them, no?"

"Yes. A simple majority. Five members."

"Who do you have with you already?"

Malik gazed up at the bright blue sky. "Oh, I think I can safely count on India and Black Africa."

"And the Russian Federation, of course."

"Of course. Latin America is doubtful; much of Randolph's operations on Earth are still headquartered in Caracas."

"Greater East Asia?"

"Yamagata still controls them."

"I see. What about the Islamic League?"

"That old fool Sibuti will jump in whichever direction he thinks will be the winner. He won't cast his vote until he sees what the others do."

"That leaves North America—and Europe."

"North America will vote in favor of confiscation."

Gaetano looked impressed. "You are certain? I thought that Jane Scanwell was—well, you know."

"She will vote my way."

"That gives you four assured votes."

"You could be the final nail in Randolph's coffin."

With a smile, Gaetano asked, "What's in it for United Europe?"

Malik noticed that the Italian was delicate enough to refrain from asking for a personal reward, although both men knew what his words actually meant. And, the Russian also noted, Gaetano was no longer watching the women strolling past. His eyes were locked on Malik's, hot with ambition.

EIGHT

Dean Ingersoll looked up from his desktop display screen and gazed out at the floor of the power plant, two stories below his office window. He smiled to himself.

Spend so much time looking at the damned screen, you can forget what the hell the numbers are all about.

He got to his feet, a solid square-shouldered man of middle years, slightly graying, his face weathered from spending as much time up in the hills as he could possibly spare from his work and family.

The fishing had gone all to hell years ago. Acid rain had devastated the woods and poisoned the lakes. There were the snowmelt streams in the spring, of course, but the state only stocked them once a year and the next day the stream banks were wall-to-wall with once-a-year fishermen who left a midden heap of beer cans and other trash after they drove back to their condos and tract houses.

Besides, the past three years in a row there had been

so little snow that the streams were too feeble to be stocked.

No, Ingersoll went up into the hills to dream about how all the forest and the deer and even the fish would come back one day. He hoped he lived long enough to see it.

What was going to make this miracle of regeneration possible was the shining, nearly silent machine he was watching now, smiling like Moses must have when he saw the Promised Land.

Beneath his appreciative eyes the fusion power generator hummed to itself as it transmuted deuterium from the sea and helium-three from the Moon into pure energy. Fusion was the hope that made Ingersoll smile. Fusion power was beginning to replace fossil fuels and even the old uranium-based fission plants. The hope of the future, Ingersoll told himself. Maybe my grand-children will be able to see the woods in bloom again.

He took his windbreaker from its peg on the back of his office door and headed out for the parking lot, where his electric bike waited. It was his own design. You pedaled most of the time, using the little electric motor only to help you up hills. Charged up the battery while you were pedaling. Clean and efficient, as long as you lived close enough to the office.

The night shift was coming in as he left; all four of them. Ingersoll's fellow day-shift workers were kibitzing with them as he waved to them all and went out into the late-afternoon sunshine.

There's a fusion generator for you, he said to himself as he squinted through the bare trees at the westering sun, red from the dust and pollution of the city down in the valley. Been shining for five billion years and has at least five billion more to go. Talk about reliability.

Don was at the parking-lot gate, trudging slowly back and forth across the entrance with a new sign. NO MORE NUKES, it said, just like the tattered old one Don had carried for so many years that it had become practically illegible.

Ingersoll pedaled up to the lone demonstrator and stopped, one booted foot lightly touching the paving.

"Hey, Don, how's it going?"

Don Knight was Ingersoll's age. They had gone to kindergarten together. But Don appeared much older, perhaps because of the long gray beard he had allowed to grow down his chest. He had always looked frail, ascetic, but he had never been sick a day in his life, as far as Ingersoll knew.

"Not bad, Dean. Nice day, huh?"

Ingersoll looked around at the dead trees and the pale sky beyond them. "Guess it was. I wouldn't know. Been inside all day."

"Thought I saw a robin," said Don.

"Going home now?"

"Might as well. Want a lift in my car? We can stow the bike in the backseat."

Ingersoll shook his head. "You still driving that gas-burner?"

"Nope. My royalty check finally came in. I bought a new Barracuda."

"Another gas-burner? Why didn't you get one of the electrics?"

Don made a face from behind his beard. "No zip. No fun to drive."

"Don"—Ingersoll had asked the question hundreds of times before, maybe thousands, but he had never been satisfied with the answer—"why in hell do you still tromp around here? I mean, nobody pays any attention to you at all."

"That's not entirely so," Knight replied, not in the least defensive. "Last August the TV news people came out for the anniversary of Hiroshima."

"But this is a *fusion* generator. It's got nothing to do with Hiroshima."

"It's nuclear, isn't it?"

"So's the Sun, for god's sake!"

Don shook his head. His beard swayed back and forth like a horse's tail. "My father was anti-nuke. My mother was anti-nuke. I know that there's hardly any of us left, but *somebody's* got to keep the protest going."

"Why? It's wrong. It's stupid."

Don did not get angry. Instead, he smiled benignly, like a saint listening to the foibles of a sinner. "Nuclear power is wrong, Dean. Radiation is bad. I don't care what you think or what the rest of the world thinks. I know what I believe."

Ingersoll shrugged. He had been through this with his old friend since boyhood.

"Want to have a beer down at Suder's?"

"Good idea," said Don.

"See you there."

The nuclear engineer got on his bike. The protester ambled to his shining new convertible, tossed his sign in the backseat and took off with a roar and a cloud of exhaust gas.

The Yamagata family estate was set on a rugged hillside high above the towers and apartment blocks of Kyoto. Built like a medieval Japanese fortress, the solid yet graceful buildings always made Dan think of poetry frozen into shapes of wood and stone. Much of the inner courtyard was given to an exquisitely maintained sand garden. There were green vistas at every turn, as well: gardens and woods and, off in the distance, a glimpse through tall old trees of Lake Biwa, glittering in the sun.

The helicopter settled down, turbines screeching, in the outer courtyard. Dan unbuckled from his seat and was through the hatch before the pilot was able to stop the rotors. Squinting through the dust kicked up by the downwash, Dan saw Nobuhiko waiting at the gate to the inner courtyard. Saito Yamagata's only legitimate son was wearing a Western business suit of pale blue. His lean, angular face looked solemn as Dan approached him.

By damn, he must be nearly thirty-five by now, Dan thought, struck all over again by how much Nobo looked like his father did when they had been building the first solar power satellite. But almost a foot taller. It always surprised Dan to realize that Nobuhiko was taller than he was himself, by several inches.

The two men bowed simultaneously, then grasped each other's hand.

"Nobo, how is he?"

The younger man made a tight smile. "Drinking sake and complaining about the GEC's new tax ruling."

"He's not in pain?"

"He doesn't show any pain."

They walked along a path of stones set in the carefully raked sand garden. Dan noticed that a few new rocks had been placed off in one corner of the garden, by the miniature olive tree he had given Sai many years earlier. Half the year the tree was covered by a transparent plastic dome, heated and protected from the winter wind.

"How are you?" Dan asked.

Nobo's nostrils flared slightly. "I am going to miss him."

They removed their shoes at the open door to the main house. A woman in a carnelian red kimono silently took Dan's travel bag the instant they stepped inside: a servant or a family member, Dan could not tell which. Doesn't matter all that much, he knew. The servants have all been part of the Yamagata family for generations.

He heard Saito from halfway down the hall. The old man's rasping voice made the shoji screen walls quiver.

"Stop looking so morose! I want to see happy faces, not these long sad frowns. Must I bring in a band of geishas to please me? Can't I have pleasant looks around me on my final day?"

Women were scurrying along the hall, some bearing

trays of food, others jars of sake. They all looked distressed, close to tears. Two men in business suits backed out of the room at the end of the corridor, bowing so deeply Dan thought they could wipe their noses on their kneecaps.

"Where is that idiot who calls himself my personal attorney?" Saito was shouting. "With all these papers I have to sign, why isn't he here to witness my signature?"

The two business suits nearly bumped into Dan and Nobuhiko, they were in such a hurry to get away from their master. Flustered, they bowed again, bobbing up and down several times. Nobo gave them a single curt nod of his head; Dan bowed with more respect.

Then they stepped through the open doorway.

"Ah! My son and heir," said Saito. "And Dan, you are here at last."

Saito Yamagata scrambled to his feet and came around the low, paper-cluttered table at which he had been sitting to grip Dan's outstretched hand. His kimono was deep blue, decorated with white herons. Strangely, Sai looked ten years younger than he had the last time Dan had seen him. The cancer had burned away the fat Sai had accumulated over the years of rich living. He was almost as lean as his son, though considerably shorter.

Dan searched his old friend's eyes. There was no pain there, not even anxiety.

"Sai . . ." Dan's voice nearly broke. Surprised at his own emotion, he swallowed tears and forced a cheerful "By damn, Sai, you look better than I do."

"I feel well," Saito said, gesturing Dan to the low lacquered table. The three of them sat on the tatami floor mats. Saito pushed aside a small mountain of paper and poured sake into delicate little cups that had tiny whistles built into their lips so the drinker could show his appreciation by making as much noise as possible.

"Is there anything I can say," Dan asked, "that will talk you out of this?"

Sai drained his cup, whistling thinly, then banged it

down on the table. "You would prefer that I die in agony?"

"But if you feel so good, why end it now?"

"It is only a matter of time before the damnable tumors begin to torture me to death." Saito's face showed no fear, only resolution. "I must make an orderly transition of all my holdings, so that my son can step into my place with a minimum of difficulties."

"Yes, but . . ."

Saito made a noise that might have been a grunt. "The only regret that I have is that my son has not yet seen fit to present me with a grandson. It would be a great relief to me to know that the family will go on for another generation."

Nobuhiko kept his face immobile and said nothing.

"However," Saito sighed heavily, "there are some things that even the most devoted father cannot do for his son."

Dan felt a slight nervousness inching through him. "Sai—what am I supposed to do here?"

"There are several documents you must sign. Do you realize we are still in partnership on three separate operations?"

"Three? I know there's the solar power company and the water production factory at Alphonsus. What's the third?"

Saito rummaged through the stack of paper on the corner of the table, muttering, "With all the advances in computers and information storage, still the lawyers demand signatures in ink on sheets made by killing trees."

Dan felt himself grinning. The paperless office had been promised for more than a century, yet there was always more paper.

"Ah, here—remember this?"

Dan took a stapled sheaf of papers from his friend's hand and flipped through the first two sheets.

"By double damn! The asteroid retrieval operation. I

haven't even thought about that since . . ."

"Since all that trouble with Malik was resolved, ten years ago," Yamagata said.

Nodding, Dan said, "That chunk of rock is still in the orbit we left it in; maybe we ought to go out and start mining it, after all."

"There is not much of a market for asteroidal metals," Nobo said. "Lunar resources are cheaper."

"Yeah, sure," Dan said, growing excited. "But the Moon doesn't have anything heavier than iron—except where meteorites have hit, and most of them are buried too deep to be profitable."

"You would like to mine the asteroids?" Saito asked.

"We'll have to, one day." Dan kneaded his thighs; he was unaccustomed to sitting cross-legged. "There ought to be enough gold and platinum in that one asteroid to pay for a dozen flights."

"The GEC has set a firm price on precious metals," Nobo pointed out.

Dan felt his spirits sink again. "The goddamned GEC. What a pain in the butt those bastards are."

Saito laughed. "You haven't changed at all, Dan."

Dan grinned back at him. Then he remembered why he was here.

"Okay," he said. "What do you want me to sign?"

Ruffling through the papers again, Saito replied, "Our partnerships are personal arrangements, legally. Since Nobuhiko is going to take charge of Yamagata Industries, it will be necessary for you to sign new agreements with him."

They spent the next several minutes in silence, Dan signing almost blindly where Saito indicated, Nobuhiko adding his signature with a felt-tipped pen both in Roman script and Japanese hiragana characters.

"Good," said Saito, when they finished. He glanced out the window at the miniature garden and the reddening sky beyond. "Now we can have dinner and then . . ."

"What am I supposed to do?" Dan asked. "How are you going to do it?"

Saito smiled at him. "There is nothing for you to do except to wish me a pleasant journey. The doctors will take care of everything. All is prepared and ready."

Feeling somewhat relieved, Dan asked, "You're not going to slice your belly open?"

For the first time in all the years that Dan had known Saito Yamagata, the man looked stunned with surprise.

Nobuhiko said, "What do you think my father is going to do?"

"End it," Dan replied. "That's what you told me. Hara-kiri."

Saito burst into uproarious laughter. Even Nobo laughed until tears streamed down his cheeks. Dan felt like a dolt, staring at them.

"You mean you're not . . . ?"

Shaking his head, barely able to control his voice, Saito said, "Dan, my old and dear friend, you've always had a flair for the dramatic. I am honored that you were willing to help in a ceremony that is so far removed from your own culture. You are truly a brave man, Dan. And an honored friend."

"Well, what in hell's going to happen?"

"Cryonics," said Nobuhiko.

"I am going to have myself frozen," Saito explained. "I have not worked in high-technology industries all my life without absorbing some faith in the future."

"Frozen." Dan felt as numb as if he were on ice.

"Yes! My condition is incurable today. But tomorrow, perhaps ten thousand years from tomorrow, medical science will conquer cancer. Then I can be revived and returned to health."

Dan sank his head in his hands. "Cripes almighty. I thought maybe you wanted me to whack your head off with one of those Samurai swords."

Father and son laughed. But after several moments the laughter quieted.

"I will be leaving you," Saito remarked. "Just as though I were going to die. I might never be revived. Or it might be so far in the future that neither of you will be alive. We are truly departing from one another, my friend."

Dan let a grin creep across his face. "I'll be waiting for you, pal. If it comes to that, I'll have myself frozen, too. We'll see the future together, Sai."

"I would like that."

"Damned right!"

Dinner was long and filled with laughter and reminiscences. Saito regaled his son with tales of Dan's first days on the Moon, his battles with his fellow workers, his pursuit of the few women living on that rugged frontier.

"Do you still chase the women?" Saito asked.

Dan shrugged. They were sitting at a Western-style table on elegant chairs of Philippine mahogany: Yamagata's concession to the comfort of his friend.

"From what I hear," Nobuhiko joined in, "the women now pursue you."

Grinning, Dan replied, "They love me for my money."

"You must send a few of them my son's way," Saito said, his lips smiling but his eyes more serious. "I despair of the boy ever marrying."

"Wouldn't you want him to marry a good Japanese woman?" Dan asked.

"I want a grandson! I don't care who the mother is, as long as the child is legitimate."

Nobo said to Dan, "My father doesn't realize that men of my generation tend to marry much later in life than he did. The women, too. We have plenty of time."

"But I don't!"

All the smiles around the table faded. Saito huffed unhappily.

"I apologize," he said in a low voice. "I have ruined the spirit of felicity with my selfishness."

"I will make you a grandson, Father," said Nobuhiko.

"You may depend on it."

Nodding, Saito said, "I know, my son. I was merely trying to be humorous. I was not cut out to be a comedian."

"As long as we've gotten so damned serious," Dan said, "there's something that you can check out for me, Nobo."

He told them about Zach Freiberg's calculations of the greenhouse cliff.

"That could be disastrous for Japan!" Saito exclaimed once he understood what Dan was saying. "Half our population lives on the seacoast. If sea levels rise abruptly—a catastrophe!"

Dan grumbled to himself, Great going, guy. His last damned night on Earth and you tell him half his countrymen are going to be drowned or driven from their homes. Nice way to send off an old friend.

Aloud, he said, "It's only numbers in a computer, Sai. It might not mean anything at all in the real world." Turning to Nobuhiko, "But I'd like to see if your scientists come up with the same numbers, given Zach's input."

Nobo said, "I will have the chief of our research section contact Dr. Freiberg first thing tomorrow."

"Good."

Saito pushed his chair back from the table and got to his feet. "It is time," he said.

Wordlessly, Dan and Nobuhiko followed the elder Yamagata out into the courtyard. A bright, nearly full Moon was scudding in and out of silvery clouds. Dan could make out pinpoints of light at Aristarchus and Copernicus. Alphonsus, almost dead in the center of the Moon's lopsided face, was lost in the natural glare.

"A beautiful night," Saito said as they approached a building Dan did not recognize. "If I were a poet I would write a haiku about this night."

They entered the new building. Inside it was like a hospital: shadowless lighting from overhead panels, dry cool atmosphere, a faint antiseptic odor, silence except for the slightest whisper of air coming through the screened ducts up near the ceiling.

"My mausoleum," Saito explained, as he pushed open another door.

A team of green-clad medics sprang to their feet and bowed deeply. In the middle of the room stood what looked to Dan like an operating table, with a cluster of big lamps above it and tables of surgical instruments to one side. Along the far wall rested a large metal canister, a dewar big enough to hold a man. A twenty-first-century sarcophagus, Dan thought. Next to it stood a row of cylinders: liquid nitrogen, for freezing Sai's body.

A nurse helped Dan and Nobo into green surgical gowns and sterile masks while the rest of the team stripped Saito naked and laid him on the table. Dan saw the chief doctor bend over his old friend and inject him in the left arm with a hypodermic syringe.

Sai beckoned to Dan with his other hand.

"These are my last moments," he said when Dan was beside him. "At least, for a while. Take care of my son, will you, old friend? I ask nothing more of you."

Dan gripped Saito's hand as if it were his only lifeline. "I'll look after him as if he were my own son."

Saito smiled weakly. "Good. Good. Perhaps you can find him a suitable wife, too."

Despite himself, a grin broke across Dan's face. "I'm probably not the best man in the world to give marriage advice."

"Better than you think, Daniel. You have always been a much better man than you believe yourself to be."

Dan felt at a loss for words.

"Please . . . send Nobo to me now."

Dan stepped away and gestured Nobuhiko to his father's side. The two spoke briefly in tones too low for Dan to make out. Then the son let go of his father's hand. It dropped to the sheeted tabletop lifelessly.

"It is done," said the chief medic. "I declare him clinically dead."

One of the assistants bowed deeply to Nobuhiko and presented a legal form attached to a clipboard for his signature.

NINE

Dan's dreams that night were filled not with memories of Saito but with strange shifting apparitions of Jane Scanwell and Lucita, his ex-wife, and other women he had known. He woke before sunrise, sitting up in his Western bed, beaded with sweat, an oppressive sense of doom weighing down on him.

"Sai's not really dead," he muttered to himself as he stumbled through the dark bedroom toward the toilet. "They could revive him tomorrow if they wanted to."

Yeah, maybe, a voice inside his head replied. If they don't kill him all over again in the thawing procedure.

After a quick shower and a decision that he could skip shaving, Dan strapped on his wristwatch and checked the time in Paris. A little after eight in the evening. He used the phone by the bed to put through a call to Jane. She was not at home, her answering machine said, but all messages would be forwarded to her hourly.

Must be in some double-damned GEC meeting, Dan grumbled to himself. He spoke into the phone, "Jane, it's you-know-who. I'll be there in twelve hours or so, unless I hear from you. Bye."

Then he pulled on a pair of slacks and a loose velour shirt, trying to remember exactly where the kitchen was. He always got a kick out of shocking the servants by getting his own breakfast.

Jane Scanwell was in her office, poring over the reports and memoranda that she never seemed to have the time to read during the nominal working day.

You either have to be an early bird or a night owl, she told herself. The only way to get any real work done is to do it when nobody else is around to bother you. Once the regular working hours begin it's nothing but meetings and conferences and phone calls all the blessed day long.

Phone calls. Her computer scrolled all her incoming messages at the top of every hour. And there was a message from Dan, finally. Still being cute, signing it "You-know-who." It infuriated her. According to the computer the call had originated in Japan. Lord knows where Dan really is. He's as devious as a used-car salesman.

She leaned back in her chair and closed her eyes. Close to midnight. Where is Dan? What's he doing? And will he really be at Tetiaroa in twelve hours or less?

She found that she almost wished he wouldn't be. She felt disappointed at that. But not surprised.

It was well past midnight when Rafaelo Gaetano returned to his apartment on the Boulevard Saint Germain. Even before he switched on the lights he sensed that someone was already in the apartment. Then his conscious mind realized that there was a faint trace of a woman's perfume: not the expensive kind that was meant to be seductive, this was more like a simple floral aroma.

There was no concierge in the building. That function had been taken over by electronics ages ago. So Gaetano silently flicked his fingertips across the security keypad next to the door, guided only by the crack of light from the hallway coming through the nearly closed front door.

The pad's little screen lit up with a numeral one, and a time: 11:48. Gaetano silently closed the door and smiled to himself. He knew who his visitor was. Or at least, who it should be. Either way, he tiptoed across the thick carpeting to the window that overlooked the street. Plenty of traffic out there, although the double-paned glass effectively soundproofed the apartment. Slowly, quietly, he closed the blinds, then tapped on the side panel of the window frame in his private code. The panel slid open noiselessly. Gaetano reached in and curled his fingers around the waiting nine-millimeter Beretta.

Silently, like a commando or a hired assassin, he made his way to the bedroom. The door was half open. She was already in his bed, probably asleep.

Grinning, he put the gun down on the easy chair by the doorway and swiftly stripped down to his briefs. Then, armed and ready, he stepped into the bedroom and switched on the lights.

Katherine Williams blinked in the sudden glare and sat up in the bed, her flame red hair tumbling over her bare shoulders, the sheet slipping down from her breasts.

"Hands up, thief!" Gaetano said.

She frowned at him. "For lord's sake, Rafe, I'm in no mood for your silly damned games."

He leveled the gun at her. "I said hands up!"

She sighed and raised her hands over her head. The sheet slipped further down, to her hips.

"Caught you trying to burglarize my apartment," he said, grinning. "Now, should I call the police, or are you willing to make amends?"

"What do you want, a blow job?"

His grin widened. "That would be nice. For a start."

An hour later he was lying on his back in the darkened bedroom and Kate was saying:

". . . so I left Alphonsus right after he did and came straight here. But I felt so damned tired in this gravity that I had to go to bed."

"A good place for you to be," Gaetano murmured.

"Good for you."

"You didn't enjoy yourself?"

She did not answer.

"Those screams of ecstasy were faked? You should be an actress, then, not a lawyer."

"A lawyer has to be a good actress, sometimes."

"Come on now, you had a good time, didn't you? Didn't you?"

In the shadowy lighting from the room's curtained window, she could not make out the expression on his face. But she heard the anxiety in his voice, and she knew that she did not want to make him unhappy with her.

"I wasn't acting," she lied. "You know I couldn't do that. And I don't have to. Not with you."

"Am I as good as Dan Randolph?" Gaetano asked.

She shrugged her naked shoulders. "I don't know. I've never been to bed with him."

"Never?"

"He's never pushed it that far."

"But he has a reputation."

"I think he's getting too old for his reputation."

"Really?"

"He's never done anything more than make jokes to me."

Gaetano fell silent. Then, "Do you think he suspects you?"

"No way. He fell for the Mitchell acquisition without a quaver."

"Malik thinks it was all his idea. He thinks you're working for him."

Kate said, "I am. And for you."

"For me," he said sharply. "You work for Malik only because I want you to."

"Right. I know that."

"How is your sister?" he asked, maliciously.

"She's almost through rehab. She's been clean for six months now."

"It will be difficult for her to find employment, you know, with her record."

Kate snarled to herself, I know, you olive-oil bastard. I know!

"I will help you there, as well," Gaetano went on. "We can be of great help to one another."

Bitterly, she replied, "Maybe we ought to get married, then, if we're so damned helpful to each other."

Even in the darkness she could see his eyes go round. "Married?" Then he laughed, loud and so hard that he ended up coughing.

Cough your lungs out, bastard. You and your Russian friend, both. But she knew that she was tied to this man and his schemes. There was no way out; each step she took to help him gain more power tied her to him all the closer. Christ on the cross, we might as well be married, she thought. I hate him enough to be.

TEN

To his surprise, Dan found Nobuhiko already in the silent kitchen of the Yamagata house, sitting alone at the table closest to the big walk-in freezer. A bowl of cereal and fruit stood in front of him, next to a steaming mug of tea. He was wearing a white shirt and a tie of deep blue with the inevitable white herons on it. His suit jacket was neatly folded over the back of the chair beside him.

Business costume, Dan knew. He's the head of the company now; probably going to Tokyo to meet with his board of directors.

"You're up early," Dan said.

"You too."

"I need to charter a plane."

"I'll get you one of the company's planes. Where are you going?"

"Tetiaroa. It's a coral atoll near Tahiti."

Nobuhiko's brows rose a fraction of a millimeter.

"A romantic tryst?"

With a displeased shake of his head, Dan replied, "I'm

in no mood for romance right now."

"Ah, yes." Nobo took a crunching spoonful of his cereal while Dan followed the aroma to the automatic coffee maker that had been set up the night before.

"Did you sleep well?" Nobo asked as Dan poured himself a cup.

"So-so. How about you?"

"Hardly a wink. I feel as if a great weight has been hung on my shoulders."

Dan slid into the chair opposite his young friend's. "It has. You've got the responsibility for the entire Yamagata empire now."

Nobo looked as if he wanted to say something, but stopped himself. Finally he asked, "Don't you want something more than coffee?"

"I'll find something. Smoked salmon, maybe."

"In the freezer, I think. I doubt that there are any bagels, though."

He can make a joke, Dan thought. A weak one, but at least he's trying. That's a good sign.

He got up from the table and rummaged through the floor-to-ceiling cupboards, the big restaurant-sized refrigerators and finally the walk-in freezer. When he returned to the table, Dan was carrying a tray laden with smoked salmon, cream cheese, a tin of caviar, a handful of thin crisp biscuits, a large glass of grapefruit juice and the entire pot of coffee.

Nobo's bowl was empty, his tea mug half drained. The younger man was plainly unhappy, and making no attempt to hide it.

"Anything I can help with?" Dan asked as he sat down again.

After a moment's hesitation, Nobo replied, "Yes. There is."

"Tell me." Dan slathered cream cheese on one of the crackers.

"Your fusion fuel operation."

Surprised, Dan asked, "What about it?" as he forked

a thin layer of pink salmon onto the cream cheese.

"It's going to cut into our solar power sales. You're going to be competing against us."

The brittle cracker snapped in Dan's hand. "Damn!" Crumbs and gobs of cheese and salmon spattered over his dish, the table, his slacks.

"I've upset you," Nobo said.

"No, I'm just too double-damned clumsy." Dan brushed at his slacks. "I don't see fusion power competing against the solar satellites. They should complement each other."

"Our marketing department believes otherwise. Already, projected sales for solar power are showing a slight downward trend, for the first time since we built the original sunsat."

Dan took a deep breath. "Look, Nobo, it's only natural for people making long-term energy commitments to hedge their bets when something as revolutionary as fusion power comes on the scene."

"Fusion power has been available for more than a decade. It was never a threat to our sunsats because it was much more expensive. But now, with helium-three from your lunar mining coming on-stream, the new fusion power plants will undercut the price of solar power."

"Hey, I'm your partner on the sunsats, remember? If any throats get cut, mine will be one of them."

"But you own the entire fusion fuel operation."

"You want to buy in? I'll sell you as big a share of the helium-three business as I own of your sunsats. Okay?"

Nobuhiko closed his eyes and bowed his head, as if deep in contemplation. Dan watched him, thinking, It's less than ten hours since Sai was put away and already he's acting like a captain of industry. Good for you, Nobo!

"If current projections are accurate," Nobuhiko said at last, "the long-range trend will be for the world to move toward fusion power and away from power delivered by solar satellites. That will be very bad for

Yamagata Industries."

"Then buy into fusion," Dan urged. "Do it now, while the price is still reasonable."

"Eventually," Nobo continued as if he had not heard Dan's words, "solar power satellites will find *no* markets on Earth. Fusion generators, fueled with helium-three from the Moon, will effectively take the entire market for large central-station electrical power production."

Dan waited several heartbeats to make certain Nobo had finished his little speech. He saw that his young friend was trying to keep his face impassive; the result of his effort was something like a scowl.

Leaning his elbows in the mess on the tabletop and hunching toward Nobo, Dan said, "Listen for a minute. It's always a mistake to try to hold on to a market in the face of radical changes. I think your marketing analysis is probably pretty close to being accurate: fusion power will eventually drive out solar power. Not the small-scale kind of solar, private homes covering their roofs with solarvoltaic cells. Not that kind of thing. But the big multi-gigawatt sunsats—yes, cheap fusion power will take away their existing markets."

Nobo took in a deep breath.

Before he could say anything, Dan went on, "The smart thing to do, in such a situation, is to buy into the innovative technology that will eventually take away your existing market. If you can't beat 'em, join 'em. Your father understood that."

The young man's eyes blinked rapidly, several times. "I am not my father," he said flatly.

Dumb mistake, Dan told himself. Never throw the old man at the son. That's stupid.

"The fact remains," Nobo said, "that your fusion fuel operation will be competing against our sunsats for some time to come."

"Then buy in!"

"Why should I have to spend capital that we could use

to develop other new industries to buy into your operation?"

"What alternative do you suggest?" Dan asked.

"Limit your sales of fusion fuel."

"What?"

"Limit the sales. You have a monopoly on the mining and processing of lunar helium-three. Limit sales and you will drive up the price. That will give you a higher profit margin."

Dan could not believe what he was hearing. "Nobo, I've got a monopoly because I'm producing helium-three cheaper than anybody else can. If I start cutting down on production, everybody and his brother will jump into the game!"

"It will take them years to get into the market."

"The years fly by, pal."

"If you agree to limit production we can work out market shares, divided between sunsats and fusion generators."

"That's conspiracy in restraint of trade! The GEC would be all over us in ten minutes!"

"My lawyers assure me . . ."

"Your lawyers are full of shit if they're telling you we can carve up the energy market between us without the GEC slapping us both in jail!"

"We can handle the GEC."

"And rain makes applesauce."

"You would have made such an arrangement with my father!"

That stunned Dan into silence.

"Wouldn't you?" Nobo demanded.

Dan had no reply.

"You don't wish to make such an arrangement with Yamagata Industries now that I am at its head?"

"Nobo, I can't."

"Then you have decided to try to drive us out of the energy business."

"No! Not at all! I'm offering you a share of the fusion

operation. And you ought to get your marketing people to start looking at how the sunsats can be used to deliver power to other space facilities. Hell, you could beam power all the way out to the asteroid belt if you wanted to."

"There is nothing in the asteroid belt that needs giga-watts of power."

"But there will be! Things don't stand still, Nobo. Don't try to freeze everything in place. You'll get swamped by the changes that can't be stopped."

"Stop lecturing me. I'm not a child."

"Double-damn it to hell and back, Nobo. You're taking this personally. It's not personal; it's business!"

The younger man got to his feet and reached for his suit jacket. "You must pardon me. I am to chair the board meeting in Tokyo this morning. I will leave word to make a plane available for your flight to Tahiti."

"Tetiaroa," Dan corrected glumly.

"Wherever. Good-bye."

Nobuhiko left without a bow, without a handshake, clearly furious and not even trying to hide his emotions.

Dan stood at the table, thinking, Great way to start the day. I've just made an enemy out of my old friend's son.

Jane had not slept well, either. She suppressed the memory of her dreams, recalling only vague images of scenes from her childhood, and of Morgan, her dead husband. I pushed him into politics, Jane said to herself as she showered. I made him president. I killed him.

But not before Morgan himself had killed the love that they had shared. I pushed him into politics, but I didn't force him to take up with those other women: groupies, power-hungry bitches who slept with the high and the mighty regardless of who they might be. Then her anger dissolved as she realized that it was indeed truly her fault, all of it was her own fault. If she had let Morgan alone, allowed him to live the quiet obscure life he had originally wanted, he would be alive today and he would still love no one but her.

But would I love him? Jane asked herself as she dressed. Did I ever really love him? Or did I merely see in Morgan a man who could be guided to greatness? Maybe I was his original groupie. Until I met Dan.

With an effort of steel-hard will Jane shut off her thoughts. I have a job to do, and I'm going to do it.

She had her limousine drive her to Orly, where she boarded the Air France flight for Papeete. The hypersonic jet would whisk her to Tahiti in just over two hours. There a chartered plane waited to fly her to Tetiaroa. And there, Dan Randolph would be waiting.

Maybe.

With a start, she realized that she had not told Vasily Malik that she was on her way to rendezvous with Dan. I could call him from here in the plane, she thought, before the reentry blackout. Or at the airport in Papeete. Or, better yet, I'll wait until I actually see Dan on Tetiaroa.

Yes, she said to herself. I'll wait. It will be better to make certain he's really there before I tell Vasily the good news.

ELEVEN

Winging over the broad Pacific, Dan thought how convenient it would be if he had a seaplane at his disposal. A flying boat that could travel at supersonic speed and land anywhere on the ocean, or a river or a lake. But supersonic speed was just not enough for a man with global interests. The Yamagata plane he was in could do Mach 3, and it was taking hours to reach Tetiaroa. A commercial hypersonic spaceplane, the kind that arched high above the atmosphere and came back down like a reentering rocket, could cross the Pacific in less than an hour.

I'll have to phone Jane and tell her I'm at the island, he thought. She won't come over until she's certain I'm there. She never wants to be the first one there, wherever it is. She'd rather be six hours late than two minutes early.

He felt a worrisome uneasiness about calling Jane to confirm that he was on Tetiaroa. Too many other people could find out. Somebody like Malik, or one of those other paper-pushing bureaucrats at the GEC. Dan did not like to let his enemies know his whereabouts too precisely. Not unless he was safely ensconced in one of his own strongholds, surrounded by friends.

Friends. He thought about Nobuhiko again. *Maybe I ought to at least try to work out something with him. He's right, Sai and I would've put together some kind of a deal. I shouldn't have shut him off so abruptly. No wonder he's sore. I'll have to get back to him, try to work out some kind of plan.*

The plane droned on. Dan was the only passenger in the six-seat compartment. The flight attendant, an attractive, slim young Japanese woman, was sitting in the front row, raptly watching a No drama on video. Dan gazed out the window at the glittering Pacific, nothing but sea and sky as far as the eye could see in any direction. And towering cumulus clouds reaching up beyond their cruising altitude.

"Mr. Randolph-san," the pilot's voice came humming over the intercom, "we are being routed around a major storm system by traffic control. It will cause an unavoidable delay in our scheduled arrival, sir."

The flight attendant glanced back over her shoulder at him, as if to ask what he intended to do about the news. Dan shrugged at her. She turned her attention back to her video screen.

Dan tried to work. He called his office in Caracas and then his headquarters at Alphonsus. He plugged his pocket computer into the video screen on the back of the seat in front of him and went through the day's inputs of data. Bored by it, he switched to the global news channel and saw that the big story was the unseasonal typhoon that had torn across Samoa and was now bearing down on the Gilbert Islands.

The screen showed a devastated city on one of the Samoan islands, Dan had not caught which one: buildings blown down, trees scattered across streets and roads like tenpins, cars crushed, people homeless, fierce gray surf still pounding the beaches, UN Peacekeeping troops flying in with their sky blue helicopters to build shelters and bring food and medicine.

Then the scene shifted to the peaceful atoll of Tarawa. "Scarcely five meters above sea level at its highest point," the voice-over said in a crack-of-doom tone, "this scene of one of World War Two's bloodiest battles may soon face an even more disastrous fate: Mother Nature on a rampage."

Dan stared at the flat sandy islands of the atoll. Cripes, it's just like Tetiaroa. If that kind of a storm hit Tetiaroa there'd be nothing left afterward.

He waited until the newscast turned to its resident meteorologist and his maps. With considerable relief, Dan saw that the typhoon—named Alphonse—was moving west by north, away from Tetiaroa.

"It is very early in the season for a killer typhoon of such mammoth size and strength," the meteorologist was intoning, while the screen showed a satellite view of the storm. It *was* mammoth: its huge swirling bands of clouds covered thousands of square kilometers. "And this is only the first storm in what promises to be a very long and very dangerous hurricane season."

No mention of the greenhouse. Dan switched off the video as the newscast switched to the sports report. Looking out the plane's window, he could see a gray smudge far off on the horizon. Alphonse. Silly name for a killer.

Greenhouse warming of the atmosphere does more than melt glaciers, Dan knew. The warmer the atmosphere, the more energy it stores. The more energy, the bigger and more frequent storms such as hurricanes and typhoons.

It's a good thing I'm going to see Jane, he realized. I've got to convince her about Zach's greenhouse cliff data.

At one time the "airport" at Tetiaroa had been a strip of sand on the atoll's largest island alongside the hotel. A small plane could taxi right up to the open-air registration desk; passengers stepping out of the plane would be greeted by the room clerk and a grinning, bare-chested bellman.

Supersonic jets required longer and stronger runways, however. The French government had started to build a jet landing strip on the next islet in the coral chain, but the people of Tahiti had won their independence before the project could be completed, and for years the jet airport languished half-built. Finally a Japanese-Australian consortium bought the hotel, finished the airstrip, and even connected the two isles with a paved road and a concrete bridge arched high enough to allow dugout canoes to pass under it.

The consortium went broke eventually, and the government of Tahiti took over the entire tourist facility until a new commercial buyer could be found.

Now, as Dan stepped out of the Yamagata jet onto the hard surface of the jet runway, a smiling pair of young Polynesian women dressed in flowered red *pareos* greeted him with kisses on both cheeks and leis of colorful fragrant blossoms.

Slipping his arms around each slender waist as a husky young man took his battered travel bag, Dan started toward the waiting electric cart, wondering, Why would anyone want to live anywhere else in the world? These people are wonderful. Too bad Christianity ruined their morals.

The hotel's registration desk consisted of a bamboo counter beneath a thatched roof supported by four stout pillars, open to the salty sea breeze. By the time the cart had crossed the guano-spattered concrete bridge and pulled up at it, Dan was thinking, As long as Jane's not here, I might as well invite these lovely creatures to have dinner with me this evening. And then some.

He was shocked when he saw Jane standing in the shade of the roof off to one side of the registration desk. Tall and regal, her long auburn hair flowing past her bare shoulders, she too was wearing a wraparound *pareo,* forest green with a white floral pattern. Tied at the neck, it came to a modest midthigh on her.

Dan grinned at her and disengaged from the two Polynesian women, who giggled and jumped off the cart. He got off more slowly, and walked toward Jane with his smile fixed on his face. Stepping out of the tropical sun into the shade of the roof plummeted the temperature twenty degrees. Or is it just Jane refrigerating the atmosphere? he asked himself.

"I didn't expect you'd be here waiting for me," he said.

"Obviously," said Jane.

"Very friendly natives." He took one of the leis from around his neck and draped it over Jane's head, then bussed her on both cheeks. It was like kissing a statue.

Stepping back from her slightly, Dan said, "I'd better sign in with the room clerk."

"That's all been done in advance."

"Oh? Thanks." Dan realized that the kid with his travel bag had disappeared. He grinned again. "Are we sharing a room?"

"Not even in your dreams," Jane snapped.

"You'd be surprised what I dream about."

"Probably not."

"So which hut is mine? Are we next door to each other, at least?"

"It doesn't matter. We're the only two guests in the hotel, at present."

"The only . . . ?" Dan blinked. "I had heard that business out here wasn't all that good, but there's *nobody* else here?"

"No one but the staff," said Jane.

"That's damned romantic!"

Jane made a sound that he swore was a snort. "I'll see you at dinner," she said. Turning abruptly away, she headed off toward the rows of thatched huts that served as guest rooms.

Dan shrugged and turned to the room clerk, a chunky

middle-aged woman who was eying him doubtfully. The two young women who had greeted him at the airstrip were standing uncertainly at the far end of the registration desk.

Dan took a deep breath of clean, sweet island air, heavy with the scents of tropical flowers. The Yamagata jet roared overhead, rattling his bones with its noise, then dwindled into the bright cloud-flecked sky.

The sound of the plane ebbed into silence. The sea breeze blew, the palm trees swayed. After a few minutes of just standing there admiring the peace and beauty, Dan crooked a finger at the two young women.

They came over toward him, smiling.

"I wonder if you lovely ladies would be good enough to show me to my room," he said to them, thinking, When in Rome, do as the Romans do.

All through dinner Dan tried to figure out what was bothering Jane. *She tells me to meet her here in this isolated little paradise, I come flying out to her without asking any questions, and she's pissed as hell about something. The two little wahines? Can't be that; we're both too old to get sore at each other's sex lives. Hell, it isn't as if we're committed to each other. Why should she be sore that I'm friendly with the local entertainment committee?*

No, he decided, watching her pick at her dinner, something else is bothering Jane. Something inside her. Something that really hurts.

The dining area was out in the open air, as was almost all of the hotel. The patio was not even roofed over; they could see the stars glittering gloriously in the dark tropical night. The food was good, better than good; Dan knew that a Cordon Bleu chef had been flown in from Rome for the hotel.

He had not known that they would be the only two guests on the island. That had surprised him. As they sat in private splendor, watching the stars and the luminous white sand beach, listening to the surf booming out along the reef, sipping a chilled rosé Tavel, Dan thought how idyllic this evening would be—if only he and Jane could forget the past and begin anew.

"You picked a marvelous spot," he said, putting the wineglass down on the tablecloth.

Jane's wine had hardly been touched. She pushed her plate of delicately grilled *apakapaka* away and glanced at the empty patio, lit by Japanese lanterns and tiny candles on each of the unoccupied tables.

"Yes, I suppose it is pretty."

She was wearing a soft coral pink dress with a scalloped neckline, a choker of pearls and diamonds at her throat, her hair done in an almost girlish ponytail.

"Pretty? It's gorgeous! And you look very beautiful, Jane."

The corners of her lips twitched. "I'm older than those two wahines you took to your room this afternoon, both of them added together."

"Them?" Dan laughed. "They just helped me to adjust to the jet lag."

She gave him a sour look.

"What's bothering you, Jane? Something's tearing up your insides; I can see it from here, and I'm not a very sensitive person."

Jane looked away from him, out toward the empty beach. He waited for her to speak. She did not.

With a patient sigh, Dan said, "Okay—I didn't want to add to your troubles, but I guess I'm going to anyway. While you're figuring out when you're going to tell me what's eating at you, think about this: the greenhouse effect is going to hit this planet like a ton of bricks in just about ten years."

Jane looked straight at him. This subject was impersonal, she could handle it. "What do you mean by that?"

"According to my science people, the global climate is approaching a kind of cliff. An abrupt change. What they call a discontinuity."

"In the next ten years?"

Nodding, "Ten is an approximation. Maybe it'll be more, but not much. Maybe less. If we don't start preparing for it now we're going to be flooded out."

"The greenhouse effect has been building up for a century or more," Jane said.

"Yeah, slowly. But Zach Freiberg and the other deep thinkers tell me there's going to be a sudden change. Glaciers will melt away entirely. Greenland and Antarctica will melt down. Sea levels will go way up: twenty, thirty feet, maybe."

"That's preposterous."

"This atoll will be underwater. So will New York be, and Houston, Caracas, Venice—half the cities in the world. Millions will be wiped out, Jane. Hundreds of millions of people are going to be killed. Hundreds of millions more will be homeless and starving."

"That's a scare scenario. I've heard nothing like that from the GEC's scientists."

Dan tilted his chair back. "Maybe it's all wrong. I sure don't know. But Zach's no Chicken Little. He's tried to get your people to look at his data and all they did was laugh in his face."

Jane frowned at him, but it wasn't her frown of personal disapproval. This was her "I don't understand what you're telling me" frown. Dan took it as a good sign.

"I was glad when you asked me to come here and see you," he said, "because I needed to tell you about this face-to-face. I've got Zach's data in my computer, if you want to go over it."

"Tomorrow," she said.

"Good. Then we can go to Paris and tell the rest of the Council about it."

But Jane shook her head. "No, Dan. You're not going to Paris or anywhere else. You're staying here."

A tendril of unease tingled up his spine. "What do you mean?"

"Your holdings are being confiscated, Dan. The GEC has started—"

"Confiscated?" He lurched across the table at her, grabbing for her wrist. "What do you mean, confiscated?"

Jane avoided his hands. "Just what I said, Dan. You've violated GEC regulations and the confiscation procedures are under way right now."

"Son of a bitch!"

"While the procedures are being carried out, you're going to stay here on Tetiaroa."

"What the hell is this? You mean I'm under arrest?"

She almost smiled. "You're being detained."

"I want my lawyer!"

Jane actually did smile. "You mean the same one that represented you in the Mitchell Mining acquisition?"

Dan felt his jaw drop open. The anger evaporated. "You mean Scarlett screwed me?"

"If that's her name. Yes."

He leaned back in his chair and lifted his face to the starry sky and roared with sudden laughter. "The redheaded bitch screwed me without laying me!"

Dan laughed so hard tears streamed down his cheeks. Jane sat across the little table and watched him, startled at his laughter. She had expected anything but that.

TWELVE

Dan's laughter ended soon enough.

"I don't see anything funny about this situation," Jane said coldly.

Wiping at his eyes, Dan replied, "When they hand you a lemon, make lemonade."

"What?"

Gesturing to the moonlit beach and the star-filled sky, he said, "Here we are, alone on a tropical island, far away from the rest of the crazy world. Let's make the most of it."

Her nostrils flared angrily. "Is that all you can think of?"

He quoted:

> " 'Ah, love, let us be true
> To one another! for the world, which seems
> To lie before us like a land of dreams,
> So various, so beautiful, so new,

Hath really neither joy, nor love, nor light,
Nor certitude, nor peace, nor help for pain . . .' "

Jane got to her feet so quickly that her chair fell over behind her. "Vasily Malik will be here tomorrow to explain the fine details of the confiscation procedures."

"Great," said Dan, grinning ruefully up at her.

"You will remain incommunicado on this island until the Council deems it proper for you to be released."

"Released? To where? Debtors' prison? Or will the Council send me to Malik's Gulag up at Aristarchus?"

Jane huffed at him, turned on her heel and walked away so fast that she was almost running.

Go on, Dan called after her silently. Run away. You can run, gorgeous, but you can't hide.

Then he waved at one of the waiters who had been hovering off at the edge of the patio. The young man came over and picked up Jane's chair, then asked, "Sir?"

"The best bottle of Armagnac you've got," Dan ordered. "And a large snifter."

"Armagnac?" The kid's brow furrowed. "I don't know if we have—"

"You've got it. Just ask the bartender."

Two minutes later the youngster came back with a green bottle shaped like a flat canteen and a snifter big enough to keep goldfish in. Dan smiled and poured for himself. The waiter retreated back to the shadows.

Holding his glass high, pointing it in the direction that Jane had taken, Dan finished his quotation aloud:

" 'And we are here as on a darkling plain,
Swept with confused alarms of struggle and flight,
Where ignorant armies clash by night.' "

Then he laughed softly to himself. "But we're going to clash in broad daylight, Malik and me. Tomorrow."

* * *

He awoke with the sun. And a thundering headache. Too much of a good thing, Dan grumbled to himself as he squinted blearily at the morning brightness. Armagnac goes down smooth, but leaves a reminder the next day. Or maybe you're just getting old, pal. Seems to me you could drink a whole flagon of the stuff without a twinge, way back when.

Like all the rooms at the hotel, his hut consisted of a thatched roof and bamboo screening that reached neither the ground nor the roof. Most of the insects native to the island had been eliminated by biogenetic controls, but Dan still was not happy about the sand that inevitably seeped onto the floor matting.

Shrugging, he padded naked to the bathroom, took one bleary look at himself in the mirror, and decided that corrective action had to be taken right away. Still naked, he walked out of the hut, away from the hotel's office and restaurant, toward the lagoon. He splashed into the water; it was not as warm as he had expected, but that didn't matter. He dove in, came up sputtering and spouting, then began methodically swimming parallel to the beach.

He reached the channel between islets, felt the current rushing outward, and reversed his course. By the time he got back to where he had started, one of the hotel's boys was standing ankle-deep in the water, patiently holding a towel for him.

Dan came out of the lagoon and wrapped the towel around his middle. He was puffing like an old man: swimming was a new sport to him. He had never had the opportunity to do much of it back in the days when he lived in orbital space, and somehow when he was on Earth he was always too busy to take the time to paddle around in a pool.

It was only a year earlier that he had finally allowed himself to order a swimming pool built into his quarters at Alphonsus. It had taken a real effort of mind to convince himself that water, manufactured from lunar oxygen baked out of rocks and hydrogen scooped up in the regolith, was no longer as rare on the Moon as it had once been. It took a lot of energy to produce water, which made it very expensive. But once Dan realized with a happy surprise that he could easily afford a hundred swimming pools, he had his own private one built.

As he started back toward his hut he could feel the tropical sun baking him dry. He asked the young man walking slightly behind him, "Is there a plane scheduled to come in today?"

"I don't know. I can check."

"Yeah, please do. I'll be going to the patio for breakfast."

"Yessir."

By the time he had finished a large glass of orange juice the youngster came back to report that a plane was indeed due to land shortly after noon. Dan thanked him, then started in on his breakfast of ham and eggs. The hotel kept its livestock on one of the islets on the other side of the lagoon. Even when the wind blew from that direction, the isle was far enough away so that the smell did not bother the guests.

What guests? Dan thought sourly as he ate. This operation can't be making a profit with only two people here. The double-damned GEC won't pay enough to break even. Those bureaucrats don't believe in making profits; just in getting all the privileges of living like millionaires for themselves.

Jane stayed in her hut all morning and refused to answer his phone calls. He was supposed to be kept incommunicado from the rest of the world, so Dan did not even bother to try contacting his offices. He took out one of the outrigger canoes, paddled around the lagoon, visited the pigs and chickens on the farthest islet, and managed to overturn the outrigger in the current between islands, to the uproarious delight of the Polynesian staff of the hotel, who apparently had nothing better to do than watch him from the beach.

Standing in four feet of sun-warmed water, Dan righted the canoe, tilted it to drain the water from inside it, and then rowed with as much dignity as he could muster back to the hotel's beach. He had to grin to himself, though: overturning an outrigger must be a rare sight to these kids.

Dan was lying on the beach, letting the sun dry him and his swim trunks, when Malik's plane made its appearance. At first it was only a barely visible dot in the bright blue sky, a foreign intruder in paradise. Then it came lower, grew into a dark swept-wing shape, shrieking like a turbine-powered banshee, and finally settled onto the ground, flaps dangling down, wheels kicking up coral dust when they touched the runway.

He watched Jane go across the bridge in the electric cart and, a few minutes later, come back again with Vasily Malik sitting beside her. Dan smiled to himself at Malik's light blond hair and pale pink skin. Maybe he'll get sunstroke, he thought happily.

The ozone layer was so damaged that you could get skin cancer from solar ultraviolet if you weren't careful. But Dan found that he could not wish cancer on Malik. Not that. Not even for him.

As he got to his feet and brushed the sand off, he saw the cart go back across the bridge again. The plane's staying, Dan realized. Malik's planning to leave after he has the chance to gloat over me. With a grin, he wondered what Malik would do if he swam out to the plane and took off in it.

"No," Dan muttered to himself. "The sonofabitch would probably order the Peacekeepers to shoot me down. He'd tell 'em I'm a terrorist on my way to nuke the Vatican."

So he walked slowly toward the patio dining area. Sure enough, Malik and Jane were sitting at a table shaded by a broad, gaily striped umbrella, their heads together like a pair of conspirators.

"What a surprise!" Dan shouted as he stepped onto

the ironwood-floored patio. "Vasily—you've flown all the way from Paris just to see me? I'm honored."

Malik returned his smile. "I wouldn't have missed this occasion for the world," he said.

Jane looked just as edgy as she had the night before. Maybe more so, thought Dan. She was wearing a dark blue pair of shorts and a sleeveless white blouse. Dark glasses were her only concession to the hot tropical sun overhead. She tans well, Dan remembered, hoping that she was smart enough to use sunblock anyway.

Malik always seemed to have precisely the correct wardrobe for every occasion. He looked as if he had just stepped out of a video advertisement: casual whipcord slacks of light tan, an ivory-colored short-sleeved shirt with blue-tabbed epaulets, and a woven straw hat with a snap brim slanted at a rakish angle. No sunglasses, but his icy blue eyes looked darker than usual. Contact lenses, Dan concluded. He's too damned conceited even to wear sunglasses.

In nothing but his swim trunks and an unbuttoned open-weave shirt, Dan pulled up a chair and joined them in the shade of the umbrella.

"So tell me," he said cheerfully to Malik, "how busy you're going to make my lawyers."

Malik gave him a smile full of teeth. "Your lawyers can become as busy as they like; there is no way for them to save you. You have clearly broken GEC regulations, which have the force of international law."

"And just which regulations have I broken?"

Malik explained with great patience and obvious relish, citing specific clauses and dates. Dan listened, but his eyes strayed to Jane. She looked as tense as a prisoner facing a firing squad.

"So you see," Malik concluded, "that if any of your lawyers decide to try to help you, they will have to do it on a *pro bono* basis. As of noon tomorrow, Paris time, all of Astro Manufacturing will be closed down."

"Closed down?" Dan snapped. "You mean you're

throwing all my people out of work?"

Malik raised a placating hand. "An unfortunate choice of words, excuse me. Astro will continue to operate, but it will be managed by specialists from the GEC. Under my direction."

"Holy sheep dip," Dan grumbled.

"It'll be like what happens when a corporation goes into bankruptcy," Jane said, her first words since Dan had come to their table.

"Yeah," Dan replied. "The company staggers on, profits drop to zero, and before you know it the whole organization falls apart."

"Don't be so gloomy," Malik said. "Your employees will remain faithful to Astro Corporation. They will not be allowed to quit."

Dan fixed him with a sour look. "Another one of your double-damned regulations?"

"Yes. Of course." Malik looked wonderfully happy.

With a snort of disdain, Dan leaned both his elbows on the round table and said, "Okay. Now I've got something *really* important to tell you about."

Malik looked surprised. "More important than losing your company?"

Nodding, Dan said, "I told Jane about it last night. This is global trouble: the greenhouse cliff."

"Cliff?"

Dan explained Zach Freiberg's hypothesis about the sudden warming of the Earth. After he finished, Malik remained silent for several moments.

"We haven't seen anything like this from our scientific staff," Jane said at last.

"Yes, we have," said Malik.

"We have?"

"Your scientists have come to the same conclusion?" Dan asked, suddenly eager with hope.

Malik nodded warily. "It's been kept in deepest secrecy—"

Jane blurted, "You didn't even tell the rest of the Council!"

"How could I?" Malik said to her. "This is catastrophic news. It must not leak out to the general public. There would be panic everywhere."

Dan gaped at him. "You knew?"

"Of course I knew. I knew when your naive Dr. Freiberg brought his findings to my—our—scientific staff."

"But you should have informed the Council, Vasily," said Jane.

"Break this news to doddering old fools like Sibuti? Or gangsters like Gaetano? That would be a disaster piled on top of a catastrophe."

"I don't get it," Dan said. "What in the name of hell's angels are you *doing* with the information?"

"Taking your corporation away from you. All of the Big Seven space corporations must be confiscated. Yamagata comes next."

Dan's temper snapped. He leaped across the table, hands going for Malik's throat. But the Russian blocked him, grabbed him by the hair and one arm, and flipped him expertly to the ironwood floor of the patio. Dan landed with a painful thump, the wind knocked out of him. Malik stood over him, fists clenched, hat still in place, a twisted little smile on his lips.

"We are not in zero gravity now, Randolph. I know how to defend myself. Shall I show you a few karate kicks?"

Squinting up into the afternoon brightness, Dan saw Jane clutch at Malik's arm and a pair of beefy hotel boys rushing toward them.

Dan climbed slowly to his feet and waved the boys away. "I'm okay," he told them. "No problem. We're just having a little fun."

"I've kept up my martial arts training," Malik said, smirking. "Apparently you've spent all your time in low gravity making money."

Dan picked up his chair and sat on it, fuming to himself, I'll kill this sonofabitch one of these days. Too bad I didn't do it when I had the chance, ten years ago. His backside hurt where he had landed on the floor, but his only serious injury seemed to be to his pride.

Jane returned to her seat. Malik sat down, too.

"Let me explain something to you, Mr. Capitalist," Malik said. "You may think that I am carrying out a personal vendetta against you, but believe me, that is not the case."

"Sure," Dan muttered.

"I learned about the greenhouse disaster more than a year ago."

"And you've done nothing about it."

"Not so." Malik glanced at Jane, then returned his attention to Dan. "But before I tell what I have done, tell me—what would *you* do to save the world from the coming catastrophe?"

"I'd move heaven and earth to avoid triggering that cliff!"

"Yes, of course. But how?"

"Stop burning fossil fuels, for one thing. It's the carbon dioxide and methane we pour into the atmosphere that's causing the warming."

"Not natural causes?" Jane asked.

Both men shook their heads. Malik said, "Astronomers and geophysicists agree that neither solar activity nor ordinary climate cycles are causing the global warming trend. Our friend here is correct: the greenhouse is man-made, almost entirely."

"There's some contribution from cow farts and termite burps," Dan added, "but the overwhelming cause of the warming is the crap we're putting into the air."

Malik smiled at him. "To get back to my question: How would you correct this situation?"

"Like I said, stop burning fossil fuels. Go to fusion and solar power. Move as much as possible of the world's industrial base off-Earth and into orbit. We can make superconducting electrical motors and batteries in orbit, you know. They can replace petroleum-powered vehicles."

"All around the world?"

"Right."

"In ten years?"

"What choice do you have? Maybe we can't get it all done in ten years, but we've got start *now* and do as much as we can."

Malik drummed his fingertips on the table for a silent moment, then said, "I agree entirely."

Dan blinked at him. "Then why in hell are you wasting time trying to drive me out of business?"

"I don't understand it either," Jane said.

"Think about it for a moment," Malik said, with an expression on his face almost of pity. "It is necessary to make the whole world convert from fossil fuels to nuclear and solar energy. The entire world!"

"Yes," Jane said.

"The task cannot be done piecemeal. It cannot be done on a voluntary basis. We cannot *ask* people to stop driving their petrol-burning cars and wait until we can replace them with electrical vehicles. We cannot expect major corporations to shut down entire industrial plants for months or years while their electrical power plants are replaced. For that matter, how can we raise the capital required to build all these fusion power plants and solar power satellites—in ten years?"

"What choice do we have?" Dan snapped.

Malik took a breath. "A global problem requires global coordination. And global control."

Dan felt his jaw clench. "I knew it," he muttered. "The whole frigging world facing disaster and you see it as an opportunity to establish a double-damned dictatorship."

"Dan, that's not fair!" Jane said. "Vasily has an important point here. How can you expect—"

"How can you expect free men to act in their own best interest?" Dan felt the anger rising in him again. "A lot better than they'd be able to act when some double-damned global bureaucracy is grinding them down."

Malik raised his hands in an *I told you so* gesture. "You see? That is exactly how I expected you to react. You and your fellow capitalists. That is why it is necessary to remove you from control of Astro Manufacturing. The Council needs Astro's assets if we are to avert this disaster."

"And Yamagata's?" Dan asked.

"Yamagata also. And all the other privately owned space industries; all seven of them. They are the key to the world's survival. Once the Council controls all the Big Seven space industries—"

"You'll have accomplished what you failed to do ten years ago," Dan said.

Ignoring him, Malik finished, "We will be able to begin the process of converting from fossil fuels to nuclear and solar energy, worldwide."

"And if you succeed, what happens afterward? Will you turn all the space industrial facilities back to their rightful owners?"

Malik's smirking grin returned. "Why, Mr. Randolph, you surprise me. By then, the Global Economic Council will be the legal owner of all space facilities. In the name of the peoples of Earth, of course. For the common good."

"Bullshit!" Dan answered fervently.

Malik's expression hardened. "You think that I am doing this for my own personal gain. What do you call it? A power trip?"

"An ego trip," Dan growled.

"That is not the case. What I do I do to save the world from the coming catastrophe. My own personal power, my ego, they mean nothing. I act for the good of all the world's peoples. Not for profit."

"Sure," said Dan. "And rain makes applesauce. If you actually believe that, you're the worst kind of fool. There's only one sin in the world: poverty. And there's only one crime: believing your own propaganda."

THIRTEEN

Don't you see?" Dan pleaded with Jane. "All he's after is power! He's using this cataclysm as an excuse to grab total world power."

They were walking glumly along the beach as the sunset turned the cloud-streaked sky into flaming reds and oranges.

"Dan, you're not being fair to Vasily."

"Like hell I'm not."

"I don't like what he wants to do, but I've got to agree with him. I don't see how we can accomplish what needs to be done without the authority of the law behind us. We need the GEC's control over the situation. Otherwise . . ." Her voice trailed off into silence.

Ignoring the beauty of the fading day, Dan urged her, "He wants to be dictator of the world. He'll be using economic power instead of military, but by the time the shit hits the fan he'll be a world-class Napoleon. Or worse yet, a Stalin."

"He's not like that," she insisted. "He's really concerned. He sees this course of action as the only one that has a chance of working."

"And if it does work, he'll be sitting on a throne for the rest of his life."

"If it doesn't work, he'll take the blame."

Dan grunted. "Yeah, maybe. If he hasn't taken total control of the world's media by then."

"Be fair!"

"Fair? He knew! The sonofabitch knew all about the greenhouse cliff for a frigging *year* and he didn't tell anybody about it. He didn't even tell you or the rest of the Council."

"Yes, I know. He was afraid that the news would leak out prematurely. Can you imagine what effects it will have on people when we do start to tell them? The panic?"

"The stock market," Dan muttered.

Jane stopped walking and turned to face Dan. Standing there on the beach, the dying sun behind her, the sky flaming with color, she looked to him like a tall, strong, beautiful goddess just come out of the sea.

"Dan," she said, "we've got to work with Vasily, not against him. There's no other way."

"I don't have to do a damned thing. He's arranged it that way, hasn't he?"

"He knew you'd fight against him."

Dan nodded. "He's right."

"But if you'd promise to cooperate—"

"Cooperate? While his paper-pushing desk jockeys try to run my company? It'll take those drones ten years just to rework the organization charts!"

She sighed heavily and started back toward the huts of the hotel. "I'll be leaving tomorrow morning, you know. I have an enormous amount of work ahead of me."

"And I'm supposed to stay here. How long?"

She shrugged.

Striding alongside her, he reached for her hand. "Well, at least we've got tonight together."

He could not tell in the dying light, but he almost thought he saw tears in her eyes.

"Oh Dan," she said, "it's like everything in the whole blessed world stands between us. Has always stood between us."

"There's nothing in the world between us now," he replied gently. "Tonight there's only the two of us on this beautiful island. The past is dead and gone and tomorrow doesn't exist yet. But we have tonight."

"Yes," she murmured. "We have tonight."

Dan awoke when his wristwatch's silent alarm sent its pulsed tingling signal up his left arm. It was still dark. Jane lay sleeping soundly next to him, a thin sheet pulled halfway up her alabaster body. For long minutes he sat in bed gazing down at her in the dim light of the digital clock on the dresser across the room. God but you're beautiful, he told her silently. To think of all the years we've spent apart. What a waste. What a cosmically tragic waste.

Slowly, softly, he slipped out of the bed, not wanting to awaken her. He grabbed a swimsuit and T-shirt from the pile in the corner of the hut and padded out naked into the starlit predawn. Grinning to himself, he took his pick of the empty huts, taking one as far from his own as he could. There he urinated and showered, patted his graying hair into some semblance of order, pulled on the trunks and T-shirt, and then marched determinedly to the hotel's office.

No one was at the registration desk. The kitchen looked dark and empty. Dan knew that the staff slept in the long hut behind the office building, but the manager and his wife had a private suite in the building itself. It was a small cottage, the only building on the islet that had solid walls instead of bamboo screens.

There was no lock on the building's front door. Why bother? Where would a thief go on this atoll? All the islets put together barely added up to a few square kilometers. You could see a man standing on the pig farm from all the way across the lagoon; with binoculars you could make out his face.

Dan let himself in. The entire ground floor of the little cottage was a single room: the hotel's business office. The overhead lights went on automatically as the wall sensor reacted to his body heat. Dan saw a desk with a computer and phone console on it, two rattan chairs with gaudy flowered cushions, and a small bookcase that seemed to hold brochures advertising the hotel and nothing else.

The manager gets up early, he told himself. I'll just wait for him to come downstairs.

He sat in one of the rattan chairs and was almost dozing off when he heard the sound of water gurgling through pipes. A few minutes later, the manager came downstairs, looking more angry than surprised that Dan was waiting for him.

"Mr. Randolph," he said, "what are you doing here?"

The manager was Polynesian, short and round-bellied, old enough for his short-cropped hair to be snowy white. He wore loose-fitting shorts and a brightly flowered shirt, unbuttoned: his business attire.

"I want you to phone your supervisor in Papeete," Dan said.

"You are not allowed to make phone calls, sir."

"I want *you* to call him."

Puzzled, the manager asked, "Why?"

"So that he can call his boss in Port Moresby."

"Is this some kind of a joke, Mr. Randolph?"

"Nope. Just tell him that Mr. Randolph is declaring an emergency. And give him the code number fifty-six, twenty-five, seventy-five, thirty-nine. He'll understand."

It took ten minutes of persuasion and an electronic transfer of three hundred Australian dollars from Dan's bank in Sydney before the manager reluctantly, suspiciously phoned his supervisor. Dan sat comfortably in the cushioned rattan chair as the manager's call was transferred from Papeete to Port Moresby to Honolulu to San Diego and finally to Caracas. With each transfer the man's eyes became wider.

Dan could see white all around the manager's pupils by the time he handed the phone over. Smiling his thanks, Dan heard a computer's synthesized voice say, "Please repeat the security code for voice check."

Dan said, "Fifty-six, twenty-five, seventy-five, thirty-nine."

"Voice check positive. Stand by please."

A woman's voice said, "Security, O'Dare."

"Scramble," said Dan.

"All messages on this line are scrambled, Mr. Randolph. And carried by laser link to avert tracing."

Dan grinned. She was curt and sharp, no wasted breath. Good.

"I'm on an atoll near Tahiti called Tetiaroa. I need an airlift to a space launching facility where I can get to Alphonsus City as quickly as possible."

Hardly a heartbeat's delay. Then, "Computer shows commercial flights to Alphonsus scheduled from Yamagata center in Tokyo Bay in twelve hours."

"Not soon enough. I need a high-energy boost, too. I can't afford to spend several days in transit."

"We can roll out a private booster at La Guaira, have it ready for you by the time your plane gets you here."

"What about Cape York? Don't the Aussies have anything heading for Alphonsus?"

"Not for the next thirty-six hours, sir."

The hotel manager's mouth had gone just as round as his eyes. Dan grinned at him as he said into the phone, "Get a spaceplane to Papeete. Set up an OTV at space station Nueva Venezuela for a high-energy burn to Alphonsus. Top priority and top security. Have a plane from Papeete pick me up here and fly me back to the airport. I don't want anyone to know that the plane is coming to Tetiaroa. That's vital. And it's all got to be done before noon, my time."

"Yessir, Mr. Randolph. I'm keying it in right now."

"Good work, O'Dare."

Handing the phone back to the goggle-eyed manager, Dan thought, Malik'll find out about the spaceplane as soon as its flight plan is filed. Maybe he'll be suspicious about a flight from Papeete to Nueva Venezuela, maybe not. But he can't react fast enough to stop me. And he won't know anybody's coming here to pick me up. He thinks he's got me stuck on this atoll. My people on the space station can get me off to Alphonsus before he knows what's happening.

Walking out of the office into the first pale light of dawn, Dan told himself, If we move fast enough we can get away with it. I'll be on my way to Alphonsus before Malik knows I've left Tetiaroa.

Jane was sitting up in bed, still half asleep, when he got back to the hut. She modestly pulled the sheet over her bosom. Dan grinned at her reaction, thinking back to their lovemaking during the night.

I guess the truce is over, he said to himself.

"Where've you been?" she asked.

"Took a walk."

She looked slightly suspicious, but as he got back into bed beside her, Jane's expression changed.

"How did you like your lemonade?" she asked.

"Huh?"

"You told me that when they hand you a lemon, you should start making lemonade. How did you like the lemonade?"

Grinning, "You're no lemon, Jane. You're a peach." He kissed her and she kissed back and their bodies twined together once again.

They barely had time to pull on their swimsuits and take a dip in the lagoon before they heard a plane coming in. Jane squinted up into the bright morning sky.

"It's early," she said.

"I don't think that's your plane," said Dan.

"Who—"

"It's for me. And you."

She stared at him. "What do you mean?"

"We're going to Alphonsus. Grab your bag." He started toward their hut as the plane swooped in for its landing.

"You can't leave this island!" Jane shouted after him.

"Watch me. And you're coming too."

She dashed after him. "What do you mean? You weren't even allowed to make a phone call. We warned the manager and his entire staff!"

"Honey, the manager and the entire staff work for me. I bought this joint, the whole frigging chain, the day you invited me to meet you here."

"You what?"

He stepped into the hut and began tossing his scattered belongings into his travel bag. "You ought to check up on the ownership of the places where you want to hold prisoners. Not that it would've done you much good. There're four other corporations between me and this hotel chain. You'd've spent a couple of days following the paper trail to find me."

"You sneaking bastard!"

He looked up at her, standing in the doorway, fists planted on her hips. The swimsuit she wore was a formfitting maillot, emerald green.

"You're calling me a sneak?" Dan laughed. "I didn't invite you here for the purpose of sticking you in the slammer."

"And last night—you knew you were going to do this! And this morning!"

"I knew I was going to try. I'm not going to let Malik or you or the Pope in Rome steal my company away from me. Not without a fight."

Furious, Jane pounded a fist against the bamboo screening. It rattled as if one more shot would knock it down.

"Come on, come on, we don't have time to waste."

"I'm not going with you!"

"You sure as hell are."

"No!"

Closing the Velcro seal on his travel bag, Dan said, "Jane, I may be old and slow and softened by living on the Moon too much. Maybe Malik can beat the crap out of me. But I can still fling you over my shoulder and carry you out to that plane, if I have to."

She glared at him. "You'd have a heart attack halfway there."

Shrugging, "Then I'll be dead and that'll be the end of it. Will you cry over my body?"

"I'll do something else over your body!"

"That's not very ladylike. Come on, time's wasting."

"I'm not going," she insisted.

He stepped up to her, smiled sweetly, and said, "Either you come with me conscious, or I'll knock you out cold and drag you."

"You wouldn't dare."

"I wouldn't like to."

"A minute ago you were going to carry me."

"Stop stalling. I need you as a hostage. Otherwise that damned Malik would probably use one of the orbiting lasers to blast my spacecraft."

Jane looked at him. "You're serious, aren't you?"

"Totally."

She went to the dresser and began emptying the drawers into her carry bag.

FOURTEEN

'**ve** got to remember to give O'Dare a bonus, Dan told himself. A big one.

The half-hour flight to Papeete was thankfully uneventful. The spaceplane was waiting on the runway, sleek and delta-winged and glistening white in the late-morning sun. Dan and Jane stepped from the little jet that had carried them from Tetiaroa directly into the spaceplane's big, empty passenger compartment. With only a routine holdup by traffic control, the spaceplane trundled out onto the runway and arrowed into the sky, engines screaming.

Plenty of people come to Papeete on their own private planes, Dan reassured himself. They land spaceplanes here on a regular schedule. This isn't so unusual. I hope.

The transfer at the space station Nueva Venezuela went smoothly enough. Jane behaved herself, and the two of them went from the spaceplane's hatch into the zero-g receiving area at the hub of the station and directly through an access tunnel into the claustrophobic cabin of a modified orbital transfer vehicle.

"How do you feel?" Dan asked his hostage as they swam weightlessly to their seats in the OTV's passenger deck.

"A little queasy," Jane admitted. "It's been a long time since I've been in zero-g."

Dan opened the compartment built into the seat's armrest and rummaged through its innards. Finally he pulled out a slim plastic package. Tearing it open, he handed Jane a little circular medicinal patch.

"Slap this on behind your ear. It helps a lot."

She started to nod, turned pale, and pressed the patch against her neck.

There were no windows in the passenger deck, and even if there were they would not have been able to see much of the vehicle they were in. An OTV was built for efficiency, not style. Since it flew only in the vacuum of space, it did not need the streamlining or airfoils of an airplane. It had a rocket engine, maneuvering jets, propellant tanks, cargo bay, a cramped compartment for up to six passengers (eight, the standard wisdom claimed, if they were in love) and docking probes to latch on to a space station or another spacecraft. Plus a two-person flight deck perched at its top like a single bulbous eyeball.

From the outside it looked like an ungainly, unlikely, unlovely collection of metallic spheres and cylinders and cones. This particular OTV was also fitted out, Dan knew, with two extra oversized propellant tanks and spindly, spraddly legs ending in broad round footpads, so that it could set down on the surface of the Moon.

The ship's copilot floated down from the flight deck, feet dangling in midair, only one hand lightly touching a rung of the ladder. A longtime veteran of space flight, Dan could see: grizzled short-cropped hair and a shoulder patch on her Astro coveralls that read: GREATEST GRANDMOM IN THE SOLAR SYSTEM.

"Mr. Randolph, flight control has asked us to hold for a few minutes. They said something about a message coming up from Earthside." She looked more annoyed than worried.

"Are we cleared for departure?" Dan asked.

"We've got a six-minute window. They've asked us to hold until the message comes in. It must be a message for you, I guess."

"Screw it. Let's get moving. The message can catch up with us while we're in transit."

The greatest grandmom in the solar system nodded her agreement. "You're the boss." And she pulled herself effortlessly up through the hatch and back into the flight deck.

Jane had a bit more color in her face. "You think the message is from Vasily?"

"Who else? And it's not for me, it's for the station security officer to check exactly who's aboard this OTV and why they're heading for Alphonsus."

"He must know we've left Tetiaroa."

"Yep. By now."

They felt the slightest of bumps. Detaching from the docking collar, Dan thought. Then a soft pressure, nothing more than a feeling of settling back in their seats.

"Departing for Alphonsus," came the captain's voice over the intercom speaker. "Estimated flight time, eighteen hours, eleven minutes."

That's the best we can do, Dan realized. High-energy burn, and it still takes more than eighteen hours to get there. He sighed to himself. Well, it's better than the three days the Apollo astronauts needed. But, hell, eighteen hours! Malik could take over Alphonsus and have a firing squad waiting for me by the time we get there.

Rafaelo Gaetano tried not to let his displeasure show. As calmly as he could, he took a cigarette from the silver-inlaid box on his desk and stuck it between his lips.

Malik was obviously upset. The Russian paced across the Persian carpet in front of Gaetano's desk, hands clasped behind his broad back, face sunk in a frown of deep thought.

"He got away?" Gaetano asked, in a tone that was almost teasing. "How could he get away from an island in the middle of the Pacific? Did he sprout wings?"

Malik gave him a stare that would boil water. "He is a very clever man. Extremely resourceful. And enormously wealthy. God knows how many bribes he paid out. My people are interrogating the hotel staff."

"Do you know where he's gone?"

"No, not precisely. But I have a good idea of where he's running to."

Gaetano picked up his heavy silver lighter and puffed the cigarette to life while Malik resumed his pacing.

"So?" Gaetano asked, blowing smoke toward the ceiling.

"Alphonsus. He'll be surrounded by his own employees there."

"But once the confiscation is completed they will be his employees no longer. They will be ours."

"Perhaps," Malik muttered, staring out the window. "Perhaps. Loyalty is a strange thing. They may remain loyal to him."

The Italian swiveled his desk chair around and saw that a half moon was rising, milky pale, in the late-morning sky. He smiled to himself.

Turning back to Malik, he said, "Arrest him when he arrives at Alphonsus. That should be simple enough."

"Arrest him on what charge?" Malik snapped. "The plan was to detain him on Tetiaroa. That was close to being illegal, but I was ready to take that risk. But I cannot order our handful of people at Alphonsus to arrest the man without some clear criminal charge against him. A *criminal* charge—not this confiscation matter."

Gaetano steepled his fingers in front of his face, the cigarette held between forefinger and thumb. Squinting from behind the smoke, he suggested, "Shoot him down, then, before he gets to Alphonsus. Get rid of him once and for all."

Malik started across the carpet again. *Jesuto,* he's going to wear a path through it, Gaetano thought.

"He has Jane Scanwell with him," the Russian growled.

"What?" Gaetano nearly jumped out of his chair.

"She's with him. We know that much. We can't kill the American representative to the Council. She's a former President of the United States, for god's sake!"

"She's gone with him willingly?"

"How should I know?"

Gaetano smiled and spread his hands in a happy gesture of fulfillment. "There is the answer to the problem. Randolph has kidnapped the American representative to the Council. Kidnapping is an act of terrorism, according to international law, is it not?"

Malik stopped his pacing and stared at the younger man. "Yes! Of course! Kidnapping." For the first time that morning he smiled.

"You see? There is a solution to every problem."

The Russian's smile eroded. "But Scanwell might say that she went with him voluntarily."

"Do you think there is such a possibility?"

Malik took the leather chair in front of the desk. "I don't know. They were lovers once, from what I've heard. Perhaps she still loves him."

"That would be a complication."

"Yes."

Gaetano brightened. "But you could still arrest Randolph on suspicion of kidnapping, and hold him until Scanwell gave an official statement to the security people at Alphonsus."

Malik's smile glimmered again. "Or hold him until a special investigating team can be assembled and sent to Alphonsus."

"Exactly! That would take a week, ten days—perhaps even longer."

"And by that time the confiscation procedures will be completed and Randolph will be a man without a corporation."

Gaetano took a long puff on his cigarette, thinking, You see? I have worked out the entire problem for you in less time than it took me to smoke one cigarette.

But he said nothing of the kind aloud to Malik.

All during the long flight to Alphonsus Dan had to force himself to stay away from the radiophone. He wanted to give orders to his people in Alphonsus, he wanted to fry the ass off Kate Williams, he wanted to find out what was going on and how far Malik and his GEC snakes had gotten with their confiscation order.

But no matter how much he fretted he kept silent. Maintain radio silence, he repeated to himself ten thousand times. Don't let them know for certain that you're aboard this bucket on your way to Alphonsus.

But he could listen. For hours on end he sat with headphones clamped on and had the OTV's captain tune to the business chatter between his office at Alphonsus and Astro's terrestrial headquarters at Caracas.

What he heard was not good. GEC executive orders had already been filed, notifying Astro management that the corporation was to be confiscated. Teams of GEC administrators had already invaded the Caracas offices and several other facilities elsewhere on Earth. It was only a matter of days, perhaps hours, before they showed up at Alphonsus.

Again and again he heard his top staff people grappling with the problem as best they could, always asking:

"Where's Dan? We need him to fight this."

"Where's the boss?"

"Why isn't he available? Where the hell is he?"

Nobody knew. Dan fumed in frustrated silence as the OTV plied its fixed trajectory toward Alphonsus. Malik hit it just right, he groused to himself. The Russian sonofabitch knew my people couldn't meet this threat effectively without me to okay their decisions. And my own goddamned insistence on secrecy has just muddled things worse. Nobody to blame but myself—and that double-damned Russian.

At least his board of directors had called an emergency meeting, in Tokyo. Sai— No, Dan corrected himself. Nobo's on the board. And he's pissed as hell with me. Will he let his personal anger get in the way of his business sense? Christ, I really could lose everything I've got!

Jane slept a good deal of the time they were in transit. Dan tried to nap but could not. The captain came down and fixed himself a meal at the little galley built into the side bulkhead of the passenger deck. Later on the copilot came down and prepared a tray for herself.

"You ought to eat something," Dan told Jane, halfway to the Moon. "How's your stomach?"

"I'm fine. The medication seems to be working, but it makes me feel drowsy."

"Psychosomatic."

The corners of her mouth curled upward slightly. "We didn't get all that much sleep that last night on the island, you know."

He grinned back at her. "You're bragging."

Gesturing to the headphones floating aimlessly beside Dan, she asked, "How are things going?"

"Piss poor."

"From your point of view or mine?"

Dan stared at her a moment, adjusting his thinking to recall that they were on opposite sides, politically.

"My point of view," he said. "Malik's steamrolling through my people. He's got GEC teams taking over all my offices."

"At Alphonsus, too?"

"Not yet. But they're on their way, I'll bet."

"Have you given any thought to what you're going to do once we get there?"

Dan shook his head. "Not much I can do. Not legally.

I doubt that Malik would listen to any offers from me to negotiate."

"Probably not," Jane said. "He's got the upper hand; why should he give away anything?"

"And you're on his side? Really?"

"I've got to be, Dan."

"It won't work, you know. Malik's way won't work. Not in time. They'll move too slowly. They'll want to have everything properly organized, everything neat and exact. We don't have the time for that kind of bureaucratic bullshit. We have to move fast. Now! Move!"

Jane shook her head. "We can't afford a chaotic approach to this. We need organization on a global scale."

He stared at her. "Christ, you really are one of them, aren't you?"

"I suppose I am," she said.

"So you're going to let him set up his dictatorship while the world goes to hell in a greenhouse."

Firmly, she answered, "I am going to help the Global Economic Council to coordinate all the human race's resources—all of them, off-Earth as well as on the planet—to avert the disaster that is threatening us."

"And grind me up into little pieces in the process," Dan said.

She reached out to touch his arm. "Dan, just because you're losing your corporation doesn't mean that your life is finished. You could help us—help me."

"What do you want me to do," he snarled, "run for President of the United States for you?"

Her face went white. Her nostrils flared. Finally she said, "No, Dan. As far as I'm concerned you can go to hell."

FIFTEEN

It was a gray day in Ulan Bator, although by craning his neck and looking up high, Altan Lodoi could see that the sky above was the perfect clear blue for which Mongolia was famous. Tourists flew in from all over the world to see that brilliant cloudless sky and the endless desolation of the barren Gobi.

Too much of Mongolia's economy depended on tourism to suit Lodoi. Whole clans dressed up in costumes out of the Great Khan's era and lived in round felt *gers* like nomads while the foreigners taped pictures and called the mobile tents yurts, their Russian name.

All the days were gray here in the capital, he thought as he stared out the window. Five million people have crowded into the city. Their automobiles and heaters and cooking fires draped Ulan Bator in a perpetual canopy of choking, foul-smelling smog. He wrinkled his nose, even though inside the capitol building the air was filtered and cool and almost as lovely as a spring day out in the grasslands of his home.

Altan Lodoi was the nation's Minister for the Environment, the youngest member of the powerful inner cabinet, and the least likely to be listened to.

"His Excellency the President!" called the cabinet secretary as the door to the old man's office swung open.

Jamsrangyn tottered in, a little bald man with a perpetual one-sided smile caused by a stroke that had nearly killed him more than a year ago. But the President of the Mongolian Republic was as tough as they came, physically. The only visible reminders of his stroke were the smile and the slightly uneven stumbling of his gait.

"Be seated, gentlemen," he said as he took the slightly raised high-backed padded chair at the head of the gleaming conference table.

Lodoi and the four other members of the inner cabinet took their customary chairs, Lodoi at the foot of the table. Each of the men wore Western-style business suits. Even though Lodoi yearned for the old days of legend, it would not have occurred to him to wear anything else.

The secretary sat himself slightly behind the President, his Japanese digital recorder on his lap.

"I call this meeting to order," said the President, slurring the words only slightly. "Fill in the proper time and date, Hatgal," he told his secretary.

The five ministers seated around the table used both their family and given names, a custom adopted from their neighbors. The President, however, stuck with the older Mongol tradition and allowed people to address him only by one name. His secretary followed suit, a small affectation but an annoying one.

President Jamsrangyn turned to his Minister of Energy, a lean and bony dour-faced former engineer.

"Oyun," said the President, "I believe you have good news for us—for a change."

The others laughed, even the Energy Minister. All except Lodoi. As Minister for the Environment, he knew he would have to speak out against Energy's recommendations, and that the rest of the inner cabinet would hate him for what he had to say.

"Very good news," said Energy. "For a change," he added, with a rare smile. "All the results of our test cores and preliminary mining samples confirm that the Altai deposits are enormous. We can be exporting coal to China and the Russian Federation within two years."

"The price of coal on the world market is climbing steadily," said the Minister of Commerce.

"Predictions for the next two years?" the President asked.

"Coal will increase in value as the price of oil increases. And oil prices are climbing steeply as global oil reserves continue to be depleted."

Lodoi raised his hand to be recognized, but the President instead asked the Foreign Minister, "Will the Global Economic Council enforce a limit on the price of coal?"

The Foreign Minister, sleek and overweight, with greased-back hair and manicured fingernails, said smoothly, "Even if they do, it will be at a higher figure than the world price today."

Lodoi waved his hand this time, but the President continued to ignore him by asking the Energy Minister to continue his report. Energy went back to extolling the treasures of the new coal deposits that had been discovered.

Unable to control his growing anger, Lodoi interrupted, "What is the sulfur content of this new coal?"

The Energy Minister stopped in the middle of his presentation, blinked several times. Without turning his face away from the President he said, "Sulfur content is about the same as our older coal deposits to the north."

"In other words," Lodoi snapped, "high sulfur, high pollution."

The former engineer finally turned to face him. "The sulfur can be removed by scrubbers."

"If the users go to the expense of installing scrubbers in their power plants."

"We use scrubbers."

"Yes, and look how much good it does us!" Lodoi angrily waved a hand toward the window.

The President glared down the table at his Minister for the Environment. "What does it matter to us if those who buy our coal use scrubbers or not? Let them foul their own nests if they want to, it is of no concern to us."

Jumping to his feet, Lodoi pleaded with the older men, "Don't you see? Can't you understand? It *does* matter to us! Even with scrubbers, coal-burning is turning our city into a cesspool. Cases of asthma, emphysema, tuberculosis and even lung cancer are rising faster than our medical facilities can handle them!"

"That's not true!" the Foreign Minister snapped. "And even if it was, such tales should not be told where foreigners could hear them."

"It's worse than that," Lodoi said, inwardly surprised at the pain and sorrow in his voice. He wanted to sound strong; to himself he sounded like a crying old woman. "No matter who burns the coal, no matter where it is burned—it adds to the greenhouse effect. It makes the world hotter. Don't you realize that the climate is already changing?"

The Foreign Minister chuckled. "Yes. In a few more years we'll be able to grow rice in the Gobi."

"And build seashore resorts with the profits from our coal sales," laughed the Minister of Commerce.

"We've got to stop burning coal!" Lodoi insisted. "And oil, too. All the fossil fuels are destroying our global environment. We must stop exporting coal—"

"Never!" snapped the President. "Our coal exports are a major source of foreign income. With the new Altai deposits, coal revenues will top our income from tourism and all other foreign trade. We cannot afford to stop exporting coal and we will not do so. Never."

"But the greenhouse . . ."

"That's a problem for our grandchildren to worry about," said the President.

Everyone around the table agreed, except for the one man who understood the problem.

You've done a great job of alienating anybody who can help you, Dan told himself as he waited impatiently to get out of the OTV. Jane was sitting stiffly in her seat, looking anywhere but at him.

The cramped little spacecraft had finally landed at Alphonsus. Dan could hear through the open hatch of the flight deck the captain going through the landing procedures checklist with the ground crew. The access tunnel had been rolled out and connected to the OTV's airlock hatch. Now they were checking the air pressure and the integrity of the hatch seal. All done remotely; the ground crew remained in the safety of their underground offices and teleoperated the machinery out on the open lunar surface.

"Check. Air pressure in the green. Cracking the hatch now."

The copilot slid gracefully down the ladder in the low lunar gravity and went to the hatch built into the side of the passenger deck.

"Hold your breath," she said over her shoulder, with a wink.

She pulled the hatch open. A puff of air sighed into the spacecraft. It smelled fresh and clean after more than eighteen hours in the cramped compartment.

Dan had phoned his office the instant the OTV had touched down and made hard-wire connections with the Alphonsus spaceport. Now a quartet of worried-looking men stood at the hatch to the terminal as he and Jane made their way through the ribbed plastic of the access tunnel in the stalking, long-striding walk of one-sixth g. The two younger men wore standard lunar garb: single-piece coveralls, color-coded by job specialty. Dan saw that these two wore the policeman blue of Astro's security department.

The other two, older, grimmer-faced, were in identical

business suits: pearl gray cardigan jackets over white turtleneck shirts, with sharply creased slacks of charcoal gray. The midlevel executive's uniform, Dan thought sourly. He himself was in faded old coveralls that had once been forest green. Jane was wearing the business suit she had come to Tetiaroa in, beige slacks, tan jacket and off-white blouse.

"Welcome, Mr. Randolph!" said the taller of the two executives. Dan scanned his memory and came up with the man's name: Hubert Peel. Bert stuck out his hand and tried to smile bravely. He was several centimeters taller than Dan, but his gut bulged unheroically.

Dan shook hands with him and with the other guy, shorter, balding, his round moon face cut in half by a flowing luxurious dark moustache. Harold Schmidt, Dan recalled.

"This is President Scanwell," Dan introduced, "the American representative to the Global Economic Council. Madam President will want to arrange transportation back Earthside immediately."

Each man shook hands with Jane and mumbled his own name, seemingly embarrassed to meet a former President—and one of the enemy.

Then they started toward the conveyor-belt people mover that led to the main dome of the Alphonsus complex.

"I wish you had let us have some advance warning of your arrival, Mr. Randolph. All hell's broken loose here," Bert said.

"I can imagine. Where's Kate Williams?"

"She went back Earthside a couple days ago," said Harry, scurrying to keep up with the rapid pace Dan was setting. The two security youngsters had taken Jane in hand, literally; unused to the lunar gravity, she had stumbled and almost fallen. Now the two young men held her arms and helped her along. Dan glanced once over his shoulder and saw that she was in good hands. Then he turned his attention back to his two aides.

"There's a GEC team on its way here," Bert was explaining. "We've already received legal notification that the GEC is taking over control of the entire corporation."

Harry said, "GEC teams have been hitting every one of our Earthside offices. It's like police raids."

"Or a hostile takeover," Bert said.

"Very hostile," said Dan.

"We were told we're not supposed to have any further dealings with you," Harry added. "Not even talk to you."

Dan grinned at him. "You're not obeying an official GEC order?"

"Shit, boss, you're the guy we work for."

"Not for much longer," Dan said ruefully. "They've got me by the balls."

"The GEC's really taking over?" Harry seemed aghast. "But they can't do that! They don't know how to run this operation."

"Doesn't matter to those double-damned bureaucrats. They've got the law on their side, it looks like."

They reached the sliding way and stepped onto it. Still Dan kept up the rapid pace. Jane and her escorts fell farther behind.

"What're we gonna do?" Harry asked.

"Get my legal staff together and see what grounds we have for fighting them. And call a teleconference of the heads of each of the Big Seven."

"That'll take some time," Bert said. "They're all busy people."

"We don't have time! Get them together on the phone. Open links, we won't need scrambling or secure lines. Just do it now. We've only got a few hours."

Both men nodded in unison. "Right, boss."

By the time Dan entered his office, his one human secretary rushed to him, a stricken look on her fashion model's sculpted features.

"Thank god you got here!" she gasped. "We have just received notice that a GEC legal team is on its way from Paris with a warrant for your arrest!"

Dan breezed past her and into his private office. She hurried behind him.

"What charge?" he asked as he went to the minibar.

"Kidnapping!"

Dan huffed as, kneeling, he opened the minibar and pulled out a bottle of Jack Daniel's green label. "Is that all? I thought they'd try to stick me with mass murder and kiddie rape, at the very least."

The secretary did not crack a smile. "Dan, kidnapping falls under the World Court's terrorism acts. If they convict you, you could be executed!"

"Yeah," he said, pouring a healthy slug of the sour-mash whiskey into a tumbler made of lunar crystal. "That would save us all a lot of trouble, wouldn't it?"

His secretary had been with him for four years, a new record for a man who had a reputation for bedding his hired help and then getting rid of them. Her name was Tamara Duchamps, and she had been a fashion model in Paris, where her smoldering Ethiopian beauty and flowing dark hair had set photographers and magazine editors into near-frenzy. But she had been intelligent enough to see that modeling was a dead end to all but the very few who allied themselves sexually to the high and powerful. A woman of thoroughly independent mind, she left the fashion industry altogether and entered the world of business.

Within a year she was Dan Randolph's office manager and irreplaceable assistant. Her title was "secretary," but she knew that the title meant little. Her boss knew it too, which was more important. She was aware of Dan Randolph's reputation; she evaded his early efforts, even though they seemed rather gallant to her. To her surprise, Randolph respected her caution. Everyone else in the office told her that once he had slept with her she would be transferred far away. They took bets on when the inevitable would happen. Now, four years later, all bets were off.

"Dan," she said, in her exotically flavored British English, "this is not something that you can talk your way out of. I have checked with the legal department and they are totally off the wall. They do not know what to do!"

He plunked himself in his comfortable desk chair, took a sip of the whiskey, and leaned back far enough to put his feet on the desk. He still wore the sandals he had taken to Tetiaroa.

"Tamara, honey, never *ask* a lawyer what you should do. They don't know. Their brains are so stuffed with crap that they can't find their way across the street without a court order. You *tell* a lawyer what you want him to do. Or her," he added, his face hardening.

"Kate Williams has betrayed you," Tamara said, looking angry at the thought.

"And I never laid a glove on her," Dan mused. "Maybe if I had been more persistent she wouldn't have done this to me. Hell hath no fury, you know."

Tamara shook her head. "She would have cut your testicles off, one way or the other."

"Pleasant thought."

Suddenly exasperated, Tamara nearly shouted at him, "So what are you going to do? You cannot just sit there drinking! There is a squad of GEC people on its way here to put you in jail!"

With his free hand, Dan pointed past her shoulder. "Here comes my kidnapping victim."

Jane walked cautiously into the office, like a woman on a tightrope. The two security men hovered beyond the door, in the outer office.

Before Jane could say a word, Dan told his secretary, "Tamara, please arrange transportation for President Scanwell back to Paris—or wherever else she wants to go."

Jane looked the younger woman up and down as she made her way past Tamara and sank gratefully into one of the clear plastic, foam-cushioned chairs in front of Dan's desk. On Earth, the chair would have been too fragile to bear an adult's weight; on the Moon, it bent only slightly as Jane sat on it.

"Did I hear correctly?" Jane asked, her voice calm, subdued. "You're about to be arrested?"

Dan nodded. "For kidnapping you."

"That falls under the terrorism laws," Tamara added.

"This is very serious," said Jane.

Dan grinned crookedly. "Will you testify on my behalf at my trial? Assuming that Malik allows me to have a trial?"

"Of course you'll have a trial!"

With a shrug, Dan said, "I could always have a fatal accident while I'm in custody."

"Nonsense."

"So, assuming I come to trial, will you testify on my behalf? Or against me?"

"You did take me here against my wishes," she said, with no hint of a smile.

"Yeah, I suppose I did."

Tamara looked from Dan to Jane and back to her boss again. "You cannot just sit here! You must do something!"

"What do you suggest?" Dan asked mildly.

"I don't know!"

"Well, I do," he said, getting up from his chair. "I'm going to my quarters and get some sleep."

"What?"

"When the GEC goon squad arrives at the spaceport, wake me up. Ten to one, Kate Williams will be with them."

"Is that all you are going to do?" Tamara seemed on the verge of tears.

Dan nodded. "And arrange transport for President Scanwell."

He came around the desk, bent over Jane and gave her

a peck on the cheek, then waved to Tamara and left the
two women in his office.

Once in his quarters, though, Dan did not immediately
go to sleep. First he went to his bedside phone. The
display screen glowed a cheery yellow and showed in
bright blue letters:

HAPPY BIRTHDAY!
WELCOME TO THE BIG 50

Cripes, Dan said to himself. Today's my birthday.
Tamara must've remembered. He shook his head ruefully. It's going to be some party.

He spent several hours speaking to his managers in
their offices all over Earth and in several orbital facilities.
In between calls, he chivvied Bert Peel about getting all
the space industrialists together for a teleconference.

"I'm working on it, boss," Bert exclaimed, beads of
perspiration on his upper lip. "I've got about half of 'em
lined up, but every time I call another one he or she wants
a different time and I've got to recontact all the others."

"You tell them this is an emergency?"

"Yes! Sure."

"Okay, keep at it. I've only got a few hours, at most."

Bert mumbled what might have been profanity and cut
the connection.

Dan actually managed to sleep for about twenty minutes.
He dreamed he was struggling with someone, a faceless
man, or maybe it was a woman. They were on the edge
of the roof of some enormous skyscraper back on Earth.
They fell off, and suddenly Dan was completely alone,
plummeting toward the hard pavement of the street far
below.

He sat bolt upright in his darkened bedroom, cold with
sweat, still in the coveralls he had not bothered to take off

when he had flopped on the bed.

Casting a quick glance at the digital time displayed on the bedside screen, he peeled off the coveralls as he made his way into the bathroom, showered, shaved and put on a clean outfit: another set of forest green coveralls, but these were new enough so that their color was still vivid. And he left his sandals by the bed; lunar softboots were much more practical. Then he stalked back to his office and went in through his private entrance, avoiding Tamara and anyone else who might be in the outer office.

The dumb birthday greeting was on his desktop screen, too. Dan scowled at it as he slumped into his desk chair and flicked on the windowall. It was tuned to an outside camera view of the broad, crater-pitted floor of Alphonsus. Factories dotted the plain out to the horizon, with wide spreads of solar energy farms glittering in the sunlight. A few tractors were chugging across the dusty landscape.

He told the voice-activated phone to find Peel. Almost instantly, his aide's face appeared on Dan's desktop display screen.

"Got 'em all, boss," Peel said without preamble. "Except Yamagata. His people say he's out of contact, on a field trip somewhere."

Out of contact, my ass, Dan said to himself. Nobo doesn't want to talk to me.

"Guess we'll have to settle for number two, then," he told Peel.

"Right. In that case we can get started in about ten minutes."

"Good."

Tamara opened the door from the outer office. "The GEC team will be landing in half an hour," she announced, looking angry and afraid at the same time. "And you were right: Kate Williams is in charge of the team."

"Has President Scanwell left?" he asked.

"Not yet. She decided to wait until the GEC people

arrived, and then go back with them. She's waiting out here."

Dan smiled weakly. "She wants to be here for the kill, does she? Okay, ask her to come in. She might as well see the show."

Tamara ushered Jane into his office. She was still in the same beige slacks and tan jacket. Dan gestured her to a chair as he slid his computer keyboard from its niche in his desk. He spent the next few minutes huddled over his computer display screen while Jane sat silently watching him.

Then Peel called in to say that all six of the space-industry corporate chiefs were on-line for the emergency teleconference—except for Nobuhiko Yamagata. His chief legal counsel would participate in the conference in his place. The windowall broke up into six separate images: four men and two women, representing six of the seven major corporations that dominated space industries. Each of them was on Earth; of the Big Seven, only Dan was off-planet. Dan touched one more key, and two smaller images appeared in the lower right corner of the windowall: a view of the landing pad outside, and an empty corridor deep below the office levels of Alphonsus City.

Shooing Tamara out with one hand, Dan adjusted the phone camera on his desk so that it showed only a head-and-shoulders view of himself. If Jane wants to join the conversation, I'll swivel it around, he thought.

Then he grinned crookedly at the six electronic images. "I suppose you're all wondering why I asked you here today."

It took two and a half seconds for Dan's feeble little joke to reach them and their response to get back to the Moon. They all tried to talk at once. In the sudden torrent of angry, frightened, urgent voices Dan made out the clear fact that all of them were under pressure from the GEC to turn over control of all space industrial operations to the Council.

"That means Malik," Dan said, loud enough to cut through their babble and silence them. "Malik wants to take over all our companies. He's always wanted to be the commissar of all space operations."

Jane stirred slightly in her chair but said nothing.

"I understand," said the Yamagata lawyer, a sallow-faced Japanese with narrow, suspicious eyes, "that your assets are being confiscated entirely, at this very moment."

"That's right," Dan said. Out of the corner of his eye he saw a spacecraft settling down on the landing pad outside. It bore the sky blue markings of the Global Economic Council.

"What can we do to help?" asked the Argentinean president of Astrofábrica Corporación.

"Not a hell of a lot, Jorge," Dan admitted. "But there's something even more important that you must be made aware of."

Six faces stared at him, silent, waiting. The spacecraft sat on the landing pad while an access tunnel snaked toward it. Jane watched him too, her face as close to expressionless as she could make it.

Dan began to explain to them about the greenhouse cliff. Only one of them had heard of it, the woman who headed Eurospace A.G. "The head of my research staff is working with your chief scientist, I believe, to determine whether this phenomenon is real or not," she said.

"It's real, Hilde," Dan replied. "Malik knows it. He's using it as an excuse to take over all space industries. In the next ten years we either convert the whole spinning Earth away from fossil fuels or we see the ice caps melt and sea levels go up ten meters or more."

He waited the two and a half seconds for their reaction. Then:

"In ten years?"

"That's not possible!"

"I've never heard of such a thing."

"No one informed me!"

"How can that be?"

"Your scientists can give you the details," Dan said, flicking the image in the corner of his windowall to show the corridor between the landing pad and the main plaza. Sure enough, Kate Williams was leading a dozen grim-faced men and women, all of them dressed in dark gray slacks and jackets bearing the GEC emblem.

Quickly, Dan reviewed his discussion—argument—with Malik at Tetiaroa, and emphasized Malik's decision to take over all the Big Seven space industrial corporations in the name of necessity, due to the impending global disaster.

"He can't force us—"

"Yes he can, if he has the Council behind him."

"I never trusted those politicians."

"We'll lose everything!"

"What difference does that make if the world is drowned in ten years?"

Dan quieted them down, all the while watching Kate and her band of GEC enforcers making their way toward his office. And Jane sitting almost within his reach, silent, watching, waiting.

"Now listen," Dan told the six of them. "Hilde is right. What difference does anything make if half the world's going to go underwater? We've all got to work together with the GEC to do whatever we can to avert this catastrophe."

Jane looked surprised. He grinned at her.

"Work with the GEC?"

"Let them take over our corporations?"

"Allow them to steal what we've earned over all these years?"

"No," Dan said firmly. "We can work with the GEC and hold on to our companies—at least, you can." Kate and her gang were at the door to his outer office. Tamara was getting up from her desk, ever so slowly, to manually open the door for them. Jane was looking from Dan to the picture in the windowall's corner and back to Dan again.

"We're facing a situation that's like a major war; the biggest double-damned war anybody's ever faced. We've got to stop thinking of our profits and start working with everything we've got to win. It's victory or death, there's no middle ground.

"What you've got to do," he was saying quickly, knowing that he was running out of time, "is to make a voluntary statement, announce it in the world's media, shout it as loud as you can, that your corporations will *voluntarily* place themselves at the command of the GEC for the length of this emergency period. You will follow GEC orders to do whatever is necessary to save the planet from the greenhouse cliff—but without relinquishing ownership or control of your companies. Got that? That's the only way to work it. Voluntary cooperation. That's the only way to beat this greenhouse disaster. Cooperate voluntarily with the GEC, let the bastards take all your profits—but run your companies yourselves! You know how to do that better than any deskbound paper-shuffler."

The door to his office burst open and Kate Williams strode in, with half her team behind her.

"Daniel Hamilton Randolph, you are under arrest for kidnapping," she said.

The windowall went dark.

SIXTEEN

Dan grinned at Kate Williams from behind his desk. "Welcome back, Scarlett. You're fired."

She almost grinned back at him. "You can't fire me. I resigned twelve hours ago."

"You never really did work for me anyway, did you?"

"We don't have time for chitchat," Kate snapped. "You're under arrest. Get on your feet and come with us."

Dan put his hands flat on the desktop. "Now, wait a minute. I'm being charged with kidnapping, right? Well, here's my 'victim.' Let's ask her if she was kidnapped or not."

Kate shook her head. "Nice try, Dan, but I've already spoken with President Scanwell, while we were on the way here. She'll testify that you brought her here against her will."

Dan swiveled his chair slightly to face Jane. "Is that true?"

Jane hesitated only a fraction of a heartbeat. "Yes.

That will be my testimony. That's what you did, Dan, and we both know it."

He shrugged as if defeated. *"Et tu,* Janie?"

"On your feet, Randolph," snapped one of the young men standing beside Kate. He looked like a jock: broad shoulders, burr haircut, jacket straining across his chest. Dan realized that he was carrying a gun in a shoulder holster. Probably all of them are, except for Kate. Maybe her too; be just like her to have a loaded bra.

Slowly, so as not to alarm them, Dan slid open the top drawer of his desk. "Just give me a minute here," he muttered as he pushed away the papers that covered the slim matte-gray pistol he had put there.

"I really have no intention of going anywhere with you, Kate," he said, leveling the pistol at them with one hand and pulling out his computer keyboard with the other.

"This is nonsense," Kate began. "You can't—"

But the burrhead beside her started to reach into his jacket. Dan fired once, a sudden shocking explosion of noise and smoke. The kid slammed over backward as if hit by a baseball bat and smashed into the couch along the far wall, then slumped to the floor.

Before any of the others could react, Dan said, "He's not hurt much. It's a tranquilizer dart. He'll be okay in a few hours."

No one else moved.

"I spent a lot of years in Venezuela," Dan said, tapping keys with his left hand. "The Indians out in the Orinoco River valley have developed some dandy drugs. They use them for hunting. Once in a while they hunt other people. Still a few cannibals out there, although nobody wants to admit it." He grinned wickedly.

"Dan, you're crazy," Jane said. "You can't expect to get away with this."

He pointed the gun at her. "You're a hostile witness, Madam President. The jury will disregard your remarks."

"He's gone insane," Kate said.

"Maybe." Dan swung the gun back toward her. "Is insanity a valid defense, in my case?"

She clenched her fists and took a step toward him.

"Don't let your temper trip you up, Scarlett. I'll shoot you if you force me to. And I don't know how the stuff in these darts might affect you. The dose is big enough to knock out a horse like your snoozing pal. It might do more damage to somebody of your petite size."

"You're only making things tougher for yourself," Kate said. But she stood still.

"Tougher than a kidnapping charge? Terrorism is punishable by execution. What can be tougher than that?"

Jane said, "Dan, please . . ."

He gave the keyboard one final touch, with a flourish of his left hand, then stood up. A hooting wail clamored out of the speaker set into the ceiling panels.

"EMERGENCY!" bellowed a computer-synthesized voice. "LIFE-SUPPORT SYSTEM WILL FAIL IN ONE MINUTE! ONE MINUTE TO LIFE-SUPPORT FAILURE!"

Dan hollered over the warning system's announcement, "In one minute this entire level of offices will be opened to vacuum. I suggest you haul your asses out into the corridor and run like hell to the nearest emergency hatch. Those hatches are programmed to shut automatically when they sense a drop in air pressure. You don't want to be on the wrong side of a hatch when it slams shut."

"You're bluffing!" Kate snarled.

"FORTY-FIVE SECONDS TO LIFE-SUPPORT FAILURE. FORTY-FIVE SECONDS."

Dan shrugged. "Sure I am. And rain makes applesauce." He backed away, still pointing the pistol at them, and felt for his private door behind him.

The urgent wail of the warning siren seemed to grow louder, more shrill. "FORTY SECONDS TO LIFE-

SUPPORT FAILURE."

Jane got to her feet. "I don't know about the rest of you," she said, and started for the door to the outer office.

"Hey!" Dan called after her. "Don't you want to come with me?"

Jane hesitated only an instant. Then she shook her head and kept on going.

"You always were a smart lady," Dan called after her. "See you!"

"THIRTY SECONDS TO LIFE-SUPPORT FAIL-URE. THIRTY SECONDS."

Kate and the others suddenly bolted for the outer office and safety, leaving the unconscious burrhead sprawled on the floor. Laughing, Dan opened his private door and stepped into the back corridor. He could hear the automated warning voice calling out "TWENTY SECONDS" and then "TEN SECONDS" as he loped down the corridor toward the hatch that led to the lad-derway.

Tucking his pistol into a thigh pocket and zippering it shut, Dan opened the hatch and started down the steel rungs of the ladder. He heard very faintly, "THIS HAS BEEN A TEST OF THE EMERGENCY WARNING SYSTEM. THANK YOU FOR YOUR COOPERA-TION. ALL PERSONNEL MAY RETURN TO THEIR NORMAL STATIONS. THIS TEST IS CON-CLUDED."

Chuckling to himself at the picture of Kate Williams' face when she heard that, Dan clambered down five lev-els, to the very bottom of the tubelike ladderway. There was no hatch down here; he merely stepped out into the dimly lit bottom level of Alphonsus City, a world of machinery where humans rarely bothered to go.

Most of the machinery was for life support: the air scrubbers and fans, electrical inverters and routing sub-stations, water purification systems and recirculators. The very air hummed, throbbed like the giant mechanical heart of the city that it actually was. Dan knew that there were teams of teleoperators up above, sitting in their comfortable offices and keeping tabs electronically on the machines down here. They had video cameras, too, so they could keep the entire section under visual surveillance.

He knew also that, like inspectors anywhere, the men and women responsible for monitoring this equipment rarely paid attention to their work, except when a warning light flashed red or a synthesized voice warned of trouble that the computer's sensors had detected.

Until they're specifically told to search for me, Dan told himself, they won't be looking for anybody prowling around down here. I hope.

He made his way through the shadowy light toward the tunnel that he knew existed at the back end of this bottom level. He had helped to carve it out of the bedrock of Alphonsus' ringwall mountains, back in the days when he operated a plasma torch and alternately drank and fought with his Japanese coworkers.

One of the few mobile maintenance robots suddenly came from behind a ceiling-high electrical transformer. Dan almost bumped into it.

The robot was one of the newer models, almost six feet tall and gleaming in the far-spaced overhead lights. Its head bore two round camera lenses where eyes would be, and a speaker grille in place of a mouth. It had four arms, each ending in fully rotatable pincers with the strength to break bones.

"Unauthorized personnel are not allowed in this area," said the robot's tinny synthesized voice, in Japanese.

Crapola! If I exceed this double-damned tin can's programmed commands, it'll send a warning buzz to the operators upstairs.

Thinking swiftly, Dan replied in Japanese, "This is an unannounced routine inspection tour."

"Authorization code?" asked the robot.

Dan pecked at his wristwatch for the last authorization code he had received from the system, months ago. His trembling fingers fumbled with the tiny keypad and the phone's miniature screen lit up with: BIRTHDAY. Dan fumed and tried to find the information he needed. If Bozo here detects the gun in my pocket . . .

"Authorization code?" the robot repeated.

There it was! Hoping that the code had not been changed over the intervening months, Dan rattled off the numbers.

"Thank you," said the robot. It turned and trundled away. Dan was only slightly shaken when he saw that the machine had an identical face on the other side of its head.

"I've heard of two-faced women," he muttered to himself as he resumed his hurried pace toward the tunnel. "But robots? That's weird."

The tunnel had been started back in the days when Yamagata Industries had first decided to make a major manufacturing center at Alphonsus. Saito's father had decided to ram a tunnel through the ringwall mountains, connecting the floor of Alphonsus with the broad expanse of Mare Nubium. The lunar rock had turned out to be much tougher than expected; the costs of digging the tunnel, even with plasma torches, had risen too far. So the tunnel was never finished. Instead, a cable-car system had been built over the mountains. It was more expensive to operate than a tunnel would have been but far cheaper to construct. It was still in use.

But the tunnel was still there; incomplete, unused for nearly two decades, but still there. So were the access shafts that had been drilled upward to the face of the mountain. The first of those access shafts opened into an emergency shelter where there were pressure suits and spare oxygen bottles, in case the cable-car system overhead broke down.

That was Dan's objective. Alphonsus City, like any settlement built in the harsh airless environment of the

Moon, was a tightly sealed, closely controlled community. No one got into a cable car or stepped through an airlock without being scrutinized. You could walk for miles inside the main plaza or along the city's corridors, but there were always video monitors watching. The monitors were there for safety, but they could easily be used to find a fugitive.

Dan mused as he made his way toward the tunnel that there had been amazingly few fugitives, to his knowledge. In a community as large as Alphonsus City had grown to be, there were bound to be some thieves or perverts or the occasional case of murderous violence. But living and working on the Moon apparently sorted out the unstable types very quickly. They killed themselves, and often killed those unfortunate enough to be near them when they screwed up.

He grinned to himself as he realized that most of the inhabitants of Alphonsus were Japanese. Sure, there might have been a few with larcenous souls among them, but by and large they worked hard, obeyed the regulations, and lived frugally. He remembered the rare thief that had been caught and brought to trial. Usually it was white-collar stuff: a bartender stiffing his employer, a logistics clerk jiggering the computer system so he could sell company equipment on the black market.

There is a black market here, he knew. But it's usually so small and harmless that it's not worth the trouble going after it.

As far back as he could remember, though, there had been no real fugitives from justice at Alphonsus City. Or any other lunar settlement. You can't go out and hide in the hills. Not on a world where the only air and water is manufactured in the cities.

There had been a few disappearances, of course. That was to be expected on a harshly unforgiving frontier world. But no fugitives. Not until now.

The tunnel entrance was closed, but the electronic lock on the metal hatch was easy enough to decipher. He had expected the hinges to squeal painfully, since the door probably had not been touched in years. But it opened smoothly, quietly. Are the robots programmed to oil the hinges? Dan wondered.

The air inside smelled dusty, stale. He coughed. But it was air. It was breathable, if you didn't mind the sensation of fine talcum powder choking your throat. There was no light. Dan had forgotten to bring a torch with him, and the dim light from the basement quickly petered out in the depths of the tunnel. He felt his way along the rough side of the tunnel, thankful that this was on the Moon and there'd be no unpleasant critters slithering around in the darkness.

Wrong! A pair of tiny burning red eyes stared balefully at him out of the shadows, shoulder high. Dan felt his heart clutch in his chest, then realized that it was the indicator lights of an emergency lamp, left there years ago by the construction gang, still powered by its radio-isotope system.

His fingers found the lamp's square shape in the darkness and slid across gritty dust until they touched its activating switch. The sudden light made Dan squint, but his eyes quickly adjusted.

It was easier going with the lamp. In a few minutes Dan found the hatch to the access tunnel and started climbing up the ladder toward the emergency shelter up on the surface. As far as he knew, the access tunnel had never been used to rescue stranded cable-car passengers. Never had to be. The cable system had worked fine ever since it had been erected, except for a few minor glitches that stranded cars for an hour or less—well within the air supplies the cars themselves carried.

At the top of the access tunnel, the hatch leading into the shelter had no security lock; a simple spin of a well-oiled wheel opened it easily. Dan felt some puzzlement as he pushed the metal hatch back and climbed up into the shelter. The robots from down below didn't come up here for maintenance work. Would the Yamagata safety people who maintain the cable cars take care of this hatch too?

The shelter reminded him of the old days, when construction crews lived in "tempos": temporary shelters made of expended spacecraft sections, thin aluminum cylinders that they buried under a few feet of rubble scooped up from the regolith. Life in the tempos had been spare and rugged, no place for a person of delicate sensibilities. Or a keen sense of smell, for that matter. Tempos. He had lived in them for nearly three years, and here he was back in one.

It was a curved-roof tempo, sure enough. Almost bare inside, Dan saw in the light of his hand lamp, except for tall green cylinders of oxygen, a phone console sitting on an otherwise empty desk, a couple of shelves of emergency medical kits and rations—and a quartet of space suits, standing stiffly in their racks like knightly armor of old, complete with helmets on shelves above the empty torsos.

The first suit he picked had only a quarter of its normal supply of oxygen in its tanks. Annoyed, Dan went to the next suit. Its tanks were dry.

"They maintain the damned hatches," he muttered, "but not the suits. That's brilliant."

The other two suits were almost empty, as well. Fuming now, Dan went to the oxygen cylinders to start refilling one of the suits. They too were low; each of them was missing from half to three-quarters of its normal capacity.

This is crazy, he said to himself.

It was laborious work, even in the low gravity. It took more than an hour for Dan to fill the backpack tank of one of the pressure suits. Then he waited, worriedly, for two hours more, watching the suit's gauges to make certain that the tank did not leak.

No leaks, he decided with relief. But then, how did the tanks lose oxy? And the standby cylinders, too?

His wait had accomplished another purpose: the sun

should have set by now. Checking his wristwatch computer, he found that it was indeed nighttime outside. It would be more difficult for them to spot him out in the open. Not impossible, by any means. But the cover of darkness gave him a bit more of an edge.

If I don't break my damned neck out there, he groused.

Very carefully he stepped into the leggings of the suit he had selected and pulled on the thickly insulated boots. Then he wriggled into the hard-shell torso and wormed his arms through the sleeves. Stomping around the cramped shelter, he tested the suit's flexibility. Then he backed into the backpack, still hooked to its rack, and felt its latches click against his suit's fittings. It had been a long time since he'd carried a fully loaded backpack and pressure suit. Even in the Moon's gentle gravity it felt like a ton of dead weight on his shoulders and back. The damned pistol still in the pocket of his coveralls jabbed against his thigh annoyingly.

Dan pulled on the suit's gloves and sealed them to the wrist cuffs. He flexed his fingers, thinking, *They haven't made much of an improvement on these things. Feels as stiff as rigor mortis, and the damned suit's not even pressurized yet.*

Finally he slid the helmet over his head and sealed it to his collar ring. He pulled the visor down and locked it, then clumped over to the only oxygen cylinder that still had some gas in it. Fitting its extension hose to the port on his suit, he overpressurized his suit until it bulged out like a balloon, making it awkward to move his arms or legs.

Then he waited, watching alternately the watch and the pressure gauge on the instrument cluster on the suit's left wrist. With nobody here to check him out, this was the only way to test that the suit was properly sealed and there were no pinhole leaks anywhere.

There are old astronauts and there are bold astronauts, Dan remembered the old saying, *but there are* no old, bold astronauts. Haste is the enemy of safety, he knew.

At last, satisfied that the suit was tight, he let most of the overpressurizing oxygen hiss out of the port and stepped slowly, like some monster from a horror video, to the airlock of the shelter.

It took several minutes for the lock to cycle. Then the indicator light turned red and Dan slid the outer hatch open. The smooth gentle slope of Mt. Yeager confronted him. Downslope he could see the humped mass of rubble that covered Alphonsus City's main plaza. Directly overhead ran the cable-car line.

His wristwatch tingled against his skin. Glancing at the watch on his suit cuff, Dan realized what the programmed wristwatch was telling him. This was the exact moment of his birth, fifty years ago, precisely.

"Happy birthday," Dan muttered as he stepped out onto the glassy, pitted slope of Mt. Yeager.

SEVENTEEN

Four hours later he was still climbing the tallest mountain of the Alphonsus ringwall. Sandpapered by eons of micrometeorite infall, most of the Moon's mountains looked tired and old. They slumped, rounded and softly curved, their slopes usually very gentle. But the sandpapering had made their slopes very smooth, as well, almost glassy. Traction was not easy.

Dan was puffing with exertion. Malik was right, he thought. I've let myself get out of shape. Fat and fifty, that's me. He stopped and looked downslope toward the floor of Alphonsus. Even though the sun was down, there was seldom true darkness at this latitude. A gibbous Earth hung in the black, star-flecked sky, fat and gleaming, blue seas and white clouds, glowing with life and warmth. Even the nightside of Earth glittered with lights of cities and highways.

There was enough light to see the little pockmarks of mini-craters in the stony ground. Enough light to spot a lone man walking—if you knew where to look. Dan doubted that the space station all the way out at the L1 point could pick him up visually, or even in the infrared. And he knew that the satellites orbiting the Moon at closer altitudes were not equipped for such detailed surveillance work.

I'll be okay, he told himself. Unless they pop a surveillance team into an OTV just to look for me. Or maybe send out a cable car full of guys with telescopes. Better get a move on.

To where?

That had been the first question he had asked himself when he had realized, back on Tetiaroa, that Malik intended to jail him. Where can you go to hide from the Global Economic Council? As one of the richest men in the Earth/Moon system, Dan had always kept a few special hideaways for himself, and a few false identities so he could travel undetected and undisturbed. But with all his assets confiscated, he was down to the few emergency things he had tucked away in safe deposit vaults in various cities on Earth.

For more than ten years he had played this seemingly pointless game. At times he himself had thought that he was being paranoid—or at least childish. But deep in his gut he had known that power-hungry men like Malik would topple him if they got the chance. Now they had done it, and he was running for his life.

To where? The question popped up again to confront him as he slogged upslope, following the cable-car line overhead as a rough guide. His immediate goal was another one of those "temporary" shelters that had been emplaced along the cable line. He worried that the next tempo would be largely gutted of its supplies, as the first one had been. Or that Kate Williams' team of goons would have figured out where was going and be there waiting for him.

He pushed on.

Fifty years old, he thought. Some double-damned birthday this is. Some guys retire by the time they're fifty.

Or chuck their careers and start out on something new.

He grinned to himself. That's what you're doing, Daniel old pal. Change of life. Time to start a new career. You're going from being a billionaire to being a penniless fugitive from the law. How's that for progress?

Well, he answered himself, maybe this time around I'll figure out what I want to be when I grow up.

Feeling strangely cheerful, Dan trudged on up the slick, almost slippery face of the mountain. He stumbled here and there; once he slid on his rump for nearly thirty yards, stopped only by the rim of a new-looking crater. Sitting there, helmet visor fogged with his ragged breath, peering down into the shadowed depths of the crater, he realized that sizable meteoroids still struck the Moon with some regularity.

That would be the icing on the cake, to get killed by a meteoroid. God's sniper. He laughed and clambered laboriously to his booted feet once again. At least, he told himself, you can make yourself a moving target.

I panicked, he admitted. I panicked and ran. But what alternative did I have? Once Scarlett's goons had me in their grip they weren't going to let me go. Whether Malik sent me to Tetiaroa or Devil's Island, I'd be tucked away someplace where I'd never get out. I had to run. Or end up in the penal colony at Aristarchus.

Shouldn't have come back to the Moon. That was my big mistake. You can get around on Earth. Twelve billion people down there; not even the GEC can keep track of all of 'em. I could have faded into the background while I figured out some way to fight back. Now I'm stuck up here. My next big accomplishment will be to find some air to breathe once this backpack runs dry.

And every step I take moves me farther from the launchpad where spacecraft take off for Earth.

He spotted the tempo, a rounded hump of rubble that looked at first like an abandoned slag heap. But there was an airlock on one side of it, and an antenna poking up from its top.

And a parade of bootprints in front of the airlock, Dan saw. In the undisturbed airlessness of the Moon it was impossible to tell how fresh the prints were. They could have been left by Armstrong and Aldrin, if the Apollo 11 crew had landed at this spot. Dozens of prints, overlapping, exposing the bright sandy-looking underlayer of the regolith. In a few millions years' time they would be darkened by solar radiation, just as the undisturbed top layer was.

The prints appeared out of nowhere, seemingly. Then Dan realized that people came this far in a cable car, got down from the car by ladder, and walked to the tempo's airlock. How recently? He studied the prints for a few swift moments. There seemed to be just as many heading out as heading in, but he could not be certain.

Shaking his head inside the helmet, Dan decided to push on. I'm not walking into any trap they've set up for me, he told himself. I'd rather run out of oxygen first.

Nearly three hours later he was wondering when he would run out of oxygen. The tempos had been placed an hour's walk apart. That was the theory. It had taken Dan considerably more than an hour to reach the next one, and it too had plenty of bootprints around its airlock hatch. So he went on.

Trudging up the mountainside, Dan eyed the poles that held the cable. There were sensors atop each pole, he knew. The scientists used them to study the electric fields set up by the incoming solar wind, and the Moon's faint magnetic field. Have they put cameras up there? Are they watching me? He pictured Kate Williams laughing her head off, watching him stumbling along, knowing exactly where he was every moment of his supposed escape.

"Bust your guts laughing," he muttered. Then he remembered his suit radio. He clicked it on and tuned to each frequency it could reach. No calls to him demanding his surrender. No security traffic at all. Nothing but the usual bored chatter between workers and the regular Alphonsus news and entertainment stations.

Dan stayed with the classical-music station. They were playing Sibelius' *Valse Triste*. He wished it were something more energetic and less gloomy.

The suit smelled funny. Maybe the oxygen's contaminated, he thought. Or whoever was in this shell before me left a powerful body odor in it. Or maybe I'm starting to crack up. Whatever, the next shelter is *it*. I'm going in no matter what.

He had reached a ridge of flat ground, something of a shelf that jutted out from the shoulder of the mountain. The crest seemed within reach, but there in the middle of the ridge sat the unmistakable humped pile of bulldozed rubble that marked another tempo.

Dan clumped tiredly over to it. Sure enough, there were plenty of bootprints all around the airlock hatch.

"What the hell," he said to himself.

He slid the hatch back and stepped in. The airlock cycled automatically and most of the stiffness of his suit wilted away as the air pressure built up to normal. The light panel turned green and Dan slid the inner hatch open.

A huge, shaggy-maned, red-bearded man was standing at the hatch, massive fists planted on his hips, a fierce scowl on his flushed face.

"Who the hell are you?" Dan blurted.

The man snarled back, "And just who the fook are *you?*"

EIGHTEEN

Dan stared at the big, red-bearded stranger. Beyond his giant bulk, the shelter looked as if it had been turned into a home. He saw two pairs of double bunks, a desk with a computer atop it, and rough shelves stacked with canned foods all the way up the curved ceiling.

"I asked you a question," the big man said. "Who are you? What're you doing here?"

"I asked you first," said Dan, taking a booted step further into the shelter.

The man looked like anything but a GEC enforcer. Or a Yamagata employee, for that matter. His coveralls were frayed and faded, even patched at the knees, stained with oil and dirt. His wild hair hadn't seen a scissors in months, and his beard looked as if it could be home to an entire biota of its own. He's sure not one of *my* people, Dan told himself.

"Now, look," the man growled, "I've asked you twice. I won't ask a third time. Who the fook are ya?"

Grinning, Dan slid his helmet visor up. He had been in his share of fights on the Moon. This big goon was in his coveralls, while Dan was still encased in his pressure suit and helmet. If it came to a fight it would be no contest, despite the stranger's size.

"You're trespassing on Yamagata Industries' territory," Dan said. "And from the looks of it, you're stealing equipment and supplies, to boot."

The man roared and made a grab for Dan. Inside his cumbersome suit, Dan made no attempt to evade him. He jabbed with a stiff left, ready to follow it with an overhand right. But the giant let the left bounce off his chin with no apparent effect, and before Dan could throw his haymaker, he grabbed Dan by the armpits and lifted him off his feet, suit and all.

Suddenly Dan was dangling in midair, feet pedaling uselessly, his arms flailing, while the giant roared in his face and shook him like a terrier breaking a rat's back. Dan rattled around inside his suit, banging his head inside the helmet. He could not breathe. He tasted blood in his mouth. His whole world was shaking and roaring. He saw stars flashing and everything started to go gray.

"That's enough, I said! You don't wanna kill him until we find out who he is and what he's doing here."

The giant let Dan fall to the floor with a thunderous thump. Pain shot through him. Cripes, he's broken every bone in my body, Dan thought.

"Lemme talk to him."

Dan looked up through bleary eyes and slowly focused on the wrinkled, shriveled face of an ancient black man. He was tiny, the smallest and skinniest man Dan had ever seen. And old, far older than anyone Dan had seen on the Moon. Like the giant, the black man's coveralls were tattered and grimy.

The scrawny little man squatted beside Dan's prostrate form, bent his face close to Dan's, and said in a voice like sandpaper, "You gotta excuse my big friend. He's got a real short fuse."

Dan nearly gagged at the man's breath. Every part of his body hurt.

"We don't get a whole lot of visitors here," rasped the old man.

Dan nodded weakly.

"Now I'd 'preciate it if you'd kindly tell us just who the hell you are."

Slowly, painfully, Dan propped himself up on one elbow, still breathing hard.

"If you don't talk to me, Big George here'll go back to kickin' the shit outta you."

Grinning weakly, Dan managed to say, "No . . . thanks."

"Then who are you?" the old man asked sharply.

"Whatchya doin' out here?"

"Give me a minute . . ."

"To think up a story," growled Big George.

The old man held up a hand. "Let him catch his breath, Georgie."

He finally managed to say, "I'm Dan Randolph. I'm on the run from the GEC—"

"Dan Randolph!" blurted Big George. "Not fooking likely! I worked for Dan Randolph. He's one of the richest bastards in the fooking universe."

"I was," Dan said, pulling himself up to a sitting position. "Double-damned GEC stole everything I own."

"We ain't heard nuthin' about that," said the old man.

"Just happened today. I took off before they could grab me and send me back Earthside."

"And you just happened to drop into our shelter," Big George said, his bearded face full of suspicion.

"That's right."

The old man rose to his feet. "Help him up, Georgie."

Before Dan could react Big George leaned down, grabbed him again, and lifted him upright.

"Get that suit off him. We can use it," said the old man. His voice sounded like an old-time diesel rig grinding its gears.

"I've told you my name," Dan said, as he lifted his helmet off. "What about yours?"

The old man cast him a sour look. "This is Big George," he said, pointing with his thumb. "They call me Pops Tucker."

"They? Who?"

"None of your fooking business," George snarled. "Now peel off that suit or I'll take it off for ya."

Dan started to open up the seals on his cuffs. He heard the chugging of air blowers and thought that the square anodized blue case sitting in the far corner of the shelter looked like an air regenerator from an OTV. They obviously don't work for Yamagata, he thought, and they sure don't work for me. They've turned this tempo into living quarters—for more than two people, if the other bunks mean anything. And the little guy said "they" call him Pops Tucker. Who the hell are "they"?

Lifting the hard-shell torso of his suit over his head, Dan told them, "I'm going to be pretty goddamned stiff and sore, thanks to you."

Tucker frowned at him, but said, "George, find some liniment and aspirin in the medical supplies." To Dan he added sarcastically, "I'm sorry we don't have diathermy equipment or a whirlpool bath for you, Mr. Billionaire."

"Don't worry about it," Dan replied. "My own stuff is probably being used right now by a redheaded lawyer who was a spy for the GEC."

When he finally had removed the last part of his suit, Tucker motioned for Dan to come with him to the table they had set up at the far end of the shelter.

"Our dining room," he said. "You must be hungry."

"Now that you mention it," said Dan, sitting down gingerly.

Tucker took the slim plastic chair on Dan's right. "Before we eat, tell us what happened to you."

"Yeah," George said, straddling the chair on Dan's left. He leaned his buffalo-sized forearms on the table; it groaned and sagged. "Prove to us that you really are Dan Randolph."

Dan felt the pistol in his pocket pressing against his thigh. Whoever these guys were, they weren't security types. Professional security men would have searched him thoroughly. He felt a little better, knowing that these two men were more like babes in the woods than anything else. The pistol gave him an edge, even against Big George.

"Well?" Tucker prompted.

Dan started to tell his story, getting angrier inside with each sentence. Kate Williams, Nobo Yamagata, even Jane Scanwell had betrayed him. Now Malik's people were taking over the empire he had worked all his life to build up. Now he was broke, alone, friendless, seemingly at the mercy of two crazy men. And burning with helpless rage. He didn't know which was making him more furious: his hatred for Malik or his frustration at being unable to do a thing about it.

"You mean you expect those other bigwigs to work with the gov'ment on this greenhouse cliff?" Tucker asked incredulously.

Dan sighed heavily. His back felt like a board that was on fire. "I don't know what the hell they're going to do. If they can't convince the Council that they'll cooperate voluntarily, Malik'll sure as damnation take them over, just like he's taken my company."

His wizened chin barely clearing the tabletop, Tucker looked across at Big George. "Whattaya think, Georgie?"

"I never saw Randolph when I worked for 'im," George replied. "But this bloke tells a good story, at least."

"When did you work for Astro?" Dan asked. "What kind of job did you have?"

George scratched at his shaggy beard. "Two years ago. Came up here to maintain the surface skimmers. For the big helium-three project, you know."

"Right. We were hiring teleoperators then. And technicians to maintain the skimmers. They're pretty complex pieces of equipment."

"Yeah. Well, to me they weren't anything but big bulldozers with some fancy toys built onto their backs."

The skimmers scooped in the top few centimeters of the lunar regolith, separated the dirt into basic elements and fed the ores to solar-cell manufacturing plants, all completely automated. They separated out the helium-three, turned the silicon into solar cells, and deposit the cells back on the ground as they moved along.

"Damned expensive toys," Dan said.

Big George actually smiled at Dan. Or he seemed to; it was hard to tell what was going on inside that beard.

"We used to call 'em cows. Grazed on the regolith and shat solar cells."

Laughing, Dan added, "All automatic, too—or under remote control by teleoperators back inside the city."

George's smile turned into a scowl. "That's what they fooking told you, maybe, but it's not the way it fooking worked."

"What do you mean?"

"Fooking skimmers needed maintenance all the time. Otherwise they'd be down more often than they'd be working. Bosses had us out on the surface every fooking day, fixing the bastards."

"Fixing what?" Dan asked.

"Dust! You ever try working on the surface? Fooking dust gets into everything."

"I've worked on the surface," Dan snapped. "I was working up here when you were in diapers, for God's sake. We designed those skimmers with electrostatic dust screens—"

"That aren't worth a cow flop," George said. "I'm telling you, they had us out on the surface every fooking day, just about."

"But that's against safety regulations. The radiation buildup could be dangerous."

"Tell me about it. I complained, but my supervisor said it was either go out on the surface or get fired. I tried to go over his head. No way. I tried to get the other technicians to refuse to go outside—bring the problem to a boil, so to speak."

"And?"

"And they fired me."

"I never heard anything about this."

"I suppose not. You're too high above us working blokes to be bothered with such petty problems."

"Who fired you? What was his name?"

"Hers. And what difference does it make? What're you going to do about it?"

Dan started to reply, then realized George was right. There wasn't a damned thing he could do about it.

"So what happened then?" he asked quietly.

"Well," George said, "Astro guarantees your return fare Earthside, even if you're fired. Part of the pension fund. That's one good thing about the company, I've got to admit."

"So how come you're still here?"

"I took it out in cash and hung around for a while. Figured I could get another job. I had a girlfriend at Alphonsus that I didn't want to leave and she couldn't go back Earthside because she was making five times what she'd get back home."

Dan waited for him to say more, but George lapsed into silence.

"You gotta understand," Tucker said in his rasping voice, "that there's a whole underground community here. People like George who just sort of faded into the background—"

"Now, wait a minute," Dan said. "People don't just fade into the background up here. Everybody's accounted for. Computers keep track of every person who arrives and every one who departs. And in between, too."

Tucker smiled widely, showing teeth that looked artificial to Dan and creasing his wrinkled face even more deeply than usual.

Pointing to the desk a few feet away, he said, "There's a computer. You find George Ambrose in it. Or Freeman Tucker. I can name a hundred more, too."

"A hundred?"

"More," George said.

"How in the name of hell can you live in a closed society like Alphonsus? I mean, it's a self-contained community, ecologically and economically."

Tucker gave him a nasty smile. *"Almost* self-contained. *Almost* completely closed. We live on the almost."

"How?"

"That's none of your business, not yet. Right now, we gotta figure out what to do with you."

Dan glanced at Big George. The shaggy giant was watching him the way a lion stares at a gazelle.

"Way I see it," Tucker said, in his harshly grating voice, "there's three possibilities."

"Three?"

Ticking his fingers, "One: you're a spy from management, sent here to root us out. Two: you're some nut case who thinks it'd be fun to be in the counterculture. Three: you're telling the truth and you're really who you claim you are."

George held up three of his fingers. "So you got one chance out of three of staying alive."

Dan mulled it over for a moment, then leaned back in his chair—painfully—and tried to look nonchalant. "One out of three is a good batting average, in baseball."

NINETEEN

The weather forecast had been for partly sunny skies with a forty percent chance of afternoon showers. But it had started raining in Miami Beach about eleven in the morning, a steady, cold rain driven by a stinging wind from the Atlantic. The ocean looked gray and angry, as if displeased with what it saw ashore.

The mayor of Miami Beach sat beneath the protective canopy, of course. It had been intended to shield the VIPs from the sunshine, but some thoughtful soul had attached rain flaps of clear plastic on three sides of the bright blue canopy. Now, as rain lashed against the flaps and wind buffeted the entire stage so hard the mayor feared it would blow away, the governor droned on endlessly with his prepared speech.

". . . with the foresight and courage that have always marked the truly courageous pioneers and innovators who have made Florida the great state that it is," the governor thundered into the microphone, trying vainly to outhowl the wind.

The crowd had dwindled to almost nothing. Many of the folding chairs that had been carefully arranged out in front of the wooden stage had been blown over. Only a handful of people remained out in the wet, beneath big, swaying beach umbrellas that the mayor's public-relations people had frantically scrounged from every shop they could find along Collins Avenue.

The TV crews were at their posts, thank goodness, swaddled in slickers and plastic tarpaulins. Doesn't really matter how many people are in the live audience, the mayor thought, as long as this ceremony gets onto the evening newscasts. As long as the cameramen don't show all those empty seats.

At last the governor finished, to a spattering of applause, and the master of ceremonies—a nationally recognized talk-show host—introduced the mayor as "the man who has been the guiding light behind this project from its very inception to this moment of its dedication."

The mayor's ears were finely attuned to measuring crowd reaction, and he calculated that the applause for him—sparse as the audience had become—was slightly more than the governor got. That boded well for next year's election campaign, even though the mayor had more of his dependents out there than the governor had.

"Today," the mayor said, after thanking the emcee for his glowing introduction, "we dedicate more than a structure of concrete and steel. We dedicate ourselves to the proposition that Miami Beach will remain a viable community despite the worst that Nature can hurl against us."

Behind him, behind the stage and its billowing canopy, rose a wall of gray concrete that stretched the length of what had once been a beautiful beach. Now the beach was completely gone, replaced by a seawall twenty feet high, gray and grim and resolute. It protected the line of hotels and condominium high-rise buildings that stood shoulder to shoulder along the former beachfront, towers of glass and steel and developers' dreams.

Florida's seaside resorts and retirement communities had been devastated by the gradual rise in sea level and the increasing violence of storms powered by the rising greenhouse effect. Many cities and towns had lost their beaches, their seafront palaces, even their marinas and canals to the encroaching ocean. Causeways had been inundated or even washed away entirely. Whole towns had gone bankrupt. Mass migrations northward and inland had already begun.

The Miami Beach Seawall Project was the answer to the problem, the gauntlet thrown down in the face of Nature by a combination of desperate private developers, frantic Florida bankers, and frenzied local and state politicians. Using federal, state and even private funding, they had built a seawall that would protect Florida's showcase resort city from the rising sea and the raging storms.

In truth, the mayor had been a driving force behind the project. Scientists from Washington had said that no seawall could stand against the full might and fury of a mammoth hurricane. Yet other scientists (especially those from Florida universities) maintained that a wall could be built that was strong enough to do the job.

Now it was completed, and the mayor stood basking in the glow, figuratively, of his mighty accomplishment. It had cost billions, as the media and the mayor's political enemies pointed out repeatedly. But it would save the hundreds of billions already sunk into the city's buildings, streets and infrastructure.

"Now Miami Beach is safe," the mayor proclaimed, straining his voice against the growing bluster of the wind. "Now we no longer have to fear rising ocean levels or damaging storms."

Behind him, waves crashed against the seawall, thundering harder and harder against its concrete face. Driven by an ever-fiercer wind, the ocean seemed to be smashing itself against this new challenge. The seawall held, for the time being. But an especially powerful gust of wind ripped away the canopy that protected the VIPs up on their makeshift stage.

Screams, shouts and a horrible groaning of timbers. The plastic canopy, suddenly torn loose, flapped wildly and knocked the mayor and several other VIPs off the stage, twelve feet down onto solid concrete. Then the entire stage shifted and tilted and came crashing down.

The mayor, his wife, four others onstage and the three closest TV camerapersons were killed. The governor escaped with only a few broken bones. In the tumult and confusion, no one noticed that the ocean waves were already lapping over the top of the seawall, sending dark gray fingers of water down its other side and onto the protected ground behind it.

And this was not a hurricane, not even a tropical storm. Merely a few gusts of wind.

Dan Randolph knew nothing of the tragedy in Florida. He had finally been allowed to share a meager meal of frozen fish and rice from packages that bore the heron symbol of Yamagata Industries. The microwave oven in which Pops Tucker heated the food was not original equipment for a temporary shelter, Dan knew. It had been brought in from somewhere else.

Big George talked expansively during the meal of his younger days growing up in the opal mines of Australia.

"After living in Coober Pedy most o' my life, I thought these underground cities on the Moon would be downright luxurious. And they were."

Tucker stayed silent throughout dinner. But every time Dan glanced at him, the sour old man seemed to be watching him, eying him carefully, craftily. Like a judge sizing up a convicted man before sentencing. Or like a salesman trying to figure out how much he can charge for a used piece of merchandise.

Dan said nothing to the wrinkled, gnomish little man. He wondered if the pistol in his thigh pocket made a big enough bulge to be recognized. He realized that it was only a matter of time before the GEC put a price on his head. That's what Tucker's trying to figure out: how much am I going to be worth to him.

Dan and Big George talked for a couple of hours after dinner, with Tucker making rare contributions to their conversation. George bragged about the work he had done on the Moon's surface, braving the dangers of radiation and the billion-to-one chance of a meteoroid hit. Despite himself, Dan began talking about his days on the early construction jobs in orbit, and the first rugged mining operations on the Moon. After a while, George went silent and Dan found himself narrating story after story about those pioneering times. He did not even have to embellish the truth to keep the big Aussie spellbound.

"I'm goin' to sleep," Tucker said at last. He made it sound cranky, accusative. "If you guys are gonna keep spinning yarns at each other, do it quietly, okay?"

George shook his shaggy mane as if awakening from a trance. "Yeah, it's getting late. Time to sleep."

"You can have the upper bunk, over George," Tucker said to Dan, pointing. "And I'm a very light sleeper, so don't try anything funny."

Dan gave him a laugh. "What do you think I'm going to do, run away and hide?"

Tucker snorted disdainfully. "That's how you got here, ain't it?"

Dan acknowledged his point with a shrug. They took turns in the toilet, then climbed into their respective bunks without removing their coveralls. Dan's body still ached from George's pounding, but he fell asleep almost immediately, exhausted physically and emotionally. If he dreamed, he did not remember it the next morning.

Rafaelo Gaetano sat on the flagstoned patio in the warm evening breeze and gazed up at the sliver of a moon dancing in and out of the clouds. Then he looked down into the streets and sighed. At least the stench of the city did not reach up this far to the hillside villa.

Reggio di Calabria had been a beautiful city once. Down at the toe of the Italian boot, across the strait from Sicily's Messina, Reggio's waterfront had once been described as "the most beautiful kilometer in Italy" by no less than the poet D'Annunzio.

Now the city was bursting to overflowing with people driven off their parched farms by the drought. The streets were choked with garbage. Homeless people fought the rats every night. The waterfront was awash in filthy water half the time. In daylight you could see the high-tide marks on the buildings, creeping higher all the time. Drought and flood. Gaetano wondered how they could both be happening at the same time. Perhaps this greenhouse business was real, after all.

"Escaped, you say? How could the man escape? Where can he run to, up there?"

Gaetano returned his attention to the fat, wheezing old man sitting across the patio table from him. Don Marcello Arcangelico had been at death's door ever since Rafaelo had been a boy. But the old man refused to cross death's threshold. Beneath his pasty, sagging skin was a heart pacemaker, an artificial hip, a transplanted kidney and plastic tubing in place of worn-out arteries. The man was a tribute to modern medical science and his own indomitable will to continue living at any cost.

In the evening shadows, with only the lights from the house and a few flickering fireflies, it was difficult to read the expression on Don Marcello's fleshy face. But the tone of his voice was unmistakable. He was not pleased.

Gaetano reflected swiftly that it did not matter to Don Marcello that he was a Council member of the GEC, one of the most powerful men in what was in effect the government of the world. Governments did not impress Don Marcello. He saw them merely as impediments to business, as greedy bureaucrats with their hands out for bribes or, worse, honest do-gooders who wanted to rid the world of businessmen such as himself.

"So?" the Don asked impatiently. "How could he escape? Where has he gone?"

With great care to keep a tone of respect in his voice, Gaetano replied, "I don't know how he escaped. He was in his own headquarters, however. There must have been many men there who are loyal to him. He must have had considerable help."

"Yes, yes," Don Marcello muttered. Personal loyalty to one's leader was a concept he could understand and agree with, even when the loyalty was to an enemy.

"As to where he's gone," Gaetano went on, "what does it matter? He can't show his face in any of the cities on the Moon. He can't get off the Moon: all the launching facilities are under tight control. He is probably already dead out on the surface someplace."

"And if he's not?"

Gaetano shrugged elaborately. "What difference? He can't go anywhere that matters. He can't do anything to interfere with us. As far as our plans are concerned, he's as good as dead."

Don Marcello was silent for several moments. Gaetano could hear his heavy, labored breathing in the darkness. "And what does the Russian think of this?" he asked at last.

"Malik? He is concerned. With him, Dan Randolph is a personal affair. A vendetta."

"Vendetta," Don Marcello mumbled. "What would a Russian barbarian know of a vendetta?"

Gaetano wisely chose not to reply.

"Well?" the old man snapped. "Is he *doing* anything?"

"Who?"

"The Russian, you cucumber!"

Through clenched teeth Gaetano answered, "Malik ordered that all the satellites in orbit around the Moon be used to scan the surface for signs of Randolph."

"Satellites? Machines. What about a search with people?"

"Don Marcello," Gaetano said as politely as he could, "the Moon is not like Earth. They don't send out search parties with dogs. There's no air on the surface. No water."

The old man considered this for several moments, mumbling wheezily to himself. Then, "If they do not find his body it means that he is not dead. If he is not dead he can still be a threat to us."

"I don't see how. He's been stripped of his power. All his wealth has been confiscated. Even if he is alive, he's hiding like a rat someplace almost half a million kilometers away from us."

"He is dangerous, I tell you."

And so is Carthage, Gaetano thought to himself. But he knew that Don Marcello's kind of stubborn ruthlessness was what had made Rome a great empire and what made their family enterprise an international power.

"What of the Russian?" Don Marcello asked. "Does he suspect?"

Gaetano shook his head. "Not a thing. He thinks this plan to confiscate the Big Seven space corporations is all his own idea."

Again silence, except for the old man's labored attempts to breathe. Down the hillside, Gaetano could see the distant lights of cars passing on the highway.

"The scientists actually believe," Gaetano said in a hushed voice, "that the sea levels will rise so high that cities like Reggio will be completely flooded. Messina, Palermo, even Naples will be underwater."

"Bah!"

"They say it will really happen."

"Even if it does," said Don Marcello, "it only means more power and money for us. People will want new homes. They'll come running up here to the hills, willing to pay anything for a shack to live in. And in the meantime we'll be skimming the cream off the Big Seven— almost legally!" He laughed, a coughing, painful, ugly gargling sound.

Gaetano nodded in the gathering darkness. Don Marcello Arcangelico saw the world in very simple terms.

What was good for him was good for his family. The rest of the world, the rest of the universe, he did not care about.

What a name for him, Arcangelico. Then Gaetano remembered that Lucifer had been an archangel.

TWENTY

"Now we see if you're really who you say you are,"
Pops Tucker said in his sour, grouchy manner.

It was morning. Not sunrise; that would not
happen out on the worn old mountains of the Alphonsus
ringwall for another three hundred and thirty hours. But
inside the shelter where Dan had slept with Big George
and Pops Tucker, the digital clock on the comm console
said 0745 hours. The overhead fluorescents had switched
on automatically. Morning.

Dan sat on the edge of his bunk, feeling grungy, unwashed, still stiff and sore from the rattling George had
given him. In the darkness, before falling asleep, he had
tucked his gun under the thin mattress of his bunk. It was
safer there than bulging in his pocket, he reasoned.
Tucker eyed him suspiciously. George was in the lavatory; they could hear him gargling ferociously, sputtering
like a drowning man.

"If you really are Dan Randolph," the old man said,
"and what you told us last night was the truth, you can

be a big help to us."

"How?"

"You'll see."

George came out of the lav wearing only his skivvies. He looks like an ad for bodybuilding, Dan thought. More muscles than a squad of weight lifters.

Over a breakfast of coffee and thin, flavorless wafers, Tucker outlined his plan.

"If you're really the head of Astro Manufacturing, you oughtta be able to access Astro's logistics inventory programs pretty easy."

Dan sipped at the hot, bitter brew in his plastic cup. "What makes you think I'd have anything to do with inventory programs? I hire people to deal with that for me; I don't handle it myself."

"You used to hire people," George reminded him.

"That's right," Dan admitted. "I used to."

Tucker was undeterred. "Those gov'ment assholes took over your office yesterday, right? I'll bet they haven't touched the company's inventory programs. Not yet. They'll be busy with personnel files and organization charts and crap like that. They don't know from the *real* stuff. They're just paper-pushers, not real workers."

With a shake of his head, Dan insisted, "The first thing they did, most likely, was erase my access codes to all the company programs."

"Your personal access codes, maybe. What about the emergency codes, though?"

"Probably not. But what makes you think I carry them around in my head?"

"You've got 'em," Tucker said firmly. "If you're really Dan Randolph, you either got 'em or you know how to get 'em."

Dan put his cup down on the table. Tucker had a crafty look on his wizened face. Big George was munching on one of the wafers, but he too had his eyes on Dan.

Heads you win, tails I lose, Dan thought as he stared back at Tucker. If I can't access the inventory programs you throw me out the airlock. If I can, you get what you want and maybe *then* you toss me out. I'll have to get that damned gun when they've both got their backs turned.

"Well?" Tucker prompted.

Dan gave him a crooked grin. "Let's see what's in my wristwatch."

He slipped it off his wrist. It was easier to work the tiny keyboard that way. Dan knew that the emergency access codes to the logistics programs were not stored in the wrist unit's minuscule computer, but the gadget did hold the phone numbers of every department head at Alphonsus and Caracas. This early in the morning hardly any of them would be at their offices, but their phones would be linked to the company's central mainframe.

It was almost ridiculously easy. While Tucker and George watched, Dan used the name of the head of the logistics department to get the mainframe to produce a string of access codes.

"You were right," he muttered as he watched the numbers scrolling past on the wrist unit's tiny screen. "Don't even need the damned emergency codes; the idiot program's about as secure as a virgin in the men's locker room." Dan frowned, thinking that he would have to beef up the system when . . .

Then he remembered that it was no longer his system, or his company.

Tucker borrowed his wristwatch and went to the desktop computer, began tapping in the access codes.

George smiled happily. "Now we'll be able to find out what your blokes are moving from one location to another."

"What good will that do you?"

"Can't steal what you can't find," George said.

"Steal?"

"Right. How do you think we live out here? Charity from the Big Seven?"

Tucker looked up from the screen, its bluish glow

casting a ghastly light on his wrinkled face. "There's a shipment of spare parts for the skimmers goin' out to the base camp on the outslope."

"Crew?" George asked.

"None indicated. Just a cargo run."

"Sounds good. When?"

Tucker glanced back at the screen. " 'Safternoon. Leaves the city at sixteen hundred."

George rolled his eyes ceilingward as he did a swift mental calculation. "Ought to be here by sixteen-twenty, sixteen-twenty-five at the latest."

"You're going to hijack a cargo trolley?" Dan asked.

Tucker made a disdainful grunt. "Nothing so grand, Randolph. We're not big thieves; we're just small ones. All we're going to do is pilfer a little."

Jane Scanwell had spent the night in the transfer station at the L1 liberation point, thirty-six thousand miles above the lunar surface. She had left Alphonsus within an hour of Dan's escape and now, after a sleepless night, was sitting uneasily in the passenger compartment of a regularly scheduled shuttle heading for Earth orbit.

Weightlessness still bothered her. Although she was strapped into her seat, her innards still felt as if she were falling endlessly and her head was throbbing. The passenger compartment was very much like the interior of an airliner; the flight attendants even walked almost normally along the central aisle, thanks to Velcro slippers. Still, Jane fought down the queasiness in her stomach, the feeling of stuffiness in her sinuses.

And her roiling emotions. Damn Dan! she said to herself for the hundredth time that hour. And damn me for caring about his foolish, arrogant hide. Running away! What a stupid trick to pull. Where's he going to run to, on the Moon? He'll just get himself killed, that's all he's going to accomplish.

Well, what can you do about it? she asked herself. Is there any way you can help him?

She was surprised at her own question. Help him? He's a fugitive from justice. How can I even dream of trying to help him? And when did he ever ask for my help? He ran away from me. He always runs away from me. We could have stayed on Tetiaroa together. But he didn't even give me the chance to tell him that I'd resign my Council position if he'd quit Astro and retire peacefully.

Now it's too late, she realized. Now he's a fugitive in hiding. Maybe he's already dead.

Good riddance! He's been nothing but heartache and pain to me ever since I met him. Time to forget Dan Randolph and get on with my life. No tears. No regrets. If he's not dead already he will be soon and there's nothing I can do about it. Not a damned thing.

She refused to cry. But suddenly her guts churned with acid and she grabbed for the retch bag in the seatback in front of her.

Katherine Williams sat in Dan's swivel chair and studied the data on his desktop screen. The takeover was proceeding smoothly. Each department and section of the company was functioning as it should—somewhat raggedly, perhaps, in a few cases, but that was to be expected when there had been such an abrupt change in management. Now the computer system was patiently, remorselessly, thoroughly rooting Dan Randolph's name and all his various access codes from every branch of Astro Manufacturing. Within a few hours, as far as the computer programs were concerned, Dan Randolph will cease to exist. It will be as if he never had existed, Kate thought.

But where is he? she wondered as she leaned back in his chair. It was utterly comfortable: its midnight black covering was something like butter-soft leather, but warm to the touch and gently yielding, so that it conformed to the contours of her body as if the chair had been custom built for her alone.

Kate smiled to herself. Not a bad idea, actually. Instead of going back to San Francisco, why not stay here and run Astro for the GEC? I can bring Kimberly up here; she'd be better off away from her old haunts, once she's out of the rehab center. We'd both be better off up here on the Moon: Kimberly away from her drug culture and me a quarter-million miles away from Rafe.

Gaetano was not a bad lover, once they got down to the pleasure of lovemaking. It was the damned silly games he liked to play beforehand. He really didn't like women, Kate realized. No, it's not that, exactly. He's afraid of women. He's got to put himself in a position of absolute power before he can get it up.

What would Gaetano do if I told him I wanted to stay here and run Astro's operations for the GEC? And bring Kimberly up here with me? That would just about break his hold over me. Would he care? He can always find some other woman to dominate.

She shook her head, frowning. No, he wouldn't want to give up his power over me. Not unless I could give him something in return. Something he wants more than his feeling that he can control me. Something . . .

The answer was displaying itself to her in the desktop screen. Dan Randolph! If I could deliver Dan to him, Rafe would let me have Astro as my reward. That would work.

She broke into a happy smile as she leaned forward across the desk to reach the computer keyboard. I'll have Kim here safe *and* Astro Manufacturing. Terrific! All I've got to do is find Dan Randolph.

She began pecking at the keyboard with single-minded intensity, telling herself that it wouldn't matter if Dan was dead or alive. All she had to do was find him. Or his body.

"Are you sure this is going to work?" Dan asked dubiously.

"I've done it before," Big George's voice replied in his helmet earphones. "It's not as crazy as it looks."

It looked pretty crazy to Dan. He and George were climbing up one of the slim concrete pillars that held the cable-car line, clambering in their space suits slowly up the steel ladder rungs imbedded in the pole like a pair of ungainly oversized bear cubs struggling up a tree.

Pops Tucker had remained in the shelter, too old and frail for the athletics that George was contemplating.

"It's simple," George said. "We wait at the top of the pole. The fooking trolley comes by. We jump down onto its roof, then climb down and enter it through the airlock. Nothing to it, practically."

The pillar looked about ten meters high to Dan, from the ground. Halfway up, climbing laboriously in the awkward pressure suit, it seemed more like a hundred meters high. He leaned over to see the ground from inside his helmet. Make it two hundred meters, he said to himself.

"The main thing is the timing," George was explaining. "When I say to jump, jump. Don't want to miss the fooking bus. Even in this gravity, a ten-meter fall can break your bones."

Dan's back still hurt sullenly. At last they reached the top of the pillar. He clambered up beside George and the two of them hung there like high-tech monkeys. Suddenly a new thought popped into his head.

"Hey, once we're inside the trolley, how the hell do we get out again? We can't wait until it gets to the end of the line, there'll be people waiting for it there."

He could not see George's face behind the heavily tinted visor of his helmet. But he heard the big man chuckle. "We stop the bugger, that's what we do. Stop her and use the emergency escape line to get back to the surface."

"Then they know somebody's been aboard it."

"Sure they know."

Inside his helmet, sweating from the exertion of the climb, Dan frowned with puzzlement. "But I've never heard of a trolley being hijacked."

"Doesn't happen very often," George's voice replied. "We don't do this every day, y'know."

"But I would have been informed about it," Dan insisted. "My security people would have reported it up the chain of command to me."

"Maybe," said George. "Maybe not."

"I don't understand—"

"Hold it! Here she comes."

Dan had to turn his entire upper torso to look in the direction of the cable, hanging tautly a few feet below them. It was still night on the Moon, but there was enough Earthlight for him to make out the bullet shape of the trolley whizzing along the cable toward them. Cripes, it's coming fast. If we miss . . .

"Jump!" George yelled.

Dan jumped. He seemed to hang in emptiness forever. Then he landed with a bone-rattling thud on the trolley's roof. His boots scraped and slid on the slick hard surface and he felt himself going over sideways in the dreamy slow motion of the Moon's low gravity. He reached out for something to grab hold of but there was nothing, not even thin air, nothing but vacuum. He was falling over the side, slipping like a man in a nightmare toward the ground rushing by so far below.

Something grabbed him hard and yanked him back onto the flat surface of the trolley's roof. Dan lay on his belly, gasping.

George's voice in his earphones sounded amused. "I forgot to tell you—grab one of the handholds on the roof when you land. Otherwise you'll fall off."

"Thanks . . ." Dan puffed, "for the . . . advice."

"C'mon, no time to waste."

I'm too old for this, Dan said to himself. But, taking a deep breath, he slowly got to all fours. George was already clambering down the side of the moving trolley to work its airlock hatch. Dan got shakily to his feet. The car was moving along at a good fifty knots or more, he estimated, but there was no real sensation of movement.

No wind, certainly, and the car seemed steady as a rock beneath his feet. A little vibration, but nothing much. If he didn't look at the ground hurtling past it would be hard to tell they were moving at all.

"C'mon," George called. "In we go."

Dan lowered himself down from the lip of the roof and swung into the open airlock. Within minutes he and George were inside the main cab of the trolley. It was stuffed with crated mechanical parts and boxes of electronics equipment.

George whistled happily. "A fooking cornucopia!" He went to the display screen built into the front bulkhead. "Can you work this?"

Clumping in his boots, Dan walked up beside him and pecked at the keyboard mounted on the wall. The car's manifest appeared on the screen.

"Fair dinkum, mate. Now let's see what we want to take."

To Dan's surprise, George selected only a half-dozen small electronics items from the cargo.

"Is that all?" he blurted, when George indicated they would stop the car and get off now. "I damn near broke my neck just for this?"

George must have nodded inside his helmet, though Dan could not see it. "Enough," he said. "If we get too greedy it'll upset people."

"Upset who?"

Stacking the half-dozen boxes he had selected beside the airlock's inner hatch, George answered, "The people in your security section who look the other way when we steal from you, that's who."

TWENTY-ONE

But we have the legal authority to take over your entire company," said Vasily Malik, his face somber, almost grim.

"The authority perhaps," answered Nobuhiko Yamagata, equally serious, "but I doubt that you have the power."

Jane Scanwell sat with Malik on the settee. Across the low coffee table from them sat Nobuhiko and the Japanese consul—a government official low enough to offer no real threat to the GEC Council members, but high enough to make it plain that the Japanese government was vitally interested in the fate of Yamagata Industries.

Beyond the windows of Nobo's hotel room rose the spires and rooftops of New San Francisco, still rebuilding after the mammoth earthquake of six years earlier. At least the city has insisted on keeping the view of the bay clear, thought Jane. That's one benefit of the quake. But it had taken seventeen thousand deaths to overcome the greed of builders who had raised constantly higher towers in the old days.

Malik glanced at the Japanese consul, an undistin-
guished-looking man of middle years dressed in a conser-
vatively dark business suit, his face as expressionless as a
blank mask.

For three weeks he had been pressing for a personal
meeting with the new head of Yamagata Industries. Finally Nobuhiko had agreed to meet him in San Francisco: a neutral ground between Japan and the GEC's
Paris headquarters. They were in one of the company
suites in the rebuilt Yamagata Hotel. Nobo was wearing
a casual knit shirt and shorts, fit more for a tennis match
than a duel against the powers of the GEC. Both Malik
and Jane were in business clothes: her pants suit was a
shade of light blue that complemented her auburn hair
beautifully; Malik wore a summer-weight suit of pearl
gray.

"Are you saying," the Russian asked Nobo, "that the
Japanese government would resist a GEC order of confiscation?"

"Yes, that is precisely what I am saying," Nobuhiko
replied.

"That would be . . . unfortunate."

Nobo leaned forward earnestly across the bare coffee
table. "I cannot speak for the government of Japan officially, but I assure you that Tokyo will take a very dim
view of any attempt by the GEC to take over Yamagata
Industries the way you have taken over Astro Manufacturing and several others of the Big Seven."

Jane offered, "We're only talking about Yamagata's
space facilities, not your terrestrial operations."

"I understand that."

"Your government would oppose that?"

"To the point of exercising its option to withdraw
from the Global Economic Council."

"That would be an extreme move," Malik said uneasily.

"And if Japan withdraws," Nobuhiko pressed his advantage, "China and all the Little Tigers of the Pacific Rim will undoubtedly withdraw also. Perhaps Australia and New Zealand, as well. Who knows how far the movement might spread?"

"That must not happen," said Malik.

"Don't you understand?" Jane pleaded. "We *must* have control of the space facilities. In the next ten years or so—"

"The greenhouse cliff. I know," Nobo said.

"Then you must understand why all the space facilities have to be under a unified control."

"Control is not the same thing as confiscation."

"Astro was confiscated because it broke the law," Malik insisted.

"And Rockledge? Arianespace? What pretexts did you use to take them?"

Malik stiffened. "We are here to discuss the fate of Yamagata Industries, not the GEC."

"The two seem inextricably intertwined," Nobo said, the faintest of smiles playing at the corners of his mouth.

"In the face of a global catastrophe, you refuse to cooperate with the GEC."

Nobo raised a finger. "Not so. Yamagata Industries will cooperate fully with the GEC. We understand the gravity of the greenhouse problem, the severity of the challenge that faces the world. Japan is very sensitive to this issue; after all, the rise in sea level will be especially disastrous for Japan. We will certainly cooperate—but we will not be coerced."

Jane glanced at Malik's grim face, then turned back to Nobuhiko. "You will cooperate voluntarily?"

"That is what Dan Randolph advised us to do, just before he disappeared."

"Randolph." Malik growled the name.

"He called us together, you know, the day he disappeared; all seven of us."

"I know," said Jane, her voice low. "I was in his office."

Nobo looked away from her. "I was . . . unable to attend the teleconference. But Dan urged us to cooperate fully with the GEC's effort to avert the greenhouse cliff. Even if the GEC expropriates all our profits. He said we are facing a wartime situation, and we must act accordingly."

"Wartime?" Malik snapped.

"Dan's position was that we must make the same sacrifices we would if we were at war, if we are to beat this greenhouse cliff. Yamagata Industries intends to do so."

"I see," Malik said stiffly, the way a man accepts a situation he hates. "That is good news, I suppose."

"On the other hand," Nobo went on, "if the GEC continues with its efforts to take over Yamagata's space facilities, we will fight you in the World Court."

"But that could take years!" Jane said.

Nobo acknowledged her assessment with a single nod of his head.

"And in the meantime the greenhouse cliff will draw even closer," said Malik.

"That is true."

They all fell silent for several moments. The two Council members clearly saw the offer that Nobuhiko was making: stop the effort to confiscate Yamagata's space facilities and the corporation will cooperate fully with the GEC's effort to avert the greenhouse cliff. Otherwise, the entire GEC itself might be torn apart and the greenhouse warming will devastate the planet.

"Complete control," Malik muttered at last. "We must have total control of all space facilities. That is imperative."

"I am willing to grant you total control of all Yamagata space facilities—provided," Nobo raised both his hands, "that you recognize legally that such control is voluntarily granted by Yamagata and can be withdrawn whenever Yamagata desires."

Malik slapped his thighs angrily. "Impossible! How can we set long-range operations in motion when you can pull out at any moment?"

"How can you expect me to give you control of my space facilities with no time limit? You could keep them forever!"

Jane leaned toward Nobo. "How about a time limit written into the agreement, then? Say, ten years?"

"Twenty," said Malik.

"Five," said Nobo.

They glared at each other over the coffee table.

"Five years," suggested Jane, "with an automatic renewal for another five, unless one party wants to end the agreement."

"We need ten years at least," Malik insisted. "Even that will not be enough. How can we convert the entire planet's energy and transport systems in ten years? It can't be done! All we can hope for is to make a significant start on the problem."

Nobo said to Jane, "I believe a five-and-five agreement will be workable."

Malik leveled an accusatory finger at him. "I know what you are after! With the whole world looking to you and your other space industrialists to provide fusion fuels and solar power, you intend to gouge incredible profits out of this opportunity!"

Nobuhiko forced a smile. "I presume that if I allow you to control all of Yamagata's space operations, that control will include a limit on our profit margins. In fact, I thought that was the real reason behind your insistence on control."

"The operations must be done at cost," Malik said, not taken aback for a moment by Nobo's placating tone.

"It will be necessary for us to vastly enlarge our facilities in space," Nobo countered. "How will the GEC provide capital for such expansion?"

"Cost plus a percentage for expansion," Jane suggested.

"But no profits," said Malik.

Nobo leaned back in the settee, forcing the consul to

move slightly, the first indication since their meeting began that the man was actually alive.

"The GEC will provide any additional capital needed?" he asked.

"Yes," Jane said before Malik could open his mouth.

"All salary levels will be maintained? We have a rather liberal policy of bonuses and salary reviews, you know."

"You will continue to operate the facilities as you see fit," Jane said. "The Council will take the responsibility for management."

"Including price-setting," Malik added.

"Five years, with renewal option."

Malik hesitated, then said, "Over a total of twenty years."

"Three renewal options, then," said Jane.

Nobuhiko closed his eyes for a moment, as if communing with spirits. When he opened them again he said, "Very well. I will sign such an agreement."

"And you will get the others in the Big Seven to sign similar agreements?"

"Those you haven't already seized," Nobo said.

"Excellent."

All four of them rose and shook hands across the coffee table. Not one of them smiled.

In Paris it was two in the morning. Rafaelo Gaetano sat on the sofa in his living room, swathed in a burgundy red silk robe, his bare feet up on the pillows, his eyes fixed on the video screen. Transmission quality of the picture was good, considering that the camera was about the width of a human hair and set into the ceiling of the hotel room in San Francisco. The sound was weak, though; he had to strain his ears to understand what they were saying.

When the four stood up and shook hands, Gaetano fished the remote control from the pocket of his robe and clicked off the TV.

Unconsciously he bit his lower lip as he thought, We wanted total control of Yamagata and the others, but

Malik's made this half-assed deal with the Jap. Five years. That ought to give us enough time to put our own people in charge. By the time the renewal comes up, we could have Yamagata Industries and the others in our pocket, if we play our cards right.

He nodded to himself, satisfied that his report to Don Marcello would be acceptable. At least, he thought it would be.

Dan Randolph had learned a lot in three weeks. There was an underground community on the Moon—an illegal, unacknowledged subculture that lived by theft, barter and bribery. And now he was part of it.

He was walking through the main plaza of Alphonsus City, heading toward the grand entryway of the brand-new Yamagata Hotel, grinning to himself that he could get away with it. Of course, he had changed considerably. He had not shaved, and although his three-week beard was depressingly gray rather than the youthful sandy blond he would have preferred, it effectively kept his face from being recognized by the men and women walking along the plaza. And he was thinner, tauter. Three weeks of living as an outlaw had burned off some fat.

The people in the plaza were almost entirely Japanese, of course. Still, Dan felt a pang of surprise. And he felt annoyed with himself that he was surprised. He had known that Alphonsus was basically a Yamagata facility; his own Astro operations merely leased space from Sai's corporation. But he had surrounded himself with his own people so much that he had forgotten, down in his gut where it counted, that his Americans were a small minority of the men and women who lived and worked in Alphonsus.

I insulated myself too much, he thought as he walked along the pedestrian thoroughfare. How easy it is to separate yourself from the real world. Big-shot Dan Randolph, sitting in your office and giving orders, watching your flunkies jump, ignoring the world around you because it was so much easier to let yourself think you knew what was going on. So much more pleasant to tell yourself you were in charge, to watch people hop when you gave an order. You took up swimming while the rest of 'em were working to steal it all.

No wonder Malik was able to take my company away from me. It was my own damned stupid fault.

The main plaza was an immense domed structure, big enough to hold six football fields. But the city was all underground, buried deep below the plaza level. The area up here was devoted to green trees and flowering shrubbery, an open-air theater with a gracefully curved acoustical shell, small shops and restaurants and pleasant winding walks through the greenery. A few fliers were gliding high up above on rented plastic wings and their own muscle power. Soft music wafted through the air over the hum and hubbub of the crowds on the thoroughfares. To Dan it all seemed like a giant shopping mall, the kind he had known in Houston that had created an environment just as artificial as this vast dome on the Moon.

A pair of young Japanese whizzed past him on a skateboard. Probably a married couple, from the looks of them. Maybe not: she's holding him awfully tight. They shouldn't be in the pedestrian lane, Dan grumbled to himself. Sure enough, they were stopped by a robot traffic monitor only a few hundred feet up ahead, the spinning light on its head glaring red. The young man looked abashed as the robot recited its programmed lecture on traffic safety and a printed summons chugged out of the slot on its side.

Dan grinned at them as he sauntered past. He noticed that both the man and his lady friend had earphones clamped to their heads. God knows what kind of brain-numbing music they were pumping into their skulls. The traffic robots were equipped with radio overrides, so their lectures and instructions were piped right into the earphones. The long arm of the law.

Just be careful that the long arm of the law doesn't tap *you* on the shoulder, he warned himself. He was carrying a fake ID that Pops Tucker had cooked up for him, based on data from Astro's personnel file that the grumpy old man had hacked into. It would not bear close scrutiny, but a simple robot might be fooled by it. The secret was not to be stopped and asked for identification. Accordingly, Dan walked with the flow of pedestrian traffic, as innocuous and unremarkable as the shrubbery planted along the thoroughfare. The coveralls he wore were old and faded from their original sky blue, but clean and not too frayed. The ID·badge clipped to his breast pocket identified him as R. Jones. His shoulder patch claimed he worked in Astro's logistics department. He had left his pistol back in the tempo shelter he shared with Tucker and Big George; hidden it behind his bunk. He still did not trust his two new acquaintances enough to show the gun to them.

He sauntered through the entryway of the hotel, past the built-in X-ray detectors and security cameras and the two burly Japanese doormen in their bright new uniforms. Anybody could come into the hotel's lobby area; there were restaurants and shops open to the public. It would be a different matter to try to get into one of the residence suites.

The lobby was gorgeous, floored with basalt from Mare Nubium polished to a mirror finish. Like all lunar facilities, the hotel's various floors were deeper underground than the main plaza's level. There were no staircases on the Moon; too easy for newcomers unaccustomed to the lower gravity to trip themselves. Dan descended a wide rampway, walking slowly like the rest of the crowd to admire the sheets of water sliding noiselessly down tilted panes of glass on either side of the central rampway, into spacious fish ponds at the bottom level. Freely flowing water was still a rare sight on the Moon, even though aquaculture provided much more protein for the lunar diet than agriculture could. Tourists tossed bread and other goodies to the beautifully colored fish. Dan wondered if they realized that they would be eating those same fish in another day or two.

Dan felt strangely happy. For the first time in years, in decades really, he felt free. No obligations, except to his stomach. And his groin. No responsibilities, except to avoid getting caught. At the age of fifty he was starting a new life, almost as if he were a kid again.

So half the world's going to be flooded out in ten years or so. Not a damned thing I can do about it. I would've tried to help, but they stopped me. Not my responsibility anymore. I wanted to help, but Malik saw to it that I won't be able to. Tough luck, world. I could've saved you a lot of trouble. But they won't let me. Malik. And Jane—even she turned against me. We could have had a great life together, the two of us. But it was never meant to be.

He shrugged as he walked, trying to accept it all philosophically. But inwardly he seethed. The more he thought about it, the less he liked his thoughts. Malik. And Jane. Nobuhiko turning his back on him. And Kate Williams. The traitor. The damned smiling, long-legged, redheaded, sexy-looking traitor.

I'd like to wring her neck, he told himself. But he knew that was not what he really wanted to do. With an angry huff he realized that what he really wanted was to get her in bed.

Or anybody, come to think of it. The one problem with this new life-style is getting laid. It's a lot easier when you're filthy rich.

Katherine Williams was speaking to Rafaelo Gaetano from her office in Astro Manufacturing's complex in Alphonsus. In the three weeks since she had spearheaded the GEC's takeover, Kate had come to think of Dan Randolph's former office as her own.

It had not changed much, physically. The pictures on the walls were still mostly photographs of rocket laun-

ches and space facilities that Randolph had built. Kate
had replaced one especially pointless engineering sketch
with a print of colorful flowers in a vase. She kept a small
photograph of her sister and herself in the top desk
drawer, where no one could see it. It had been taken
when they were teenagers, arms around each other's
waists, smiles full of milk-white teeth, no marks of pain
or disappointment or responsibility on either of their
happy pretty faces.

"He's not dead," she was saying to Gaetano. "I'm
certain of that, Rafe."

It took two and a half seconds for her words to reach
Earth and his response to return. She was smoothing her
hair when he replied:

"How can you be so sure? He hasn't shown up for
three weeks. He can't live out in the open that long."

"He's not out on the surface," Kate said firmly. "He's
somewhere here, around Alphonsus, using an assumed
identity."

Gaetano seemed annoyed by the transmission lag. He
glowered into the screen.

"You're guessing," he said at last.

Kate shook her head. "Nobody's found his body. But
I've found something that's maybe more interesting than
his corpse." She stopped, smiling, knowing that he would
be impatient to hear what she had to say.

"So? What is it?"

"People are living in the emergency shelters that are
scattered around up on the surface. People who aren't
registered on the personnel files of any corporation up
here."

Gaetano's frown deepened even further when her
words reached him. "People? What people?"

Kate waved an uncertain hand. "The lunar version of
the homeless, Rafe. People who have no IDs, no jobs, no
permanent abode. I'm digging into this; there's apparently an entire underground community here at Alphon-

sus. I'll bet the same situation holds at all the other lunar facilities, as well."

"I thought everybody lives underground up there."

"I mean underground like—well, like crooks. Black market. Illegal aliens, sort of. They must be criminals, Rafe. They can't hold down regular jobs, or they'd be on the personnel files and have regular living quarters assigned to them."

His scowl turned thoughtful. "You mean there's a whole nest of illegals at Alphonsus?"

"Yes. And Copernicus, and the other communities, too. Just like any city on Earth, Rafe."

"And you think Randolph is in with these bums?"

"He must be."

Gaetano ran a finger across his moustache. "Then you'd better find him. Don't even think about coming back until you do."

Kate tried to look upset at the thought that she was not to return to Earth until she had rooted Dan Randolph out of his hiding place. She kept herself from smiling until several seconds after the phone link had been ended.

TWENTY-TWO

Randolph Jones—Dan's assumed persona—was a lowly computer programmer in Astro Corporation's logistics department. In other words, a high-tech clerk. The actual Randolph Jones was enjoying two days of fun and games with some of the women that Big George played with over in the mining facility out on the plain of Mare Nubium.

Horny though he might be, Dan had not been able to bring himself to bed one of Big George's playmates. No wonder the company's group insurance rates keep going up, he thought the first time George had taken him out to the camp. They looked sleazy and dirty, not at all the kind that Dan felt comfortable with, even after several rounds of locally brewed "rocket juice."

One of the whores had plunked herself on Dan's knee and whispered into his ear, "Even if you're too old to cut the mustard, honey, you can still lick the jar." Then she shrieked with wicked laughter. For the rest of that evening Dan was glad that his beard was coming in gray.

Now, after an hour's walk through the Yamagata Hotel shops, ogling jeweled baubles and pricey clothes and handsome women that he could no longer afford, Dan headed for work as Randolph Jones at Astro Manufacturing's logistics office. The women bothered him. It was fine to feel free of responsibilities, to live from day to day, almost like a teenager. No worries. No cares. But no women, either. I've got to do something about that, he told himself.

Astro's logistics office was two levels below the main plaza, connected to the big enclosed garage where the surface skimmers and tractors were housed and maintained. The personnel computer accepted R. Jones' ID badge without a quiver, simply checking the retinal pattern coded onto the badge against Dan's eyes. It was not programmed to check the pattern on the badge against R. Jones' pattern in the personnel file. Dan realized that this was a hole in Astro's security procedures that you could drive a tractor through. But who would have thought that the company needed tight security procedures at a lunar base? Besides, every piece of equipment and item of supplies was constantly monitored by the logistics computer, wasn't it?

The past three weeks had taught Dan how fallacious that assumption was.

"Hey, man, you're not Randy Jones."

Dan clipped his badge back onto his pocket as he surveyed the man accosting him. He was another maintenance tech, a black American somewhere in his early thirties, tall and gangly in blue coveralls that were just as faded as Dan's own. His face looked more curious than suspicious.

"Randy's taking a couple of days off. He asked me to fill in for him so he wouldn't lose any pay."

"Yeah?"

Dan sidled closer and lowered his voice. "He's with a couple of girlfriends."

The black man huffed. "Sounds like him. Tryin' to live up to his name."

Glancing at the man's ID badge, Dan said, "Listen, Bob—you're not going to give me away, are you? Randy and I are splitting the pay, and I sure could use the money."

Robert Thomas obviously did not like the situation. But he said, "I won't give Randy away; he's a friend. A screwball, but a friend. Just don't you fuck up on the job, man. Then we'll all be in the soup. You know anything about tractor maintenance?"

Dan said, "Randy told me his job was running the inventory program."

Thomas smiled. "Okay. I guess you really do know the old motherhumper. Yeah, you handle the inventory while the rest of us do the real work."

Letting out a breath that he had not realized he had been holding in, Dan followed Bob Thomas up the power ladder to the big, echoing garage where the tractors and skimmers were kept. Men and women were already at work, welding sparks sputtering, the clang of metal on metal ringing across the concrete floor of the domed chamber.

"I'll see you at lunch break," Thomas said to Dan, then he headed for his workstation across the wide floor.

He's going to be a problem, Dan told himself as he swung onto the power ladder that carried him up to the cubbyhole office on the catwalk overhead where the logistics computer was housed.

Jeff Robertson leaned back in his squeaky old desk chair and smiled politely at his two visitors. His desk was cluttered with memorabilia: a small forest of framed photographs of family and old friends; a massive silver-plated drill bit from his first oil well, that took up one whole side of the desktop; several model airplanes; and a miniature mock-up of a fusion power reactor that looked almost puny next to the drill bit.

Through the window behind Robertson's desk, Jane
Scanwell looked out at the soaring glass and steel towers
of Houston, but the allegedly blue Texas sky was lost in
a gray haze of smog.

"I can see your problem," Robertson said, his voice a
thin tenor, "but I don't understand why you're bringing
it to me."

To Rafaelo Gaetano, sitting beside Jane in front of the
desk, Robertson looked like a canny old cowboy, or
perhaps the flinty sheriff of some frontier Western town,
hard-bitten and quick on the trigger. The old man was
whipcord lean, his face like tanned leather stretched over
an ancient skull, a strong eagle's nose jutting out from it,
his hair white and wispy. His eyes bulged, hyperthyroid
almost. But they were bright blue and keen as a prairie
scout's.

Robertson was wearing a comfortable old shirt of
sagebrush lavender with a string tie hanging loosely from
its collar. Gaetano had refused to take off his dark suit
jacket, even though Robertson had remarked that the
office might be a bit warm for them. To Jane, in a tailored
silk blouse of cream white and a knee-length navy blue
skirt, the room felt almost frigid. Texans and their air-
conditioning; her years in Europe had made her forget
how profligate her fellow Texans could be.

"You are the chief executive officer of the world's largest energy corporation," Gaetano answered smoothly.
"Who else would the Council turn to, except you?"

"Aw hell," Robertson said, "I'm just an old man who
got kicked upstairs."

His smile belied his words. His voice did quaver
slightly, and Gaetano knew that this man had spent
nearly seven decades in building Southwest Energy Corporation into the multinational giant it now was.

Jane said, "I don't think anybody could ever get away
with kicking you anywhere, Jeff."

Robertson's smile flashed wider. "Miz President, I
would never argue with you. Hell, even if I hadn't voted

for you, you're much too purty to argue with."

Jane made herself smile back at the old man. She had known Jeff Robertson since the days when his oil money had helped lubricate Morgan Scanwell's first campaign for governor. A hundred years ago, Jane thought, trying to keep the pain from showing. A thousand years ago.

"The simple fact of the matter," Gaetano said, leaning forward in his chair slightly, anxious to get down to business, "is that you are the most respected man in the world energy industry."

Robertson gave a modest shrug. "I been working in the oil patch longer'n anybody who's still around and kickin', I reckon."

"You have seen the GEC report on the greenhouse cliff?"

"Yep. Read the executive summary, at least. Got my science people going over the details for me."

"That report is Top Secret!" Gaetano said. "It shouldn't be revealed to anyone! If the public finds out about the greenhouse cliff there could be mass hysteria and panic."

"Relax," said Robertson. "My people know how to keep their mouths shut. Nobody's gonna go 'round scaring the hoi polloi."

"It's all right, Rafe," Jane said soothingly. "We can trust Jeff."

"Well then," said Gaetano, more calmly, "you know the catastrophe that is about to strike us."

"I know what your report claims will happen."

"It's real, Jeff," said Jane. "This isn't a matter of scientists making guesses. The facts are inescapable."

Robertson studied her for a silent moment, his pop eyes narrowing. "Real, huh? Then what can we do about it?"

"That is exactly why we are here," Gaetano said. "To get your help."

The old man leveled a finger at him. "Now look. I know what you've done to the Big Seven space corporations. Don't think you're going to take over Southwest that way. Or any of the energy corporations. That's out of the question."

Jane realized that his down-home accent had vanished. Gaetano's nostrils flared with suppressed anger.

"No one wants to take over the energy corporations," Jane said quickly. "Least of all Southwest."

"Good."

"But we do need your cooperation."

Robertson did not reply.

"It is urgent," said Gaetano, "more than urgent—it is *imperative* that we begin to move transportation and industry off fossil fuels."

"Hell, I know that! Knew it twenty-five years ago. Why do you think I turned Southwest Oil into Southwest Energy? When we had movie stars running around the country scaring everybody to death over nuclear, I was backing fusion as hard as I could."

"But now we've got to start phasing the auto industry into electric cars," Jane said. "And quickly."

Robertson snorted disdainfully and leaned his skinny arms on his desk. "That won't be easy. You're talking maybe a hundred billion dollars of tooling and redesign. More. To say nothing of the advertising and public relations campaigns they'll have to start."

"Yamagata has promised his cooperation in Japan," said Gaetano. "In three years there will be no more petrol-powered automobiles built by the Japanese."

"You expect Detroit to go along with that?"

"It is imperative."

With a shake of his head, the old man replied, "Don't-cha see? If the Japs go to electric cars, Detroit will see it as an opportunity to grab the import market back from them. It'll be easier to sell gas-powered cars; that's what the public really wants. Muscle cars. Not those little electric putt-putts."

"That's why we need your help, Jeff," said Jane. "You've got to be a leader on this."

"Janie, dear: you know and I know that by the time this thing strikes, I'll be dead and gone."

"But there are twelve billion other human beings who'll be hit by this disaster!" Jane insisted. "You've *got* to help us, even if it's the last thing you do!"

"Convert the whole global energy industry from fossil fuels to nuclear? In ten years?"

"Nuclear and solar," said Jane. "The Big Seven are all under GEC control now. They'll produce the fuel for fusion plants and build solar panels at maximum output. We're already developing plans to double their capacity within the next five years, and then double it again."

"But that won't do you much good if nobody down here on the ground wants to buy 'em, huh?"

"Exactly right."

"I don't know if it can be done, Janie. Especially in the time you say we've got to do it."

"We've got to *try.*"

"The alternative," said Gaetano coldly, "is for the GEC to take over the energy corporations and run them for the duration of this emergency."

Robertson glowered at him. "You try that and there won't be any GEC. We'll tear it apart."

"This is no time for threats," Jane snapped, "from either of you. There's no room for anything but cooperation. Period."

The two men stared at each other for a long, wordless moment. Finally Robertson turned back to Jane and said, "You're right, honey. We got no choice. This problem is bigger than all of us put together."

Then he turned back to Gaetano. "It's even bigger than the Mafia, isn't it?"

Gaetano's head snapped back as if he'd been slapped. "Wh . . . why do you ask me that?" he sputtered.

"I didn't get this old by being a fool," Robertson said. "I know the crooks are crawling all over this mess, like a bunch of roaches nibbling away in the dark."

"Are you accusing me—"

"I'm not accusing anybody. I'm just telling you that if you want the world's largest corporations to cooperate with the GEC, you better keep the goddanged Mafia off our backs."

"There is no such thing as the Mafia," Gaetano snapped.

"Mafia, Cosa Nostra, the international crime syndicate—call it whatever you want to. We both know it exists and the people in it are licking their chops for the chance to skim the cream off this disaster. You just make sure they keep out of our way. Because if you don't we'll blow you to hell and gone. We won't go to the police or the lawyers or the courts. We'll use whatever kind of force it takes to get rid of you cockroaches. Understand that?"

Trembling visibly, Gaetano rose to his feet. "You insult me because I am Italian. I assure you, sir, that if there actually were such a thing as the Mafia, it would not interfere with the work you will be doing."

"Like hell."

Jane said, "Jeff, you're talking to a member of the Global Economic Council."

Robertson huffed, swiveled back and forth slightly in his desk chair, then got up and put on a smile. "Well, maybe I got carried away. Sorry 'bout that. I apologize. Nothing personal, son." The old man stuck his hand out over the desk.

Gaetano took one step forward and clasped Robertson's proffered hand.

"No offense meant," said Robertson, thinking, He'll be carrying my message back to his goombah pals in Sicily, all right.

"None taken," Gaetano said, thinking, He won't live to see the end of this. That is for certain.

Kate Williams rubbed her bleary eyes. She had been staring into the computer's display screen for hours, patiently, doggedly going through the logistics inventories for the past month, item by item.

Leaning back in the comfortable swivel chair, she closed her eyes yet still saw columns of numbers parading past.

They're clever, she said to herself. Damned clever. Must be a whole network of people stealing and covering it up. And they're getting all the help they need from Astro's own employees. Those renegade people out there couldn't exist without Astro employees covering up their pilfering. They're smart enough to keep it small, keep it down at a low level so nothing disturbing shows up to alert management. No wonder Dan never found out about it. His own company is honeycombed with people who're helping these fugitives to survive.

And now Dan's one of them. Now he's part of it, I *know* he is.

Kate opened her eyes and sat upright once again. The digital clock on the desk said 1:47 A.M.

"Phone," she called in a tired but clear voice, "get me Kimberly Williams in San Francisco."

"Yes, ma'am," replied the phone, in a neutral voice. It had been a sexy female voice when Kate had taken over the office from Dan; she had immediately changed that.

"No answer," said the phone a moment later.

Kate felt a tingle of alarm. "What time is it there?"

"The correct time in San Francisco is sixteen forty-eight and eleven seconds."

Almost five in the afternoon, Kate thought. She could still be in school. Or the clinic. Or maybe just out enjoying the day. Nothing to worry about. I'll call later. She's okay. It's perfectly normal for a person to be out in the afternoon.

But why wouldn't she be carrying her phone with her? Kate asked herself. What's she doing that she won't answer my call?

She tasted blood in her mouth and realized she was biting her lips. With a groaning sigh she unclenched her teeth and reached for the computer keyboard again. Personnel files. Kate made a mental note to tell maintenance to install a voice activation circuit in the computer; Dan may have enjoyed fiddling with the damned keyboard, but she didn't.

Still, she flicked her fingers across the keys quite adroitly, determined to check every person who had left Astro's employment in the past year against the manifests of each departing flight. She wanted to know who was still roaming around Alphonsus, unemployed, undocumented, outside the system. Dan Randolph would be among those drifters, she knew.

Rubbing her weary eyes again, she thought, If only Dan would steal something big enough to be noticed right away by the logistics program. I can't keep track of all these minor pilferings. If only he'd try to grab something big.

TWENTY-THREE

I don't like it," growled Pops Tucker. "Sounds too damn risky to me."

"We can do it," Dan insisted.

Big George was sitting at the other end of the shelter, by the airlock, resealing a knee joint on the pressure suit he had just repaired.

"What do you think of it, Georgie?" called Tucker.

The oversized Aussie looked up from his work. The work light behind his shoulder cast its high-intensity beam on the suit legging, leaving his shaggy-maned face in shadow.

"It does sound risky," he said.

Tucker nodded with satisfaction across the table at Dan.

"On t'other hand," George went on, "having our own fooking hopper would make life a helluva lot easier around here."

Dan grinned back at the wizened older man. "See? George is for it."

"I didn't say that," George replied.

"You didn't say you're against it," Dan challenged.

"No. Not exactly."

Tucker gave Dan one of his patented sour frowns. "Now look, Mr. Big Shot: we get along here by keeping a low profile. As far as the corporations are concerned, we're not worth the trouble of rooting us out. But if we start stealing big, then Yamagata and Astro and the others will come down on us and we'll all end up over in the penal colony."

"They won't even know it's gone," Dan said. "I can jigger the logistics program so that it looks as if the hopper was routinely retired from service and scrapped."

Tucker looked utterly unconvinced.

"I can do it from here," Dan added. "I've already hacked into the program so we can work it from your desktop here."

"And how do we hide a rocket vehicle big enough to carry a five-ton payload?" Tucker snapped, his grating voice almost a snarl.

"You don't have to hide something that nobody's going to be looking for," Dan said. "It's not unusual for a hopper to be parked alongside a shelter. Survey parties, maintenance crews—they all use hoppers all the time."

"And the propellants?"

Dan grinned across the table at the older man. "I can make a deal with a couple of people in Yamagata's logistics center. We send them some of the designer drugs your friends in the pharmaceutical lab cook up and they divert enough propellant to us to keep the hopper running."

"You think you're pretty damn smart, don'tcha?" Tucker growled.

In truth, Dan did not feel comfortable making a drug deal. Most narcotics had been legalized when he had been a kid, but the designer drugs that the lab people made illicitly out of their employers' chemical supplies were usually untested and always more potent than the stuff available legally. On the Moon, a man or woman stoned or even a bit high was a potential killer.

Yet he shrugged and answered, "I think we can do better than we are."

"Just what the hell do you want out of this? What's pushing you, Randolph?"

"I want to get back to Earth," Dan heard himself say. He had not known that until the words formed in his mouth. "I want to fight the bastards who stole my company and make them give me back what's rightfully mine."

"Fat chance."

"Maybe no chance at all. But I've got to try."

"Even if it means dealing drugs?"

"Come on, Pops, you've bartered your share of them. We're not talking about the hard stuff. It's perfectly legal for people to use recreational drugs. They're not addictive."

"Oh no? Those lab guys brew some pretty potent shit, you know."

"Not as potent as that rocket juice booze they make out at the Nubium camp. That stuff'll dissolve your liver."

From the other end of the shelter George said, "You're talking about a lot more than the little bit o' trading we've been doing."

"It's time you guys started thinking bigger. I'll never get back Earthside on the minor little pilfering you've been doing." Grinning, Dan added, "If you're going to steal, steal big! Steal big enough so you can afford a good lawyer."

George did not laugh.

Tucker stared at Dan for several long moments, his wrinkled old face a mixture of disgust and pity, his red-rimmed eyes wary, almost feral.

"I wish I could get back to Earth too," he said at last, his voice so low Dan could barely hear him. "I got grandchildren I never seen. They think I'm dead. My own kids think I'm dead."

"Help me and I'll help you," Dan said.

Tucker made a derisive snort. "It ain't that easy, Mr. Big Shot. I'll *never* get back to Earth. Body's all shot to hell. I'd collapse and die of heart failure if I tried to stand up to a full g."

"But we could—"

"You could nothing!" the old man snapped angrily. "You think you're so friggin' smart. Do this, do that, and snap, crackle and pop you're back on top of the world. Lemme tell you, Big Shot, it ain't gonna happen."

Dan stared back at the bitter old man.

"Know how I got here? Playin' with their computers, just like you want to do. I was an expert at it. I made a friggin' fortune for myself, workin' for Astro by day and piling up a fortune in bank accounts all over the world just with a few touches on my keyboard at night."

"They caught you?"

"I caught myself. Couldn't keep my big stupid mouth shut. I was *so-o* smart! Got a couple drinks into me one night and told a pal what I was doin'. Two days later a squad of Yamagata security pigs lifted me outta my desk chair and threw me in a detention cell. Japs! Your friggin' Astro security people let the Japs pick me up."

Dan said, "Yamagata's responsible for law enforcement all through Alphonsus. What you did wasn't just an internal Astro matter."

With a sour face, Tucker went on, "They sent me to the penal colony for five years. I got out in two, good behavior and all that crap, but by then I couldn't make the trip back to Earth. Too weak. Muscles shot to hell; heart too."

"So?"

"So they put me on an enforced exercise program. Worse than the penal colony. Like bein' in boot camp. Instructor was some fanatic from Uganda; he thought Afro-Americans were nothin' but shit. Gave me hell every minute. And they were chargin' me for the service! By the time I woulda got back Earthside I'd not only be broke and have a prison record, I'd owe the friggin' Yamagata Corporation a year's friggin' salary!"

"You bugged out?"

"Damn right. That African bastard was tough but he wasn't smart. I faked a heart attack and snuck out of the hospital they put me in. Been on my own ever since. Met up with Big George a few years ago and we been livin' in these shelters, goin' from one to another every few months."

George put down the suit legging and came up to the table. Sitting down massively, he said, "You know, Pops, I been thinking that if we had a hopper we could make the move from one shelter to another a lot easier."

"We've been doing all right without a hopper."

"We could do better with one," Dan said.

"Like how?"

"We could extend your range of operations. Instead of just going as far as the mining camp on the other side of the ringwall, we could start trading with Copernicus."

"A hopper can't get that far!"

"Unrefueled it can't," Dan said. "But suppose I could get my friends at Yamagata to deposit propellant supplies for us along the route to Copernicus?"

"You're crazy," Tucker muttered.

Big George looked thoughtful, though. "Let me ask you something, Dan."

"Sure."

"What do we gain by all this? I can see the risks we'll be taking, but what do we stand to gain?"

"Money."

"Money?" Tucker snapped. "What the hell can we do with money? We live on barter, we've got no use for cash or credits."

"Money," Dan repeated. "Until now you guys have just been living hand to mouth, just eking out your survival. But now we're going to start making money. We're going to pile up credits in banking accounts."

"Why?"

"To buy what each of us wants. Freedom. With money you can buy lawyers. You can buy media reporters. You can buy your way out of this rat's nest and come back into normal society and begin to live like real human beings again."

Ever since her meeting in Houston with Jeff Robertson, Jane had been troubled by the Texas energy tycoon's angry remarks about the Mafia.

For more than a week she did nothing about it. But each time she saw Rafaelo Gaetano, whether it was in a meeting or a cocktail party or just in passing in the GEC offices, the question nagged at her. Is Rafe *really* part of the international crime syndicate? And what did Jeff mean by what he said? Is he really worried that the Mafia might in some way try to hinder our global conversion plan?

No matter how she tried to forget the matter or ignore the persistent questions that percolated through her mind, she could not drive the matter out of her consciousness. One night she even dreamed that Dan was alive, not on the Moon but in Sicily, running a vastly complex criminal organization instead of his own Astro Corporation.

When she awoke that morning, troubled and bleary-eyed, she made her decision. She phoned Jeff Robertson. From her apartment, not her office at GEC headquarters.

For several heartbeats the phone's screen remained blank. Jane sat at the little curved rosewood desk in the room she used as an office and realized that it was only a little past four in the morning in Houston.

Finally the screen brightened and Robertson's puffy-eyed face appeared, grinning curiously.

"You know I'm an early riser, Jane honey," he said amiably, "but this is kinda ridiculous, isn't it?"

"I'm sorry, Jeff," she blurted.

"If the phone had said it was anybody but you I'd have cussed 'em out and gone back to sleep."

"I just couldn't put off calling you any longer."

"It's about what I told your Italian friend, huh?"

"Yes. How did you—"

"I was wonderin' how long it'd take you to gnaw on that bone."

"Are you really serious?" Jane asked. "Is there an actual threat from some international crime syndicate?"

"You bet there is."

"It's hard to see how criminals could get in the way of the GEC."

"That's part of what makes 'em successful," Robertson said. "The victim doesn't even know he's being infected. Real parasites."

"What should we do?"

"First thing you oughtta do is hop on over here so we can talk in private, one on one. I got a lot to show you but I don't trust phone links."

Jane immediately thought that Rafe would find it suspicious if she suddenly took off for Houston. She said, "I could take a long weekend, a sort of minivacation."

"At your home in Horseshoe Bay?"

"Yes."

"Got room for a weekend guest?"

"For you, Jeff, anytime."

"I'll have to bring the wife. She don't trust me too far."

Jane laughed. "Of course. Bring Helen along with you."

"I was getting frantic, that's why!" Kate Williams nearly shouted at the phone screen.

Her sister's face stared out at her, eyes smoldering with sullen distrust. Kimberly Williams was four years younger than her sister. Even with her flaming red hair cropped militarily short, she looked enough like Kate so that a stranger would quickly realize they were sisters;

but Kim looked used, worn, pale and sick. Except for her eyes. They were fiery, tawny, defiant, the eyes of a caged leopard.

"You didn't have to call the fuckin' police," Kim said.

"I hadn't heard from you in a week," Kate replied, her inner anger building. "You hadn't shown up in the clinic for ten days."

In the two and a half seconds it took for Kim's reply to come to her, Kate studied her sister's face. No bruises. Eyes look clear, not dilated.

"I was with one of their damned doctors! It was his idea to take a week off and go have some fun!"

Kate pulled in a deep breath, trying to calm herself, trying to avoid the explosion that so often erupted when she and Kim talked to one another.

"I'm clean," Kim added, less belligerently. "The doctor wouldn't let me get started again."

"That—that's good," said Kate.

Again the transmission lag. Then Kim's pale, angry face softened. "He didn't want me stoned." She almost giggled. "I had to be awake and alert to please him."

Christ, Kate thought, there's always the damned body tax. You'd think by now a man and a woman could work together or be friends without sex.

"Listen, Kim," she heard herself saying. "How'd you like to come up here for a while?"

"To the Moon? Leave the clinic?"

"I can arrange for your treatment to continue here. I'm going to be staying here for a while. Why don't you come up and stay with me?"

She waited for her words to register on her sister's face.

"You really mean it, Kate? You want me to stay with you?"

"I love you, Kimberly. I know I haven't been the best big sister in the world to you, but I want us to be together now."

Kate had not expected the reaction she got. Kimberly broke into tears. The two sisters cried together, separated by a quarter-million miles but feeling closer than they had in years.

It was an hour later, all the details of Kim's trip to Alphonsus carefully worked into the computer, when Kate signed the authorization for scrapping a long list of defunct equipment. Computers notwithstanding, such orders had to be signed; the legal department insisted on a personal signature of authorization.

Kate signed the thin plastic sheet—paper being nonexistent on the Moon—with only a cursory glance at the list of equipment to be scrapped. She noticed that it included a full-sized rocket hopper, but she paid no real attention to that. She was thinking, instead, that it would be good for Kim to be away from her doctor friend. And with Kim at Alphonsus, Kate herself would not have to pay court to Rafaelo Gaetano anymore.

It had been a long time since Dan had piloted a hopper. Inside his pressure suit he felt a thin sheen of nervous cold sweat as the Astro technician walked him around the ungainly vehicle.

The hopper looked worn and battered. Maybe it really is ready for the scrap pile, Dan thought as he walked around it. Sitting on six splayfooted aluminum legs, it was little more than an open-grillwork platform with a T-shaped control console up front where two space-suited people could stand, and a trio of bulky cargo containers, their gold anodized finishes pitted and faded. Underneath there were six small rocket nozzles, looking black and hard-used, evenly spaced around a long flat propellant tank. The craft's minimal electronics were built into the forward console. Spare oxygen bottles were strapped against the first cargo container.

"You read the manual?" The tech's voice in Dan's helmet earphones sounded dubious. The young man knew that what he was doing was illegal, and the wreck of a "scrapped" hopper anywhere near Astro's launch facility would swiftly be pinned to him.

"You saw me go through it, right on your own screen," Dan said.

"Pretty damned fast, if you ask me."

"I'm a speed reader. Besides, I can pull up the manual on the control panel screen, can't I?"

"Helluva time to be reading the manual, when you're spinning into the ground."

"I was flying these rigs before you were born," Dan snapped.

"Yeah, sure. You came up here with Armstrong and Aldrin, didn't you?"

Dan laughed. "No, H. G. Wells."

The two space-suited men walked slowly around the hopper, checking it out by eye. It looked old and weary to Dan, but the computer said all its systems were fully functional.

"Come on," the technician chivvied, "I ain't got all day for this."

He's scared somebody will see us and realize that this clunker is supposed to be heading for the recyclers, Dan knew.

"Okay," he said, drawing in a deep breath. "Guess she won't look any better than she does now."

He climbed up the two-rung ladder while the tech quickly went to his little tractor and wordlessly started back toward the launching facility, about a kilometer away.

Dan plugged his suit radio into the console and asked for clearance to take off. Hoppers were always flitting around the lunar cities; the only need for traffic control was when they were located near a launch facility.

"Stand by, hopper," said a man's voice. "Got a tour boat about to leave."

Dan turned entirely around so he could watch the passenger spacecraft lift off, more than a kilometer away. The launch was not a spectacular display, as it would have been on Earth. No thunder of rocket engines. No slow majestic rise of the booster out of clouds of exhaust and steam. The big bulbous spacecraft merely seemed to flick itself off the Moon's surface like a flea jumping: one instant it was sitting on the launchpad, the next it was gone, flung into the dark sky so quickly that Dan lost sight of it in the restricted view from inside his helmet. A small dust storm swirled lazily around the pad in the wake of the launching, the thin clouds slowly sinking back to the ground in the gentle lunar gravity.

"Okay hopper, you are clear to take off."

Dan reached for the pistol-grip control bar, feeling both a little scared and a little exhilarated.

"Hopper taking off," he said into his helmet mike.

The craft shuddered as he thumbed the ignition switch, then rose slowly off the ground. Cautiously, Dan turned it toward the tempo shelter he had been living in, and started gaining altitude to clear the first level of the ringwall. He grinned to himself. It had been a *long* time, but now he remembered that back in the old days flying one of the hoppers had always reminded him of flying on a magic carpet.

"I'm heading back to Earth," he muttered to himself. Then he added, grinning, "Even the longest journey is started with a single theft."

TWENTY-FOUR

But I thought that when drugs were decriminalized," said Jane, "organized crime went pretty much out of business."

Jeff Robertson gave her a pitying smile. "For a former President of the United States, you're still awfully naive, Janie girl."

He was the only man in the world whom Jane would allow to call her "girl." She smiled at Robertson as they sat on the glassed-in patio of her Texas home. The spacious house was on a hillside overlooking the large, man-made LBJ Lake. Outside it was a fierce summer day, the kind that allows Texans to say they don't have to be afraid of hell. Jane kept the air-conditioning comfortable but not frigid. If Robertson wanted it cooler, he had yet to ask.

The old man was dressed up in a floral cowboy shirt and stiffly new jeans tucked into his fancy tooled boots. Jane was in an "at home" outfit: loose-fitting slacks of light tan topped with a short-sleeved pale yellow blouse.

A frosted pitcher of margaritas sat on the low table between them, next to a plate of coarse salt. Robertson held his wide-rimmed glass in both hands; Jane's was on the end table next to her chair.

"Oh, I know they're still into prostitution and smuggling and things like that," she said. "But we cleaned them out of the international banking industry years ago, and—"

Robertson shook his head. With his pop eyes and jutting beak he sometimes reminded Jane of a turtle.

He took a sip of his margarita, then said, "Look, honey: when most of the states in the Union legalized betting to the extent that they started state lotteries, did that drive the Mafia out of gambling?"

Without waiting for her to answer, he went on, "Hell no. When you legalized drugs, it didn't drive the crooks out of the narcotics business, either. Cut their profit margins, yes. But they still sell drugs: they sell the kind you can buy legally for cheaper than the legal price, and they sell the kind you can't buy because they're too dangerous to use."

"How can they undercut the government's price?"

"They steal the stuff and then resell it!"

"Oh."

"They're still into banking; more respectable now, smarter than they used to be, almost legitimate. But they siphon billions off into their own pockets every year. The bankers just take it as part of the cost of doing business and pass on the expense to their customers."

"That wasn't going on when *I* was President," Jane murmured.

"Course not." Robertson's tone of voice was not quite condescending, but close enough.

"You're telling me that the Mafia is now a worldwide organization."

"Yep. Just like the corporations, the crooks have gone international. The Mafia, the Yakuza gangs in Japan, the old Latin American drug cartel—they've all linked up worldwide. Wouldn't be surprised if they've wormed their way into the Big Seven, up on the Moon."

Jane felt angry, confused, puzzled. "But how? What do they do? How are they making their money?"

"Skimming, mostly," said Robertson. He leaned forward to refill his glass, then twirled it in his hand to find a part of the rim that was still salted. He half-drained the glass, then smacked his lips noisily. "Best margaritas this side of Albuquerque."

"You were telling me about skimming," Jane said gently.

"Yeah." Robertson leaned back in his chair and half-closed his eyes. He looked as if he were going to sleep. "Your company takes in ten dollars, let's say. But somehow only nine-fifty gets onto the books. The rest winds up in some crook's pocket."

"But how can they do that?"

"Lotsa ways, honey. They bribe one of your employees. Maybe with real money. Maybe with women, or drugs or something else the poor sucker thinks he wants bad enough to take the chance. Oftentimes the sucker himself comes to them for a loan—"

"They're still loan-sharking?"

The old man's eyes sprang wide open. "Long as banks want collateral there'll be loan sharks. Pretty often a guy'll get in over his head gambling; even legalized gambling can break your back, y'know. Then he goes to the sharks and"—Robertson banged his hand down on the arm of his chair so hard that Jane jumped—"they've got him. At the kinds of interest rates they charge, the poor slob never gets out from under. He owes them. He either does what they tell him or they break him in half."

"So he starts to work for them."

"Yep. It's almost all white-collar stuff now. More money stolen with a computer than with a gun, any day. But there's always the threat of violence. And not just to the sucker himself; they threaten his family, too."

"That's sickening."

Robertson finished off his margarita and put the empty glass down on the table between them. "You haven't hardly touched yours."

Jane said, "How do we keep them out of the conversion program, Jeff? It's going to be tough enough to make this thing work without having the Mafia leaching money out of it, making everything more expensive."

"And it won't be just money skimming, come to think of it," he said. "You better be damned alert and watch who you contract out the work to."

"What do you mean?"

"You've seen your share of recycling outfits that just dump the garbage in the dark of night instead of actually recycling it, haven't you?"

"I've prosecuted enough of them."

"Well, suppose you have an organization that's got the job of replacing gasoline cars and diesel trucks with your new electric buggies. Suppose the buggies somehow get mysteriously hijacked and later on they show up halfway across the world, selling for ten times the price the GEC has set?"

"I don't see how anybody could get away with that."

Robertson shrugged his frail shoulders. "Maybe I picked a poor example. But things like that can happen. You better keep a sharp eye out."

Jane picked up her drink and took a sip of it without taking her eyes off Robertson. At last she asked, "Jeff— will you keep a sharp eye out for me?"

He cocked his head slightly to one side, as if he hadn't quite heard her.

"You know so much more about this than I do. Will you be my eyes and ears? I'll give you complete authority to go anywhere, see anything. You'll report directly to me and no one else."

"I'm an old man, Janie. I can't go flittin' around the world the way I used to."

"Then I'll see to it that you have access to all the

program's files. If you see anything suspicious you can alert me."

Frowning, "Hell, I'll be spending twenty-nine hours a day in front of a damned computer screen."

"I need your help!" Jane pleaded.

His frown melted. "Well . . . I guess I ought to put my mouth where my money is."

"You'll do it?"

"I'll do some of it. Nobody'll be able to keep track of everything; this danged project of yours is gonna be just too big for any one person to watch over. That's what they're counting on. That's one of the advantages they have."

"But you'll help."

"On one condition." He raised a bony finger. "This is just between you and me. Nobody else in the loop. *Nobody!* I don't want that Gaetano guy knowing about this. I'd be dead in half an hour once he found out."

Jane frowned at him. "Do you actually think . . ." Her voice trailed off.

"Sure as God made little green apples, honey," said Jeff Robertson. "He's one of 'em."

Zach Freiberg squinted in the unaccustomed glare of the studio lights.

"If you think this is bad," said the elderly man who would interview him, "you should have been around before the low-light-level cameras were available. Damned lighting would melt your makeup!"

Zach knew his interviewer was trying to put him at ease. Television was new and unnerving to the scientist, even this little local public-access show. He knew that if Dan Randolph were still running Astro, he could have stayed in his lab in Pasadena; Dan himself would have handled the P.R. And been much better at it.

"I'm a planetary geochemist, not a TV personality," he had told the eager young woman who had phoned him.

Rumors of the greenhouse cliff had leaked out, of course. No matter how tight a lid the authorities in Paris tried to maintain on the story, their very own extraordinary actions against Astro and the others of the Big Seven had started the rumor mills running.

.Her bright eyes glittering like a snake's, she had answered, "But you're the man who discovered this greenhouse cliff, aren't you? I got your name from a source in the GEC's office in Manhattan."

With a mixture of flattery and cajolery she enticed Zach to the TV studio in the old, run-down area of Studio.City where he now sat in a fake leather chair up on a carpeted platform, blinking at the lights that all seemed aimed straight into his eyes. Out among the cameras positioned on the studio floor sat a TV monitor screen that showed Zach's own face, looking flustered and unhappy.

"This is going to be taped, you know," said his interviewer as a pair of technicians clipped nearly invisible microphones to their lapels and wormed a wireless receiver into the man's left ear. Ignoring them, he went on, "It won't matter if you hesitate or fluff an answer; we can start over. So don't worry about a thing."

Zach ran a nervous hand through his wiry red hair. Don't worry about a thing, he repeated silently. The whole world in danger of annihilation and he tells me not to worry.

"In five!" called a voice from the dimness out on the floor of the studio.

"Wet your lips," someone hissed at Zach.

He ran his tongue over his lower lip just as the interviewer began, "Good evening. I'm Herman George and this is 'Newsmakers,' the program that takes you behind the headlines to meet the people who move and shake our society. Tonight we are fortunate to have Dr. Zachary Freiberg . . ."

It was like testifying in court, Zach thought. The interviewer began by asking his name, his profession, and a few friendly questions about what a planetary geochemist actually does.

Then, "The whole world has been in a stir over rumors that a 'greenhouse cliff' is going to cause tremendous and sudden changes in our weather a few years from now. Yet the Global Economic Council has strongly denied that any such phenomenon exists. Are they lying to us, or is the 'greenhouse cliff' a mere figment of some environmentalist's overworked imagination?"

"It's real," said Zach. "The greenhouse cliff is as real as today's weather."

The older man smiled. "I've always thought the weather in Southern California is a bit unreal." Before Zach could respond, he asked, "Tell me, just what on Earth is a greenhouse cliff?"

Zach launched into an explanation, trying to keep it as simple as possible. Out of the corner of his eye he saw on the monitor screen news clips of hurricanes striking cities, floods washing away villages, farmlands withering under a parching sun. Somebody in the studio had done her homework.

"And all this will happen quite suddenly?" the interviewer prodded.

"That's why it's called a cliff," said Zach. "In ten years, give or take a couple, the world's climate is going to change suddenly and very radically." Before the next question could be asked, he added, "Unless we do something about it."

"Something? What can we do?"

"Stop adding to the greenhouse!" Zach replied with some emotion. "Stop burning fossil fuels. Stop polluting the seas where the algae live. Stop tearing down the rain forests."

"How can we stop burning fossil fuels? Our factories, our furnaces, our automobiles—"

"The GEC will be initiating a program to convert the whole world away from fossil fuels and into nuclear and solar."

"They've made no announcement of this."

"They will."

"Nuclear and solar energy, eh? Nuclear cars?"

"Electric cars," Zach snapped. "But their electricity will be provided by safe, clean fusion power plants. Solar energy can make individual homes self-sufficient."

On and on it went, for what seemed like hours. Without realizing it, Zach became quite passionate talking about what had to be done.

"We have the technology to accomplish this!" he insisted. "We have the brains and the muscle. We can beat this disaster if we all work together, everyone, all around the world."

"That's a very tall order," said his interviewer.

"It's the greatest challenge the human race has ever confronted." Zach did not notice that the camera now was focused directly on his animated, earnest face. "This isn't a war against another nation; it's not even a war against nature. It's a battle against ourselves, against laziness and greed and the thoughtlessness that's fouled our planet's air and water so terribly. It's a battle we've got to win, because if we don't, at least half the world's population will die. Probably more."

He was drenched with perspiration by the time the interview ended and the hot lights winked off.

"Wonderful!" said the interviewer, reaching over to pat his back. "You did a magnificent job."

Surprised but pleased, Zach mumbled his thanks and headed home.

The next morning, thinking it over after a good night's sleep, Zach concluded that on balance he had indeed done a good job.

Until Vasily Malik phoned.

"I have just seen a videotape of the interview you conducted last night."

Zach did not notice that the Russian was grim, unsmiling. "How'd you like it?" he asked eagerly.

"My dear Dr. Frieberg, you are a phenomenon on

television. A true spellbinder. Just the man to show the public how urgent this problem is."

Smiling boyishly, Zach started to say, "Well, thanks—"

"Which is exactly why you will *not* give any further interviews to anyone, under any circumstances. Is that clear?"

"What? What are you talking about?"

With great patience, Malik said, "We are working very hard to control news leaks, Dr. Freiberg. We must avoid premature disclosure of the greenhouse catastrophe. We must avoid public panic at all costs! Why do you think we have said nothing, officially? Why do you think we have denied all the rumors of the greenhouse cliff?"

"Now look, you can't muzzle me. I'm an American citizen. I've got a right to speak freely."

Coldly, "You are an employee of the GEC, Dr. Freiberg. If you do not promise to cooperate with me, you will be transferred to Antarctica. And your family with you. Do I make myself clear?"

Zach glared at the phone screen for several angry moments, thinking, The bastard knows I'm not allowed to quit my job for the duration of this emergency. He can push me anyplace he likes.

"Do you understand me, Dr. Freiberg?" Malik insisted.

Nodding glumly, "I understand you. No more interviews."

"It is all for the best," Malik tried to assure him.

"Yeah, sure," Zach muttered, wishing that Dan Randolph were around to defend him.

It took almost a month for Kate Williams to get her sister to Alphonsus. Gaetano had been immediately suspicious, of course, when the clinic that was guiding Kimberly through drug rehabilitation reported to him that she had decided to leave San Francisco. He had phoned Kate and told her that he would not permit Kim to join her on the Moon.

Kate had expected this showdown. She was prepared for it. Still, she was glad that Gaetano was a quarter-million miles away, and that they saw each other only on the telephone picture screens. If they had met in person he would have easily seen her tension, her trembling, her fear.

"Rafe," she said, sitting in Dan Randolph's former chair, holding herself together with conscious effort, "I want Kimberly here with me. I've done a lot of dirty work for you and bringing Kim here is my reward."

He raised an eyebrow. "Your work for me is not finished." Then he added, smirking, "Especially the dirty part."

Kate tried to keep her face from showing any emotion. "I've delivered Astro to you. Now you want me to find Dan Randolph. Okay, I'll do that. If I have Kimberly here with me."

She waited until he heard her words and began to shake his head. Then she said, "There's something else I want, too. Once I've located Dan for you, I want to continue running Astro Manufacturing."

That shook him. Both brows went toward his scalp. "You? Run the whole corporation?"

"That's what I want in return for finding Dan."

"That's impossible!"

They argued back and forth for nearly two weeks. But in the end Gaetano agreed to let her run Astro *if* she located Dan Randolph—dead or alive—and *if* she promised that she would continue to share his bed whenever she came to Earth. Kate readily consented to his terms, knowing that Gaetano would have to come to the Moon. She had no intention of leaving, not ever, not once she had Kim safely by her side.

It took another two weeks for all the arrangements to be made so that Kim could leave California legally and have her medical records transferred to the hospital at

Alphonsus. Kate spent the time actually running Astro; implementing the orders that were coming from GEC headquarters to develop a plan for doubling the production of fusion fuel and expanding the manufacturing capacity for solar panels.

She spent her nights, though, tediously creating a computer program designed to spot discrepancies in Astro's logistics system. And Yamagata's. The renegades who were living off Astro and Yamagata kept a low profile, pilfering such small amounts of goods that the company accountants were willing to write the losses off.

"They're down in the noise," the chief accountant told her. "It'd cost more to root them out than they're stealing from us, so why bother about it?"

Kate smiled at him and nodded and wondered if he was on the take. Maybe the renegades paid him off? But with what? They didn't steal enough to make a dent in the man's salary and bonuses. She dismissed the idea.

Instead, she slaved each night to perfect the computer program that would automatically highlight any discrepancy between what went into the logistics system and what came out. Down to a single bottle of aspirin or a cubic meter of oxygen.

Dan Randolph is among those renegades, she knew. He's one of the people stealing from his own company. And he won't be content with small-time pilfering; his ego will drive him to do bigger and better things. I want to track *everything* that's being stolen. Sooner or later I'll find a pattern. Sooner or later Dan will try to grab something big enough that he'll leave his signature on the theft. Then I'll get him.

And it better be sooner, rather than later, she told herself. Rafe is not a patient man. Neither in bed nor out of it.

Rafaelo Gaetano had other things to worry about. He thought of Kate often enough, and he did not like the idea of relinquishing her sister, who was his major hold over her. But now she wanted something else, something much bigger: she wanted Astro Corporation for her own. That gave him a bigger, more powerful control of the beautiful redhead.

Gaetano smiled to himself as he sat in his Paris office. Steepling his fingers, he leaned far back in his chair and gazed out his window at the gleaming white dome of Sacre Coeur, up on Montmartre's hill, and waited for the phone call he expected.

So Kate wants her sister to join her on the Moon. From the videos I've seen of her, she's a good-looking redhead, too. Skinny, almost scrawny, but that's from her drug addiction. Once she's on the Moon, Kate will fill her out. Maybe I'll go up there too, for a vacation, perhaps. Two redheads in the same bed are better than one. Sisters, too. That should be interesting.

The phone chirped.

Gaetano leaned forward in his chair, stretched out his arm, and picked up the handset. "Yes?" he said in English.

A man's voice replied, "I just heard that there has been an airplane crash in Texas. A friend of President Scanwell was killed. A man named Jeffrey Robertson."

"Ah," said Gaetano. "Too bad. Make certain that President Scanwell receives the news."

"I believe she already has," said the voice.

"I see," Gaetano said. "Thank you."

As he put the phone down he saw Jane Scanwell standing in his doorway, her face stricken with grief. And hatred.

TWENTY-FIVE

Dan was humming to himself as he stood at the controls of the hopper. It had been a good trip: he had carried a full load of pilfered electronic simulation equipment, erotic videotapes and the homebrew liquor everyone called "rocket juice" all the way out to the Fra Mauro complex, halfway to Copernicus. The construction team building the new mining and refining center there had paid handsomely.

Not in cash, of course. In electronic credits, which Dan immediately relayed to Pops Tucker back at their shelter, and Tucker deposited in one of the safe banks they had picked. They had three, all Earthside: one on the Cayman Islands, one in Liechtenstein, and one in New Jerusalem. Each bank had a reputation for discretion, solidity and compliant GEC inspectors. Tucker sent the credit information directly Earthward by a small communications laser that George had assembled for them. They spoke directly to a specific commsat in Earth orbit, bypassing all lunar communications nets.

Dan knew from his own early experiences that the most deadly hazard on the Moon is boredom, especially in a new, raw camp without any real facilities for entertainment. A guy could do crazy things in his empty off-duty hours; he'd known men who just walked off in their pressure suits and never came back. More often there'd be a fight over one of the women—or over one of the men. The fights could be brutal, or worse still, they could create smoldering grudges that ended in outright murder.

Rocket juice helped pass the idle hours, although it could also aggravate the tensions and confrontations. So did drugs. Dan thought that the simulation equipment would be the most help to the construction workers. There were enough electronics whizzes among them to jigger the equipment into virtual reality rigs, where a person could put on a simulator helmet and escape into a private fantasy world for hours on end.

That's why the construction camp supervisors looked the other way when Dan landed with his load of goodies. They knew better than the administrators who worked in safe, comfortable offices back at Alphonsus that their crews needed diversion and entertainment almost as much as they needed oxygen and water.

Dan Randolph, benefactor of the working man, he said to himself. And woman, he added, grinning. One of the construction workers had been especially grateful for his appearance. A rangy brunette with the kind of sculptured face he remembered from his years in Caracas, she had shown Dan to a private little shelter just large enough for two. It had been the best hour Dan had spent since Tetiaroa.

He grimaced inside his helmet at the memory of that tropical atoll and Jane and Malik and how they had all conspired to strip him of everything he had built. "I'll get it all back," he muttered to himself. "I'll get it back if I have to tear down everything between here and Paris."

His dark mood ended almost at once, though, because the beeper on his control panel began flashing its red light. The propellant tanks were sitting down there on the dusty, pockmarked Nubium plain, precisely where the Japanese guy he was dealing with at Yamagata had said he would leave them. Their minitransponder was sending out its weak little signal; you had to be practically on top of the tanks before you would know they were there.

Dan nudged his pistol-grip joystick forward and the hopper descended, flat as a carpet, no nosing down as a plane would in Earth's atmosphere. It was night once again on this side of the Moon; Dan only operated the hopper at night, less chance of being spotted by a legitimate vehicle or one of the satellites in orbit. He strained his eyes for sight of the tanks and finally saw them, sitting gray and round like a trio of natural boulders on the darker basaltic floor of the mare.

It took the better part of an hour to refill the hopper's tanks. Dan almost forgot to disconnect the transponder beacon; at the last minute he unclipped it, shut it off, and carried it back aboard the hopper. Then he took off again on the final leg of his trip back to the shelter where George and Pops Tucker were waiting for him.

Dan was bone-weary when he finally opened the inner hatch of the airlock and stepped into the shelter's familiar confines.

Even before he could slide open his helmet visor he realized that he had stepped into a trap. George and Tucker were nowhere in sight. Instead there was a quartet of strangers in dark gray coveralls holding pistols leveled at him.

"You're under arrest, Randolph," said one of the men. Dan recognized him as the burrheaded jock he had shot back in his office the first time they had tried to take him in. "And this time you're not getting away."

To her credit, Kate Williams did not gloat. In fact, she seemed more than serious: she seemed wrathful.

"Drugs!" she nearly screamed at Dan. "You've been peddling drugs to my people here!"

They had brought Dan to his former office, where Kate now stood behind his old desk, shaking with fury.

"Recreational stuff," he said, taken aback by her rage. "Nothing harmful."

"How the hell would you know what's harmful and what isn't?" Kate snarled. "Did you try any of the junk yourself?"

Dan blinked with surprise. Of course he hadn't. Alcohol was his drug of choice.

"So you've turned into a dirty drug dealer," Kate snarled. "Look at you! You even smell filthy!"

"I've been in a space suit for damned near fourteen hours," Dan said defensively. But he knew it was more than that. He hadn't cut his hair or beard in weeks. His coveralls were shabby and unwashed.

"The great Dan Randolph, a drug dealer. Smuggler. Thief. You're *never* going to get out of jail."

Dan just sat there, knowing that she was right. He felt utterly exhausted, spiritually as well as physically. There was only one way Kate could have found him, he thought. George or Pops must have turned him in. Waited until I was out by myself and they ran to the authorities. Saved their own skins, probably. The sons of bitches will probably access the money we've banked!

He felt totally alone in the world, alone in the universe. Betrayed by everyone he had known.

Including this furious redhead standing behind *his* desk in *his* office. Anger surged through Dan.

"You've stolen everything I've worked to build up," he said to her through gritted teeth. "You've got a fucking lot of nerve to call me a thief."

"You're the one who's broken the law," she snapped. She turned slightly, and said in a softer voice, "I could see why you ran away, Dan. But selling drugs—that's unforgivable."

"Taking a man's life away from him is okay, though."

"You won't be executed, you know that. Even though

you deserve it and the law allows it, we won't kill you."

"You already have."

That one look at Gaetano's face was all that Jane had needed. She knew instantly that he was guilty. No amount of evidence, no witnesses, no judge or jury could convince her otherwise. Gaetano had murdered Jeff Robertson. Or caused his murder. It was all the same as far as she was concerned.

The accident report came in a few days afterward. Jeff had been flying his own plane from Houston to Dallas, something he did almost every week. According to the coroner, he suffered a massive heart attack. He must have lost control of the plane and it crashed, killing him. What was left of the body had been cremated, as specified in the old man's will. No chance to go back and check for poison, or the kind of drug that could trigger a heart attack.

As far as the world was concerned, the eighty-eight-year-old man had died of natural causes. The global energy industry mourned his passing with impressive pomp. There was even a TV special about his life.

Jane knew it was murder. She did not know what to do about it. There was no one in the GEC she could trust, no one she was certain was not in league with Gaetano. Not even Vasily Malik. Yet she was determined to avenge her old friend's death. The burning acid of vengeance was a new emotion to Jane. Even when her husband had died and she had blamed Dan for it, she had not felt this flaming hot hatred that now seared every nerve in her body.

It was weeks later, at a conference with Yamagata Industries' chief executives in Tokyo, that she saw a way.

She knew Nobuhiko Yamagata only slightly. Through her staff secretary she invited the young man to an informal lunch. Through his staff secretary he accepted. Jane suggested her hotel; Nobo's representative came back with the suggestion that they meet at the Yamagata

Building, where they could dine in privacy and get to know each other better. Jane, who had hoped for precisely that, readily agreed.

They met in a small, luxurious dining room done in deep rich woods and decorated with exquisitely delicate silk paintings. Jane was relieved to see that Nobuhiko had provided a Western-style table and chairs, although the kimono-clad women waiting on them brought bamboo trays of sashimi and sake in thimble-sized cups.

After expressing renewed regret at his father's demise, and being politely reminded that his father was cryonically sleeping rather than truly dead, Jane turned their conversation toward business.

"It must be an immense challenge to take over the entire Yamagata complex at a time of such enormous changes."

His lean face utterly serious, Nobo replied, "Yes. There are many problems, many challenges. But I think the work is going well, don't you?"

"Extraordinarily well," Jane said.

"We have had some difficulties with your GEC administrators," Nobo said, surprisingly blunt for a Japanese. "They seem more interested in paperwork than in performance."

Jane smiled, wondering if the "we" Nobuhiko used was meant to be royal. "If there is any way I can help . . ."

He smiled back. "I think we are educating them sufficiently." When he smiled his eyes lighted up like a boy's, Jane noticed.

"Have you had any problems," she asked, slowly, "with the criminal element?"

"Criminal element?"

"What is the Japanese version of the Mafia called? The Yakuza?"

Nobo shook his head, frowning slightly. "Not the same thing at all. And, no, we have had no trouble from organized crime. None that I have been made aware of, at least."

Jane took a sip of sake. Then, "This immense program of ours, this movement to convert the world away from fossil fuels—it's like a big fat tethered cow to the criminals. They will try to milk it as hard as they can."

"Perhaps in the United States that is true. Even in Europe. Not in Japan."

"Not in your space facilities?"

He smiled again. "What can they steal in space? Or even on the Moon?"

"There are criminals on the Moon. Fugitives from justice."

"Ah. You are speaking of Dan Randolph."

Inwardly Jane flared with anger. This was not the course she had wanted this conversation to take.

Nobuhiko took her silence for agreement. "I wish I could have helped Dan. I was angry with him over something that does not seem so important now. I suppose I was upset at the time; my father had just been put away."

"I see."

"Isn't there some way Dan can be pardoned? He should be back in charge of Astro, if you want to get the best out of that corporation. In fact, if you put him in charge of all space operations you would be getting far more than is now possible."

"In charge of all of them—including Yamagata?"

Looking slightly sheepish, Nobo said, "Dan is the best manager in the business. He should be in charge of all the space operations, including Yamagata's. Then you would see results!"

"He wouldn't work for the GEC."

"He advised us to," Nobo pointed out. "He pleaded with us to cooperate with you."

"So that we wouldn't have to take over your corporations, as we did Astro."

"So that we can make this tremendous conversion in

energy and transport within ten years," Nobuhiko countered firmly.

Jane sighed. "Well, maybe it would have been good to put Dan in charge. But he's a fugitive now. A criminal. We don't even know if he's dead or alive."

Shaking his head, Nobo said, "A great loss. A great tragedy."

On impulse, Jane blurted, "The Mafia murdered a friend of mine, a man who was just starting to investigate how deeply they've wormed into the GEC."

Nobo's eyes narrowed. "Are you serious?"

"Yes. Completely serious. I've come here to ask for your help."

"What can I do?"

"That's just it. I don't know yet. But I need an ally, someone with your strength and your resources. Can I rely on you? Will you help me?"

The young man was silent for several moments. Then he answered, "I would be honored to help you in any way I can. But, frankly, it would be much wiser to find Dan Randolph, pardon him, and set him onto this problem. If anyone in the Earth/Moon system could tangle with the Mafia successfully, it would be Dan."

Once they led Dan away to a detention cell, Kate felt as if the room needed fumigating. But as she stood behind the broad gleaming desk, staring at the closed door to the outer office, she began to realize that maybe it was she who needed cleansing.

I ruined his life, she said to herself. I drove him to this.

But then she shook her head viciously. He didn't have to deal drugs. There's no excuse for that. He deserves whatever he gets.

She looked around the office with new eyes. My office! It's mine now. And Kim's on her way here. She'll be arriving in a few hours. I've got Astro and I've got Kim. Now all I have to do is get Rafe off my back and I can start to really live!

A few hours later Kate stood eagerly at the reception area, under the pads where the spacecraft landed. She had watched on the video monitor as Kim's ship settled down gently on its pad and the access tunnel snaked out and connected to its airlock.

Now the first passengers were coming through the tunnel. And there was Kim! Thinner than Kate had expected, pale and thin, like someone who had been sick for a long time. But her flaming hair, cropped so short, was thick and luxuriant, her stride confident even in the unaccustomed low lunar gravity, her face beaming with a wide smile.

She was not smiling at Kate. She was not even looking at Kate. She was smiling at the tall, darkly handsome man walking beside her.

Rafaelo Gaetano.

TWENTY-SIX

I t took all her strength to keep from screaming.

Kate sat in the posh dining room of the new Yamagata Hotel, where the giant video windows presented scenes of Hawaiian beaches in the setting sun, and watched Gaetano charm Kimberly out of her pants, almost literally.

"I have never seen anyone—man or woman—adapt to the gravity here as easily as you have." Rafe was smiling at her. Strong white teeth like a shark's, Kate thought.

Kimberly, her eyes still slightly shadowed, her cheeks sunken, smiled back glowingly. "A friend of mine warned me about the gravity. She loaned me her weighted boots—see?"

And Kim held up one miniskirted leg to show the stylish lunar softboot she was wearing. To Kate, her sister's leg looked bony, knobby.

But Gaetano said, "You mustn't put temptation so close, little one. A man's first instinct is to stroke a beautiful lady's leg."

Kim giggled. Kate fumed.

Halfway through their main course Kim suddenly excused herself. Kate watched her hurrying to the ladies' room, wondering if some lingering effect of her addiction were still in her blood. Was she perspiring? Were her hands shaking?

"A lovely young sister," Gaetano murmured across the elegant table.

"Keep your hands off her," Kate hissed.

"Jealous?"

"She's my *sister,* for god's sake. I don't want her getting involved with the likes of you. She's had enough problems in her life."

Gaetano's smile turned nasty. "Yes, I know all about it. Kimberly Williams," he recited. "Parents divorced when she was ten. While her older sister Katherine went to law school, Kimberly stayed with her mother in San Jose and became involved in the drug culture at the public school. By the time she was fifteen she was heavily addicted to narcotics. Arrested for prostitution and—"

"Stop it!" Kate snapped.

Gaetano shrugged as if it did not matter to him one way or the other. He reached for his wineglass.

"What made you come up here?" Kate asked in an urgent whisper. On the same ship as Kim, she added silently.

Gaetano sipped at his wine, red and dark as blood, then put the tulip-shaped glass down on the tablecloth and brushed at his moustache.

"Why, I came here to see you, Kate. I grew lonely for you. I miss the little games we used to play."

"And you just happened to meet my sister."

"A charming coincidence," he lied. "She's worked very hard to break her addiction, but I'm afraid that it would be ridiculously easy to turn her onto narcotics once again."

"I'll kill you!"

He laughed. "Katherine, it's so much easier to make

love instead of war."

She glared at him.

Turning serious, Gaetano hunched across the table toward her. "You have control of Astro. You thought that if you could get your sister here with you, you would be free of me." He waved an extended index finger back and forth in front of her eyes. "Not so. You will never be rid of me. Not until *I* decide that I want to be rid of *you.* Do you understand?"

Kate said nothing.

"Do you realize how easy it would be to get your sister stoned to the point where she would think it fun to come into bed with us?"

Kate could feel her teeth clenching so hard she feared they would shatter.

"Don't be angry, dear one. You have your new position as head of Astro. You can have your sister, too. All I want is for you to follow my orders. In your office and in your bedroom."

"You'll leave Kim alone?"

"Of course! What would I want from her, if you are obedient?"

Kate lowered her eyes.

"The Russian thinks you still are working for him," Gaetano said, switching to business. "That is good. Let him continue to believe so. As long as you do what I tell you to."

Looking up, Kate saw that Kimberly was threading her way through the other tables toward them. She looks okay, Kate told herself. God, she actually looks happy.

"All right," she whispered urgently to Gaetano. "I'll follow orders like a good little slave. Just keep away from my sister."

"Of course," Gaetano assured her. Kate did not feel assured.

For days, Nobuhiko Yamagata pondered the meaning of Jane Scanwell's surprising statements at their luncheon together. Organized crime fastening its tentacles to the global conversion program? Murdering a friend of hers whom she had asked to investigate the situation for her?

Unsettling thoughts. The GEC's mad scramble to avert the greenhouse cliff was an awesome undertaking in itself; to have it undermined by the international crime syndicate—if such a thing actually existed—was more than dangerous. It could be fatal for half the human race.

Nobo decided that he needed more information. He explained the problem to his chief of security, a tiny, bandy-legged, pot-bellied man whose little remaining hair was as gray as a rainy day. The man had been Nobo's own bodyguard when he was a lad, personally selected by his father. He was a master of the martial arts, pot belly and all. More importantly now, he was a brilliant organizer and administrator.

The security chief listened to his master's apprehensions, then proceeded to arrange a meeting between Nobo and the head of one of the great Yakuza families. At first Nobo thought it unseemly to sit in the same room with a crime lord, but the security chief explained that the Yakuza had their own sense of honor and the head man would try his best to be cooperative, as long as he did not feel he was risking his own interests.

"He is well known to the police," the security chief told Nobo, "and has assisted them on investigations of certain violent crimes. In his own world he is a man of high rank and honor. It is no shame upon you or this house to meet with him."

Still, Nobuhiko hesitated. Until the security chief added, "He was a good friend to your father."

So the meeting was arranged, at the family home above Kyoto. Both men wore Western business suits: Nobo's charcoal gray, the Yakuza lord's an off-white raw silk.

His name was Toshiro Kakuta: small but very solidly built, head as bald and blunt as a bullet, eyes unreadable but alert. The older man bowed to Nobuhiko, somewhat stiffly. Nobo wondered if the stiffness was from age or the fact that this man did not often bow to others.

Returning the bow, Nobo gestured to the low lacquered table already set with a tea service. No third person would enter this room until their talk was finished. Kakuta slowly, almost painfully, sank to his knees and then sat cross-legged. Arthritis, Nobo decided.

They sipped tea and spoke pleasantly for quite some time about the lovely view of the forest through the room's big picture window. That led to a discussion of the weather, and then how warm the season had been, and finally to the matter of the greenhouse and the GEC's global effort.

"I have been told," Nobo said, glad to be on the subject at last, "that in other parts of the world, organized crime syndicates are stealing money and resources from this vital program."

Kakuta bowed his head ever so slightly. "I have been informed of the same. A terrible thing to do."

"I have not heard of any such interference with this necessary work in Japan."

Lifting his chin again, he said, "No. We recognize how crucial this work is. There is nothing to be gained by robbing one's own nest."

"I am pleased to hear you say it," Nobo said, wondering how much of the man's words were true.

"If I may explain . . ."

"Please do."

"In any large organization it is not always possible to completely control the actions of every individual member. There may well be the misguided soul, here and there, who makes some profit from your great work. I deal harshly with such foolishness when I learn of it, but I am not omniscient."

It was Nobo's turn to bow his head slightly. "I understand."

"I am grateful that you have the same wisdom as your father." A heartbeat's pause, then Kakuta added, "And at a much younger age."

Nobo kept himself from reacting to that. "Can you tell me," he asked, "is there truly an international crime cartel? A syndicate of global proportions?"

Kakuta remained silent for so long that Nobo began to think he would not answer. Finally the older man said, "That is a difficult question. There have been loose alliances from one region of the Earth to another, from time to time. Some of our own groups here in Japan have formed links with families in the United States, for example."

"But no actual organization, on a permanent basis?"

"Not yet."

Despite himself, Nobo felt his brows rise. "Not yet?"

"Within the past year there has been great pressure brought to bear to form such a continuing global organization, with permanent hierarchy and structure."

"Where does this pressure come from?"

Kakuta swung his head a few centimeters from one side to the other. "That is a question that I cannot answer."

"You mean you will not answer."

Kakuta said nothing.

"Can you tell me this much, at least," Nobo asked. "Does this pressure involve the Mafia?"

"The Mafia is already an international organization. It includes most of Europe and all of North America."

"So I have been told."

"But they do not operate in Japan, and as long as I am alive they will not."

"I see. I understand and I am indebted to you for sharing your wisdom with me."

"It is a pleasure. May you have ten thousand years of happiness."

"And you the same."

Kakuta burst into a full-bellied laugh, startling Nobuhiko. "Ten thousand years for me? Oh no, not in *my* business!" He rocked back and forth with laughter and slapped his thighs.

Nobo smiled back at him and thought, I will send President Scanwell a team to guard her—without her knowing it. She may have a GEC security team, but they might easily be infiltrated. The best security is the least visible.

Augustus Greenwell tramped through the sodden woods, grateful that his Barbour coat was truly waterproof. It had rained again last night; it had rained every night for the past six, cold, driving acid rain that was killing the woods and poisoning his lake. He had complained to the Environmental Protection Agencies, state and federal, to the idiots in the Weather Service who kept nattering about unseasonable cyclonic disturbances, to both his senators and even to the President's science adviser.

Still it rained, even on the weekends when he wanted to go hunting in his own private woods.

Slogging through the muddy underbrush, heavy laser rifle on his shoulder, he admitted to himself that the rumors about the damnable greenhouse must be right after all. The weather is changing. This greenhouse collapse or whatever they were calling it probably is real, rather than just another attempt by still yet another government agency to tell him how to run his business.

Convert all our models to electric! Ridiculous! It'll bankrupt us. Chrysler's gone, Ford's tottering on the brink, and now they want me to start making plans to convert to nothing but electric cars. And keep it secret until some leech in Paris says it's okay to announce the news! It's a ploy by those rotten Japs, that's what it is. They're way ahead of us on electric cars and now they've got the GEC to order us to stop making gasoline-powered cars. *Ordered* us! Ordered *me*!

And the damnable banks are going along with them. No loans for gasoline cars. Not even for methane or synfuel models. All fossil fuels are out, starting with the production runs two years up the line.

Greenwell spent several minutes swearing in nearly infinite detail about the GEC, the banks, and his Japanese competitors. He had a choice vocabulary of curses, which he carefully refrained from using unless he was absolutely alone. Now he trotted out his richly profane litany from beginning to end, turning the air blue as he sloshed through puddles of acid rain.

A crow cawed from high in the bare branches of a dead spruce. It was the only bird Greenwell had seen all morning. He scowled at it. The grouse and duck and other game birds were all gone. Dead or fled. That's gratitude for you; after the years I spent making this a sanctuary for them, not allowing anybody else to shoot them.

Hydrogen. The thought made him angry all over again. We could modify our existing engines to burn hydrogen. The stuff gives good performance, and in some ways it's even safer than gasoline. But those foreigners from the GEC had stared at him as if he were insane when he offered to convert to hydrogen cars rather than electrics.

"Hydrogen?" they had exclaimed.

"Too dangerous!"

"The Hindenberg!"

When Greenwell had pointed out to them that Germany's Daimler-Benz Corporation had been running hydrogen-fueled buses for half a century without mishap, they just shook their heads.

"The decision has been made, Mr. Greenwell. You will convert to electric automobiles, just like everyone else."

"There is only one GEC program, and everyone must adhere to it."

But if we can make a simple conversion to hydrogen instead of having to go into electrics—Greenwell mulled the possibilities. Hydrogen isn't a fossil fuel; when you burn it the exhaust is water. And if a hydrogen car can give performance like a gasoline car, we could run rings around the Japs and their dinky electric autos! But those motherless maggots won't hear of it. Electric cars or nothing. Damn them all to hell a thousand times over!

The crow cawed again, as if mocking him. Taking a deep breath of relatively clean air, Greenwell put his rifle to his shoulder, aimed the laser sight at the squawking crow, and pulled the trigger. The camera built into the rifle's former firing chamber clicked, and Greenwell was satisfied that he could have killed the noisy black bird.

He had never killed a living creature in all his life. Above everything else, August Greenwell prided himself on being a conservationist.

Dan sat in his windowless cell deep underground, staring blankly at the electronic chess game his captors had given him. He had asked for a cyberbook reader with some of the classic novels he had never had the time to read, or a television set so he could at least see the news and try the opera channel to see if he could learn to enjoy something deeper than *West Side Story*.

All they gave him was this stupid little chess set that had only eight levels of play programmed into it. Trouble was, the damned machine beat him consistently on level two and higher.

Dan's cell was bleak. Bare concrete walls. One bunk, one toilet, one sink and one table with a single chair. The ceiling was glareless light panels that stayed on twenty-four hours a day. Monitoring cameras watched him from behind those panels.

He sat hunched over the chess game wearing a prisoner's gray coveralls. A team from the GEC was on its way from Paris to bring him back Earthside, where he would stand trial for kidnapping, terrorism, drug dealing, grand larceny and anything else they could think of. Dan did not look forward to the interrogation he knew Malik would order. They'd want to get the names of the other renegades living around Alphonsus. Dan was determined not to tell them, but he did not know how long he could hold out against even the legal interrogation techniques—to say nothing of the kind that Malik would prefer using.

What difference does it make? he asked himself, sitting alone in his bare, chilly cell. George and Tucker ratted me out, why should I protect them?

He pushed away from the plastic table and got up slowly. The cell always felt cold to him. Must be my imagination. Certainly can't be damp down here; the only damned water around here is the stuff they make in the factories.

Why hold out when they interrogate me? Dan knew the answer: To screw Malik. Not to protect George or Tucker or any of those bums. They weren't loyal to me, why should I be loyal to them? But if Malik wants their names then I won't give them. The Russian sonofabitch can turn me inside out and I won't tell him a double-damned word.

I hope. Dan had no doubts about his ability to withstand psychological pressure. But he also felt certain that Malik would quickly resort to more physical methods. For the good of the world's people, of course. All the heinous tortures in history had been done for the purest of motives. Just like Torquemada working so hard to save all those souls by ripping apart all those bodies.

If only I could get loose once I'm back on Earth, Dan thought as he paced the five steps from one end of his cell to the other. I've got half a dozen bankrolls stashed away down there. I could offer a pretty hefty bribe for some help in breaking loose. Then I could disappear and live a decent life under an assumed identity. Maybe even some plastic surgery . . .

He stopped short. And do what? Spend the rest of my life sitting on my ass in Argentina or Taiwan, hoping nobody spots me? While Malik and the rest of them run the world straight into the greenhouse cliff?

He reached out his right hand and touched the concrete wall facing him. He pressed both hands against it, then leaned all his weight on them. The wall did not budge. Who are you trying to kid? he snarled silently at himself. You're going to spend the rest of your life in a cell like this. Or worse. Malik's not going to let you go. And nobody's going to help you. Not Jane or Nobo or Kate Williams or anybody.

Straightening up, squaring his shoulders, Dan told himself, Okay. Let's face reality. There's only one possibility. Sooner or later, Malik's going to come within my reach. The damned smiling, gloating sonofabitch is going to get close enough for me to grab him by the throat. Then I'll kill him. It'll have to be quick. Smash his double-damned windpipe before he realizes what's happening. Drive the cartilage in his nose up into his brain. Snap his neck. Quick.

Then they can put me on trial for a real murder instead of these phonied-up charges.

Dan nodded, satisfied that he was right. It was a discussion he had held with himself every day since they had tossed him into this cell. He came to the same conclusion every time.

Now, as he did after each of those self-discussions, he got down on the floor and started doing push-ups. His first day in captivity he could do only ten. Now he was up to fifty. Next he would do sit-ups to flatten his gut. Then he would jog around his cell until his legs were too shaky to carry him.

He was on his seventy-third sit-up, sweating and grunting, when he heard the *beep-beep-boop* of the door's electronic lock being worked. Too early for dinner, he thought. They had taken his wristwatch from him, but he had a fair judgment for time.

The door swung open and the huge shaggy form of Big George pushed through. Behind him, like a tiny spacecraft eclipsed by a massive asteroid, was Pops Tucker.

Dan almost laughed, sitting there on the floor. "So they got you too."

"Not fooking likely," said George, in a near-whisper.

"Get up," Tucker said. "We're takin' you outta here."

Dan scrambled to his feet. "You're what?"

"We're springin' you. Come on!"

Instantly suspicious, Dan growled, "What's going on? Am I supposed to be shot while trying to escape? Is that it?"

Tucker curled a lip at him. "You don't trust us, huh?"

"Why should I?"

"Because we didn't give you away, in the first place," answered Tucker, looking and sounding disgusted, "and we're risking our goddamned asses to spring you, in the second place."

"We don't have much time," George said, glancing down the corridor outside the cell.

Dan noticed that he was holding a pistol in one huge hand. It looked like the same gun Dan himself had brought from his office.

"Where'd you get that?" He pointed at the gun.

George grinned from inside his wildly tangled beard. "Where you left it, behind your bunk. Pops went over the shelter with a detector array that first time you and me went out to meet the trolley. Remember? Didn't find any electronic bugs but we found this."

"And you left it there?"

"Sure, what'd we need it for?"

"We're wastin' time," Tucker said.

Dan made a decision. He started for the door. Outside, he saw that the corridor was empty.

"How long will a man stay out when he's been hit with one of these darts?" George asked as they started down the long narrow blank-walled corridor.

"Depends on his size," Dan answered, hurrying to keep pace with the big man. "Ten, twenty minutes. Maybe half an hour."

"Then we gotta run like hell," Tucker puffed, already jogging to stay with them.

"Here we go!" George scooped up the frail old man and bolted ahead like a football runningback. Dan raced after him.

A few minutes later they were in the sublevel where Alphonsus' life support machinery chugged away. George set Tucker down on his feet again, and the sour-faced old man slipped on a pair of dark goggles. He bent over even more than usual, seemingly studying the floor.

"EMERGENCY!" blared the overhead speakers. "EMERGENCY! A PRISONER HAS ESCAPED FROM THE DETENTION CENTER. HE HAS AT LEAST TWO ACCOMPLICES. THEY ARE ARMED. USE EXTREME CAUTION!"

"Why the fook are they piping that down here?" George complained. "Nobody here but the maintenance robots."

"There might be a few human technicians around," Dan suggested.

"Or they're tryin' to scare us," said Tucker.

Dan shook his head. "More likely they just put the announcement on the whole damned comm system. I'll bet it even went out to the tourists up in Yamagata's new hotel."

"All right," said Tucker, returning his attention to the floor. "Now we sprayed a dye that's only visible in the infrared—that's where we walk. Georgie bent the camera supports enough along our path so we can sneak under 'em and they won't see us."

"Had to shoot the two guys at the monitor screens in the detention center," George said, somewhat ruefully. "One of 'em was a girl. Cute, too."

"Hell, you think Hogface Martha is cute," Tucker growled.

George laughed.

They walked slowly along the path that only Tucker could see. Dan wondered how long they had before a maintenance robot crossed their path or a live security team was dispatched to scour the area. I won't be able to fool a robot, he realized. I don't have the current codes.

Then they passed a familiar alcove. The metal rungs of a ladder were set into the wall, leading up.

"Hey, wait," he called to the others.

"What?"

"Let's go up this way," he said.

"Are you crazy?" Tucker snarled. "That's not the way to the outside. That goes up to—"

"My office," Dan said. "Last place they'd think of looking for us."

"You *are* crazy."

"Like a fox. Come on." And he started up the ladder.

There are two possibilities, Dan reasoned as he climbed. One: George and the old man are working for Malik and I'm supposed to be shot while trying to escape. Maybe there's a goon squad up at that shelter at the top of the vertical shaft waiting to kill me. It'd be just like Malik to have George and Pops snuffed too; clean up the whole mess and leave no witnesses.

Two: the pair of them are really on my side and risking their asses to free me. But there could still be a squad waiting for us at the shelter. If Kate Williams is still running the show around here she's too smart to let me get away with the same escape route twice.

He glanced down in the dimly lit shaft and saw that George was following below him. Probably Tucker's behind him, too small to see behind Georgie's bulk.

Sure enough, he heard the old man's voice echoing sourly off the shaft's walls, "This is the dumbest damn thing I've seen since Harry Kline decided he could breathe vacuum."

Grinning, Dan hissed a *shhh* down at him.

TWENTY-SEVEN

They came out into the service corridor that ran behind the offices. Dan knew the area by heart and led them, tiptoeing like a trio of naughty schoolboys, to a closet where the janitorial staff kept its equipment.

Most of the closet was occupied by a pair of janitors: squat, sturdy robots whose once-gleaming metal skins were now scuffed and scratched from wear. The closet walls were lined with shelves containing cleaning solvents, dust absorbers, and maintenance equipment for the robots.

"As long as nobody comes in to refill the robots' tanks we're okay," Dan said as they quietly closed the door. He added silently, *And as long as nobody happens to be looking at the monitoring cameras watching the corridor.*

It was utterly dark with the door shut. Dan heard a dull thud and an "Ouch!" from Big George.

"Watch it," he whispered.

"Now you tell me. Thanks a fooking lot."

"What do we do now?" Tucker hissed.

"We wait. Anybody got a wristwatch?"

A brief glimmer of fluorescence. "It's seventeen thirty-eight."

"Too early. People'll still be in their offices. We sit here and wait. The robots are programmed to go out at ten P.M. We'll wait till then."

Dan hunkered down on what little floor space was available, arms clasped around his knees. He heard Tucker grumbling and George huffing as he strained to squeeze himself into a semicomfortable spot.

In the darkness Dan pictured Kate Williams working in his office, at his desk. I'd like to bust right in there and grab the traitorous bitch, he seethed to himself. Slap her flat on the double-damned desk and show her who the boss really is.

Then he grinned to himself, remembering Tamara's warning that Kate would cut his balls off. Tamara. I wonder where she is? What's she doing now? Kate wouldn't keep her as an assistant; the kid was too loyal to me.

"I still think this is crazy," Tucker grumbled, his whispering voice grating angrily. "We're sitting ducks here."

"They won't expect us to be here," Dan countered. "They've probably got goon squads combing the lower levels and searching outside for us. This is the best place to be, for now."

"For how long?" George asked.

"Till I get a chance to pop into my office and check the computer files. There's a few things I want to know."

Tucker mumbled something too low to understand.

"Pops, how long will it take you to hack a permanent access for me into Astro's files?"

"Once we're into them? Ten seconds."

Dan chuckled softly. Nothing wrong with Tucker's self-image. "Might as well get some sleep while we're waiting," he said.

"Sure," Tucker groused. "Let 'em take us while we're snoring."

"You're the one who snores," George whispered.

"That's right. You never snore, do you? I never heard so goddamned much noise in my life."

"Cut the chatter," Dan hissed. He closed his eyes, wondering if he would be able to sleep at all.

The two robots lit up abruptly and began to hum, snapping Dan from a deep slumber. The door to the closet swung back and both the stubby thickset machines trundled out into the corridor on nearly noiseless little wheels. The door swung shut again.

"Fooking pile of junk near ran over my foot," George muttered.

"It's twenty-two hundred," Tucker said before Dan could ask the time.

Wordlessly, Dan pushed the door open a crack and squinted up and down the corridor. No one in sight. The monitor camera, up near the ceiling more than twenty meters away, showed a single baleful red eye.

We'll have to chance it, Dan said to himself. They can't be watching every monitor screen all the time. Even if they've programmed the system to sound an alarm whenever the cameras see somebody in the corridors, they can't possibly check out everybody. I hope.

"George, you wait here," he said. "They're looking for three men, not two. Pops, we're going to walk slowly, like a pair of maintenance men. Keep your head down and try to look natural."

"You'd look a helluva lot more like a janitor without that beard," Tucker muttered.

"Yeah. I know."

Beard and all, the two of them stepped out into the corridor and walked to the back door to Dan's office, with the video camera staring at them. Maintenance personnel go into the offices to check that the robots haven't screwed up, Dan told himself. There's nothing unusual enough to alert security. Again he added, I hope.

Kate had changed the security code on the door's electronic lock, but it took Tucker a scant few seconds to press a palm-sized analyzer against the lock and then tap out the new code, while Dan stood between him and the camera.

The lights went on in the office automatically as they stepped in. Dan took in the familiar surroundings with a single glance. His pictures had all been replaced by paintings, mostly Impressionists, very high-quality reproductions. Scarlett's got good taste, he admitted to himself.

Swiftly he went to his desk and flicked on the computer. His chair felt odd to him, slightly uncomfortable, as if its shape had subtly changed. He knew that all his old access codes to the company's files had been erased. What would Kate Williams use? He tried her first name, then her last, then both together. No go. On a whim he typed in "Scarlett."

The screen lit up, ready for his next command.

"I'll be damned," Dan muttered. Then he went to work.

It took more than an hour for Dan to scroll through the basic information he wanted. Tucker fidgeted at the edge of his awareness, becoming more nervous each second. At one point Dan told him to bring George from the closet.

"And relax," Dan said to the wizened little man. "If they haven't come down on us by now, then they don't know we're here."

The company records told him a story as bad as he had feared he would find. Worse, in some ways. Astro was being micro-managed by bureaucrats from the GEC who had no understanding of how to run a working company. Production was faltering while the GEC put major emphasis on paperwork. Every move had to be okayed by the new management. Filling out the proper forms had become more important than getting the job done.

There were plans to vastly increase the company's production of helium-three. Plans to double the production of solar panels. Plans to triple the tonnage of silicon and aluminum shipped to the factories in orbit.

Or rather, there were memorandums and reports and impact statements about such plans. Plans to make plans. Committees to study the proposed plans. Other committees to study the committees' recommendations.

Dan pushed his chair back from the desk with a disgusted snort. Christ, what a putrefying mess. At this rate the whole damned world could be underwater and the only way anybody'll be saved is if they stack their double-damned reports on top of one another and climb up to the top of the pile.

"It's almost midnight!" Tucker whispered hoarsely. "How long—"

"I'm just about finished," said Dan. "Here, make me an access that nobody else can find. I want complete access to all the files in the system."

The dour little man perched on Dan's chair, his frail legs dangling off the floor, his fingers flying over the keyboard like a concert pianist's. Big George sprawled dozing on one of the couches across the office.

It took more than ten seconds. Nearly ten minutes. Finally Tucker gestured to the glowing screen. "It's done. You can pop into the system any time you want. What code name do you want?"

Dan thought a moment. "Freedom."

Tucker hiked his brows, but tapped in the word. "Now can we go?" he asked sourly, shutting down the computer.

"Wait," said Dan. "One more thing."

He went back to the desk, booted up the machine again and, using "Freedom," asked the system to locate Tamara Duchamps. The screen showed that she had been assigned to the transportation department. Her job title was secretary to the manager of freight exports. Got her stuck out at the mass driver, Dan realized, as far away from comfort and safety as they could put her.

He shook his head. Kate's a real bitch, he thought. But

then he brightened. It ought to be a lot easier for me to see Tamara out there at the Nubium facility than it would be if she were still here inside Alphonsus.

"For god's sake!" Tucker hissed at him. "Let's get out of here!"

"Relax," Dan said. "This is the safest place in the city for us, right now."

"Then why's my stomach feel like there's ten thousand frogs jumpin' around in there?"

Dan crossed the thick carpeting and entered the lavatory. The cabinet drawers under the sink were filled with Kate's things now: perfumes and cosmetics and even some skimpy, frilly underwear that made Dan grin appreciatively. "So that's what she wears underneath it all," he muttered. No pills. Not even aspirin.

He was about to give up when he finally discovered his shaving things crammed into the back of the bottom drawer. Even the barber's scissors and electric razor were jumbled in there. Greatest luxury in the world, Dan remembered, is having somebody else shave you. Shaking his head at the memory of a particularly gorgeous Swede who took her tonsorial duties seriously even while topless, Dan started the onerous chore of chopping off his beard.

Tucker was fidgeting nervously when he came out clean-shaven. George was still snoring on the couch.

"How do I look?"

"Great. Now let's get *out* of here!"

Eying the shaggy Aussie, Dan said, "Might be a good idea if we cleaned him up, too."

Tucker looked as if he were about to have apoplexy.

Muhammed Shariff Sibuti rose from his knees and carefully rolled up his prayer rug. He kept his office locked during the times of prayer. Even though his staff were all faithful to Islam, he did not want unbelievers such as Malik or, worse, the Catholic Gaetano to intrude on his prayers.

God knows that we will need all the help and strength that only He can provide, Sibuti said to himself as he carefully placed the tasseled rug into the cabinet behind his desk. And all the patience, too, he added as he sat in his desk chair once again.

He touched the button that unlocked his door, then with the same long slim finger activated his phone. "I will see Minister Malik now," he said, noticing that his finger was trembling.

It had been nearly two months since Malik had dropped his bombshell about the greenhouse cliff, yet Sibuti still felt stunned, shocked. Slowly, carefully the word was being passed on to leaders in the various national governments and multinational corporations. Sibuti imagined he could see the shock waves spreading from Paris to the capitals of nations and the seats of the great industrial empires.

"Minister Malik is here, sir," said his secretary's voice over the phone.

"Send him in."

Malik had not changed a whit over the past weeks. Sibuti felt as if he himself had aged a century, but Malik looked as youthful and determined as ever, dashing even, in his military-style tunic of deep blue. Sibuti felt very old in his ordinary gray business suit.

"You wanted to see me?" the Russian asked, taking one of the chairs in front of Sibuti's desk without waiting to be invited.

The older man nodded, pressing his lips together. "Yes. I am beginning to prepare the agenda for next week's Council meeting. I think it is time that we began to discuss how we will break the news of this impending catastrophe to the general public."

Malik's ice blue eyes flickered briefly. "It is too early to inform the public at large."

"Too early? But rumors are already beginning to spread. The media—"

"The media can be controlled. And rumors always

spread. What of it?"

"Rumors can be very damaging, very dangerous," said Sibuti.

Malik shot him a glance filled with scorn. "Nothing but hot air."

"You think so! Let me tell you, sir, that rumors can be deadly. Do you understand me? Deadly! When I was first appointed to the Council, every year the mighty rivers of Bangladesh overflowed and killed thousands on the coastal plains. Then we began to build the big hydro dams up in the mountains."

"And controlled the flooding," Malik interrupted. "And provided the electricity that has brought the standard of living in the region up by several hundred percent."

"Yes. True. But the year that the third dam was being finished, do you remember that? A rumor began to spread in the coastal cities that the dams had failed. The rumor spread like wildfire."

Malik leaned forward, interested in the older man's story despite himself.

"Anyone with a television could see that the dams were perfectly all right," Sibuti went on, his thin voice rising. "But the people did not trust reports by the news media, they did not even trust the evidence of their own eyes. They reacted to the *rumor*! They fled in terror from the cities in a mad dash to get to higher ground. They emptied the stores, looted what they could not buy, burned what they could not carry off with them, killed one another on the roads."

Somewhat subdued, Malik said, "I do remember something of that."

"The cities were abandoned in panic. Thousands were killed. By panic. By a rumor. The national economy was crippled for several years before things settled down to normal once again. *That* is what rumors can do!"

Malik spread his hands. "But my dear Minister, your own story proves how hard we must work to avoid panic.

Imagine what would happen if we suddenly announced that half the world might be flooded out in the next ten years. It would be like Bangladesh everywhere!"

Sibuti glared at the Russian, but his expression slowly softened as Malik's point sank in. "Yes, I see. I understand. We are on the horns of a dilemma. A very painful dilemma."

"We are making progress," Malik said. "The politicians whom we have informed are dithering and flapping around like a pack of geese, as usual. But the corporate leaders seem to be facing the situation much more realistically."

"I see where the Americans have renewed their request to develop hydrogen-fueled automobiles."

Malik frowned. "We must resist that request. Our program calls for electric cars; we can't have the Americans pulling an end run on us."

"End run?"

"I will speak with Jane Scanwell. She can handle the American industrialists."

Still blinking with confusion about Malik's Americanism, Sibuti asked, "What about Japan?"

"Yamagata is being very cooperative. Not only has he pledged his corporation's assistance, he has even volunteered to form a steering committee that will serve as liaison between the major multinationals and our Council."

"Very good! But what of the Big Seven?"

Malik's eyes narrowed. "The confiscation of Astro Manufacturing had its desired effect on them. They have all fallen neatly into line and permitted us to install our own administrators to manage them for the length of the emergency."

"That could be ten or twenty years," said Sibuti, the beginnings of a smile on his thin lips.

"Or more," agreed Malik.

The older man rocked back in his desk chair for a few moments. Then, hunching forward again, "I still believe we must face the very urgent need to inform the public about this. It is imperative!"

"In time," Malik said placatingly. "In time. Look at what happened when we informed the leaders of the environmental movement."

"A disaster," Sibuti agreed.

Under a promise of secrecy, a dozen of the world's leading environmentalists had been brought to Paris and briefed on the greenhouse cliff. The GEC wanted their help in formulating plans for recruiting environmentalists all over the world to help in the battle against the impending catastrophe. What they got instead was chaos. Suspicion and distrust. Three of the prominent European "greens" flatly refused to believe the data before their eyes. Several of the Americans expressed the opinion that the GEC could not solve the problem, and one actually seemed to believe that a worldwide flood would be a *good* thing! As if the world deserved such a cataclysm!

"We must control this news very carefully," Malik was saying. "Very tight control of the media is absolutely necessary."

"But you don't seem to understand," Sibuti countered, "that the news is already leaking out. The politicians we have briefed, the environmentalists—they will not keep our secret. Not for very long, at any rate."

Nodding, Malik admitted, "I know. That is why our next move must be to gain a firm control over the news media, worldwide. Once that is accomplished, then we can begin to break the story to the public in our own way, on our own terms."

Sibuti nodded back. "Ah. I see. Yes, that is the way to do it, I suppose. It shouldn't be too difficult to gain control of the media in most nations. Even in Great Britain the government can censor the news whenever it feels the necessity."

"It's the Americans who will be the problem, as usual," said Malik. "Them and their quaint notions of freedom of the press."

"There are the international news networks, as well."

"Yes, but they can be handled the same way we got the cooperation of the Big Seven. A little show of force and a plea for voluntary cooperation—or else."

"A formidable task," said Sibuti.

"But it must be done."

"Yes. I agree. I shall place it high on our agenda for next week's meeting."

"Good."

The Russian got to his feet. Sibuti rose too and extended his hand. The two men left on a much friendlier note than they had displayed earlier.

But as Malik strode back toward his own office, he thought, Let the old fool prepare his agendas and chair his meetings, as long as he stays out of my way. I've got it all almost within my grasp. Once the news media are under control, then I'll have the power I need to get this job underway.

Sibuti sank back into his desk chair once Malik left his office. His thoughts were not on next week's agenda, but on his nephew in Jakarta. His nephew owned a small construction company that was bidding on a major project to construct a seawall meant to protect the Indonesian capital against the rising sea level. Sibuti had discreetly funneled much information to his nephew, helping him to prepare his bid for the project.

Now my nephew wants me to put in a personal word for him. All I have to do is call the contracting officer and suggest, ever so mildly, that the Indonesian project should go to a local firm.

He stared at his phone console, its screen blank. The seawall will be useless, he knew, if the greenhouse cliff raised sea levels more than ten meters. Moreover, his nephew had complained that he was being forced to pay an exorbitant "priority fee" to an outfit of thugs who controlled the concrete business in Jakarta. Rumors were that they were associated with some international crime syndicate.

Rumors again. Sibuti saw his own reflection scowling in the dark phone screen. Do I want my nephew mixed up with such criminals? Yet how can he remain in the construction business without access to concrete? Does it really matter? Write off their excess "fees" as a cost of doing business. Everyone else does.

But should I personally intervene? It is not proper. Yet—he is my nephew.

Sibuti stared at the phone console for a long time, struggling with his conscience. Finally he reached for the handset, thinking, Blood is thicker than rules and regulations. After all, he is my nephew. And everyone does it. If I don't help him, someone else will help one of his relatives.

TWENTY-EIGHT

I t had almost come to a fistfight, but finally Dan and
Tucker convinced Big George that his beard had to
come off. Dan did the honors, sitting George on the
toilet in his lavatory and chopping away for what
seemed—even to Dan—like hours.

Tucker was almost climbing the walls when Dan
straightened up, his back popping with strain.

"Want me to shave the stubble for you, George?"

"I can do it myself," the big Australian muttered, sullen and subdued.

Dan stepped back into the office. Tucker jabbed an
impatient finger at the pile of hair clippings on the floor.
"You don't have to be Sherlock goddam Holmes to figure
what you guys have been doin'."

With a grin, Dan said, "That's what the cleaning robots are for. They ought to be popping in here pretty
soon; usually come into this office around one A.M., unless Kate's reprogrammed them."

Tucker growled, "Like you were in here that late, to

see what time they arrived?"

"I burned some midnight oil in this office," Dan said, glancing around. All of a sudden he hated the paintings on the walls, the slightly odd feel of the desk chair. This has been stolen from me, he said to himself. They've stolen this office, the furniture, the whole company. Everything I have.

"Well, I hope you two are fooking satisfied."

Dan whirled to admire Big George's freshly shaved face. And understood immediately why the oversized Aussie had grown the beard in the first place. George had a baby's pink, smooth face; wildly out of joint with his massive physique.

"How the hell old are you, George?" Dan asked.

"Twenty-three," mumbled the Aussie.

"Holy shit," said Tucker. "I must've been twenty-three once, but it was so damned long ago I forget what it was like."

Laughing, Dan went back to his former desk.

"Now what?" Tucker fairly screamed.

"I just realized," Dan said, flicking on the computer again, "that if I can get into the company's system I can also get into some of the personal files I buried in here years ago. If nobod—aha! There it is!" He looked up at his two friends, beaming. "Fellas, we may have been fugitives when we came in here, but we're going to leave like gentlemen."

Just to be on the cautious side, however, Dan told Tucker and George to leave by the back door, the same way they had come in.

"I'm going out the front door, just like I owned the joint."

"Where do we meet up again?" Tucker asked.

"At the registration desk of the new Yamagata Hotel."

"What! Are you crazy?"

"Like an owl. Give me half an hour. Then come to the registration desk and ask for Roger Wilcox. That'll be me. I just pulled up Roger's old file, transferred some of the money he had left in a bank Earthside, and made him a reservation at the Yamagata. Topflight suite; you'll enjoy it."

"He's fooking nuts," said George.

"You got a better place to squat?" Dan snapped. "They'll have all the tempos staked out by now, don't you think? Certainly all the airlocks will be under close surveillance."

Tucker shook his head wearily. "You're right, Georgie. He's nuts. But he's right, too. By now we couldn't get out of the city unless we had a platoon of U.S. Marines with us."

Dan flipped him a military salute. "See you in half an hour."

There was a human clerk at the registration desk, even at half past midnight, that's how posh a hotel the Yamagata was. He was Japanese, of course, much too polite actually to ask where in the world Mr. Roger Wilcox was coming from. There were no passenger flights arriving at this time of the early morning. And Mr. Wilcox had no luggage.

Yet his reservation was there in the computer, along with Wilcox's credit data, absolutely authentic.

Dan saved the tired young man the embarrassment of asking. "Damnedest thing," he said, trying to remember what a Texas twang sounded like. "I been coming up here for years. Usually stayed at the Astro habitat, you know, 'cause I'm on company business. One of their biggest goddamned investors, and I like to see what they're doing with my money, you better believe. But ever since that GEC gang took over, you know, there's so many new people over to Astro that they just don't have room for one of their investors anymore. Can you imagine that! I spent the whole damned day arguing with them, and half the night waiting for them to come up with some decent accommodations for me and my two assistants. Finally I told 'em, 'Fuck it! I'll got over to

Yamagata's. They know how to treat a visitor.' "

He asked where the nearest computer link was. Looking somewhat dubious, the clerk pointed to the phone console at the end of the registration desk. Dan went to it, tapped into the Astro accounting system, and had ten thousand U.S. dollars transferred to the hotel in the name of Roger Wilcox. Then he asked the clerk to give him cash. "Ten one-thousand-dollar bills, please."

The clerk's expression went from dubious to curious. Hardly anyone used cash on the Moon. But he read his own computer screen carefully, saw that the money was in Mr. Wilcox's account, then unlocked the cash drawer and counted out the money.

"I 'preciate your help very much, son," drawled Dan, handing one of the bills back over the counter to the room clerk. He hesitated a heartbeat, glanced over his shoulder as if afraid the manager was watching, then snatched the thousand-dollar note. The young man bowed and smiled with pleasure.

"My friends will be along directly," Dan said, hoping he wasn't overdoing the accent. "Please see that they get to my suite." He said nothing about luggage, leaving the clerk to assume that his two assistants would be carrying it.

Like stout Cortez when with eagle eyes he first stared at the Pacific, TV reporter Harvey Yeats struck a pose and gazed out on the glittering blue sea. The other two members of the news crew—cameraman and audio woman— knew that Harvey was already rehearsing how he wanted to look on the videotape they were here to shoot.

Their two Eskimo guides paid attention not to Yeats' pose, but to the shining new space-age parka that each of the news team wore, light yet warm, stylish and brilliant of hue. They were not jealous so much as covetous of those expensive, handsome parkas.

It was too warm to keep the hood up. Besides, Yeats knew, he would look better on the tape with the hood down and his golden hair catching the slanting rays of the sun that barely rose above the horizon.

"Don't look like much," said the cameraman. "Just a stretch of water and some of those flat ice floes out in the distance."

"Moron!" snapped Yeats. "Up here the ocean freezes over. Open water at this time of the year is unheard of."

The cameraman shrugged. "Still don't look like much."

"It's the greenhouse effect. There's hardly any ice in the whole Arctic Ocean."

"What was all that white stuff we flew over?" asked the audio woman, grinning at the cameraman. They were both accustomed to Yeats' exaggerations.

"Oh, further out, yeah, sure. But it ought to be solid ice all the way up to the shore here." The reporter turned to the two Eskimos. "Isn't that right?"

One of the Eskimos, who held a degree in climatology from the University of Alaska, nodded solemn agreement. "There hasn't been this much open water here at this time of the season in the memory of living man."

"See?" said Yeats.

"It still don't look like much," argued the cameraman. "Just some water. We could get a shot like this in New Jersey, for Chrissake."

Yeats screwed up his handsome features into a dark scowl. His crew people knew that he was thinking, not angry.

"Okay," he said, "how about this? I take one of those little kayaks and paddle out to the ice floes. You shoot me from here; show how far away the ice really is."

"I wouldn't do that . . ." said the climatologist.

Yeats waved him down. "I've done plenty of kayaking. Went down the length of the Grand Canyon last year."

The cameraman brightened. "Yeah. We could set up a remote on the kayak, just like we did then."

The audio woman nodded agreement. The two Eskimos glanced at one another. They tried to argue against it, but Yeats would not listen. "We've only got a couple hours of sunlight left, right? We're not going to stay here until the sun comes up again, that'd take months, right? So stop arguing and get me a kayak."

Thus it was that, as the pale Arctic sun touched the flat horizon of sea and ice, Harvey Keats paddled a kayak out to the nearest of the ice floes, a remote camera attached to the boat's prow trained on his tousle-haired face, a remote microphone catching every word of his nonstop narration.

Thus it was that an orca, driven close to the shore by hunger because the seals had been largely killed off, rushed up from the depths, overturned Keats' kayak, and crushed him in its jaws.

The cameraman and audio woman stood on the shore, aghast but recording every instant of Keats' untimely death. The two Eskimos looked at one another sorrowfully, grieved by the loss of that spanking new parka.

The mass driver stretched in a straight line for slightly more than two miles across Mare Nubium, just outside the ringwall mountains of Alphonsus.

The original planners of the Alphonsus complex assumed that workers at the mass-driver facility would be quartered in the city and commute to their jobs via the cable-car system that crossed the ringwall. Over the years, however, a small, makeshift, rugged community grew around the mass-driver facility. Men and women lived there for months or even years at a time, going to Alphonsus City only for vacations or to return Earthward.

Except for the long straight track of the electric catapult itself, the mass-driver complex was underground, a warren of interconnected shelters and tunnels. One of the shelters housed the complex's only bar, named Hundred Gees after the nominal acceleration that the mass driver imparted to its cargo containers to fling them into space trajectories.

Tamara Duchamps did not feel comfortable at Hundred Gees. She was accustomed to the more refined cabarets of Paris or the quiet lounges of Alphonsus City; the bar felt rough and rowdy to her. The men who gathered there were little better than grease monkeys, for the most part, and miners who drifted in from the camps farther out on Mare Nubium looking for a night's entertainment. The women were hardly better.

Tamara seldom went to the bar, but after weeks of living in this dreary underground nest, exiled from the comforts of the city, she found herself driven by loneliness, the need for some human companionship. The Hundred Gees was crowded, smoky, noisy with raucous talk and blaring canned music. But she went there anyway; there was no place else to go.

She never dressed provocatively; usually she wore plain coveralls, as she did this evening. Yet not even the drabbest of outfits could hide the lithe grace of her long-legged body or the sculptured dark beauty of her face.

"Hey, princess, you drinkin' alone?"

Tamara looked up from the minuscule table to see a lanky, red-faced guy with a bushy moustache grinning at her. Almost leering at her. The name badge on his breast said Rollins; his shoulder patch identified him as an electrical engineer.

"The place is awful crowded," he said, not giving her a chance to answer. "Mind if I sit with you?" Again without waiting, he took the chair next to hers and pulled it close. He already had a tall drink in one hand.

"My name's Jon. Without an aitch. I'm from Oklahoma, where the wind comes whistlin' down the plain."

Tamara hesitated, then said, "My name is Tamara."

"Wow! Sexy name. Where ya from?"

"I was born in Addis Ababa. Ethiopia."

"Wow!" he repeated. "Like out of the Arabian Nights."

Tamara sipped at her drink, thinking how ironic it was that she badly wanted some company but wanted even more badly to be rid of this lout. Scanning the crowd clustered thickly around the bar, her eyes smarting from their smoke, ears hurting from the noise of their so-called music, she desperately wished she were back in Paris. Or at Alphonsus, working for Dan. No matter what his reputation, he was civilized.

"Howdja like to take a little walk outside, see the Earth? It's real romantic."

"From inside a pressure suit?"

"Ever done it in a suit?"

Tamara put her unfinished drink down on the table. "Excuse me. I'm leaving."

"What? Ya just got here, didn't ya?"

She pushed through the crowd and the smoke and the noise, heading for the door.

"Just a minute, lady." Someone grasped her shoulder.

The man turned her around. It was not Jon from Oklahoma. This man had a lean face, like a weasel, and sallow skin. He did not look like one of the workers from the mass driver, and certainly not a miner. Too slick. And he wore a business suit instead of the coveralls that the workers wore.

"You're coming with me. We got things to talk about."

Without a word, Tamara snapped her arm upward, breaking his grip on her shoulder, while simultaneously driving a knee into his groin. The man grunted like a ruptured airlock and doubled over.

A couple of the men around the bar laughed. One of the women said, "That's it, honey, kick 'em where it hurts." Nobody else thought much of the brief encounter. Tamara pushed her way toward the door.

But now two burly grim-faced men in dark suits grabbed both her arms.

"That wasn't polite, Ms. Duchamps," said one.

"You made our friend look bad."

"What is this? Who are you?"

"Never mind. Come on along with us."

"No! I don't want to!"

She struggled but they began to drag her toward the door. The patrons of the bar watched; a couple of the men began to stir.

"Security police," announced the bigger of the two men dragging Tamara, who still struggled furiously to get free. "She's under arrest."

"The hell she is."

Another man stepped out of the crowd to stand grinning before them. Tamara recognized him: Dan Randolph.

"Now look, buddy," said the bigger of her two captors, "you could get hurt pretty bad sticking your nose into what's none of your business."

"Let go of her," Dan said calmly. "If you're security police, let's see some ID. And an arrest warrant."

The bigger man let go of Tamara's arm. Before he could take a step toward Dan, though, a *really* big man with the smooth-cheeked face of a child came up behind them and—grabbing them both by the backs of their necks—whacked their heads together with a resounding hollow thud that sounded like two billiard balls colliding at high speed. Down they both went, glassy eyes rolling back into their skulls.

The crowd cheered.

"Thanks, pal," said Dan to Big George. He offered his arm to Tamara. "Shall we leave this den of depravity?"

She saw the weasel lurching toward Dan. He spun around, warned by her glance, and smashed an overhand right into the weasel's chin. He fell forward, flat on his face.

"Such violence," he muttered, turning back to Tamara. Taking her arm in his own, Dan turned briefly back to the onlookers. "If anybody finds a security ID on any one of these clowns, tell them my name is Dan Randolph. That'll make their day."

And he marched grandly out of the Hundred Gees, Tamara on his arm, Big George following him.

* * *

"What are you doing here?" Tamara asked, once they returned to her quarters.

"Came to find you," said Dan, flexing the aching fingers of his right hand. At least he hadn't broken it.

Tamara's room was nothing more than a cramped compartment with a lavatory alcove in one of the buried shelters connected to the rest of the underground complex. Big George waited outside, guarding her door. Pops Tucker had remained at the bar, an inconspicuous little old gnome, to see what developed when the three goons came to.

"Nice place you've got here," Dan said sarcastically. "Kate really put you in Siberia, didn't she?"

Tamara felt suddenly weak-kneed. She sat on the edge of her bunk. Dan was already astride the room's only chair.

"Who were those goons, anyway?" Dan asked. "Are you in trouble?"

"Yes, I think I am," she said, surprised at how her voice fluttered.

"From Kate?"

"No. From—it sounds melodramatic to say it, but I think they're from the Mafia."

"The Mafia?"

"Some variation of it. An international syndicate of organized crime."

"On the Moon?"

"Why not? Who do you think you were doing business with when you were smuggling drugs into the city?"

TWENTY-NINE

Pops Tucker joined them at the cable-car terminal on their way back to the Yamagata Hotel. None of the three men who had accosted Tamara had security identification on them. The crowd at the bar threatened to put them into one of the catapult cargo containers if they ever showed their faces at the Hundred Gees again.

"Rough bunch," muttered Dan.

"They had a hopper waiting for them. They're on their way to the city," Tucker said. "Maybe they'll be waiting for us."

Dan shook his head. "No, they'll slink off to their boss, whoever it is, with their tails between their legs. They don't know we're staying at the hotel."

"How can you be at the hotel?" Tamara wondered. "Your photograph, your retinal prints—Kate has spread them all over Alphonsus and the other settlements, as well. How can you ride in this car without the security department recognizing you on the monitor cameras?"

They were alone in the cable car. This late at night,

hardly anyone traveled between the Nubium facilities and the city.

"Two safeguards," Dan said, grinning tightly. "One: my wrinkled old friend here has hacked into the security files and transferred the photograph and prints of a long-dead mining engineer for my own. So the dumb computer is looking for a dead man, not for me."

"But there are still people who might recognize you."

"That's where bribery comes in. Like the room clerk at the hotel when we checked in a couple nights ago. He knew something was slightly askew, but I tipped him enough to make him happy about it. Money talks, kid. It talks loudly. But when you want it to, it can whisper."

Despite his avowed confidence, Dan was edgy and hyper-alert when the cable car reached its terminal in the city. Hardly anyone in the underground corridors at this time of night. They took a powered walkway to the hotel and went immediately down to Dan's suite.

The sitting room was huge, ornately decorated with Oriental carpets flown in from Earth and furniture made on the Moon to resemble classic styles. One entire broad wall was a video window.

Jabbing a finger toward a closed door, Dan said to Tamara, "You can have the master bedroom. Pops and George are sharing the other bedroom. I'll sleep out here tonight."

Half an hour later Dan and Tamara were sitting on the couch that would convert into his bed. Tucker and George had retired to their own room. A pair of brandy snifters stood on the coffee table before the couch. The room lights were turned down almost all the way. The picture wall was showing a video scene of a crescent Earth glowing blue and white in the infinite black sky above Mare Nubium.

". . . so that's how Kate caught you, I'm sure," Tamara was saying. "She was tracking the logistics program, looking for where the steady leaks are."

"While I was getting people to smuggle propellant for

the hopper I snagged," Dan muttered. "I should've known better. Never leave a straight trail behind you."

"It was while Kate was searching the logistics files that I began to see how somebody was bleeding away five to ten percent of the company's assets. That's when I began to suspect that there were criminals burrowing into Astro's business."

"And you told Kate about it?" Dan asked.

She nodded solemnly. "That's when she transferred me out of her office, to the mass-driver complex."

"So she's in on it."

"She must be."

"And she wasn't satisfied just exiling you to the mass driver. Those goons were sent to shut you up permanently."

Tamara shuddered.

"Damn!" He smacked a fist into his open palm, making Tamara jump. "I thought it was Malik and his double-damned GEC bureaucracy. But it's an international syndicate of criminals that we're up against. Both of them."

"The crooks see the GEC's greenhouse project as an opportunity to steal on a global scale."

Dan shook his head. "It's more than that, kid. They've always been around, nibbling at the edges. Like a pack of rats, hiding in the dark, biting off what they can when you're not looking. We've had problems like that at Astro since I first got into business."

Tamara smiled at him. "For a while there you were one of the crooks."

"Yeah, I guess I was."

He got up from the couch and began pacing the big, plush room. "But now they're organizing on a global scale. They're not after just money anymore. They wouldn't have to organize globally for that. They could just continue operating the way they always have."

Tamara watched him striding, thinking out loud.

"No, they're after power now," said Dan. "This greenhouse project is giving them the opportunity to focus all their efforts. They want to take over the GEC. That's what they're after."

His eyes ablaze, Dan came back to the couch and sat beside Tamara once again. "That's what it's all about! They're letting Malik and the others on the Council turn the GEC into an effective worldwide dictatorship. Then they take over the GEC! They'll be running the whole double-damned world!"

"Do you really think so?"

"Hell yes! What do they care if half the world sinks beneath the waves? They'll control everything that's left."

"That's . . . frightening."

"There's plenty to be frightened of. Anybody who gets in their way is liable to be killed."

"Like me," she said, her voice small, hollow.

Dan nodded.

"I'm scared, Dan. They want to kill me."

Tamara pressed close to him, close enough for Dan to smell the scent in her hair, to see into the depths of her jet black eyes. She was trembling. So was he. She slid her arms around his neck and kissed him. Dan held her tightly, his mind spinning. His body reacted.

Lifting her up in his arms he walked across the big shadowy silent room, the glow of the distant Earth throwing highlights on her ebony hair, the classic curve of her high cheekbones, the sensuousness of her half-opened lips. Dan carried her into the bedroom and forgot about the world and all its cares.

In the morning he felt almost embarrassed. You took advantage of a scared kid, he accused his mirror image as he brushed his teeth. You saved her from a scary situation and then you carried her off to your bed like Gonzo the Caveman. Back to your old tricks.

But, hell, it *had* been a long time. And she was just as happy about it as I was.

Tamara was sitting demurely in the bed, sheet pulled to her chin, when he came out of the bathroom. Feeling unaccustomedly flustered, Dan padded to the closet where his two newly purchased suits were hanging in the otherwise empty expanse.

"You talk in your sleep, do you know that?" Tamara called to him while he hastily dressed.

"Not me. And I don't snore, either."

"You didn't snore. But you talked. Quite a lot."

Pulling on his slacks, Dan asked, "Anything intelligible?"

"Mostly mumbles," she said. "Only one name came through clearly enough to understand."

"One name?"

"Jane."

Dan felt the breath sink out of him.

"That would be Jane Scanwell, wouldn't it?"

He remembered the dream. It was about Jane, all right: angry with him and loving him all at the same time. A real jumble.

"Wouldn't it?" Tamara insisted.

He stepped out of the closet fully clothed in a sandy brown lightweight suit that he had bought at the hotel's men's shop for an outrageous price.

"Yeah," he admitted. "Jane Scanwell."

Tamara smiled at him. "I think you should marry the woman. You definitely are in love with her."

He made a sour face. "Thanks for the advice."

Tamara laughed and got out of bed, heading for the bathroom. Dan stood watching her lithe naked body until she shut the door. He shook his head. Women. How can a woman spend the night making love to you, parade herself naked in front of your feasting eyes, and at the same time tell you that you're in love with somebody else and you should marry her?

The trouble was, Dan knew, that she was entirely right.

* * *

Jane realized she was taking a chance. She had no certain way of knowing where Malik's loyalties stood. She wanted to believe that Vasily was exactly what he appeared to be: a hardworking member of the Council, a dedicated representative of the vast Russian Federation, a man intent on orchestrating this enormous global effort to save the world from the greenhouse cliff.

But he could be secretly working for Rafe. Or perhaps working with him, rather than for him. If that's the case, Jane knew, if he's on *their* side, then I'm stepping into a minefield.

Their meeting had to be away from the GEC offices. Jane knew that Malik's relationship with his wife was strained, at best. She hardly ever saw the two of them together, even at social functions. So she felt almost no qualms when she asked him to have dinner with her, alone. And she was not surprised when he swiftly agreed.

Now they sat at a table by the big picture window of Les Trois Anges, looking out over the Seine as evening spread its soft purple shadows over Paris.

Smiling over his aperitif at her, Malik said, "This is a very romantic restaurant, isn't it?"

Jane did not return his smile. "I picked it because it's away from the office. We're not likely to be disturbed here. Or overheard."

He cocked his head slightly. "Then this is strictly a business meeting?"

"Of course. What did you expect?"

"Nothing. Only business, naturally. Still . . ."

"Strictly business, Vasily."

"Of course."

Jane sipped at her drink while Malik looked out at the people sauntering along the street, couples sitting on benches along the river. It would be pleasant to walk with Lucita along the Seine, he thought. Or to sit on one of those benches and watch the Moon come up over Paris' rooftops. But Lucita's heart still belongs to Dan Randolph. Malik knew that, and it fueled his hatred for her—and him.

"Vasily," Jane said, pulling his attention back to her, "I think the Council is being undermined by organized crime."

His smile turned sardonic. "Not that again."

"Again?"

"Just because Gaetano's an Italian, half the Council thinks he's connected with the Mafia."

"He is," Jane said firmly. "He had a friend of mine murdered."

Sighing, "Yes, Rafe told me he thought you blame him for Robertson's death. He was eighty-some years old, wasn't he? A heart attack is not uncommon—"

"He was starting to investigate how organized crime is infiltrating our greenhouse project. They killed him."

"I'm sorry, Jane. I can't believe that. Not without some hard evidence."

She studied his face, trying to determine if he was being honest with her or covering up his own connection with Gaetano.

"If I bring you hard evidence," Jane asked, "what will you do?"

Malik's eyes flared. "I will do whatever needs to be done to wipe out the criminals. Our program to avert the greenhouse cliff is too important to allow a pack of hoodlums to get in our way."

He seemed honest enough about that, Jane thought. Now comes the hard part.

"Vasily—has it occurred to you that Gaetano and his kind want our project to succeed? That they want the GEC to take control of the global economy, because it will be easier for them that way?"

"I don't understand how—"

Jane hunched closer to him, leaning across the little table, and lowered her voice to a whisper. "Once the GEC is effectively running the entire world's economy, if the criminals have successfully infiltrated the Council, then *they* will be masters of the world."

She saw a flash of understanding cross his face. Then it hardened into an immobile mask. "So you think that I am merely a pawn for Gaetano to push about as he chooses?"

"I think that we are all running the danger of packaging the world with a big ribbon and handing it over to the international crime syndicate."

Malik was obviously angry, and obviously trying to control the rage he felt. "Very well," he said through gritted teeth. "I will keep a careful watch on Gaetano. If you have this hard evidence you mentioned a moment ago, I would like to see it."

Jane nodded slowly. "I'll get it for you."

"Rest assured that I have no intention of allowing criminals to take over the Council. I have decided to run for the chairmanship when Sibuti's term is over."

"But it's Europe's turn next."

"Do you want Gaetano in the chairman's seat?"

"No."

"Then we must break with tradition and force a vote, a true vote. Will you support me?"

"One hundred percent," said Jane.

"Good," Malik replied. "Now let's order something to eat."

To himself he added, And once chairman I will see to it that I remain in the post for the duration of this emergency. No one else has the guts to deal with this greenhouse problem, not even this former President of the United States.

THIRTY

"Not only does she suspect me," Gaetano was saying, his voice high with anger and fear, "but now she's got the Russian to oppose me in the vote for chairman!"

Marcello Arcangelico sat calmly in his powered wheelchair, his eyes following the furious pacing and wild gesticulations of his young henchman.

"Softly, Rafaelo. Softly. This isn't *Aida;* you don't have to bellow."

Gaetano stopped his raving and stared at his chief. In the sudden silence he could hear the faint chugging hum of the biomedical equipment built into the wheelchair that kept the old man alive.

"Come, sit down here. Beside me." Arcangelico patted the seat of the chair next to him.

They were in the old man's study, a dark and somehow menacing room lined with bookcases from floor to ceiling. The windows were covered with tasseled drapes, heavy with dust. Medieval suits of armor stood in the corners and on either side of the double sliding door, brandishing lances and battle-axes and spiked truncheons. Scant glimmers of sunlight leaked around the thick draperies; dust motes danced in their wan beams.

Don Marcello had parked his powered chair beside the heavy mahogany table in the center of the darkened, somber room. There were four chairs placed perfectly around the table, and a small lamp exactly in the middle of it, shining feebly, throwing the Don's face into wrinkled highlights and deep shadows.

Gaetano sat obediently on the proffered chair, complaining, "But the chairmanship was supposed to go to United Europe. To me. The rotation is traditional. It's unheard of for another Council member to contest the election! It's a slap in my face!"

Don Marcello shook his head sagely. "Let them have the title," he said, his voice wheezing slightly. "What do you care? Titles mean little. Power is what counts."

"What about respect?"

"The Council chair is an empty title. Some prestige, I know, and more responsibilities. But what additional power does it gain you? Very little."

"It should be mine, by right," Gaetano mumbled.

"Yes, I understand. But now I will show you how to gain more power than the chairmanship would give you. And respect, as well."

Gaetano leaned forward slightly, eager to hear.

Raising a trembling finger, Don Marcello said, "You will withdraw from the election."

"I will what?"

The old man coughed, then continued, "You will withdraw and allow the Russian to be elected unanimously. In the name of peace and harmony."

"But—"

"You will tell the other members of the Council that you agree with the Russian: in this time of extreme emergency the Council needs an experienced man at its head, not the youngest of their members."

"But Don Marcello!"

"Once you do that, they will all be indebted to you. They will be very grateful that you did not cause a rift in the Council's ranks. They will respect your willingness to step aside in the name of harmony and efficiency." The old man laughed wheezily. "They might even become convinced that you are not a Mafioso, after all!"

Reluctantly, feeling very downcast, Gaetano said, "I see. I understand."

He knew that Don Marcello's suggestion was a command. Give up the chairmanship. It would be a humiliation, a personal affront. But perhaps giving it up voluntarily would be better than being beaten in a vote. Still, Gaetano glowered in the shadows of the dusty old room. I am a member of the Global Economic Council, he told himself. I represent all of United Europe. Nearly three-quarters of a billion people. And I must accept this humiliation? I must grovel in the dust? Why? Why must I allow them to show such disrespect for me?

He knew why. Don Marcello had raised him to his present height and Don Marcello could push him down into oblivion, quite literally, whenever he chose to.

He looked down at the old man, sunken into his wheel-chair, his face half-hidden in shadows, his mind spinning intricate webs of power. How much longer can this ancient wreck of a man keep on living? Why don't I just reach over and turn off his batteries for a couple of minutes? No one would know. Then I could step into his place.

"Another thing," Don Marcello murmured, totally unaware of the younger man's murderous thoughts. "There will be a meeting soon, perhaps as early as next week. In the Cayman Islands. Top people from Japan, Latin America, the States, everywhere. You will represent me at this meeting."

Gaetano blanched. "I shouldn't be seen with such people!"

"You won't be seen. The meeting will be totally private. Not even the news satellites will notice it; we have taken steps to see to that."

"But still—"

"I want you to give them the complete layout of the GEC's program on the greenhouse. And I want them to vote for you to coordinate all our actions in this regard. That is an election I want you to win!"

Gaetano felt as if he were soaring up among the clouds. "Me? You want me to be the head?"

"Capo di tutti capi," Don Marcello said. Then he made that wheezing laugh again. "Except for me, of course. You can be boss of all the other bosses, but I am still your boss. Understand?"

"Yes. Of course. Thank you, Don Marcello." And he thought, You will be my boss for as long as you live.

For such a powerful office, the room looked small and indecently shabby. It was high in a skyscraper in midtown Manhattan, and if the windows had been clean they would have offered a fine view of the old Rockefeller Center and even a glimpse of Central Park's threadbare greenery.

But the four people in the office were focused entirely on their own problems. Two of them were reporters, a man and a woman, both in their early thirties, both aggressive, ambitious and angry. Josh Pollett was the wiry, high-strung type; he had wadded his suit jacket into a ball and flung it across the room an hour ago. Harriet McIntyre had shouted so much that her throat was sore and rasping.

The third person was the news network's president and CEO, sleek-looking with a beautifully groomed silver gray toupee and a hand-tailored silk suit that cost a month of the two reporters' pay, combined. Although the argument had been raging for more than an hour, neither of the reporters had said aloud what was commonly gossiped in the office hallways: that Wayne Manley had risen to his present post on the strength of his skin color rather than his abilities.

Sitting at the head of the wobbly steel table was the owner of the network and chairman of the corporation's board of directors. To her back she was called the Empress Theodora.

"But I've got corroboration!" Pollett was yelling. "I've got ten different sources all telling me the same story!"

"Leaks," muttered Manley, his eye on Theodora rather than his reporters. "Try to put them on the air and they'll clam up. Then they'll sue."

McIntyre, coolly blonde on camera, tried to cool things off here. "Let's all calm down a little and see where we stand."

"Fine idea," said Theodora. Even seated at the rickety table she looked tall, austere, regal.

"Okay," said Pollett. He sucked in a deep breath, then, glaring across the table at Manley, said, "There's a global catastrophe coming down. The greenhouse effect is going to hit with a vengeance. Sea levels up thirty feet. Killer storms all the time. Half the world flooded out."

Manley muttered, "Nonsense."

"I've got Zachary Freiberg's word for it," Pollett insisted. "He's a distinguished scientist from CalTech."

"He's not with CalTech," said Manley. "Hasn't been for ten years."

"He's a visiting professor there," countered Pollett. "He's also lectured at MIT, University of Texas, and half a dozen countries overseas."

"But he works for Dan Randolph, doesn't he?"

"Dan Randolph?" Theodora's eyes snapped. "I met him once. I wouldn't trust him as far as I could throw this building."

Harriet McIntyre wondered if Randolph had made a pass at her. Or failed to make a pass at her.

"Freiberg's top talent," Pollett was saying. "He says that this greenhouse will hit in ten years, maybe less."

"Absolute nonsense," Manley said.

"There's more," McIntyre interjected, throat rasping.

"Three months ago the GEC confiscated Astro Manufacturing. Just took it entirely away from Dan Randolph, for some little infraction of the rules."

"It must have been more than a little infraction," said Theodora.

"And the GEC has been quietly muscling every major corporation on Earth," McIntyre went on, "especially the Big Seven space companies."

"Over this make-believe greenhouse cliff?" Manley sniffed.

"Right," she croaked. "The GEC is trying to line up all the major corporations—especially those in energy and manufacturing—to follow some master plan that they're drawing up."

They went into another hour of fevered discussion, slightly calmer this time; at least there was no screaming. But when all the arguments were laid out on the table and the two reporters sat back exhausted, Manley still said:

"You don't have anyone who will admit to this greenhouse thing on camera. Not even Freiberg."

"He's being muzzled," said Pollett wearily.

"They're all being muzzled," McIntyre added.

Shaking his head again, Manley said, "We can't go on the air with rumor and innuendo. We'd get sued!" Turning to the Empress, "And our FCC license renewal comes up in eight months."

"But this is an important story!" Pollett pleaded. "It's vital! Millions of lives are at stake and the goddamned government's suppressing the story!"

"The GEC," McIntyre corrected gently.

"But Washington's going along with them." Pollett's voice sounded agonized.

"We've got to do *something*," McIntyre said.

All three of them turned to Theodora.

She sat there for a long moment like a true empress: calm, aloof, all-powerful.

Then, "What I am about to tell you is in strictest confidence. If you repeat it anywhere, to anyone, I will deny it totally and you will not only be fired but black-balled throughout the industry. Do you understand?"

They nodded dumbly.

"The greenhouse threat is real. The GEC is putting together a monumental effort to stop it from happening. I have been asked by the President himself to keep the lid on this story until the GEC is prepared to make it public. This network will cooperate with the GEC and the United States government in every way possible. Is that understood?"

More nods.

"Good. Then this is the last word any of us will utter on this subject until the GEC is ready to make its announcement."

"When will that be?" Pollett found the strength to ask.

"When they're ready." With that, the Empress got to her feet and headed regally for the door. Manley scrambled to catch up with her.

McIntyre stared at her colleague. Pollett was sweaty, his shirt a rumpled mess, his eyes bloodshot.

"Well," she said, "that's that."

"Maybe," he said tightly.

"Don't go off the deep end," she warned.

"Sure. We'll just sit here until the sea level reaches our floor, huh?"

Like similar facilities back on Earth, the Yamagata Hotel's gymnasium was called a "fitness center." It was filled with shining equipment, had thick, dark blue wall-to-wall carpeting, soft music piped in through the ceiling speakers, and air fresheners sprayed through the air to mask the stink of sweat.

Unlike similar hotel facilities on Earth, this lunar gym was almost always filled with men and women, even children, puffing, bending, lifting, grunting, pedaling away in grim determination. Anyone who stayed on the Moon for more than two weeks was not allowed to return Earthward until they had put in enough exercise hours to convince the authorities that their hearts were ready to face a full one g once again.

Dan pedaled on a stationary bike next to Tamara, knowing that he was in a race against time and chance. Sooner or later someone would recognize that Roger Wilcox was actually the wanted fugitive, Dan Randolph. Or one of the well-bribed hotel employees would turn him in for the reward that the GEC was offering. That must have been Kate's idea, putting a price on my head, he thought as he churned away at the bike. Ten thousand dollars. Damned piker. I'm worth a lot more than that. Hell, I've put out more than that in bribes already.

Across the gym, Big George was lifting enormous barbells, lying flat on a padded bench and hefting the tremendous weights like a cartoon-character strongman. It would take weeks before either George or Tucker could condition their bodies properly, after years of lunar living. Tucker, convinced that at his age he could never get back into good enough shape, had flatly refused even to come to the gym.

I don't have weeks, Dan knew. I'll have to leave them here when I head back to Earth.

He had ensconced Tamara in her own room at the hotel once Tucker had cranked out faked identification for her. The old man's a whiz with the computer. Dan realized that Tucker could make himself a multimillionaire with his talented fingers any time he wanted to. But he feared being caught again, and kept as low a profile as he could.

So Dan would head for Earth with Tamara. The Mafia couldn't threaten her if they didn't know where she was. Tamara Duchamps had already disappeared, as far as the security computer system was concerned. The exotic dark beauty pedaling alongside Roger Wilcox, her gym shorts revealing long smooth-skinned legs, was a tourist named Emelia Temple. From the Caribbean island of St. Croix.

The odometer on the bike's console beeped.

"Ten miles," Dan said. "I'm finished." He slid off the bike's seat, backside aching, sweat dripping everywhere except into his eyes, thanks to the headband he wore.

"I still have one-point-seven miles to go," said Tamara, hardly puffing.

"Dinner in my suite," he said.

She nodded and went back to the video she was watching on the bike console's built-in screen.

Tamara had slept in her own room since that first night they had shared, a week earlier. It's better that way, Dan told himself as he lingered in the gym's shower, letting the gloriously hot water sluice over his body. We shouldn't be complicating each other's lives; they're complicated enough as it is.

Besides, he admitted ruefully to himself, she's right. I love Jane. I've loved her damned near all my life. The thought made him grin. That's the way the world works, buddy: you can get just about any woman you want, but you want the one you can't get.

As he dried off and began to dress, his grin slowly evaporated. There's one woman you want, and she's right here, within reach. Kate. The treacherous Scarlett. She's in with Malik and it looks like she's in with the crime syndicate, too. There must be a helluva lot of valuable information stored in that pretty head of hers.

Tucker had tried to hack into Kate's private files, but unlike most of the Astro programs, Kate's were strongly protected with programs that would trigger alarms if anyone tried to access them without the proper code.

But I could access her, all right, Dan said to himself as he rode the lift up to his suite. I could grab that red-headed bitch in my two hands and access the hell out of her.

THIRTY-ONE

That evening, after dinner, after Tamara had gone back to her own room, Dan asked Big George to come with him. He did not say where until they were well out of the hotel, riding a powered walkway through the underground corridors that led to the Astro office complex.

"Kate Williams?" George was aghast. "The one who's running Astro now? Are you out of your fooking mind?"

"I've got to see her," Dan said grimly.

"You'll get us all caught and sent to the penal colony!"

"You can go back to the hotel if you want to."

"What good would that do? They catch you, they pump you full of babble juice, and then they catch us."

"I wish I had some truth serum with me right now."

George shook his smooth-cheeked face. Under Dan's orders he had faithfully shaved every morning, complaining loudly each time about the pain to his sensitive skin.

"Let me get this straight," George said as they rode past homebound Astro employees heading the other way. "You're going to go back to your office, say hello to her and ask her to spill her guts to you?"

"Something like that."

"You're fooking daft, my friend."

"She screwed me out of my company!" Dan blurted.

"And now you want to rape her? Is that it?"

"No!"

"Then what?"

"I want to—" He hesitated, groping for words. "I want to make her know that she hasn't finished me. I want to spit in her eye and tell her that I'm going to take back everything she's stolen from me. And I'll break her back in the process. Figuratively, not literally."

"And the thought of sticking it to her has never crossed your mind," George said.

"Well . . ."

"It's a fooking enormous risk, just to impress a woman."

Dan shrugged. The big kid is right, he knew. This is crazy. But I've got to do it. I can't leave the Moon without seeing the expression on her face when I tell her that I'm going to get even.

"You had a lot of women in your day, didn't you?" George asked.

Dan looked sideways at him. "In my day."

"I've only been with the ladies over at the camps on Nubium."

A sorry bunch, Dan knew. But he said, "In the dark, pal, all cats are gray."

"I've heard that," George said. "Is it really true?"

The big kid looked almost melancholy. Dan could not lie to him. "No, it's not, Georgie. Women are as various and marvelous as fine wines. You can spend your life tasting and still not be halfway through the list."

George brightened considerably. "Really?"

"There's hope for you, Georgie. Why don't you try smiling back at some of the women who watch you in the gym?"

"Oh, I don't think—"

"Try it. Break the ice. They'll come over and talk to you. You'll see."

They were coming to the end of the powered walkway. Beyond lay the corridors of the Astro complex. Glancing at his wristwatch, Dan saw that it was well past nine P.M. Most of the regular staff was gone, even the eager beavers who worked late. But if Kate's taken over my office, then she's probably living in my quarters as well. If she's not in one of them she'll be in the other.

Mad dogs and Englishmen, thought Zachary Freiberg as he jogged along the broad, flat Santa Monica beach in the noonday sun. The surf was down, but the public beach was busy with shapely young ladies in skimpy bikinis sunning themselves while muscular young men showed off for them, playing volleyball, hoisting weights, or just flexing well-oiled biceps. They'd better be well oiled with sunblock, Zach thought, or else the UV coming through what's left of the ozone layer will give 'em all skin cancer.

There was a lot of skin visible to worry about. Zach felt distinctly out of place, old and puffing and potbellied, in his sweat-stained running suit.

He had bolted from his office, unable to stand the pressure that was building up inside him. Invited to an international conference on the greenhouse effect being held at a hotel just minutes from his CalTech office, Zach had been refused permission to attend by the GEC bureaucrats who feared "a premature disclosure of the impending crisis that would cause widespread public panic and have a deleterious effect on the global economic balance."

I should have told them to shove it and gone to the conference anyway, Zach said to himself as he jogged along the beach. Yeah, and then they'd send you to Zaire or Patagonia or some other sweetheart of a location, you and Jessie and the kids too.

Premature disclosure. They'd better disclose some-thing soon. Time's ticking away and from what I can see all they're doing is holding conferences of their own and shuffling papers. And trying to keep the lid on the situa-tion.

He stared at the soft swells surging in toward the beach. Is it my imagination or is the beach narrower than it was last year? I ought to call the local parks department and have them make a measurement.

"Hey, Zach! Wait up!"

Surprised, Zach halted and turned to see who was calling him, one hand raised to his brow to shield his eyes.

He recognized Terry O'Doul loping across the sand toward him, suit jacket swinging from one hand, shoes in the other, shirt unbuttoned, a big grin on his lantern-jawed face.

"What on earth are you doing here?" Zach blurted as the lanky O'Doul caught up with him.

"Why the hell weren't you at the conference?" O'Doul shot back. "It was right around the corner from your office, for god's sake. You were invited, weren't you?"

Zach tried to keep the bitterness from showing. "I was too busy, Terry. Couldn't make it."

"Too busy—jogging?"

The hell of the GEC's security measures was that Zach was not allowed to tell anyone why he was not allowed to say anything.

"Come on." He pointed toward the refreshment stand up the beach. "I'll buy you a beer."

They talked about the conference, the papers deliv-ered, the people who were there, as they sat in the shade of the refreshment stand's awning. Neither of them drank much of their beer.

"Everybody was asking for you," O'Doul said. "Brud-noy was especially disappointed that you didn't show up."

"Couldn't be helped," Zach muttered.

"Why not?"

"I told you. I'm too busy."

"Doing what?"

Zach did not answer.

"Your work's related to the greenhouse, isn't it?" O'Doul probed, his eyes showing more curiosity than suspicion. "We all expected you to give us the latest on what the new landers have found on Venus."

Zach gave a single shake of his head and reached for his beer.

"What the hell is it, Zach? What's wrong? This is me, Terry, remember? We used to make up limericks about Brudnoy when we were in grad school, remember? You can tell me."

"No," Zach said. "I can't."

"Why not?"

He gulped at the beer, almost strangled on it. Sputtering, he managed to choke out, "Job security."

"I don't understand."

Zach coughed down the beer, cleared his throat. His old classmate was staring at him, alarmed, worried about him.

"Listen, Terry, you still go down to Antarctica every winter?"

"It's summer down there."

"To McMurdo?"

"Yes, most of the time. I make a trip to the station at the pole now and again."

"I shouldn't be telling you even this much," Zach said, lowering his voice. "But you'd better start drawing up plans for evacuating those bases."

"Evacuate? McMurdo?"

"All the Antarctic bases."

"But why?"

Zach flicked a glance at the youngster running the refreshment stand. He was at the other end of the stand, chatting with a couple of bikini-clad teenagers.

"Because all the bases in Antarctica are sitting on top

of a mile-thick sheet of ice."

"So?"

"So the ice isn't going to be there."

"What?"

"It's going to melt down, Terry. It's probably started melting already."

O'Doul's expression went from incredulous to thoughtful. "Well, the Ross shelf has thinned noticeably, but that's just a long-term climate swing. The ice will thicken up again with the next sunspot cycle."

Zach said nothing.

"Won't it?"

"Be prepared to evacuate. Just in case the ice keeps on melting regardless of the sunspot cycle."

"What are you trying to tell me?" O'Doul asked.

Zach got down from his stool. "I've already told you too much. Got to get back to the office now. It was good to see you, Terry. Don't tell anybody you saw me, okay?"

He started trotting to the parking lot where he had left his car, leaving O'Doul standing there scratching his head.

"But you haven't even been here two weeks!" Kate Williams said, nearly shouting.

Kimberly slumped in one of the chairs in front of Kate's desk. "There's nothing to do here. It's a bore."

"Nothing to do? What about flying in the big dome, or low-g acrobatics? There's—"

"It's a bore!" Kimberly snapped. "Everybody up here is boring. A bunch of Japanese who stick to themselves and some Americans who're mostly engineer nerds. I don't need this! I want to go back."

Kate held her breath, trying to make herself as calm as possible before replying to her sister. In just two weeks Kim had gained a healthy bit of weight, gotten some color in her cheeks. Good diet and regular exercise under the carefully metered full-spectrum lamps in the gym had done more for her than months in the rehab clinic.

"You can't go back," Kate said, keeping her voice soft and even. "There's no one back on Earth for you to go to, unless you want to return to the clinic."

Kimberly gave her a self-satisfied smile. "Rafe invited me to visit him in Italy."

Kate felt her jaw drop open. The breath gushed out of her so hard she could not answer.

"I'll be staying with his family, so it'll be okay. They have a beautiful place down below Naples. He's shown me pictures on the phone and he even sent me a set of holograms. It's a gorgeous estate—"

"Absolutely not!" Kate nearly screamed. "You're not going to see him!"

Kim's smile turned nasty. "Have I taken your boyfriend away from you?"

"I forbid it! You're not leaving this city."

"Hey, you don't own me!"

"Oh no? Where did you think you were going to get the fare?"

"Rafe will send it."

"The hell he will! I'll impound it. You're still a minor, legally."

Kimberly's tawny eyes flashed with anger. "Then I'll raise the money myself."

"And how are you going to do that? What kind of job do you think you can get up here?"

"Same as anywhere."

"Get out!" Kate screamed. "Get out of here, you little whore!"

Smirking, Kim got to her feet and started for the door.

"You're confined to your room," Kate called after her. "I'm going to instruct security that you're not to be allowed out and no one but me is allowed in. You'll sit in there until I can talk some sense into you."

"You're just jealous," Kim said, without a trace of anger. She was almost smiling as she spoke. "I thought you were finished with Rafe. Well, anyway, he's finished with you now."

She left, closing the door gently behind her.

Kate sank her head in her hands. Kimberly. Kimberly. That bastard Rafe is just using you to keep his power over me. I've got to explain that to her, tell her the whole story. Will she believe me? Probably not. Can I keep her here, keep her from running back to Earth and into Rafe's arms?

She sat up straighter in her desk chair. I'll keep Kimberly here, no matter what it takes. If I have to break both her legs I'll keep her out of that bastard's clutches. No matter what. No matter what.

She called security and explained that she wanted her sister confined to her room. The woman on the phone screen promised to send a robot to Kimberly's door.

Then Kate leaned back in her chair and lowered the room's lights. For long hours she reclined there, letting the chair's softly yielding surface soothe her, relax her. She drifted into a light, troubled sleep.

And awoke when she sensed someone stepping into the office.

Blinking her gummy eyes, she saw the figure of a man standing before the desk. In the shadowy light she could not quite make out his face, but she knew who it was anyway.

"Hello, Dan. I was wondering when you'd show up."

THIRTY-TWO

Sitting at my desk drowsing, Dan saw. A line from Hamlet came to his mind: "Now might I do it pat."

Kate stirred, eyes fluttering. "Hello, Dan. I was wondering when you'd show up."

As she rubbed the sleep from her eyes, he came around the desk. Resisting an urge to grab her and yank her out of *his* chair, Dan made himself sit on the corner of the desk. He folded his hands in his lap.

"Couldn't leave without saying good-bye, Scarlett."

"You're leaving?"

He nodded solemnly. "Going back to Earth."

"Then coming here was a pretty silly thing to do," Kate said.

"I know."

"But you couldn't leave without coming to see me," she said, looking up at him. Kate laughed softly. "I knew it. My security people went apeshit after you escaped. But once you registered at the hotel—"

"You knew about that?"

"That little old man you've got with you is pretty good at hacking into computers, but we've got the real experts."

Dan marveled at the news. "You knew and you didn't do anything?"

"I wanted to see what 'Mr. Wilcox' was up to. I didn't have to send anybody out searching for you. I figured you'd come here, sooner or later. You couldn't stay away, could you?"

"No, I guess I couldn't."

Leaning further back in the chair, Kate put her feet on the desk. Dan saw that she was wearing softboots, and the clinging fabric of her slacks outlined her calves and thighs tantalizingly.

"So what happens now?" Kate asked. "You going to tear my clothes off and rape me?"

Dan grinned down at her. "I imagine your security people are already watching us, aren't they? How much of a show do you want to give them?"

"We're not being watched. Oh, the office is locked tight now. One-way locks. I had them installed right after your friends sprang you. You can't get out until I call security to come in and open the door from the other side."

"That's cozy."

"We're not bugged, either. I have my own people go over this office twice a day."

Curious, he asked, "Who would bug you?"

She laughed again; Dan thought it sounded bitter. "Lots of people bug me, Dan. Lots of them."

"Like me?"

"You? You're the least of my worries."

That stung. "Then who?"

She straightened up in the chair, planted her feet firmly on the carpeted floor. "Do you know a GEC Councilman named Gaetano? Rafaelo Gaetano?"

"The representative from United Europe."

"From the Mafia, you mean."

Dan felt his eyebrows hike up.

Kate nodded. "That's what I said. The Mafia. They've got their hooks into this global conversion program, and they plan to take charge of the whole operation."

"How do you know?"

"Because I've been working for them, how else? Gaetano has a hold on me and he's forced me to let them infiltrate Astro."

"So I heard."

"From who?"

"Never mind."

"The Duchamps woman? I transferred her out of here so she'd be out of Gaetano's way."

"Somebody tried to kill her."

"Jesus Christ! Murder?"

"Why not? They're good at it. Centuries of experience."

"This is getting too heavy."

Feeling a different sort of anger heating his blood, Dan jabbed an accusing finger at her. "You think that milking the conversion program isn't going to kill people? By the millions? What the hell do they care, as long as they come out on top."

Kate nodded grimly. "I suppose that's right."

"And Malik's in with them, I bet."

"I don't think so," she said. "Oh, sure, Malik's efforts to get all the major industries under GEC control is making it easy for the crime syndicate to move in."

"Yeah," Dan said disgustedly. "Malik ties up everybody hand and foot and the crooks come in and pick their pockets."

"Something like that."

"So how do you like working for Gaetano and his family?"

"I'd like to kill him," said Kate.

Dan cocked his head at her. "That shouldn't be too tough for you to do. You're sleeping with him, right?"

"I can't."

"Don't like the sight of blood?"

"I told you, he's got a hold on me. My sister. If I kill him, I'm certain they'll send somebody to kill her. And then me."

Her eyes strayed to a framed photograph on the desk. In the dim lighting, Dan could make out a young woman's face, long hair billowing, a strong resemblance to Kate.

"So you want me to do your wet work."

"You don't have to kill him," Kate said. "Just expose him. Him and his whole rotten scheme. The law will do the rest."

"The same law that screwed me out of my company?"

Kate got to her feet and stood eye to eye with Dan. "That's right. The same law."

He grinned at her righteous anger. "Why should I help you?"

"I thought you wanted to save the world."

"Looks like the world doesn't really want to be saved. And I've got my own neck to worry about, thanks to you. And Malik."

Kate studied his face in the low, shadowy lighting for a long moment. Then she turned away and stepped to the farther corner of the desk.

"You really don't have much of an option, Dan. You *are* a wanted fugitive. All I have to do is call out for security and they'll burst in here and arrest you."

His grin widened. "And all I have to do is agree to get Gaetano for you and you'll let me waltz out of here?"

"That's my offer. Take it or leave it."

"You'd trust me once I'm back on Earth, out of your control?"

"I know you, Dan Randolph. More than anything else you want to get even with Malik. Destroying Gaetano will go a long way toward toppling Malik, as well. You can see that."

"Maybe."

"And beyond that, you really do want to save the

world from this greenhouse disaster, don't you?"

"Maybe," he repeated, more softly.

"So?"

"So if I go after Gaetano, won't that still be dangerous for you? And your sister?"

Kate shook her head. "They'll see the great Dan Randolph attacking them. They won't even think about me."

"I could get myself killed."

"You've got nine lives," Kate said, almost sneering.

"Maybe I did once," he muttered. "I've got a feeling that a lot of them have been used up."

She put both her hands flat on the desktop, leaning forward slightly. "That's the deal, Dan. I'll supply you with all the data you need. You nail Gaetano for me."

"Or else?"

"Or else I call security and we send you to Malik with an airtight guard around you."

"Hmm."

"And we sweep up all your friends, as well. The big Australian and your old computer hacker and all the other illegals who're hiding around Alphonsus."

"You make a strong case for yourself, Scarlett."

She did not smile. "Well?"

"There's something I want," said Dan.

"You're in no position to bargain."

Ignoring that, he replied, "I want Tamara Duchamps protected. She's got nothing to do with this game, there's no reason for her to get hurt."

"She knows enough for them to want to eliminate her."

"I want your absolute guarantee of her safety," Dan insisted. "Otherwise no deal."

"I can't give guarantees, Dan."

"You keep her here under your personal keen eye, Scarlett. Protect her the way you'd protect your sister. You can do that much."

She thought a moment. "Dan, I could agree to that. But it'd be a lie. I can't protect her. I don't even know if

I can protect my sister and myself. Do you think I'd be asking you for your help if I felt safe here?"

It was Dan's turn to be silent, thinking. She's telling the truth, he realized. She's scared and she knows she can't protect Tamara now that the goons are after her.

"Okay," he said. "I'll take the kid with me. But I want your promise that you'll leave those other people alone. They're not hurting you. They're no threat to anybody."

"The illegals?" Kate made a disdainful little huff. "They can stay. It'd be more trouble to round them up than it's worth."

"Deal?" he asked.

She let a smile curve her lips. "Deal."

Dan put out his hand. Reaching across the length of the desk, Kate extended hers. They shook hands briefly. But Dan did not let go of her.

"One more thing," he said. "I'm curious. If I had ever made a serious move on you, how would you have reacted?"

Kate pulled her hand free. "You're a hopeless chauvinist to the bitter end, aren't you? I'm not a person to you, I'm a goddamned set of sex organs!"

Dan raised both hands in mock surrender. "Just asking!" He backed away from the desk, then added, "Didn't you ever even think about it?"

"Hardly ever," Kate snapped.

"Hardly ever?"

"Security code four-eight-four!" she called out.

The phone responded, "Doors unlocked."

"Now get the hell out of here," Kate said, "before I change my mind and call a live team to arrest you."

"Okay," said Dan. "But I'll need the data you told me about."

"I'll send it to Wilcox's suite at the hotel."

"And you'll leave the illegals alone?"

"Yes," she snapped.

"That's a promise, now."

"You have my word," said Kate.

Dan nodded, thinking to himself, Not as solid as a written contract but it'll have to do.

Jane Scanwell felt utterly weary as she stepped from the limousine and went to the front door of her apartment building. The chauffeur waited, standing almost at attention beside the limo, until the electronic lock clicked and the ornate iron-grilled door swung open.

I wonder if limousines can be converted to electric motors, Jane mused idly as the lift carried her to her floor. The only electric cars I've ever seen are so little. It will be ironic if we have to give up some of our luxuries. But it might help in the public relations aspect of the program—if we ever get to the point where we reveal the program to the public.

She almost missed the note that had been slipped under the door. It was in a small off-white envelope, lying on the parqueted floor of the entry.

Frowning, she bent down and picked up the envelope. No return address. No writing on it at all. She put her purse down on the table beneath the mirror and opened the envelope. It was not even sealed.

ALIVE AND WELL AND LIVING IN PARIS. MEET ME AT THE TOP OF THE EIFFEL TOWER TO-MORROW AT HIGH NOON. YOU KNOW WHO.

Dan! Suddenly Jane's knees went weak and she sagged against the little table for support.

Dan. He's alive and well and in Paris. She struggled for a moment to regain her breath. The fool! The stupid, arrogant wonderful fool. In Paris. He's not dead. He's here and he wants to see me.

She thought she would be unable to sleep, but Jane drifted off easily that night, her dreams filled with images of Dan and Morgan and Vasily Malik, all jumbled together. The next morning, dressed in a skirted suit of deep burgundy over a soft pink tailored blouse, she could hardly keep still in the office.

You're behaving like a silly schoolgirl, she berated herself. Yes, a voice in her mind answered. Isn't it marvelous?

Jane did not even notice the drizzling rain until she went down to the porte cochere. The uniformed guard asked if she wanted a limousine called up.

"No, thank you," said Jane, thinking that the limo drivers were GEC employees and kept records of who went where. "A taxi, please."

Taxi companies kept records, too, so Jane told the driver to take her to the old Hilton Hotel. It had been bought and sold a dozen times in the past few decades, but still the taxi drivers knew it as the Hilton.

Instead of going to the hotel's restaurant, Jane went to the clothing store in the lobby and purchased an umbrella for an extravagant price. Then she walked in the chill drizzle the few blocks to the Eiffel Tower. Hardly anyone was there in the gray misty weather. She rode the elevator to the top with a young Oriental couple who seemed to be honeymooners, smiling at each other, oblivious of the weather and of the city spreading around them as the elevator rose higher and higher.

The wind was so strong up at the top that Jane feared her umbrella would be torn from her grasp if she opened it. So she hovered in the scant shelter offered by the elevator tube. Where's Dan? she wondered, glancing at her wristwatch. It was quarter past noon.

"Late, as usual."

She spun around and he was standing before her, plastic rain hat pulled low over his face, trench-coat collar turned up, grinning like a teenager.

Jane flung her arms around his neck and they kissed until even the honeymooners noticed.

"I thought you were dead," she said when they separated slightly.

"I thought you wouldn't give a damn."

"Oh, Dan, let's stop fighting. No matter what's happened in the past, no matter what's going to happen in the future, I love you. I can't fight it any more. I love you."

"And I've loved you ever since I first met you, Jane. All these years I've tried to hide it, even from myself. But I love you. You're the only woman I've ever loved."

Over lunch at the tower's restaurant Jane brought him up to date on the GEC's plans and politics. And the Mafia's interference. And Jeff Robertson's murder.

"So Rafe has actually declined the Council chair, leaving the way clear for Vasily to be elected," she was saying.

Dan frowned at the news. "That means that Malik's in with them."

"I've been wondering about that. I don't think he's working for the crime syndicate, but—"

"They wouldn't let him take the chair away from their own man if he wasn't."

"Maybe he doesn't realize it?"

"My left foot! He's in with the bastards all right. He's working hand-in-glove with the people who murdered Jeff Robertson."

Jane stared at him across their little table. "What can we do?"

Dan grinned at her. "Same thing that the Founding Fathers did when they were writing the Constitution: trust the people."

"What do you mean?"

"We're going public, Jane. With the whole sorry tale. It's the only way to smoke these snakes out from under their rocks."

"You mean you want to tell the public about the greenhouse cliff! Dan, you can't!"

"We've got to. The longer this program stays in the dark, the longer the crooks have to worm their way in. And the longer Malik has to set himself up as global dictator."

She shook her head warily.

Reaching into his jacket pocket, Dan took out a holo cube. Holding it between his thumb and forefinger, he said, "There's enough data here to blow Gaetano out of the water. But what good is it if the people you give it to are working for the sonofabitch? All it'll do is get you killed."

"But Dan, if you reveal the news about the greenhouse to the public, people will panic. The consequences could be disastrous!"

"You don't think they'll panic once the GEC does release the news?"

"Vasily is working out plans to orchestrate the information."

"Leak it out slowly. A drip at a time, like the Chinese water torture."

Obviously displeased with his words, Jane replied, "Isn't that better than throwing everybody headfirst into the deep end of the pool?"

"No," said Dan firmly. "This is literally a sink or swim situation, Jane darling. We've got to throw a strong light on it. Now."

"You're mixing metaphors," she muttered.

"But my heart is pure."

"I can't agree with you about this."

"That's okay," he said cheerfully. "All I need is to know that you'll be on the right side when the shit hits the fan. I'll do the rest without implicating you."

"You're going to disappear again?"

"For a little while. I've got to."

"I had thought . . ." Her voice trailed off.

"Thought what?"

"Can't we just chuck the whole business and go off by ourselves? Nobody's going to be able to solve all the world's problems, Dan. Not you, not me, not all of us together. We've slaved at it all our lives and what has it gotten us except heartache? Can't we just run away and live the rest of our lives in peace and be happy together?"

"I'm a fugitive from justice, remember?"

"I can fix that. You wouldn't even have to face a trial if I testified that I went to Alphonsus with you willingly."

He leaned back in his chair and studied her. "Where would we go, Jane? Tetiaroa? It'll be underwater in a few more years. Geneva? What'll the Swiss do when the snow on the Alps melts down and floods their valleys? Rome? New York? Where?"

For long moments Jane said nothing. She sat like a living statue, auburn hair perfectly coiffed, green eyes staring at Dan. Beyond her the restaurant windows showed that the drizzle had turned into a hard slanting rain. The sky, the city beneath, the whole world seemed gray and cold.

"You're right," she said, in a voice so low Dan could barely hear her, even though the restaurant was nearly empty and very quiet.

Dan sighed. "For years I've said that when the going gets tough, the tough get going to where the going's easier. But there's no place to go, Janie. This is one fight we can't avoid."

She nodded reluctantly. "It's just—I thought it would be so good if we could be together."

"We will be." He reached across the table and took her hand. "We'll be together, Jane. There's nothing in the world I want more. We'll be together—come hell or high water."

Her eyes went wide. Then she burst into laughter. "You certainly know how to choose your words!"

He laughed too, thinking how good it was to see her happy, even if it was only for a moment.

It's a myth that sea level is the same everywhere around the world, thought Amory Magee. Bending over his tabletop display, its light throwing weird shadows across his angular face, he saw the world's oceans and seas as a living, breathing creature in constant motion, flexing, reaching, writhing with currents.

Gaea is the wrong name for this planet of ours, he
thought as the display showed him the shifting patterns
of ocean currents all around the world. The computer
display was created from the sensors of three geostationary satellites, continuously and simultaneously. Ours is
an ocean world. Poseidon is a better namesake than any
earth goddess.

Magee was a solitary man, acknowledged by those in
the Oceanographic Institute who had to work with him
as a genius, but a prickly one.

"Sea level," he muttered to himself, pushing his large,
owlish eyeglasses back into place. They kept slipping
down his thin, sharp nose when he bent over the display
table. "No such thing as sea level, not really. The
Pacific's higher than the Atlantic, most places. Of course
it's much bigger. And the Arctic could get itself trapped
behind the Bering Shelf, it's been so low in the past.
Probably triggered the Ice Age that way."

He often talked to himself, alone in his laboratory. No
one contradicted him. He liked that.

His eyes focused on the Gulf of Mexico. "Now, there's
a perfect example of what I mean. Trade winds blow the
length of the Atlantic and pile the water up in the Gulf
until it's considerably higher than the ocean itself. That's
what generates the Gulf Stream, of course."

Sea levels were rising, and much faster than anyone
had anticipated. Magee had faithfully sent his reports to
his superiors at the Institute. What they did with them he
neither knew nor cared. His interest was in how the
oceans were working, how Poseidon was behaving himself. Once in a while he thought idly that, at the rate the
sea was rising, they would have to abandon these buildings. The idea of moving filled him with such anxiety,
though, that he usually pushed those thoughts out of his
conscious mind as soon as they arose.

He flicked his fingers across the remote keyboard he
held in his hand and data points appeared on the display.
Earthquake predictions from the people over in Califor-

nia. Most people thought that earthquakes on the sea-floor were nothing to worry about. Magee knew better. His favorite reading was firsthand accounts by the survivors of tsunamis. He enjoyed picturing the wall of water that could sweep miles inland, crushing and drowning everything in its path. "Serves them all right," he groused. "Poseidon is nobody to take lightly."

A new earthquake prediction had appeared since the last time he surveyed the display. "Somebody's calling for a quake in the Gulf of Mexico," he saw, surprised. "That's unusual." Tapping on the hand-held, he saw that the prediction called for a deep temblor, Richter scale seven or higher. "Big one!"

Working his remote control again, he saw that under the right circumstances a considerable tsunami could spread from the locus of the seafloor quake. "Florida?" he asked, pecking at the keys. But the tidal wave petered out before it could swamp Florida's west coast.

"That's good, I suppose," he muttered, feeling slightly disappointed. "Florida's already got enough problems with the sea-level rise. Lots of expensive condominiums are being emptied out, I hear."

The seafloor contours might guide the tsunami onto the Texas-Louisiana coast, he realized. "New Orleans is going to be hard hit if these numbers are right."

He tapped one more key and the display showed the time-frame estimate. Within one year. Magee whistled to himself. "Accuracy?" The numbers said plus or minus twelve months.

Magee blinked at the numbers. "That means it could happen any day now," he said to himself. Shaking his head, he added, "I wouldn't want to be in New Orleans when Poseidon comes calling. Hope somebody's put out a warning to them."

As they stepped out of the Eiffel Tower elevator into the driving gray rain, Jane popped her umbrella open. The wind nearly pulled it out of her hands. Dan reached for it and helped her steady it.

"Where are you staying?" she asked.

"It's better if you don't know."

"In Paris?"

"For the time being."

She looked out across the rain-swept park. "I'll have to get a cab."

"You'll never get one around here. I'll walk with you to the Hilton."

"Are you sure that's a good idea?"

"As long as you have the umbrella, yes."

The only other people out on the streets seemed to be a few Japanese tourists, looking wet and bedraggled and miserably unhappy.

"Jane, can you set up a meeting with Nobo for me?"

"Nobuhiko Yamagata?"

"Right. We had a kind of stupid argument the last time we were together. At his father's freezing. He got pretty sore at me and—"

"He's not angry anymore. I think he'd like to see you."

"Good," said Dan. "We could use his help."

"We certainly could."

They parted at the Hilton, Jane waiting in the lobby while the doorman phoned for a taxi, Dan striding off through the rain toward the apartment he had taken, hat pulled low and shoulders hunched against the rain. They did not kiss good-bye. Not at the hotel. Too many people might have seen them.

I've got to protect her, too, Dan thought, squinting into the chill rain. She may have a GEC bodyguard, but I'll bet Gaetano's put himself in charge of security for the whole board. That'd be just their style of operation. Still, he grinned his widest grin as he walked splashing through the puddles on the sidewalks. She loves me. She really loves me. He wished he could sing and dance through the storm like that what's-his-name in that old video. He wished he could feel like a kid again, so blitzed by the thought that Jane loved him that nothing else mattered.

But he knew better. He had the world on his shoulders. Now Jane's safety was an added problem. Big George and Tamara were waiting for him at the apartment. The four of us against the world, with Malik and Gaetano and the whole double-damned international crime syndicate against us.

His grin vanished. I forgot to tell Jane about Tamara. Better remember to do it next time we meet. Got to make certain she doesn't get the wrong idea about the kid. That could screw up everything.

THIRTY-THREE

Once on Earth, Dan had tapped into one of the funds he had established in Liechtenstein, at the same bank into which he had deposited the money that he, Big George and Pops Tucker had made on the Moon. The lunar account was a pittance compared to that of Mason Dickson, Dan's alias.

Roger Wilcox had disappeared; Mason Dickson had sprung to life out of the computer files of the International Bank of Liechtenstein, a charming miniature nation nestled in the Alps between Switzerland and Austria, where sleekly smiling bankers spoke in whispers and accepted deposits with few questions and low taxes. Like stoutly independent Switzerland, Liechtenstein had not formally joined the Global Economic Council. The only other nation on Earth that had similarly remained aloof was Afghanistan.

Big George had accompanied Dan and Tamara to Earth. Pops Tucker remained on the Moon, too physically debilitated to face full terrestrial gravity without a long and rigorous course of rehabilitation, which he adamantly refused even to consider.

"Besides," the wizened old man had argued, patting his tabletop computer, "I can keep an eye on your Williams woman for you."

Dan had reluctantly agreed. Big George told him, "He's living the way he wants to. Fooking old kook's been an outlaw for so long he wouldn't know how to behave in normal society."

Dan nodded, but remembered Tucker's bitter anger at being unable to see his grandchildren. Which one is the real Pops Tucker? Dan asked himself. The nasty old man who won't stir himself to get back into shape, or the sad old guy who's never seen his grandchildren?

But he put those thoughts behind him as he drove a rented car through a slashing rainstorm that was flooding the streets of Geneva. Every time I see Jane it seems to be raining, he said to himself. The car radio was babbling about the unusual warm spell, the unseasonably heavy storm and the rising level of the lake. The water was hubcaps deep in several places; the police had cordoned off several streets altogether.

Wait till the glaciers start melting down, Dan thought grimly. They'll have to borrow gondolas from Venice. If there's anything left of Venice.

The Bank of Geneva was hushed and imposing. Marble floors, vaulted ribbed ceiling, the smell of heavy money oozing out of the walls. The guard at the security desk was expecting Mason Dickson; Dan was escorted to a private conference room on an upper floor.

Dan opened the door as the guard stood a respectful distance away. Jane was already there, her back to the door, staring out at the merciless rain. Nobo sat beside her, looking glum.

They both turned at the click of the door's closing. Jane's smile warmed the room. Nobo jumped to his feet, a slightly sheepish expression on his lean face.

He came to Dan with his hand extended. "It's good to see you again."

Dan grabbed his hand. "You too, Nobo. I'm sorry about the blowup the last time we talked."

"It was my fault."

"Mine, just as much. I could've been more flexible."

"So could I."

Jane had swiveled her chair around to face the round table that dominated the small room. "Don't start another argument apologizing about the old one," she said.

Nobo laughed and Dan clapped him on the back and the argument was forgotten. Almost. Dan could not help thinking that the whole issue was moot now: he couldn't adjust Astro's helium-three output even if he wanted to. He no longer had control over the company.

As soon as the two men had seated themselves, one on either side of Jane, Nobuhiko said, "Dan, I want you to come back to my family home with me. You'll be safe in Kyoto."

Dan shook his head. "Thanks for the offer, but I'm still a wanted man, a fugitive from the GEC's brand of justice. You don't want to put yourself in jeopardy over me."

"You are my friend and you are in danger," Nobo said. "I can protect you until Jane straightens out your legal difficulties."

"You don't understand, Nobo. My legal difficulties don't amount to a thimbleful of buckeyballs compared to this greenhouse crisis."

"That's in the hands of the GEC," said Jane.

"Which means it's in the hands of the double-damned Mafia and their associates around the world."

"If you fear for Jane's safety, I have a very discreet security team guarding her night and day."

"You do?" Jane yelped.

Nobo made a small nod. "Ever since you spoke to me about your fears and Mr. Robertson's murder."

"Look," Dan said, "I've got enough data from Kate

Williams to blow Gaetano out of the water, but I don't know who to give it to."

"The GEC has tied up most of the world's media, Dan," said Jane. "I've checked. Most of the member nations have imposed their official censorship laws. In the States, the major media have privately agreed to go along with the GEC's blackout on the greenhouse crisis—at least for now."

"Will they take the material I've got about the Mafia infiltrating Astro? And their plans for all the major industries?"

"From a criminal, a man wanted for kidnapping, terrorism, drug dealing, smuggling and grand larceny?"

Dan grinned at her. "Lord, that sounds damned impressive, doesn't it?"

"It's not funny, Dan."

"There are always outlets for hot news," Dan said. "The TV tabloids, the smaller news outfits."

"Then it won't be news, it will be gossip. Put your Mafia story alongside stories about three-headed babies being born on Mars and what have you got? No one will pay any attention."

"Yeah," Dan admitted grudgingly. "Nobody except the hit men."

Nobo suggested, "You could give Dan's information to the media, Jane. You are a very prestigious person. Your integrity is unquestioned."

She gave a little shrug of her shoulders. "The first thing they would ask would be where I got the information, what's my source. That would lead right back to Dan—"

"How about an anonymous leak in the Astro office?"

"And who would that be?"

"A beautiful half-Ethiopian young woman who'd be a knockout on video."

Jane's eyes narrowed. Nobuhiko asked, "Wouldn't that expose her to danger?"

"They've already tried to kill her."

"Where is she? At Alphonsus?"

"I've brought her here. She's staying with me."

"A beautiful young woman," Jane said thinly.

Dan raised both hands over his head. "There's nothing going on between us. I'm just trying to protect her."

Jane looked totally dubious.

"Honest," said Dan, trying to look sincere.

"If she is in such danger," Nobo said, "then she must come with you to Kyoto."

"She should," Dan agreed. "But I'm not going with you, Nobo."

Nobuhiko shot him a questioning look.

"I'm going to be doing some highly illegal things, friends. I've thought it all out and it seems to be the only way to crack this nut open."

"What do you mean?"

"What are you talking about?"

Dan took a deep breath. Then, "Jane, you can go to the American news media with my information and give them Tamara as your source. That's even the truth, almost."

"And I can keep her under my protection in Kyoto," said Nobo.

"Yeah, but I'm not sure that the media will take the story, even with Jane promoting it to them."

"They'd have to!" Jane snapped.

Dan made a lopsided grin. "Jane, honey, you've been in politics all your life. You know that the First Amendment guarantees the media the right to broadcast anything they choose to. But it doesn't guarantee that they have to broadcast something they don't want to."

"They'd take this story!" Jane insisted. "One of them would and then the others would have to follow suit."

"Suppose Malik threatens a court injunction? Or the current U.S. President leans on the media executives to bury the story? He's no friend of yours, that imbecile in the White House."

"I'll get the story aired," Jane said firmly.

"And I'll help you," said Dan.

"How?"

"My way."

She's gone. Kate Williams lay sleepless on her bed, wondering where her sister was, fearing that she knew.

With Rafe. Somewhere down on Earth she's letting that bastard do whatever he wants to her as long as he feeds her whatever crap she's turned on to now.

She gripped the sheets so hard that her fingernails cut into her palms painfully. *And I can't do a thing about it! Not a goddamned motherfucking thing! How could she get away from Alphonsus? How could she even get out of her goddamned room without my permission? This whole place is honeycombed with Rafe's people. I thought I was running Astro, but he is, like a puppeteer from a quarter of a million miles away. He's stolen my sister and now he knows he can make me jump through any hoop he wants just as long as he promises not to hurt her any more.*

I'll kill him! she screamed silently for the thousandth time. *If he ever comes within arm's reach of me again I'll tear his throat out!*

But he won't come close to me again. He's too smart for that. He knows me too well. Besides, he's got my sister to fuck.

The phone chirped.

Kate sat bolt upright and grabbed at the receiver. She kept the room unlit, the video circuit closed.

"Katie? Did I wake you up?" Kim's voice!

"No," she managed to choke out. "I was awake anyway."

The delay told Kate that her sister was back on Earth.

"I just want to let you know that I'm okay. Don't worry about me."

"Where are you?"

She knew what the answer would be even while her sister's reply made its way to her.

"In Italy! It's beautiful here! The beaches are all

flooded right now but the weather's wonderful and we have our own swimming pool."

"We? You're with Rafe?"

Did Kim's voice sound slightly blurry? Was she slurring her words? Kate listened hard.

"Yes. He's wonderful. He says he sends you love and kisses. You want to talk to him? He's right here. But I can't put on the video 'cause we're both indecent!" Kim giggled like a schoolgirl.

"No," Kate said, weary, defeated. "I don't need to talk to Rafe. I'm sure that if he has any business to discuss with me he'll call later."

"Okay. I just wanted you to know that I'm fine. I'm having a great time."

"What are you taking?"

The delay seemed longer than before. "Taking? I'm not taking anything. I'm totally clean, Kate, honest."

"That's good," she said. "Stay that way."

When she hung up the phone Kate remembered all the other times Kim had sworn she was clean. She always used the same phrase: "I'm totally clean, Kate, honest."

She dropped back onto the bed, staring up at the ceiling in the dark. Where are you, Dan Randolph? Why haven't you done anything? You've got to get the bastard. Get him quick before he kills my little sister.

The Philharmonic Hall of Naples, Florida, had seen magnificent performers and illustrious audiences in the past, but never an occasion such as this. To celebrate the fiftieth anniversary of the spacious, handsome building, the Naples Philharmonic Orchestra combined with the Mormon Tabernacle Choir to gratify the crème de la crème of American society. No vulgar entertainment stars or other pop icons. No artists or authors or politicians. The one thousand elegant men and women who gathered at the Philharmonic this night were each multimillionaires, tycoons of commerce and industry, civic leaders who earned their lofty places in their communities the old-fashioned way: by buying in.

Jane Scanwell was invited not because she was a former President of the United States or the nation's representative on the Global Economic Council. She was invited for the same reason everyone else was: because Texas oil and aerospace money had made her rich.

She accepted the gilt-edged invitation to the gala evening not because she had any desire to see or be seen by the leisure class. Jane came to Naples because she knew that the Empress Theodora, head of the largest news network in the world, would also be in attendance.

The first half of the show ended with a rousing rendition of "Battle Hymn of the Republic." The hall was still ringing with the audience's heartfelt cheers when Jane swiftly left her box seat and managed to be casually strolling past the door to Theodora's box when she opened it and stepped into the corridor.

"Theodora!" Jane said over the chatter of the crowd pushing past. "How nice."

"Why, Jane," said Theodora, with equal sincerity, "I haven't seen you in ages."

They fell in step as they went with the flow of the crowd along the plushly carpeted corridor. Theodora was the taller of the two women, by an inch or so. She wore a black velvet double-breasted tuxedo jacket over a scoop-necked white silk tank blouse and black velvet slacks. Her ash blonde hair, usually pulled into a businesslike bun, fell to her shoulders in graceful waves. Jane was in a more conventional off-the-shoulder gown of jade green that set off her rich auburn hair beautifully. Both women wore enough jewelry to ransom a kingdom, but in this glittering crowd they were hardly noticed.

"I've been trying to reach you at the office," Jane said, maneuvering toward one of the quiet little alcoves off to the side of the corridor.

"It's always so hectic there," said Theodora, her voice slightly brittle. The crowd was pushing past them and she did not like being bumped, even by her peers.

"Do you have a minute?" Jane asked, gesturing toward the green marble bench in the alcove.

Looking distinctly unhappy at being trapped this way, Theodora turned to the lanky young man behind her and said, "Wally, would you get me a glass of wine, please? Not the champagne, it's awful. White wine."

Wally bobbed his head and asked, "And for you, ma'am?"

"White wine will be fine," said Jane.

They forced their way across the flow of the crowd and sat side by side on the marble bench.

"All right," said Theodora, with the air of a patient getting into a dentist's chair. "What is it you want?"

Jane made a smile. "I want to hand your network the hottest story of the century."

Theodora's brows rose slightly. "Really?"

"You've heard rumors about the greenhouse cliff, haven't you?"

"I promised the President that my people would not be party to such rumors."

"It's more than rumors, Theodora. The GEC is starting a program—"

"I said I promised the President."

"But—"

"I know he's not of your party, Jane. But he is the President and I have promised him that I would keep the lid on this story."

Jane could not keep herself from frowning.

Which brought a smile to Theodora's lips. "Why, from what I understand of it, the GEC itself has asked all the news media to keep quiet for the time being. Are you going against your own Council?"

"There's more to it than that, Theodora," said Jane. "Much more. The GEC is honeycombed by criminals. This entire effort is being undermined by the international crime cartel."

That widened Theodora's eyes. "Are you certain?"

"I wouldn't be telling you this if I weren't certain. And frightened of what might happen."

"How do you know this? I mean, do you have any hard evidence that we could use?"

"Reams of evidence. From Astro Manufacturing. And if your reporters start digging into other major corporations, they'll find—"

"Astro Manufacturing?" Theodora interrupted. "Isn't that Dan Randolph's company? Didn't the GEC throw him out for cheating or stealing or something?"

"Dan Randolph, yes," said Jane. "His company was confiscated."

"And he's the one producing your evidence?"

"It's from his former company."

"You got it from Randolph himself, didn't you?"

"Yes."

"And you didn't turn him over to the authorities?"

"He's not guilty of anything," Jane said.

Theodora's smile turned pitying. "I've heard rumors for years that you two were hot for each other. Even when he married that Latin American woman, the stories were floating around about the two of you."

"That has nothing to do with the current situation," Jane said.

But Theodora clearly did not believe her. "Jane, how can I put any credence into a wild tale told by a wanted criminal?"

"But the greenhouse cliff is the greatest threat the human race has ever faced!" Jane insisted. "And the Mafia's crippling our attempts to avert the disaster!"

"The Mafia." Theodora sighed.

"It's all true!"

"Jane, dear, even if it is all true, I have promised the President that I will not allow my people to report this supposed disaster story. He doesn't want people unnecessarily frightened and I agree with him. I am not going to promote a scare story."

Jane got to her feet. Looking down on Theodora, she snapped, "Then you'd better be a damned good swimmer."

She turned and stamped off into the crowd still milling around the bar at the end of the corridor. Wally came back with two fluted glasses of white wine, looking surprised that his boss was alone.

The mayor of New Orleans frowned at the somber faces around her. She tapped the report on her desk, lying closed in its forest green plastic binder. She had read the executive summary before convening this meeting. She had neither the time, the inclination, nor the technical understanding to read the full report. Now she scowled at the men who had come to talk about it. They all looked dismally grave, as if they had to make her take medicine she didn't want to take. All men, all of them.

"Do you know how much it would cost to build the levees higher?" she asked accusingly. She had been a prosecuting attorney who had toppled the previous administration in a sensational series of trials for outrageously inept corruption.

"No matter what it costs," said the state's environmental man, "it's going to have to be done."

"And how much will the state put in to pay for this?"

"The city's more than five feet below sea level, for the most part," the man insisted, ignoring her question. "Do you want five feet of water covering everything?"

"We won't have to improve the river levee," said the city engineer. "Just the lake."

"Just the lake?" the mayor asked acidly.

The city engineer flapped his hands. "We can do the river later. The lake seems to be the first problem."

"The existing levee is too low for the worst-case situation," said the environmental man.

"It's ten feet above the level of the lake," the mayor snapped.

"But, Yor Honoh, the lake's level *has* been rising, that's the lord's truth," said the majority leader. "Y'know, I live out by Metarie and I tell you, ol' Pontchartrain is on the rise. Why, you can see it on the causeway. Gettin' higher all the time."

"How much in the past five years?"

The environmental man flipped through the copy of the report he held on his lap. "Two inches," he replied.

"How much in the next ten years?"

Squinting at the numbers, "Four inches, maybe six."

"And the existing levee is *ten feet* above the water level?"

The man from the federal Severe Storms office piped up. "It's not the average water level that causes the problem, Miz Mayor. It's the worst-case scenario."

"Worst case."

"Exactly. For example, usually the Mississippi stays within its normal banks. But when it floods, well, you certainly need those concrete levees, don't you?"

"Pontchartrain has never risen ten feet above its normal level."

"Not even in a hurricane?" the federal man shot back, smirking at her.

"And we've got the pumping stations."

"But what if—"

"No what ifs!" she snapped. "This city has all sorts of problems and they all require money. Do you think I can go to the voters and tell them they've got to pony up how many hundreds of millions of dollars because Pontchartrain is rising two inches every five years?"

"Somebody's got to do it," muttered the environmental man.

"Not in my administration," she said coldly. "Maybe in twenty years or so the lake might be getting high enough to warrant raising the levee. Maybe in twenty years it'll all dry up and disappear! Who knows?"

The city engineer said, "If there's some disaster, like a

really strong hurricane or—"

"We'll face that problem when we come to it," said the mayor. "I'm not about to spend the taxpayers' money on some scientific theory."

THIRTY-FOUR

Vasily Malik strode onstage like a conquering hero, with a broad smile and a happy gleam in his eyes. Dressed in an impeccably tailored blue suit, he went straight to the podium and gripped it with both hands. The hall was filled to overflowing with news reporters; video cameras focused on the newly elected chairman of the Global Economic Council. Two big TV monitors flanked the podium, one displaying the BBC's broadcast, the other CNN's. Both pictures were the same, except for a minute difference in the angle at which the cameras were focused on Malik's triumphant expression.

Jane Scanwell sat in the balcony section reserved for VIPs. All the other Council members were there: Muhammed Shariff Sibuti looking slightly nonplussed, as if he did not fully understand what was happening; Rafaelo Gaetano with a smile that looked decidedly forced, Jane thought.

It had been three months since she had last seen Dan.

For three months Jane had hammered at her so-called friends high in the corporate world of the news media. They had listened to her story of criminal corruption in the GEC, promised to study the situation, and done nothing. They always asked for her source of information. When she told them it was Dan Randolph they invariably shrugged her off. "He's trying to get back at Malik; everybody knows the two of them hate each other. We can't be party to a personal vendetta—we'd be sued for billions! And Randolph's a fugitive from justice, to boot."

Only two of her media contacts actually promised to examine the information Jane brought with her. Again, no action from them. It was like pouring a cup of water onto the Sahara. The information disappeared somewhere in the network's labyrinth of departments and bureaus. Jane began to understand that the Mafia had people in the news networks, too. They wanted Dan's information, not to broadcast, and certainly not to use as the starting point of an investigation. They wanted it to help them track down the leaks in Astro Manufacturing.

Now Malik stood before the media reporters, fresh from his unanimous election to the GEC chair, the sky blue emblem of the GEC serving as a backdrop for him.

Smiling for the assembled reporters and the hundreds of millions of TV viewers, Malik said, "Good afternoon, ladies and gentlemen. You will be happy to learn that I do not have a prepared speech to give you."

A titter of laughter rippled through the reporters.

"However, I do have an announcement to make. After it, I will be happy to answer your questions."

He paused, took a breath while the hall fell absolutely silent except for the barely audible sound of the cameras humming and the faint hiss of the lights.

"My first act as chairperson of the Global Economic Council is to institute an Industrial Coordinating Committee, which will consist of the CEOs of each of the world's leading industrial corporations. The ICC will serve as a focal point for the GEC's continuing efforts to ameliorate the effects of industrial pollution on the Earth's atmosphere."

"He's lying," said a voice.

The hall stirred.

"He's not telling the whole truth," said Dan Randolph, whose image filled the BBC monitor screen. "Ask him why he needs an Industrial Coordinating Committee."

Just as suddenly as it appeared, Dan's image winked off, leaving Malik's angry red face on the screen.

Malik turned and glared at his aides, standing openmouthed with shock in the wings of the small stage.

"Who was that?" somebody asked.

"Was that Dan Randolph?"

"Please!" Malik raised his hands for calm and put a reassuring smile on his face. "There must be some crank somewhere in the BBC system—"

"I'm not a crank," Dan said, this time from the CNN monitor. "But I think maybe you're a crook."

Pandemonium among the reporters. They were on their feet, shouting questions—not at Malik, but to Dan's image in the screen.

Dan grinned at them. "Hey, this is Vasily's media conference. Ask him your questions, not me. He's got all the answers you want."

Malik angrily strode off the stage and Dan's image winked out, leaving the reporters with no one to question. The TV screens showed only the GEC emblem and a bare stage.

"I want him found and I want him found immediately!" Malik was screaming into his phone. "Dead or alive, it doesn't matter. If I don't get results immediately I'll have you replaced! Do you understand me?"

Gaetano had brushed past the Russian's distraught secretary and come into Malik's office looking as tense and angry as Malik himself. He stood before the desk as the Russian turned off his phone with a furious bang of his fist against the keyboard.

"And what do you want?" Malik snapped.

"To help you," said Gaetano.

Malik rose from his chair and leaned his knuckles on his desktop. "The only help I want is in finding Dan Randolph."

"Dead or alive, I know."

The Russian made a furious snort.

"I can help," Gaetano said, pulling his silver cigarette case from his jacket pocket. Malik saw that his hands were trembling slightly.

"Is it true, then?" Malik asked. "You have connections to the Mafia?"

Gaetano lit the cigarette and puffed a cloud of bluish smoke toward the ceiling. "I have friends who can help you find Randolph."

"The Mafia," Malik insisted.

"Call them whatever you want to," said Gaetano. "You want the man dead. So do I. We can work together to see that he never bothers us again."

"The Mafia," Malik repeated. He turned his back to Gaetano, went to the windows and stared out at the gray Paris sky. It always seemed to be gray, these days, he thought. It seems as if I haven't seen a blue sky in years.

"You can't turn your back on us," Gaetano said, his voice brittle with suppressed anger. "You and I have been working together for many months now. You are part of *my* organization, whether you like it or not."

Malik said nothing. He wished that Gaetano would disappear.

"I will see to it that Randolph is found. And done away with. Then we can go on with our plans for organizing the world's industries."

Malik waited until he heard his office door click shut. When he turned around he noticed the new nameplate that his secretary had placed on his desk for his approval: V. S. Malik, Chairman. He tasted ashes in his mouth.

Gaetano strode along the hallway to his own office, thinking furiously. Malik is a reluctant ally, but he'll go along with what I want him to do. He has to. He has no other choice. Jane Scanwell is the dangerous one; she's in league with Randolph, probably in love with the bastard.

By the time he reached his office and closed the door behind him, though, he was smiling. Why not use Jane to lure Randolph into the open? That would work. And then both of them can die in the same accident.

The more he thought about his idea the more he liked it. And once the two of them are out of the way, he told himself, Don Marcello can at last have the fatal heart attack I've been waiting for.

Gaetano actually whistled happily as he sat at his desk and picked up the telephone handset.

There was no way to hush up Dan Randolph's brash interruption of Malik's media conference, not when Dan had been seen by more than a hundred million TV viewers.

GEC public relations flacks tried to deflect reporters' questions. Randolph is a criminal, a fugitive from justice. He's sore because the GEC stripped him of his company.

Yes, but how did he break into the BBC and CNN transmissions? How did he do that?

We're investigating that. Both those networks are beefing up their security. And we're installing new protective circuits in all the communications satellite ground stations.

You mean he broke into the ground stations?

Electronically, yes. That seems to be what he did. We're checking out that line of investigation. There was no physical break-in. It looks as if he managed to override the uplink transmissions from Earth to the satellites and insert his own transmission in place of what the uplinks were carrying.

But how could he do that? Where did he transmit from?

We're looking into that.

You don't know?

Not yet. But one thing is for certain: with the new protective programs we're adding to the ground stations, he'll never be able to do it again.

Two days later, the UNESCO educational channel was running a program about global warming. Schools all around the world tuned in to see the top experts from major universities discuss the possibilities of drastic changes in the global climate.

"Much of the problem stems from human activity," said a geophysicist from Kenya, his thick white hair a startling contrast to his deeply black skin.

"Yes," agreed the moderator, a world-famous actress who had turned activist when her career began to slump. "As I understand it, atmospheric pollution from human sources is now a bigger factor than all the natural sources of pollutants combined."

"If by 'natural sources of pollutants' you mean volcanic eruptions and animal wastes, then, yes, it is true. Humans are ruining the atmosphere at an alarming rate."

"What about the greenhouse cliff?" asked Dan Randolph. His grinning image suddenly appeared between the moderator and the scientist.

The moderator and scientist went on speaking as if nothing had happened, because the show had been taped in advance of its airing. But their sound went off and Dan Randolph's image seemed to hover between them like an elf or a leprechaun.

"They're not telling you about the greenhouse cliff, kids," Dan said cheerfully. "There's a strong chance that the climate is going to shift abruptly, within a few years. Think about it. What would *you* do if the sea level was going to rise by ten meters or more?"

Before the shocked schoolchildren could react, before their stunned teachers could think to turn off their TV sets, Dan's image disappeared and the original show droned on as if nothing had happened.

But that evening a dozen million children asked their parents what a greenhouse cliff was.

Both the World Cup soccer game and cricket match were interrupted by Dan Randolph. His image seemed to appear randomly on television broadcasts ranging from daytime soap operas to a live presentation of *Aïda* from the Baths of Caracalla in Rome. Dan appeared during one of the intermissions; opera lovers appreciated his courtesy.

He never was on the screen for more than thirty seconds. He spoke about the greenhouse cliff and the fact that the world was facing an inexorable crisis.

"The GEC's answer is to take control of all the world's industries," Dan said, for once his elfin smile gone, his face grim. "That means they're taking control of all the world's jobs. They stole my company from me. What will they be stealing from you?"

Reporters all over the world beat themselves into exhaustion trying to find Dan Randolph, trying to get Malik or anyone in the GEC to reply to his charges. Zach Freiberg appeared on nationwide TV in the United States and explained what the greenhouse cliff was. But two dozen other scientists gave interviews belittling Zach's views and casting doubt on his credibility.

"After all," said one kindly-looking white-haired woman, "he did work for Dan Randolph, didn't he?" She herself worked for Rockledge Industries, under GEC management.

Finally, after two weeks of uproar, Jane Scanwell announced that she would give a news conference in Paris to respond to Dan Randolph's charges on behalf of the GEC.

Malik knew that Jane would confirm everything Randolph had been saying.

"It will be a disaster for us," he moaned to Gaetano.

"Then we must not permit her to meet the reporters," said the Italian.

THIRTY-FIVE

Dan shivered slightly as he sat in the bare wooden chair and hunched closer to the fire. It can't be the radiation, he told himself for the fortieth time that morning. I'm just not accustomed to the cold.

It was snowing again. Through the cabin's only decent window Dan could see the white flakes sifting down gently, quietly, cold and still as death. He shuddered again inside the quilted coat he had thrown over his shoulders. Then he got up from the chair to toss another stick on the fire.

Now I know how Sai must feel, he thought, bottled in liquid nitrogen.

His campaign was going well. It was fun to twist their tails, those pompous asses at the GEC. Must be twenty-two zillion security agents and news reporters trying to figure out how I'm able to break into the TV transmissions. Flatlanders, all of 'em.

It had been ridiculously easy, although physically arduous. Nearly four months ago Mason Dickson had taken a vacation in space. From Liechtenstein he drove to Milan and caught the spaceplane to Rockledge Industries' tourist hotel in orbit. He chose Rockledge's space station because, in addition to its famous Zero-G Hotel, the satellite also housed a considerable satellite repair and refurbishment facility.

For a suitable exchange of money, one of the Rockledge technicians spent a week in Mason Dickson's plush luxury suite at the hotel while Dan replaced him at his job. The man was a maintenance technician whose specialty was working on the communications satellites in geostationary orbit, 22,300 miles above the Earth.

Dan rode an orbital transfer vehicle to the Clarke orbit together with a team of human and robot technicians. He spent most of his time inside the shielded OTV, as did the rest of the humans, directing the robots who went out to work on individual satellites in the high radiation flux of the upper Van Allen Belt.

At week's end he returned to the hotel, became Mason Dickson once again, and—after a weekend of rest—returned to Earth.

Each of the commsats that his crew worked on now carried a miniaturized electronics package that allowed Dan to override the signal coming up from Earth and beam his own signal down the receiving antennas around the globe.

The price, though, had been high. Dan had to pay hush money to each of the other four technicians in the OTV. And he been exposed to more radiation than he liked to think about. Dan had to go EVA several times, to make sure that the small-witted robots had done their jobs correctly. Even inside the OTV the radiation dosimeters constantly hovered in the yellow warning area. The standing joke among the four other men and women of the crew had been that they not only belonged to the Zero-G Club, they also belonged to the Zero Population Growth movement.

Now he sat in the austere shack in the foothills of the

Himalayas, shivering with cold. Or was it radiation sick-ness?

It was unfair to call the building a shack. The lamas had built it solidly, with loving care, as they did every task they undertook. To them it was a retreat house, a remote place of solitude where a man could contemplate his place in the universe without interruption from the outside world. Nobo had made the arrangements for Dan to use it, at the same time he had taken Tamara with him to Kyoto.

Dan pulled his chair closer to the fire. He grinned when he thought about the look on Nobo's face when he first saw Tamara. Talk about being hit by the thunderbolt. Nobo nearly fell over his own feet trying to be polite and helpful to her.

The door banged open and Big George stamped in, a blast of frigid air swirling into the room.

"It's snowing again," George growled.

"I thought you liked the snow."

George had never seen snow any closer than a satellite view before he had come to this remote retreat house with Dan. For the first few days he had reveled in the white purity of it. But then he began to grumble that the stuff was "fooking damned cold. And wet."

George tossed his fleece-lined parka onto the bench by the door and came over to the fireplace, rubbing his big hands briskly. He had begun to let his beard grow back; he was starting to look shaggy and fierce again, rather than pinkly cherubic.

"How do you feel, Dan?"

"Got the shakes."

"I ought to get a doctor for you."

Dan laughed humorlessly. "How? By oxcart?"

"By picturephone," George replied. "We could access one of the medical libraries, find out if you've really got radiation sickness or not. Don't have to call a real person and let them know where we are."

"I'll be okay," said Dan. "Even if it is rad poisoning,

I've got plenty of pills for that."

George looked unconvinced.

"It can't be a very bad dose," Dan said. "My gums aren't bleeding and my hair isn't falling out."

"Then what's bothering you?"

With a painful sigh, "Old age, I guess. I haven't been exposed to winter in a long, long time."

Changing the subject, George asked, "When's your next broadcast?"

Dan glanced at the gray electronics boxes piled in a corner of the room. *Wonder what the lamas would say if they knew their retreat house had become a television studio?*

"Did you hear me?" George asked.

"I'm not deaf," said Dan. "Some of my faculties are still working."

"So? When?"

"They'll be expecting me to pop in on Jane's news conference. So, instead, I'll hit the evening news shows the night before. Give the reporters more questions to ask when Jane meets with them."

"That's tomorrow, then."

Dan nodded. "We might as well do it on the Japanese news networks. Won't have to worry about time zones so much. Then all the others will pick it up, all around the world."

"Sounds good to me," said George. "Wish you looked better, though."

Dan grinned at him. "You want me to wear makeup for the camera, George?"

"I just wish you looked better."

Gaetano flew from Paris to Naples aboard a regular commercial airliner the night before Jane Scanwell's scheduled news conference. *It will be best if I am far from the scene of the crime,* he told himself, *with plenty of witnesses to vouch for my whereabouts.*

Besides, Kimberly was waiting for him in Naples. In so

many ways she reminded him of Kate: the same red hair, the same fiery spirit, the same wild heat when her passion overwhelmed her. And yet they were different, as well. Kate was reluctant and had to be controlled. She disliked the little games that Rafaelo enjoyed playing. Kim, on the other hand, invented games of her own. She could be demanding, but they were demands that he enjoyed meeting. And exceeding.

She did not even know that she was on a drug-induced high virtually all of the time. Gaetano's servants saw to it that the drugs were in her food. Nothing truly harmful. Just enough to keep her wired. When he wanted her to be obedient, like the time he invited his friends from Messina to share their bed, he saw to it that other dosages were applied.

And then there was always Kate. *It's probably better that she remains on the Moon. If she knew what's happening to her precious sister, she would probably try to murder me.* Gaetano smiled to himself as the plane crossed the Alps. *No, better to keep Kate where she is. Whenever I have to go to Alphonsus I will have her there waiting for me, obedient to my command, willing to turn herself inside out for me, because she is afraid for her sister.*

He almost laughed aloud. *If she could have seen what that trio from Messina did with her, she would know that her worst fears have already come true.*

Then he sobered. *What will happen once Jane has been removed? Will she lead us to Randolph? Everything depends on finding that American bastard before he does any more damage.*

He paid no attention to the magnificent Alps gliding past outside his plane's window. Nor did he notice how brown they looked, how little snow remained on their jagged peaks.

Josh Pollett was literally quivering. Like a hunting dog who knew there were birds hiding in the bushes, the wiry, sharp-featured reporter was atremble with anticipation as he sat at the tape console. He was running videotapes of Dan Randolph's unauthorized broadcasts.

Harriet McIntyre and Wayne Manley stood behind him in the darkened workroom. She too was wide-eyed with eagerness. Manley was frowning, his sleekly handsome face distinctly unhappy.

"How does he do that?" Manley asked, his voice a low rumble.

"What difference does it make?" Pollett snapped. "He's doing it."

"Every network on Earth has teams of experts checking their equipment. The GEC has an army of investigators looking into it."

"I've been pushing every source I've got," said Pollett. "Nobody can figure out where he's broadcasting from, or how he's breaking into the regular broadcasts."

On the screen, Dan Randolph was saying, "This is real, folks. We're all facing a terrible disaster. Don't take my word for it. Ask the scientists. Ask Zach Freiberg at the California Institute of Technology. Ask Vasily Malik or your own representative on the Global Economic Council. They've got to act! And fast! But they won't unless *you* make them act."

Pollett flicked an eye to the digital timer beside the screen. "That's the longest he's stayed on the air: fifty-three seconds."

"He's looking grimmer," McIntyre said. "More desperate."

"He's got good reason to be desperate," said Manley. "They'll catch him soon."

"I wish we could catch him first," McIntyre said. "Nobody knows where he is, or where he's broadcasting from."

Pollett swiveled his chair around and got to his feet. "Listen, Wayne, we've got to do something about this. Whether Randolph is right or not, this is the biggest story of the decade—maybe of the century!"

"Don't go off the deep end," Manley warned.

"We're all going to be in the deep end if Randolph's telling us the truth," McIntyre snapped.

Manley turned and made a move for the door, a well-fleshed man in an expensive three-piece suit. His two reporters, in faded jeans and T-shirts, scampered to cut him off. Manley glared at them in the dim light coming from the viewer's screen.

"Come on, now," Manley said.

"No, you come on," Pollett said heatedly. "We can't sit on this story any longer. Holy shit, Wayne, we're talking about half the world being flooded! This is bigger than Noah and the ark!"

"Any 'gentleman's agreement' that the network might have made with Washington is out the window now," said McIntyre, more reasonably. "Surely even the Empress can see that."

"That's no way to speak of Theodora."

"Come on, Wayne," Pollett chivvied, "let me interview Freiberg. I've interviewed him before. He's a responsible scientist, not some nutcase or quack."

"And I can get to Jane Scanwell," McIntyre said.

"And maybe this guy Malik, through her," Pollett suggested.

Manley put up his hands. "I'll speak to Theodora about it."

"When?"

"It's got to be today!"

"This evening," Manley answered, clearly irritated. "I'm having dinner with the family."

"Okay," said Pollett. "I'm catching the next flight to L.A."

"And I'll go to Paris."

The two reporters burst out of the viewing room like eager schoolchildren running out to play, leaving Manley standing there alone. A slow smile crept across his fleshy face. Let them go, he told himself. Even if Theodora refuses to listen to reason they can get their interviews and then we'll present the Empress with a fait accompli. She wouldn't fire me if things go sour. She'll fire Pollett and McIntyre. After all, I didn't authorize these interviews, did I?

Jane sat at the gracefully curved little walnut desk in the study of her apartment, bent over the screen of her laptop, poring over every detail of the data Dan had given her. She knew the give-and-take of a live meeting with the reporters. She wanted to have as much information in her head as possible for the morning's news conference.

She had come home from the GEC office and immediately launched into her preparation for the morning's news conference, stopping only to get out of her business clothes and into a comfortable terry-cloth robe and to fix a light dinner tray. Far into the night she sat studying, memorizing facts, numbers, dates, names. The dinner tray sat on the desk untouched.

A noise. Just a soft whisper, really, but it made her jerk her head up and glance around the little room. The window was closed and locked. It must have been something down on the street, Jane thought. Nothing to be alarmed about. Still, she got up from the desk and walked through the apartment, checking all the windows and especially the French doors that led out onto the balcony. Then she went back to her computer and accessed her own security system. All the lights were green. Everything was fine.

You're being melodramatic, Jane told herself.

On the roof of the apartment building two Japanese men in ordinary business suits walked slowly along the edge, speaking quietly of their plans to enter the martial arts tournament in Saigon during their vacation time. A third sat in the deep shadow of the air-conditioner shed, visible only by the tiny red glow of his cigarette.

Down on the street across from the building's front entrance another pair of Japanese, one of them a woman, loitered in a dark doorway. In the alley behind the building, a lone Japanese man prowled, fading into the shadows at the slightest sound. In an apartment on the first floor of Jane's building, an older Japanese man sat in front of a TV screen. He seemed to be drowsing, except that every few moments he lifted his hand to inspect the small black electronic box it held. Six green lights shone steadily. All was well with the people he had deployed. His TV screen showed the lobby of the apartment building, quiet and empty except for the concierge, who was truly asleep behind his desk.

Jane knew nothing of this. Nobuhiko had informed her that she was being guarded, but she had never noticed any bodyguards. She had the right to ask for protection from the GEC security department, but she feared that Gaetano had infiltrated that office before any of the others.

So she checked her electronic security system, then shut down her computer and went to her bedroom. For the first time in her life she felt personally endangered. It was not exciting; it was frightening. She wished there were some way to avoid the danger that she knew was pressing in on her. But Gaetano and his criminals had to be exposed, she told herself. If we're going to save the world, we've got to get rid of the crooks.

She knew that her real reason was Dan. He loves me and he needs me. He'll get himself killed if I don't help him. The silly fool, butting his head against the GEC and the Mafia and anyone else who stands in his way. Silly, stubborn, egotistical, glorious, wonderful fool.

She stopped and looked at herself in her bedroom mirror. "And what are you?" she asked the image. "Just as foolish as he is." Then she laughed, knowing that this was the way it had to be.

The phone buzzed. She called out, "Answer," and the screen lit up with:

MUST SEE YOU AT MIDNIGHT AT SACRE COEUR. IMPERATIVE. YOU KNOW WHO.

Dan's here! He's back in Paris.

The digital clock on the phone said 11:18. Jane called for a taxi as she whipped out of her robe and hurriedly pulled on a cinnamon turtleneck blouse and suede skirt. She was out the front door of her apartment building by 11:29, tugging on a leather coat. A taxi was waiting at the curb.

"Sacre Coeur," she said as she ducked into the cab's backseat.

The elder man in the first-floor apartment was galvanized into action when he saw Jane race across the lobby. He pressed the emergency button on his hand-held communicator and dashed to the stairs that led down to the lobby. The couple in the doorway sprinted out into the street; the man took a snapshot of the departing taxicab while the woman raced for the sleek black sedan they had parked half a block away. By the time she drove up their chief had come out. The three of them piled into the car and raced after the taxi.

The three on the roof came down the elevator to the basement garage. They jumped into their gray minivan, the slamming of their doors echoing through the garage, and roared out into the street, barely slowing down to pick up the man who had come around the building from the alley. Inside the van they had enough communications gear to link directly to a commsat, if necessary. And a small arsenal of weaponry.

"This isn't the way to Sacre Coeur," said Jane as the streets slid by in the dark, silent night.

The driver did not answer. She rapped on the thick plastic partition and said it louder, in French. Still no reaction from the driver.

"Stop!" she hollered. *"Arrete!"*

When the driver still played deaf Jane realized that she was being abducted. She sat rigid on the rear seat of the taxicab, her stomach ablaze with fear. It's happening! They're kidnapping me!

For a moment she thought this might be Dan's way of

spiriting her off to meet him. But Dan wouldn't frighten her. He'd be in the driver's seat himself, grinning into the rearview mirror. She peered at the mirror and saw the driver's dark eyes watching her coldly. His eyes reminded her of Gaetano's.

In the car following the taxi, the young Japanese said excitedly, "Don't let them out of your sight."

The woman driving the sedan wanted to snarl at him. Instead she said nothing and concentrated on her driving, constantly reminding herself that in France one drove on the right side of the road, not the left, as in Japan. It was not difficult to follow the taxicab; it was not speeding and there were hardly any other cars in the streets now, in this quiet part of the city. The difficulty was in following it without letting the driver know he was being followed.

"It's a pity we don't have a bug on the taxi," said the young woman. "Then we could track it without their seeing us."

"Well, we don't," the young man snapped. "Keep your eyes on it or we'll lose them."

In the backseat their chief was speaking through his wrist communicator to the other four in the van, following some distance behind them.

"You must assume that the abductors will notice us following them and be prepared for a fight when they finally come to stop. Under no circumstances are you to risk the life of the Scanwell woman! Nonlethal weapons only. Understood?"

A single "Hai!" issued from the wrist comm's tiny speaker, like the voice of a sprite or a gremlin.

Past the city limit the taxi drove, past the sprawling modern suburbs that ringed Paris, gaining speed once they were out into the countryside. Jane had tried both doors; they were locked. The driver had not said a word, but his eyes kept flicking up to the rearview mirror. Turning, Jane looked out the back window. Far in the distance a pair of headlights gleamed, disappeared when the ground dipped, appeared again.

We're being followed, she realized. Nobo's body-guards? Dan? Or more of the kidnappers?

The driver picked up a radio microphone and spoke into it. His words were muffled by the plastic partition, but Jane thought she detected the musical cadences of Italian. He's calling for help, she thought.

She looked at her watch. Its glowing digits said 12:29. They had been driving for exactly an hour. The night was dark out here. No moonlight lit the countryside. They might be passing spacious farmlands or rivers or anything at all. Jane had no idea of where they were or where they were going. Once every few minutes a village flicked by, ancient stone buildings and a few streetlamps standing like forlorn sentinels in the night. The taxi whizzed through their narrow twisting streets without slowing. God help anyone or anything in its path, Jane thought. She caught blurred glimpses of signs bearing names, but they meant nothing to her.

Jane's bodyguards knew where she was heading before she did. In the minivan, one of them bent over an electronic map, his finger tracing the road that the sedan and taxi were following.

"There's an abandoned airport less than two miles ahead, on the right," he said into his radio microphone. "They must be heading there."

The older man in the backseat of the sedan grunted his agreement. Reaching forward, he tapped the woman driving the car on the shoulder. "Faster. Get closer. They are heading for an airport."

At last the taxi whipped past a chain-link fence where two other cars sat on either side of the gate. An airport? Jane wondered. The road became bumpy, the taxi jounced and rattled. Then she saw a helicopter up ahead, sitting next to a crumbling old building that looked as if it might once have been the control tower of a military airport. A single lamp on a tall pole lit the scene.

And she heard gunfire.

As the sedan pulled onto the access road to the airport
the two cars that had been parked by the gate pulled
together, hood to hood, to block the entrance. Without
a word of discussion or command, the young woman
swerved the sedan to the left, smashed right through the
aged chain-link fence, and plunged in a swirl of dust and
gravel past the two parked cars.

Men from the two cars turned and fired at them with
pistols and assault rifles. The young man in the front seat
leaned out his window and fired back with his pistol as
the car plunged ahead, swerving and bucking. Bullets
slammed into the car. A burst caught the young man,
exploding his head into a pulpy spray of blood.

The woman flinched but did nothing more. Teeth biting into her lower lip, she hunched over the wheel and
doggedly closed in on the cloud of dust that the taxi was
kicking up. Her chief, ducked down between the seats,
said calmly into his wrist comm, "Use whatever force
necessary to eliminate the team at the gate to the airport."

The gunmen at the gate were ducking back into their
own cars when the minivan came zooming up the road
and hurtled through the break in the fence. An anti-tank
rocket blew the first car into a blazing ball of flame,
which ignited the gas tank of the second car. The double
explosion masked the screams of the men roasted alive.

The taxi lurched to a stop so hard Jane was thrown off
the seat. One door popped open and the driver, gun in
hand, waved her out. She saw the black sedan boiling
down toward them.

Someone yanked her by the arm, pulling her out of the
taxi. People were shooting at the sedan; Jane saw its
windshield shatter and its hood go flying as the engine
blew steam and the big heavy car plowed its front end
into the soft billowing bare ground. A gray minivan
pulled up beside it, unscathed except for muddy dirt
spattered along its side.

A pair of men grabbed her arms and she felt something

cold and hard pressing against her temple.

Everything went quiet. Jane was gasping for breath, her heart thundering in her ears. But the people around her seemed to be standing absolutely still, frozen in the harsh bluish light from the single lamp pole.

"Outta the car!" shouted the man holding the gun to her head. "Outta the car or I blow her fuckin' head off."

Nothing happened. No one moved.

"You understand English?" he yelled louder. "I said get out of the car! Now!"

Jane heard the metallic click of the pistol being cocked.

The driver's door of the sedan opened and the young woman stepped out. Jane saw that she could hardly be out of her teens, slim, wearing black slacks and blouse, her hair pulled back tightly. She raised her hands to shoulder level. Jane saw from the corners of her eyes that there were at least five men leveling guns at her.

"You in the van, too," called the man with the gun. "Out."

The four men in the van came out slowly, reluctantly.

Jane heard the high-pitched whine of the helicopter's engine starting up. Then the man beside her said, "Scratch 'em."

"The girl too?"

"All of 'em, stupid."

"But we could have some fun with her."

The man cursed in Italian, then said, "Have your fun, then snuff her. And make it fast!"

The blaze of gunfire made Jane jump. The four men fell like scythed wheat. Jane smelled the acrid smoke from their guns. Her ears rang.

The man tugged at her arm and she realized that he had put his own gun back in his shoulder holster and was pulling her toward the helicopter. A second gunman accompanied them, cradling a vicious-looking assault rifle in his arms. Through the ringing in her ears she heard the deeper roar of the chopper's engine. Stunned, stumbling, she let the man half-drag her to the helicopter while she looked over her shoulder at the three gunmen advancing on the lone girl.

They pushed Jane into the helicopter. Her hands were trembling too hard to fasten the safety belt. The man did it for her while she stared at the crumpled bodies sprawled by their cars and the smoky pyre that still flamed out by the gate. And the three grinning men surrounding the girl by the shot-up sedan.

The helicopter's engine roared up to full power, its big rotor kicking up a sandstorm as the pilot yelled, "All strapped in? We're taking off."

The young woman stood trembling beside the sedan, her eyes flicking from one of the leering gunmen to the other. They had all holstered their pistols as they advanced toward her.

"She's kind of skinny," said one of them, in English. "Maybe we can fatten her up."

"Yeah. We'll stuff her good!" All three of them laughed. The closest one reached out for her.

She brushed his hand away and struck with the heel of her palm under his chin so fast that her hand was a blur. The guy's head snapped back and he staggered, arms flailing, and fell onto his back. The other two grabbed for her but she ducked under them, rammed her clenched hands into the groin of one of them and rolled away. The man's eyes rolled up in his head and his breath gushed out of him as he collapsed to the ground.

The third was reaching for his pistol when the old man bashed his back with the car door, then sprang out of the car and broke the guy's neck with a single chop of the edge of his hand. By then the young woman was sprinting for the helicopter, just starting to lift off the ground.

The old man snaked a small slim dead-black pistol from his belt and calmly shot the two gunmen that the girl had incapacitated. For good measure he put a round into the skull of the man he had already killed.

As the helicopter began to lift off the ground the young woman leaped as high as she could, stretching her arms to their utmost, and just managed to grab one of the landing skids.

The chopper bounced and swerved under the sudden unbalanced weight.

"Hey, what . . ." The pilot grappled with his controls.

"One of them's hanging on to us!" yelled the man sitting beside the pilot.

The man beside Jane snarled, "Fucking idiot!" and yanked his pistol from its holster. He opened the door and leaned out into the blast of wind from the rotor. The young woman was hanging on to the landing skid with one hand, staring up at him, swinging as she tried to hide beneath the helicopter's bottom.

"Bitch," muttered the gunman. He unbuckled his seat harness, leaned out farther and fired three shots into her face point-blank. Just as Jane, suddenly filled with flaming anger that boiled over her fear, shoved at his back with all her strength.

The girl fell silently, already dead, to the ground. The gunman screamed as he plunged. Jane leaned back in her seat, a terrible smile on her pale face.

THIRTY-SIX

The old man stood with his pistol in his hand still smoking, his eyes wide at the sight of his daughter sprawled and broken on the ground. The Mafioso who had killed her lay not more than a meter away, broken and bleeding. The helicopter dwindled into the dark night sky, carrying Jane Scanwell with it.

The three other gunmen lay dead around him. He stepped past their bodies and went to the minivan, where his four men lay, their bodies riddled.

They died well, the old man thought. But my daughter died the best of them all.

He had much to do. First, he slid back the door of the van and climbed inside. Crouching before the electronics hardware that lined one side of the van's interior, he flicked several switches. A display screen lit up, a single red dot blinking off to one side of its circular grid. The elder Japanese touched two keys and the red dot moved to the center of the screen. Another touch, and a map appeared on the screen.

It is well, he thought. My daughter succeeded in planting the tracker bug on the helicopter. Now at least we will know where they are taking the Scanwell woman.

He powered up the satellite link and made his report to his superiors in Kyoto, knowing that he had to take care of the bodies of his team before the sun rose and anyone could see what had happened here. Knowing that he had really failed in his mission to protect the Scanwell woman. Knowing that as soon as the proper services were conducted for his daughter he would take his own life as payment for his failure.

"Kidnapped?" A bolt of almost electrical intensity raced through Dan.

Nobo's face on the phone screen seemed wretched with anguish. "Abducted, kidnapped. They took her from Paris last night."

Dan had just finished the latest of his pirate broadcasts, breaking in on evening entertainment shows in the western hemisphere with his abrupt warnings about the greenhouse cliff and corruption in the GEC. He felt tired, as if he had been struggling to reach the top of a hill for ages yet still had a long, long way to go.

Snow was banked against the window. The wind was howling outside, moaning down the chimney so strongly that Dan feared it would blow out their meager fire. George was squatting by the fireplace, feeding sticks while glancing over his shoulder at Dan.

"Kidnapped," Dan repeated. "Not killed."

"They are holding her as a hostage," said Nobo. "We received a message from them this morning."

"We? Who do you mean?"

"Gaetano spoke to Malik about it this morning."

"Gaetano. The Italian. He's come out into the open, has he?"

"Dan—he says they're willing to release Jane."

"Malik told you that?"

"Yes. He gave me the message because he knows I can reach you."

"Malik wants me to know that Jane's been kidnapped," said Dan. "Nice of him."

Nobo closed his eyes briefly, tiredly. "It has nothing to do with your rivalry. The message Gaetano gave him was that they will release Jane—in exchange for you."

"Oh?"

"And the data file you have from Astro."

Dan thought swiftly. "I suppose they've swiped the copy that Jane had."

"Her apartment seemed undisturbed, but no trace of the file was found when the police searched it."

"They want me, huh?"

Nobo answered tautly, "In forty-eight hours. They have set a deadline of forty-eight hours."

"That doesn't give us much time."

"They will kill you, Dan."

"They'll kill Jane, too. She knows as much about them as I do, now. Maybe more."

"Dan, I will throw the full weight of the House of Yamagata into finding Jane and rescuing her."

Dan thought, Your team of bodyguards didn't do much good, pal. What can you do for her now?

As if he could read Dan's thoughts, Nobo said, "We know where the helicopter took her."

"You do?"

"One of our agents managed to plant a bug on it before she was killed."

Killed, Dan said to himself. Of course. Nobo's team wouldn't let Jane out of their protection without a fight. "How many casualties did they take?" he asked aloud.

"Six dead."

"Damn! I'm sorry, Nobo."

"The important fact is that we know where the helicopter landed."

"Where?"

"At a private airport just outside Lyon."

Dan leaned back in his chair. "They must have transferred her from there."

"Yes. And we don't know where they've taken her."

Dan swept the room with his eyes: the bare wooden floor, the sturdy beams of the ceiling, George hulking by the fireplace, the snow piling up outside. They're holding her hostage someplace and I'm stuck here in the ass end of Shangri-La.

"I've got to get out of here," he said to Nobo.

"I have already dispatched a plane to the airport nearest you."

Dan pictured the bumpy grass strip that passed as an airport, down in the valley below this monastic retreat house. "It'll be covered with snow, Nobo."

For the first time, the trace of a smile played across Nobuhiko's face. "I am aware of the climate in the Himalayas, my friend. And the team I have sent is well acquainted with the region. Three of them have scaled Mount Everest."

Dan grinned back at him. "I should have guessed."

"In the time until they reach you," Nobo asked, his face going somber again, "what should I say to Malik?"

Dan shrugged. "Tell the sonofabitch that I'm on my way to Paris."

"Paris?" Nobo seemed startled. "Is that wise?"

"No," said Dan. "But it's necessary."

Luther Clay leaned back in his creaking leather chair and wondered why the whole world seemed to conspire to make his life miserable. He had fought and struggled and scrapped for every little step up the ladder of success. Now, at his age, life should be easier, much easier. Instead, it got harder every blessed day.

Clay had been appointed to head the state's environmental protection office only a year earlier, the culmination of a long and dedicated career in the state bureaucracy. He had a right to expect a long and uneventful reign as the state's top environmental man, and then a peaceful and well-paid retirement.

Instead, he had troubles with the mayor of New Orleans and these federal pests who insisted that the levee on Lake Pontchartrain was no longer sufficient to meet their theoretical worst-case scenario.

And now he had an assistant who had just dropped a worse-than-worst-case scenario on his desk.

Damn!

He peered over his glasses at Regina Cartmill, sitting nervously on the front two inches of the chair before his desk. She was a mousy type, plain brown hair and plain vanilla skin blotched here and there with acne.

"An earthquake?" asked Clay, his voice dripping with disbelief.

Bobbing her head up and down, Ms. Cartmill said, "That's what the report predicts. A Richter scale seven earthquake in the Gulf sometime within the next twelve months."

Clay pushed his glasses back into place. "There hasn't been an earthquake in these parts within the memory of living man. I don't even think there's one on the records."

"There is. I checked. Eighteen-twelve. The New Madrid fault. It was one of the biggest earthquakes in history."

Clay shook his head. "Eighteen-twelve? More than two hundred years ago?"

"Maybe we're due for another one."

"My sweet lord."

Ms. Cartmill said, "But the prediction is for the quake to be out in the Gulf, hundreds of miles from here."

"Then why the warning?"

"There might be disturbances in the water. You know, a tidal wave."

"Tidal wave?" Clay yelped.

She nodded unhappily.

"What on earth are we supposed to do about a tidal wave?"

"According to the report, all we can do is evacuate all the low-lying coastal areas."

"Evacuate?"

"That includes New Orleans," she said, her voice so low that Clay could barely hear it.

He seemed to shrivel before her eyes, sinking into the chair as if he wanted to disappear altogether.

"Mr. Clay? Are you all right?"

"Oh, I'm fine," he said, his voice little more than a croak. "Our budget's being cut again. Our lawsuit against the companies who've been dumping raw sewage into the river has been thrown out of court. There's a madman on television telling everybody that the greenhouse is going to drown us all. My wife is hysterical because our daughter wants to marry a white boy.

"Now you've just told me that half the state might get flooded out. That means I've got to go to the mayor of New Orleans, who already hates the sight of me, and tell her that on some unknown day sometime in the next twelve months she's going to have to give the order to evacuate the city because a potential tidal wave caused by a theoretical earthquake might possibly wipe out her city. That's fine, just perfectly fine. That's *wonderful.*"

Despite the dogged weariness that was draining him, Dan paced the main room of the retreat house, half mad with impatience. He was perspiring beneath his heavy woolen shirt and leather vest, yet he felt chilled, as if his bones were turning to ice. The fire flickered fitfully, throwing gleaming highlights on the polished wooden beams of the low ceiling.

Big George banged through the door, looking like a fuzzy bear in the long-haired coat he wore. For once, no blast of wind followed him into the room.

"Storm's over," he announced, trying to sound cheerful. "Moon's up. You can even see the lights of Alphonsus and Copernicus. It's really a pretty night out there."

"Any sign of them?" Dan asked.

George shook his shaggy head. "We might be the only two fooking people left on Earth for all the signs you can see out there. Not even a paw print in the snow." He pulled off the coat and tossed it onto the chest by the door. "Fooking beautiful, though, what with the moonlight on the new snow."

"They should have been here by now," Dan said, still pacing.

"You eaten anything?"

Dan shook his head. George muttered to himself and went to the smaller room that served as a kitchen. When they had first arrived at the retreat house, they had been surprised to see a modern refrigerator, a sizable freezer, electric stove and even a microwave oven. The lama who had guided them up the steep and narrow mountain path to the house explained with a gentle smile that although the lamas themselves were forbidden to use such luxuries, they knew that Western guests regarded them as necessities. Then he had gone outside and started the diesel generator that powered the house.

Dan could not help thinking, at the time, that even in this remote site, in a house built by religious ascetics for peaceful contemplation, they were adding their little bit to the greenhouse effect. Later, he grumbled that the lamas had not bothered to wire the house for electrical heating, relying only on the pitiful fireplace—which also added its jot to the greenhouse.

George made a meal from the dwindling supplies they had brought with them and insisted that Dan sit at the table with him and eat.

"You've got some strenuous days ahead of you, mate," George said, almost cheerfully. "Better keep up your strength, eh?"

Dan spooned whatever it was into his mouth, his mind focused on Jane. Where is she, what are they doing to her, is she all right, have the bastards already killed her, how can I help her sitting here in this godforsaken shack at the ass end of nowhere with a dose of radiation sickness eating away at me?

"Where in the seven levels of hell are they?" he shouted, slamming his spoon down on the table.

George eyed him from beneath his bushy red brows. "If you'd keep quiet for half a tick you'd be able to hear them."

Dan's breath caught in his chest. Yes, in the stillness of the night there was a faint thrumming sound. Then he huffed and said, "It's just the damned generator."

George shook his head. "No, it's not. Listen."

It seemed as if each second stretched into eternity. But soon enough Dan realized the young Aussie was right. It was definitely the sound of a helicopter.

He bolted from the table, grabbed his parka and dashed out into the snow. The sky was bright with moonlight, the snow glittered clean and untouched except for George's own tracks around the cabin. And up in that sky, clattering and thundering like a giant mechanical insect, Dan saw the black silhouette of a helicopter approaching.

"Hey, you're right, Georgie! It's a beautiful night! A gorgeous night!" He laughed and pounded the big man's back.

THIRTY-SEVEN

You don't look so well," said Vasily Malik.

"Never mind that," Dan snapped. "We have work to do and less than twenty-four hours to do it."

They sat facing each other on the fantail of a luxury yacht under the warm Mediterranean sun, beneath the shade of a molecularly thin plastic awning, reflective white on top and UV-absorbent blue-green underneath. Barely an hour had passed since the Yamagata supersonic jet transport had landed Dan and George at San Remo, on the Italian riviera. From the deck of the yacht the magnificent old hotel and casino stood white and colonnaded against the hills that glittered with row upon row of hothouses where Europe's finest flowers were cultivated.

Malik had suggested a meeting place outside Paris, claiming he was afraid that Gaetano had him under surveillance. Dan did not entirely believe the Russian, but Nobuhiko suggested the yacht at San Remo. It belonged to Yamagata Industries; it was safe and unbugged.

Now Nobo sat between Malik and Dan; Big George was up on the bridge with the skipper, hugely enjoying the first time he had been on the water in more than ten years, even though the yacht lay at anchor.

"I have a medical team on its way," said Nobo.

"We're here to get Jane back," Dan said. "Everything else can wait."

Malik inclined his head slightly, as if conceding the point. But he said, "May I remind you that, technically, you are under arrest? You are in no position to make demands."

Nobo's eyes shifted from the Russian to Dan, who put on a grim smile and replied, "May I remind you, in the real world, that Jane's being held hostage by a bunch of bastards who say they'll let her go only when they get their hands on me. I'm a valuable property, pal."

"That is the only thing that is keeping you out of jail, at the moment," said Malik.

Dan's nostrils flared. "And the only thing that's keeping me from throwing you the hell over the side and into the drink is that I double-damn *need* you and the capabilities of the GEC to find where they're holding Jane and rescue her."

"You have no intention of trading yourself for her?" Malik asked. He was almost smirking. "What a surprise. I thought that at last you would show some shred of altruism, some particle of self-sacrifice."

The air between the two men seemed to crackle like the filaments in a spark tube.

"Listen, Vasily," Dan said, hunching toward the Russian until their noses were barely an inch apart, "I'll do what has to be done, but I have no intention of going in like a lamb to the slaughter. They're not going to let Jane go no matter what I do and we both know that."

"I do not know that," said Malik.

Dan leaned back in his canvas chair. He looked into Malik's ice blue eyes. "Just how much do you know?"

"What do you mean?"

"Are you working for them? Are you part of this double-damned Mafia operation?"

"Certainly not!"

"Then prove it." Dan jabbed a finger at the Russian. "Cut all this bullshit and give us the help we need to find her."

Malik stared back at Dan intently. Finally he made a small smile and waved one hand in the air. "Very well. I propose a truce between us, until Jane is safe once again."

"A truce," Dan echoed.

"I will forget that you are a wanted fugitive," said Malik. "Until Jane is safe."

A small grin returned to Dan's face. "And I'll forget that I'd rather feed you to the fishes."

"That seems like an excellent arrangement to me," said Nobo.

"Okay." Dan put out his hand. Malik hesitated for just a moment, then took it. Dan was surprised by the strength of his grip.

If I find out he really is working with Gaetano and the rest of those thugs, I'll kill him, Dan said to himself.

At the same time Malik thought, Perhaps the hoodlums will kill him and save me the trouble afterward.

"Shall we go to work now?" Nobo asked.

"By all means."

Nobo picked up the portable phone beside his chair and said, "Please bring up the map."

A moment later, Tamara Duchamps emerged from below deck, wearing a flowered bikini beneath a filmy beach coat. She carried a square electronic display map in both hands.

Dan saw Malik eying her and it made him angry the way a father would simmer at a man's lecherous ogling of his daughter. Then he noticed how Nobo looked at her. And how she looked back at him. He's really fallen for her, Dan saw. He's in orbit. And she doesn't mind it a bit.

Tamara put the flat display map on the low table before the men and managed to touch Nobo's hand before she stepped back behind his chair. He reached up and nuzzled her hand. She beamed a smile at him.

Dan grinned widely. Looks like Sai's going to get the grandson he wanted.

Then Nobuhiko became businesslike again. Pointing to the map, he said, "The security team that I had watching over Jane was under orders not to risk her life. That is why they allowed the kidnappers to take her."

Malik muttered, "That is their excuse for failing to stop the kidnappers."

Nobo glanced at Dan, who let his disgust with Malik show on his face.

"Sir," he said to the Russian, "five men and one woman let themselves be killed rather than risk Jane's life. The leader of the team killed himself after making his report to me."

Malik said nothing.

"Before she died," Nobo went on, "the woman managed to plant a homing device on the helicopter that carried Jane away from Paris. The helicopter landed here, near Lyon." He tapped the map.

"And then you lost track of her," said Malik.

Before Nobo could reply Dan said, "But *you* can help us pick up the trail, Vasily."

"I? How?"

"The surveillance satellites. The World Meteorological Center keeps the satellite tapes on file, don't they?"

"I suppose they do, but—"

"Jane's abduction happened less than forty-eight hours ago. They took her to this private airport and we assume that they transferred her to another plane and flew her somewhere else. We can scan the satellite tapes to see the planes that left that airport during the critical time period and track them to their destinations."

Malik rubbed his chin. "Yes, I suppose that is possible. If the tapes have sufficient resolution."

"If they don't, there're the military systems in the Peacekeepers' satellites. They can read the flyspecks on a postage stamp."

"Then we should go to the Peacekeepers first," said Malik.

"Okay. Good," Dan said. "Two things, though. It's got to be done fast. No hang-ups from the usual red tape. And it's got to be done in absolute secrecy. If they know we're tracking them they'll move Jane again."

Malik nodded. "I can get the commander of the Peacekeepers to help us. He is a Swede; I know him well. And I doubt that even the Mafia has infiltrated the International Peacekeeping Force."

"Assume nothing," Dan warned. "If you and the IPF commander can work this out with nobody else in the loop, that would be best."

"I understand."

"What do we do in the meantime?" Nobo asked. "The forty-eight hours are almost up."

"I will contact Gaetano and tell him that you are on your way to me," said Malik. "I will ask him for instructions on how and where to deliver you in exchange for Jane."

"Good enough," said Dan, adding silently, I hope. He turned to Nobuhiko. "We won't be able to use Peacekeepers' troops, Nobo. They're forbidden from anything that doesn't involve aggression between national groups."

"I know," said Nobo. "Yamagata will supply you with all the muscle you need. It would be difficult for me to stop my people from trying to avenge their friends' deaths."

It was night. A cool breeze swept across the water, pushing low clouds past the smiling moon. Dan saw the twinkling lights of San Remo as the anchored yacht bobbed on the swells. People there are going to dinner and gambling at the casino and living their lives just as if there's no greenhouse cliff, no disaster staring them in the face. Everything we've done so far hasn't put a dent in their awareness. Maybe nothing will until it's too late.

The breeze gusted and he shivered.

"You should get medical attention," said Tamara softly in the shadows.

Dan turned and saw that she had wrapped a windbreaker around herself, though her long lithe legs were still bare. She held another jacket out to Dan. He was still in the woolen shirt and chinos he had been wearing since the helicopter picked him and Big George out of the snow of the Himalayas. In the heat of the Mediterranean afternoon he had felt comfortable. Now he was chilled.

"Thanks," he said, pulling on the nylon jacket.

"We just got word from the Yamagata spaceport at Alphonsus. Kate Williams left yesterday."

"Yesterday? Where's she heading?"

"The space station Nueva Venezuela."

"And from there?"

She shrugged.

Dan thought a moment. "Wherever she's going, it's probably where Gaetano is. Which is probably where Jane is, too."

"Very likely," said Tamara.

"I'd better tell Nobo. Maybe he can track her."

"I've already told him. Yamagata personnel aboard the lunar shuttle will follow her."

"Good." He looked into her almond eyes. "You and Nobo have hit it off very well."

Even in the darkness he could see her dazzling smile. "He says he loves me."

"And you?"

"I think I love him."

"Think?"

"Everything has happened very quickly. I want to give this time, to see if this is really love or not."

"He's a fine young man," said Dan.

"He thinks the world of you."

Dan grinned. "You see? A man of rare perceptions and fine discriminations."

But she did not laugh. "You really must see a doctor. George told me that you received a severe radiation dose."

"Mild," Dan said. "Not severe. I've had worse and I got over them."

"But you are much older now than you were in those days."

Dan's grin turned bitter. "Ah, the innocent cruelty of youth."

"Oh! I did not mean to hurt you, Dan. . . ."

With a sigh that was only partially a put-on, Dan said, "How keener than a serpent's tooth is a reminder of a man's age from a beautiful young lady."

Before she could reply, Big George stuck his head up from the main hatch. "Hey, Dan. Malik's got the tracking data from the Peacekeepers."

"Come on," Dan said to Tamara as he headed for the hatch.

Down in the yacht's main salon, Nobo and Malik sat side by side on a leather couch, poring over the electronic map board. Dan tugged at an armchair; when it barely moved, George picked it up and deposited it at one end of the couch.

"According to the satellite data," Nobo said, "there were five departures from the airport where the helicopter landed."

"Five?" Dan asked. "Over what time period?"

"Within twelve hours of the time the helicopter landed," said Malik.

Dan nodded. It was reasonable to assume that they wouldn't keep Jane at the airport for more than a few hours. They'd want to move her to a safer, better-protected location.

Nobo was working the control dials of the map. It showed five red lines radiating from the airport. The map expanded, as though their point of view were rising like a rocket. Two of the red lines went to Orly airport outside Paris, a third to Milan, the fourth and fifth to Oran, on the coast of Algeria.

"Would they take her back to Paris?" Nobo wondered.

"If they have it will be extremely difficult to find her," said Malik.

"Or Milan, too," Dan said. "Big cities are easy to hide in and tough to find anybody who's being hidden."

"Oran is not that much smaller than Milan," Nobo pointed out.

"It must be Milan," Malik said. "It's in Italy. That's where Gaetano would take her."

Dan asked, "Did those two planes for Oran leave at the same time?"

Nobo checked the data on the map display. "Within five minutes of one another."

"That's where she's gone," Dan said eagerly. "I'd bet on it! Two planes full of hoods."

Malik was shaking his head. "I doubt it."

Tamara, standing behind the couch, touched Nobo's shoulder. He twisted in his seat to look up at her.

"You can have Kate Williams followed. She will most likely lead you to Mrs. Scanwell."

"Yes, that has already been arranged."

"Where'd those planes go after they landed in Oran?" Dan asked, still poring over the map.

Nobo tapped the map's control keys. "One remained in Oran for two hours, then returned to Marseille. The other stayed in Oran for forty-five minutes and flew to—" A new red line appeared on the map. "—to Cagliari, on Sardinia."

"Sardinia?" Malik looked shocked.

"Holy shit." Dan groaned. "They must have a strong-hold there that's right out of the Middle Ages."

It's a castle, Jane said to herself. An honest to goodness castle, just like in a fairy tale.

She stood on the roof, by the crenellated parapet, and gazed down into the green valley below. The Sardinian sun was blazing hot out of a brilliant blue sky, but the breeze was cool. In the shadows it was chilly, and inside the castle's thick walls Jane had felt positively cold. On the long climb up to the roof, along the dark, steeply winding stone stairway, she had seen her breath steaming in the air.

They had brought her here the previous night. Her captors had treated her with deference. If they realized that she had pushed the gunman from the helicopter they gave no indication of it. They had delivered her to a plane, flown to another airport, changed planes, and finally brought her here. All with the exaggerated for-mality of handling a very high-ranking prisoner of war. No threats, no cruelty, but no warmth or kindness either.

This must be the way the British treated Napoleon after Waterloo. He was from Corsica, though, not Sar-dinia. And they took him to Saint Helena, little more than a barren rock out in the middle of the Atlantic.

The Sardinian countryside was harsh but not barren. The castle sat perched atop a steep cliff of bare rock, thrust like a fist through the forest below. Down in the valley Jane could see a tiny village and some cultivated fields. Vineyards, she thought, and wondered how the local wine tasted.

Her quarters in the castle were reasonably comfort-able, though too small and confined to be royal. The door was thick and bolted from the outside. Her win-dows were narrow and barred. Peering over the edge of the parapet, Jane tried to locate her room. If those are my windows, she thought, there's a sheer drop down the wall and the cliff. Even if I could get past the bars on the window there's nothing but a straight drop of a couple hundred feet.

She sighed. At least I've got my own bathroom. The kidnappers had been very thorough. When they solemnly escorted her to her room they assured her that a complete wardrobe had been assembled for her, everything in the correct size. Jane had seen that they told the truth, and wondered how they got her bra size. Now she stood in the morning sunlight, wearing the same turtleneck and skirt she had when they had captured her. It was her only sign of defiance, that she refused to put on the clothes that they had provided.

Otherwise there was no fight left in her, not even any fear. She was here and there was nothing she could do about it. If Dan or anyone else on Earth cared about her abduction and was trying to do something about it, she had not the slightest inkling. She had been kidnapped. She had witnessed the cold-blooded murder of five people. She herself had killed a man, deliberately pushed him to his death. It was if all the emotion, all the adrenaline in her had been used up. Now she felt numb, almost dazed, totally unable to do or even think of anything that could help her escape from this.

"Are you enjoying the scenery?"

She turned and saw Gaetano ducking through the low doorway of the winding staircase. As he started toward her he pulled a pair of sunglasses from the breast pocket of his jacket and put them on like donning a mask.

"You should not stay out in the sun more than a few minutes," Gaetano said. "The ozone, you know."

"You're concerned about my health?"

"Of course."

"How touching."

Gaetano smiled at her and took his cigarette case from his inside pocket. Automatically he offered a cigarette to Jane, who refused it with a shake of her head.

After he lit up, Gaetano said, "I'm sorry it had to come

to this, Jane. But believe me, we have no desire to harm you."

"And those Japanese people who were trying to protect me?"

He shrugged nonchalantly. "Soldiers killed in a skirmish. It happens."

"It was murder and you know it."

"So? Salvatore tells me that you might have helped Carlo out of the helicopter."

"He was murdering a helpless girl."

"And you murdered him?"

Jane glared at him.

Gaetano puffed on his cigarette, smiling. "Come on, Jane, there's no sense arguing over spilt milk. Or blood. I have good news for you: Dan Randolph will be coming here for you."

"Dan?" She tried to control her sudden surge of emotion; almost succeeded.

"Once he's here we can let you go."

"What do you mean? What are you going to do to Dan?"

"We just want to keep him quiet, that's all. He's been a pain in the ass for a long time. Now we can hold him here and get on with our plans."

Jane swiftly pieced it together. They want to get Dan out of their way. So they take me, knowing that Dan will come after me. I'm the bait, nothing but bait.

"Once Randolph has come to us we can let you go back to Paris," Gaetano said. Then his smile clicked off. "But you will say nothing about us, or about this, eh— episode. Nothing to anyone, understand? Otherwise Randolph will die."

"You use me to get to Dan, and then you use him to keep me quiet."

Gaetano nodded. "As long as you remain quiet, Randolph will remain alive." He spread his arms wide, the smile reappearing. "And it's not so bad living here, is it? Princes and kings fought to take this castle, centuries ago. We'll let Randolph live like a king!"

The memory of Napoleon flashed again through Jane's mind. Once the British had him safely tucked away in exile on Saint Helena, they slowly poisoned him to death.

THIRTY-EIGHT

Beneath more than two and a half miles of water and another mile of bottom sediment and ooze rests the bedrock of the basins that make up the Gulf of Mexico and the adjoining Caribbean Sea.

The fault line that marks the border between the Caribbean tectonic plate and the North American runs roughly from Cuba to Mexico's Yucatán peninsula, buried so deeply that most geologists were uncertain whether the Caribbean basin is truly a part of the North American tectonic plate or a small plate of its own.

Their uncertainty ended abruptly. After centuries of inactivity the fault line slipped slightly, a minor readjustment in geological forces, a tiny shudder of the Earth's rocky crust. Seismographic stations as far away as St. Louis recorded an earthquake that registered 7.2 on the Richter scale.

"Thank god the epicenter was far out at sea," said the public relations woman for the Mexico City seismographic center. "An earthquake of that severity would

have caused incredible damage had it been located anywhere near a populated area."

Jane had arrived at the castle late the previous night and
had been taken directly to her locked and guarded room.
One of the guards had brought her a supper tray.

This evening, however, she ate in the castle's dining
hall with Gaetano and a very young red-haired woman
who was introduced to her as Kimberly Williams.

"My fiancée," Gaetano said, with a smile that bor-
dered on smirking.

Jane had reluctantly changed into a simple jacketed
frock that she had found in the closet waiting for her.
Kimberly wore a clinging metallic blue sheath that might
have looked sexy if she had more meat on her bones. Jane
thought the kid was pretty in an immature, freckled way.
But there was something nearly haunted about her face.
Her eyes glittered, almost like a feral animal's. She talked
too loudly, too fast, and laughed far too easily.

It was a tedious dinner in the dusty, shadowy old hall.
Jane had little to say, Kimberly had too much to say and
Gaetano obviously enjoyed having the two women on
either side of him as he sat at the head of the long heavy
wooden table.

"I will be away on business tonight," he announced, as
an ice cream dessert was being served by a silent, heavyset woman in a black maid's uniform.

"Tonight?" Kimberly fairly shouted. "Why tonight?
Can't you go tomorrow?"

"I should be back tomorrow around midmorning,"
said Gaetano. Then he turned toward Jane and added,
"With Dan Randolph."

Jane gripped her spoon hard enough to bend it. But
she said nothing.

"Why do you have to leave tonight?" Kimberly
pouted. "Why do I have to be all alone tonight?"

"Important business," said Gaetano. "Don't worry,
little one. I'll bring you a present."

The kid literally bounced up and down in her chair. "A present? What? What is it? Tell me!"

"Someone you would like to see, I think. Someone who wants very much to see you."

"Kate?" Kimberly's excitement died immediately. She looked across the table at Jane and explained glumly, "My sister. My *older* sister."

Jane said nothing. But she remembered that Kate Williams was the leader of the GEC team that had taken over Dan's office at Alphonsus. Now that she knew the relationship she could see a family resemblance in Kimberly. She turned back to Gaetano, who had the self-satisfied smile of a snake on him.

He'll be bringing Dan here. And despite all his oily assurances, Jane was certain that Gaetano fully intended to murder Dan. And herself.

"Are you certain that this thing's going to work?" Dan asked, staring at the tiny flesh-colored plug he held in his palm.

"It performed almost perfectly in the lab tests," said Nobuhiko.

Dan looked up at Nobo, then across the cabin to Malik, who was already worming a similar plug into his left ear. The only sound in the cabin was the gentle lapping of waves against the yacht's hull.

"It is practically invisible once it's in your ear," Nobo went on, encouragingly. "And since it's made entirely of protein it won't show up on any kind of metal detector. They can strip-search you and they still won't find it."

"Electronic chips made of protein," Malik murmured. "Remarkable."

"And very new," said Nobo. "So new that your Mafia kidnappers have probably never heard of them."

"You said it worked almost perfectly," Dan countered. "What's the 'almost'?"

Nobo smiled. "Apparently it can cause a slight ringing in the ear when it's activated. And perhaps a slight loss of balance. The radio frequency may interfere with the middle ear's balance mechanism. It's only temporary, of course."

Dan frowned at him.

"Come on, Randolph," said Malik, "it's too late to chicken out now."

"Famous last words," Dan muttered. But he screwed the biochip radio transceiver into his ear. It felt huge, bulging.

"To be on the safe side," Nobo explained for the twelfth time, "don't activate it until you are actually at the place where you want the assault squad to hit."

Nodding, Dan said, "I know. I know." The biochip plug felt like a watermelon jammed into his ear. He could barely hear anything through it.

Their plan was simple. Malik had already contacted Gaetano with the news that Randolph was ready to give himself up in exchange for Jane's safety. Malik would bring Dan to Gaetano, leave him and return with Jane. Both men would be wearing the protein-chip transceivers so that an aerial assault team of Yamagata special forces could locate them and swoop in—but not until they had definitely seen Jane and knew exactly where she was.

As a backup, a smaller team of Yamagata personnel was trailing Kate Williams, who had transshipped from the Nueva Venezuela space station to a shuttle for Milan. That worried Dan. One of the planes that might have been carrying Jane had landed in Milan. He was certain that Gaetano had taken Jane to Sardinia, but Milan was bothersome.

Malik sighed as they clambered down the ladder to the power launch that would take them to the floatplane waiting for them. "This is going to be very risky," said the Russian.

"You can stay here," Dan said. "You don't have to put your neck on the line."

Malik shook his head with the stubbornness of a man who had struggled to make up his mind and, once it was made up, had no intention of changing it.

"We have no way of knowing that they will take you to the same place that they are holding Jane," he reminded Dan. "I can demand to see her and bring her out with me. You are in no such position."

Dan knew that the Russian was right. Gaetano's people aren't fools. If anybody connected with this situation's been a fool, it's been me. Breaking in on the commsat broadcasts the way I did forced their hand. I shook them up, all right. And Jane's in danger because of it. Because of me.

Yet he found himself grinning at Malik as the powerboat headed for the sleek, twin-engine plane. "Who would have thought that the two of us would ever be working together, Vasily?" he shouted over the roar of the boat's motor.

Malik made a pale smile as he squinted against the spray. He mumbled something that Dan could not hear through the transceiver plug in his ear.

"What?" Dan shouted, instantly hating the fact that he sounded like a deaf old man.

"Certainly not I," Malik yelled back.

Once they had climbed into the plane and strapped themselves into their seats, Dan's smile faded. Maybe we're not really working together, he thought. Maybe he's on Gaetano's side after all and he's just bringing me to the slaughter. And Jane, too.

Big George leaned his heavy forearms on the yacht's rail and watched the sleek twin-engine floatplane lift off from the calm Mediterranean water. Nobuhiko and Tamara stood beside him.

As the plane dwindled into the cloud-flecked sky, Nobo turned to Tamara and said, "I have much to do." He started toward the hatch to the main salon.

George grabbed him by the arm, turning him around.

"I'm going with your rescue team," George said.

Nobuhiko's eyes flashed wide for an instant. Then he

smiled and said, "I'm sorry, that will be impossible."

"I'm going," George said, still holding Nobo's arm.

"Perhaps you don't understand. The team is composed of paramilitary specialists. They are all highly skilled, highly trained."

"Dan's my friend and he's going to need all the fooking help he can get."

"This will be an extremely difficult and dangerous operation," Nobo said.

"If it was a fooking piece of cake I wouldn't bother with it," George said, his temper rising.

Tamara stepped between them. "Let him go with your team," she said gently to Nobo. "He is concerned for Dan."

"But the team—"

"Let him go with them," Tamara urged.

"Have you ever jumped in a parachute before?" Nobo asked George.

The big Aussie scratched at his half-grown beard. "When I was a kid, back home in Queensland."

"How many jumps?"

"Oh," George waved a ham-sized hand, "dozens of times."

Nobo knew he was lying. "Can you speak Japanese?"

"Wakarimashita," George said. I understand. Then he added, "You can't work on the fooking Moon without learning some Japanese. I can understand it if you *motto yukkuri hanashite kudasai."*

"The soldiers may not have the time to speak slowly to you," Nobo said.

"Look," George said, looming over Nobo and Tamara like a glowering thunderhead, "I'm not going to sit here and bite my nails while Dan's got his neck on the chopping block. I may not be a fooking ninja but I can fight."

Nobo glared back at the giant.

Tamara suggested, "What about the other team, the one that is following Kate Williams?"

Nobo said grudgingly, "I could ask the team leader to take you with them."

George grinned like a kid in a candy shop. "Thanks! You won't regret it." He rushed to the hatch and ducked down belowdecks.

Nobo shook his head. "This is a mistake. George will be a drag on them. He'll make matters worse, not better."

Tamara slipped her arm around his waist and leaned her head against his shoulder. "You did the right thing. He wants to help Dan." Silently she added, And he might have broken every bone in your body if you refused to allow him to go.

THIRTY-NINE

The underwater earthquake lasted only seventy-two seconds. Some of its impact on the sea above was absorbed by the soft mud of the seabed sediments. Still, a tremendous jolt of energy was imparted to the water.

Monitoring satellite sensors detected a deep swell in the Gulf of Mexico, a spreading ring of waves like the ripples caused by dropping a pebble in a pond. But these waves contained megatons of energy. They were not high, so far away from land where the water was more than two miles deep. But they were spreading in all directions, racing across the face of the Gulf, and steepening as they ran toward the shallower waters of the coast.

The satellite automatically sent its data to the ground stations beneath its flight track. None of the automated equipment was programmed to recognize a tsunami. There had never been a tidal wave in the Gulf of Mexico within the history of the satellite monitoring system. No alarm bells rang. No human observer shouted out a warning. The data were entered in the monitoring system's computer files, where they would be analyzed someday.

While the tsunami silently, relentlessly surged toward shore.

Don Marcello Arcangelico found himself on the horns of a delicate dilemma.

On the one hand, it was his policy never to allow himself to be physically connected with a crime of any sort. Other people committed the acts that he deemed necessary while he sat safely in his home, surrounded by witnesses. He had never been charged by the police with so much as a misdemeanor.

On the other hand, he felt that he had to see this man Randolph with his own eyes. Gaetano was ambitious enough to cut his own deal with the big shots in the GEC. Randolph had to be silenced and the Scanwell woman neutralized. And Gaetano kept firmly in hand. Don Marcello could not rest easily on any of those counts until he saw Randolph with his own eyes. Trust did not come easily, not when the whole world was at stake. This was no time for a slipup, no time to let Gaetano think that the old man was getting careless.

So he commanded Gaetano to bring Randolph to his home in Reggio. There was little risk that Randolph would ever identify him as being involved in Scanwell's abduction. Randolph would be dead within hours.

About an hour after the floatplane took off Dan whispered to Malik, "We're not heading for Sardinia."

"Are you certain?"

Pointing at the placid sea and puffy cumulus clouds outside their circular window, Dan said, "The sun rises in the east and it's ahead of us on our left. Sardinia is a little west of south from where the yacht was anchored. If we were heading that way the sun would be almost behind us."

Malik unbuckled his safety strap and made his way forward to the flight deck, hunched over because of the plane's low ceiling. He spoke briefly with the two pilots and then returned to his seat.

"Well?"

"They told me to mind my own business."

Dan shook his head. "It's not Sardinia."

"What can we do?"

"Get some sleep," said Dan, cranking his chair back. He closed his eyes, but he was far too restless to sleep. He felt a sullen fatigue sapping at his strength. Maybe I really have radiation sickness, Dan thought. I feel like a squeezed-out dishrag. And that damned earplug hurts.

He knew there was a plane full of Yamagata paramilitary following them at an extreme distance, guided by mini-satellites that Nobo had launched specifically to monitor the region. But what good is all this if they don't take either one of us to where Jane is?

Gaetano had left the castle immediately after dinner. Up in her room, Jane heard a car crunching on the gravel driveway that circled the castle's inner courtyard. Going to the window, she saw a flash of headlights against the main gate, and then the car was heading down the switchbacks of the road cut into the cliff's face.

Someone knocked at her door.

From the barred window Jane called out, "Who is it?"

"Me," came a muffled voice. "Kim."

She let out a pent-up breath, suddenly aware that she was alone in a castle full of armed men, except for Kimberly.

"Come in," she called.

The bolt slid back and the door creaked open. Jane caught a glimpse of the young man guarding the door, his dark face solemn as Kimberly stepped into the room. She was still in the glittering blue sheath she had worn at dinner.

"Wow! They gave you the biggest bedroom in the place."

"I suppose they did," said Jane.

"But no TV."

Jane had not noticed until Kimberly mentioned it. "I think Rafe would rather I didn't see any of the news broadcasts," she said flatly.

"There's nothing much on anyway," said Kim, moving slowly through the room, touching the sturdy old bureau, the faded mirror atop it, the massive hand-tooled armoire, the dusty tasseled spread across the canopied bed.

"You're lonely," Jane said.

"Kind of."

"Are you really Rafe's fiancée? Has he proposed marriage to you?"

Kimberly laughed brittlely. "Marriage? Not for me! I'm never going to marry Rafe or any other man."

"Then . . . ?"

"Oh, he was kind of fun for a while. But I get the feeling he's just using me to make my sister sore."

"He's not a decent man."

Kimberly shrugged. "Who is?"

Jane went to the couch, sat down and patted the cushion beside her. "Come here and tell me about yourself. And your sister."

Luther Clay took his family to Biloxi for the weekend. As head of Louisiana's environmental protection agency, Clay had phoned his opposite number in Mississippi to make certain that the beach at Biloxi was reasonably clean of oil and the Gulf water was all right for swimming.

His daughter had whined and complained all through the long, sweltering Friday-night drive. She wanted to be with her boyfriend, not stuck with her medieval parents. But as soon as they hit the beach early Saturday morning she found that there were plenty of guys there who were quickly attracted to her. Clay fretted about the amount of skin she was exposing in her bikini. Even black skin was no protection these days. But his wife told him that it was better than her spending the weekend with that white trash she thought she was in love with.

It was a hazy, cloudy day. The sun seemed pale and too weak to harm anyone despite the warnings about skin cancer. The tide seemed to be out farther than Clay had ever seen it before. Tides around the Gulf were never that big to begin with, but this morning it seemed as if the water had just picked up and walked away. Wet gray sand stretched out for what looked like a mile or more.

Clay stood staring at the uncovered beach, the tiniest hint of a worrisome thought nagging at the back of his mind. He saw his daughter laughing and horsing around with a bunch of boys, some of them white.

Then he noticed something really odd. Far out on the horizon the sea seemed to rise up. Like a wall of water, just lifting up, its top edge as straight as the horizon itself. Clay thought his eyes were playing tricks on him.

He had never seen a tidal wave before.

"So you are Dan Randolph," said Don Marcello.

Dan looked down at the corpulent old man in the wheelchair. There was a smell of corruption about him, a stink of fear in the way the other men in the room walked on tiptoe and spoke in whispers. Even Gaetano seemed subdued in this darkened, dusty, closed-in chamber with its heavy ancient furniture and its lone feeble lamp casting more shadow than light. It was high noon outside, but in this room there was no sunlight, no time. Like a gambling casino, thought Dan.

He and Malik had indeed been strip-searched and walked through an X-ray metal detector identical to the type used at airports. Now they stood in the gloomy study of Don Marcello's dreary house, under the scrutiny of the balding old man and a roomful of guards.

"You know who I am," Dan said, standing before the

wheelchair. "Who are you?"

Don Marcello waggled a fat beringed finger. "That is not important," he said in heavily accented English. Dan noticed that his rings dug deeply into the flesh of his fingers; the old man had been wearing them for many years.

"We were supposed to see Mrs. Scanwell," said Malik, standing beside Dan. "Where is she?"

"You will see her," Don Marcello replied. "Mr. Randolph will not."

A bolt of fear sizzled through Dan. *I should have known better. They're too smart to take me to the same place they've taken her.*

"Then it's no deal," he said sharply. "If I don't see her with my own eyes, the deal is off."

Don Marcello's mouth dropped open for a moment, then he threw his head back and laughed, laughed so hard his eyes squeezed shut and tears ran down his baggy cheeks, laughed until he began coughing and sputtering. One of the silent men standing in the shadows behind the wheelchair came up and handed him an inhalator. Hacking and coughing, the old man stuck the nozzle in his mouth and pressed the plastic plunger.

Maybe he'll choke to death, Dan thought.

"They didn't tell me you are a comedian," said Don Marcello, once he got his breath under control again.

"The deal was that I see Mrs. Scanwell and make certain that she's safely on her way back to Paris," Dan insisted.

"You're in no position to make any demands," Don Marcello replied. Pointing to Malik, "This one will see the woman and take her back to Paris. You stay here."

"No," said Malik.

"What?" It seemed to be a word that Don Marcello did not often hear.

"We have honored our commitment. You must honor yours. Randolph is entitled to see Mrs. Scanwell. You pledged that he would. You must honor that pledge."

"Honor? You talk to me about honor?"

Malik leaned down slightly to put his face closer to the old man's. "You cannot keep the woman silent if she fears that Randolph has been murdered. Unless she sees him, she will not cooperate with you."

Don Marcello glared up at him.

Malik turned to Gaetano. "You know Jane, Rafaelo. Am I speaking the truth about her?"

"Yes," said Gaetano reluctantly. "She is in love with Randolph. If she thinks we've killed him—well, we'll have to kill her too."

"So?"

"And you will have to kill me also," Malik said. "I will not stand idly by if you murder Jane Scanwell."

Dan's eyes flicked from one of them to the other as he thought, Malik doesn't mind them knocking me off, but he's sticking his neck out for Jane.

"How will the world react to the death of two members of the Global Economic Council?" Malik asked. "One of them its new chairman."

Gaetano shifted uneasily on his feet. Don Marcello stared at Malik, one hand stroking his chins.

"There are limits to what you can get away with," Malik went on. "Murdering two GEC representatives will bring down the full power of the international community upon your heads. And you know it."

Dan was silently urging, Don't tell him we're being tracked, for Chrissakes! Don't blow it!

Don Marcello finally replied, "You will cooperate with us if we satisfy the woman?"

With a glance at Dan, Malik allowed a tiny smile to creep across his lips. "Naturally. What do I care if you kill this American? He's been nothing but a thorn in my flesh for years. But Jane Scanwell is another matter. Let her see Randolph. Then I will take her back to Paris. What happens to this Yankee afterward is of no concern to me."

He sounds as if he means it, Dan thought. Aloud, he

said, "Jane won't go along with you if she realizes I'm dead."

"She will not realize it," Gaetano said. "We will make a few tapes of your voice and then use a synthesizer to send her telephone messages every few weeks."

"You'll need my cooperation to make those tapes."

Gaetano snickered. "You'll cooperate. First you will scream a lot, but soon enough you'll do whatever we tell you to."

FORTY

The wall of water that drowned Biloxi hit the inlet to Lake Pontchartrain less than half an hour later. It surged through the inlet, steepening and speeding up in its narrow confines, smashing everything in its path—boats, wharves, locks, bridges—and surged into the broad lake like an invading army searching for plunder.

The concrete bridge carrying Interstate Highway 10 was inundated, cars, trucks, buses swept away into the churning muddy waters. The central span of the bridge collapsed, never designed to stand up to latitudinal stresses of such force.

Within minutes the expanding wave surged over the north-south causeway that spanned the lake and smashed against the concrete levee that protected the city of New Orleans and its suburban communities.

Whole sections of the levee were gouged away; rotting concrete and rusting steel reinforcements that should have been replaced years earlier simply tore loose under the tidal wave's enormous pressure. Millions of tons of water poured through. The city's pumping stations were overwhelmed before they could even start up. A frothing smashing wave of dirty gray water rushed through the streets, knocking down poles and highway bridges, collapsing buildings, tossing automobiles and diesel trucks and city buses like flotsam. Over the unstoppable roar of the water came the screams of a million people and more as they were drowned or crushed by the raging water.

Downhill toward the river the water raced, carrying half the city with it. Electrical wires snapped and fizzed, sewer lines literally exploded with overpressure. Basin Street, Rampart Street, Bourbon Street disappeared beneath the raging floodwaters. At Duncan Plaza the water smashed through the doors and windows of the City Hall and other government buildings in an unstoppable torrent, tearing away desks, file cabinets, bookcases, people. The mayor found herself stranded on the roof of the City Hall, clinging to a useless radio antenna.

She sobbed hysterically as she looked out on what had been a city. There was nothing to see except the ghosts of buildings sticking out of the surging filthy water. The water itself was thick with debris and the floating bodies of the dead.

The same twin-engine floatplane took Dan, Malik and Gaetano westward through the late afternoon toward Sardinia. They were totally unaware of the disaster that had struck the Gulf shore and New Orleans.

Dan leaned back in his chair and closed his eyes. That old man is the boss of these hoodlums, whoever he is. Then Dan grinned sardonically. They were bargaining over my life, Malik and the old man. Deciding when they would kill me. Not if. When.

He wondered where the Yamagata plane was. They can't have stayed aloft all this time. They must have had to put down somewhere and refuel. Have they picked us up again? Inadvertently he reached toward his ear, where the biochip transceiver was lodged, but pulled his hand away when he remembered that Gaetano was sitting behind him. They haven't detected it so far, he thought. But if I activate it now to give Nobo's people a signal to home on, would the pilots up in the cockpit be able to detect it on their instruments?

He glanced over at Malik, sitting tensely in his seat. Not yet, Dan decided. The plan is that we don't activate the chips until we see Jane. Then the Yamagata team can attack. If they're still close enough to get the signal.

No matter what happened, Jane would be safe. Malik's playing a dangerous game, tightrope-walking between Gaetano and his own interests. But he wants Jane safe almost as much as I do. At least he says he does.

Dan tried to sleep. But no matter how exhausted he felt, no matter how weak and old he felt, sleep would not come. I'm scared, he realized. For the first time in my life I'm really scared. These guys are going to kill me. Or try to. I'll be okay once the action starts, he told himself. It's this damned waiting, just sitting here with nothing to do but think and wait and worry.

Eventually he drifted into a troubled sleep, dreaming of formless monsters and hovering faces that shifted before he could truly recognize who they were.

As they drove slowly up the switchback road cut into the cliff's face, Dan craned his neck for a view of the castle. It loomed up at the top of the cliff, dark gray crenellated stone walls outlined against the bright blue Sardinian sky. It's not all that big, Dan thought. But those walls look plenty thick.

He felt sick in the pit of his stomach. Whether from fear or radiation or just the fact that he had not eaten anything in almost a full day, he could not tell. Maybe they plan to starve me to death, he thought. Didn't one of the Roman emperors do that to somebody? Walled him up in a cell beneath the Senate building and let him starve to death?

He searched the cloudless sky for a trace of a contrail,

some evidence that the Yamagata plane was near. Nothing. The sky was a flawless bowl of blue, unmarred by any planes whatsoever.

As their car trundled over the warped wooden boards of the castle's moat bridge, Dan saw that there were six men standing at the main gate. They were in shirtsleeves, dark lean men with stubble on their faces and short-barreled shotguns slung over their shoulders. Rabbit guns. *Luperia*. The kind that armies all over the world had adopted for close-in killing.

Another half-dozen armed men were sitting around the sunny inner courtyard. One of them trotted alongside the car as it slowed to a stop. The driver clicked the door locks and the shotgun-armed man pulled Dan's door open.

Ducking through, Dan stretched tiredly and felt his spine and tendons pop. He let the late-afternoon sun soak into his bones. It felt good, although his legs seemed wobbly. Must be the gravity, he told himself. Looking up at the fitted stone walls around the courtyard, he saw a face in one of the narrow barred windows.

Jane.

Dan's stomach did a flip. He grinned foolishly and waved to her. Jane's face disappeared from the window and another took its place, a red-haired young woman who looked enough like Kate . . . Dan remembered Kate's sister. So she's here too. Wonder if Kate's really going to join the party.

Gaetano came around the car with a smarmy smile on his face. "You see? I spoke the truth, eh? There she is, waiting for you."

As Malik pulled himself out of the car, an older man, dressed in a dead black suit, stepped out of the doorway and beckoned to Gaetano. He went to the man, who looked to Dan like a butler or some sort of house servant. The man spoke briefly to Gaetano.

"What do you suppose he is saying?" Malik asked, sounding slightly nervous. Dan barely heard him through the earplug.

"Telling him what's on the menu for dinner," Dan said, shifting to put Malik on the side of his good ear.

Malik huffed. "Us, most likely."

"Us," Dan agreed.

"I have more good news for you," Gaetano said. "An old friend of yours has come all the way from the Moon to be with us. She should arrive here in a few minutes."

Kate Williams, sure enough. Dan wondered why she would leave Alphonsus, then remembered that she wanted more than anything else to protect her sister.

"We will wait here for her to arrive," Gaetano said. "Her car is halfway up the cliff already."

"I want to see Jane," said Dan.

"You can wait a few minutes. Then we can have a big, happy reunion, all of us together."

They also serve who stand and wait, Dan said to himself. Malik looked more apprehensive than ever. The seriousness of this pickle is just starting to sink in to him. We could all get ourselves killed.

Dan strolled slowly away from the car, across the sun-lit courtyard, noticing that at least two of the guys with shotguns watched him with beady eyes, hands on their weapons. If Gaetano knows that Kate's car is halfway up the cliff, maybe he's got guards posted along the road. Or maybe Kate just phoned him from the car to let him know she's almost here.

He enjoyed the warmth of the sun through his woolen shirt. He felt perspiration trickling down his ribs. Bake the bad stuff out of me, he said to the sun. Boil away the fear. Make me strong again.

He heard the boards of the bridge thudding, and an executive limousine swung through the gate, crunching across the gravel of the courtyard. It stopped behind the car that Dan had come in. A strapping big chauffeur hopped out and opened the door for Kate Williams.

Dan stared at the chauffeur. There was no mistaking

his size or his rough red beard, even in an ill-fitting suit of livery and a cap that was almost comically too small for him.

How in the hell did Big George get into this game?

FORTY-ONE

Jane waited impatiently for them to open the door to her room, striding from the barred window to the locked door and then back again. Gaetano was keeping them down there in the courtyard, stretching out the minutes, torturing her. Dan was there, he had seen her, he had even waved. Close enough to touch, almost. Almost.

"What are they waiting for?" Jane blurted, one hand fidgeting with her hair. She had pinned it back, smooth and sleek, but now she wondered if it wouldn't look better falling loosely to her shoulders.

Kimberly's hair was a helmet of molten copper. She was watching Jane curiously, a sly little half smile curling her lips.

"Relax," Kim said. "They'll be here soon enough."

But Jane rushed back to the window. She saw a limousine pull through the guarded main gate. The chauffeur trudged around and opened the door for a woman to step out. Kate Williams.

"Your sister's here," she called to Kimberly.

"Big deal."

"They're starting inside!" At last, at last, she thought.

Jane's eyes darted to the dusty mirror in the corner of the room. She had picked a simple forest green jumpsuit from the closet full of clothes Gaetano had provided. Sensible low-heeled shoes. No need for glamor today. If I know Dan, there's going to be a ruckus before this is all over.

Kimberly, in a pastel miniskirted sundress, seemed to be catching Jane's nervousness. Her lips had become a tense thin line, her hands knotted into fists.

"Why did he bring her here?" she asked, her voice brittle. "Rafe and I were getting along fine. We don't need her here."

Jane answered, "Rafe is a lying, murdering, scheming bastard. I imagine he'll enjoy watching you and your sister hurt each other."

"Hurt? I never hurt Kate!"

"From all that you've told me, that's not true," Jane said. Then she added as gently as she could, "And you know it."

Kimberly looked away without answering.

The bolt of the door clanked and the heavy door groaned inward. Jane held her breath. Gaetano stepped through, followed by Malik, Kate Williams and finally Dan. Four armed men stood out in the hallway. Jane ran to Dan and threw her arms around his neck.

Dan grabbed her as if she were life itself and held her to him as they kissed, ignoring all the others for a long sweet moment.

"I love you," she whispered into his ear.

Dan barely heard her through the biochip plug. He whispered back, "I've always loved you."

Gaetano clapped his hands slowly, sardonically. "Bravo," he quipped. "Bravissimo. Now let's get down to business."

Dan grinned crookedly as he let go of Jane. She stood

beside him, their backs to the door.

"You have arranged transport for Mrs. Scanwell and myself?" Malik asked.

"In due time, Vasily," said Gaetano. "There are one or two points we must clear up first."

Dan scratched at his ear, then stuck his little finger in and touched the biochip transceiver. It felt warm. But nothing happened. No ringing in his ear. No way to know if the damned thing worked or not. He glanced over at Malik. Sonofabitch hasn't activated his unit. The Russian's hands stayed down at his sides.

"Rafe, you'll have to make your transportation arrangements for the three of us," said Jane. "I'm not leaving here without Dan."

Gaetano's eyebrows rose slightly. "I'm afraid that will be impossible, my dear Jane. Dan remains here. He will be kept well and happy, as long as you behave yourself once you get back to Paris."

"I don't believe you," Jane said. "I won't believe that Dan's safe as long as he's in your hands."

Smiling, Gaetano gestured toward Kate Williams. "Look, I've even brought him an old friend from the Moon. He'll have plenty to amuse himself with while he's here."

Dan laughed. "I'd rather amuse myself with a nest of cobras."

"I am not leaving here without Dan," Jane said firmly.

"Yes, you are," said Gaetano. "You have no choice. And his continued good health will depend entirely on your continuing cooperation."

"He's right," Malik said, stepping toward Jane. "You'll have to come back to Paris with me, Jane. We have no option in the matter."

Jane glowered at the Russian, then at Gaetano.

"It's all right," Dan said. "Do what they're telling you. I'll be okay."

She studied Dan more closely. He seemed pale, thinner than she had ever remembered him. He was wearing a heavy woolen shirt and rough Levi's. There was perspiration on his brow, his upper lip.

Dan made himself smile for her. "I'm okay," he said, anticipating her question. "Just a little dose of radiation. Nobo's medics have already stuck enough counteractants in me to shut down a nuclear reactor."

But he felt weak, knees shaky. If the Yamagata medicines were doing any good he had yet to feel it.

"Then it's settled," Gaetano said. "You two can return to Paris tomorrow morning. Randolph stays here as a guarantee for Jane's good behavior."

"Tomorrow morning?" Malik asked. "Why not now? The sooner the better."

"We still have much to discuss," said Gaetano.

"Discuss?"

"Yes. I want to show you what is expected of you back on the Council. We have a worldwide program to implement, and your cooperation will be very important to us."

Dan saw how Jane's face hardened. Even Malik looked angry. Gaetano seemed amused, terribly pleased with himself.

"After all, I may not be the GEC's chairman," he made a mocking little bow to Malik, "or its most prestigious member," another bow, lower, with a flourish, to Jane, "but I do expect the two of you to help me in every way." Gaetano's smile vanished. His voice became iron hard. "In other words, I will tell you what to do and you will do it. I will be the master of the GEC. Me, and no one else."

Dan clapped his hands exactly as Gaetano had a few minutes earlier. Furious, the Italian whirled around and raised his fist. Dan saw the punch coming but could not move fast enough to block it.

Malik grabbed Gaetano's wrist and held his arm in midair. The Italian tried to twist free, but Malik held him in a grip of steel.

"There is no need for violence," the Russian said.

"Violence is for fools." Then he released Gaetano's wrist.

Wringing his hand and glaring at Malik, Gaetano said, "Yes, you're right. Violence is for fools." Then he shifted his seething gaze to Dan. "And for my hired help."

As he took his place at the heavy dark dinner table Dan thought that Jane looked furious, Malik tense, Kate worried, her sister puzzled and Gaetano as pleased as an operatic tenor who had just been asked for a third encore.

Gaetano had spent the remainder of the day locked in conference with Jane and Malik. Giving them their orders, Dan knew. Kate and her sister had gone off together. Dan had taken a nap. No sign of Big George. No sign of the Yamagata assault team. No indication that the double-damned biochip plug had worked at all.

Dan had been tempted to pull the transceiver out of his ear once he was alone in the bedroom to which Gaetano's guards had escorted him. But he feared that he might be watched by hidden cameras. So he flopped on the narrow bed fully clothed, the transceiver feeling like a boulder lodged in his ear, and stared at the ceiling, knowing that he was far too wound up to sleep.

When the guard's unlocking the door woke him, it was dark outside. Nothing had changed except the time. Dan splashed some water on his face and went down the castle's broad stone main staircase to the dining hall, escorted front and rear by silent, grim-looking guards whose shoulder holsters showed through their unbuttoned leather vests.

Gaetano sat at the head of the table, almost vibrating, he was so wired. He chattered about the antiquity of the castle, the family that had built it, the foreign invaders who had never been able to conquer it. Jane and Malik, at Gaetano's right and left, respectively, exchanged worried looks with each other and occasionally stole a swift glance down to the end of the table, where Dan sat.

He thinks he's got it made, Dan told himself. He thinks

he's won it all. I guess neither Jane nor Malik put up much resistance to him this afternoon. He gave them their orders and they agreed to do what they're told.

Kate and her sister hardly said a word as a pair of sullen-faced heavyset women in black uniforms served dinner, shuttling in and out of the swinging door to the kitchen like a pair of silent morose robots.

Where in hell is Nobo's team? Dan asked himself for the thousandth time. Do they know we're here? Has something happened to them? And what's George up to?

Gaetano's monologue had shifted from the history of the castle to the history of the family who had originally owned and defended it. Now he was talking about his own family, but Dan realized that he did not mean merely his parents and siblings.

"Related by blood," Gaetano said. "That is what makes us strong. Blood ties are the most binding. We are a family. Every man who joins takes a blood oath that follows him to the grave and even beyond."

"Beyond?" Jane asked.

"Generations beyond," said Gaetano. His dark eyes were glittering like the wine in his crystal goblet as it caught the candlelight. "What is the vendetta except a keeping of faith with the generations that preceded you?"

"I thought it was nothing more than a primitive thirst for vengeance," said Malik.

"Like a family feud in the Ozarks," Dan added, raising his voice to be heard down the length of the table.

Gaetano's smile turned sinister. "You make jokes about things you don't understand. The vendetta is an expression of family loyalty that extends from one generation to the next."

"And damned near depopulated parts of Sicily," said Dan.

"Organized murder," Malik said.

"Organized," Gaetano agreed, emphasizing the word with an upraised finger. "That is the key. Organization." He looked down the table at Dan. "You are correct,

Randolph. At one time vendettas had taken so many lives in Sicily that whole towns were abandoned, there were not enough men left to till the fields. But those days are gone. Now we are organized."

With a sad shake of his head Dan said, "Blood oaths and family loyalty—it's all so medieval. Your so-called organization is a throwback to the Dark Ages. People have learned to develop higher loyalties than that. While the rest of the world created nation-states and multinational corporations and even a double-damned Global Economic Council, you benighted pricks still act like it's the frigging ninth century."

Gaetano's nostrils flared with anger. "For thousands of years our people have been invaded by foreigners! Greeks, Romans, Goths, Huns, French. Even today our land is ruled by strangers in Rome. We created our organization to protect ourselves against the outside world."

"By stealing from your own people. By murdering and terrifying them."

"What ruler has ever succeeded without cowing his people into obedience?" Gaetano asked. "Besides, as I told you, we no longer kill amongst ourselves."

"Now you kill other people."

Gaetano conceded the point with a tilt of his head. "When we must. But violence is for fools—unless it is absolutely necessary."

"You prefer kidnapping and extortion."

"I prefer bribery," said Gaetano, a fingertip brushing his moustache. "It is usually the safest and cleanest. You would be surprised at how easy it is to bribe people. And not always with money, either. Take Kate, here. All I had to do was to give her Astro Corporation."

Kate stiffened. She did not look at Dan, or even at Gaetano. She stared at her sister, across the table from her.

"Touché," said Dan.

Gaetano turned back to Malik. "You think that the GEC is running the world; that you, as Council chairman, are in charge. But *we* are really controlling everything. From the cockfight pits of Bangkok to the agenda of the Global Economic Council, *we* are in charge! We have ended the vendettas and expanded throughout Europe and North America. We are bringing the Latin cartel under our control, and the Asian gangs as well. Soon we will have the entire world in our grasp. And the Moon, as well."

"Like Genghis Khan," Dan said.

"Eh?"

"He got the warring Mongol tribes to stop fighting among themselves by turning them outward, to conquest."

"Yes, and he built a mighty empire, didn't he?" Gaetano said.

"Is that who the old man is? The man we saw this morning? Is he your Genghis Khan?"

Gaetano's expression hardened. "Who he is is none of your business."

Dan shrugged. "Vasily, do you see where all this is leading? You wanted to get the whole world's economy under your control—for the good of the people, of course. But once you've done that, some piece of shit like this jerk can steal it from you and all you've accomplished is to hand the world over to a pack of thieving, murdering bastards."

"You need a few lessons in manners," Gaetano said.

"It's never been my strong point," Dan replied.

Malik sat silently, as if lost in thought. Jane's eyes darted from Dan to Gaetano to the Russian and then back to Dan.

The lights went out.

The chandelier and the lights in the wall sconces flicked off, leaving the table dimly lit by the decorative candles.

"The emergency generator will come on in a moment," said Gaetano.

Several moments passed. The room remained candle-lit. Gaetano spoke in Italian to one of the dour swarthy guards and he left the room. Dan heard excited, exasperated voices shouting from the kitchen.

Nobo's team has arrived, he told himself. They got here!

The guard came back into the room, bringing a palm-sized two-way radio to Gaetano. Nothing came from it but a hiss of static. In the shadows cast by the candles Dan smiled grimly. The Yamagata team's knocked out every electrical and electronic circuit in the place. Must have thumped the castle with a hell of an electromagnetic pulse.

"On your feet, all of you!" Gaetano snapped. "Something is happening here. You will each be taken to separate rooms. Do not try to leave those rooms until we have things under control. The doors will be locked and guarded. If this is an attack on the castle you will be used as hostages. All of you."

Jane looked over her shoulder toward Dan as one of the guards took her by the arm and headed for the door. Malik was pushed forward by another guard, none too gently. In the semidarkness it was hard to make out the expression on Gaetano's face. At least, thought Dan, he doesn't seem so cocky anymore.

Two guards grabbed his arms and moved him toward the kitchen, away from the others. Going to keep us separated, Dan realized. They passed Gaetano, who was banging the two-way on the table. Dan laughed inwardly: when it doesn't work, hammer it. That'll do a lot of good.

The kitchen was even darker than the dining hall, lit only by a pair of battery-powered emergency lamps placed above each of its two doors. In the thick shadows the rows of heavy pots and skillets hanging from their overhead racks looked like an arsenal of medieval weapons. Dan knew there were plenty of knives around, too, but he could not see any in the thick shadows.

But there was a big steaming pot on the stove. Dan stumbled, staggered, let his arms go limp in the grasp of his two guards. They tried to yank him to his feet but Dan hung limply between them, moaning as theatrically as he dared.

They lowered him to the floor, speaking to each other in swift Italian. Dan realized that they intended to carry him, one at his shoulders, the other at his feet.

He kicked with both feet at the guard's knees, knocking him to the floor with a surprised yelp of pain, and pulled the other one down headfirst to sprawl on top of him. Wriggling to his feet Dan grabbed the steaming pot as the guard reached for his shoulder holster. He saw the boiling water coming and tried to duck out of its way but Dan flung it at him, pot and all. He screamed as Dan wrung his hands in pain; the pot's metal handgrips had been scalding hot.

The other guard was scrambling to his feet. Dan reached overhead, grabbed a heavy iron skillet and banged him on the head with it. He fell sideways. Dan swung the skillet again, ignoring the pain in his hand. It sounded like a cathedral clock's gong. For good measure he bashed the scalded one, too. They both lay silent on the tiled floor. As Dan pawed the two bodies for their pistols he heard gunshots, muffled, far away. But definitely gunshots.

The battle's on, and Gaetano's going to use Jane as a shield for himself. Jamming the two pistols into the belt of his Levi's, wringing his painful hands, Dan headed back toward the dining hall.

FORTY-TWO

The dining hall was empty, the table still set with food in the dishes and wine in the goblets. The candles flickered fitfully in the draft from the open door at the far side of the chamber.

Dan made his way to the central hall. It was as dark as a cave, not even moonlight sifting through the long narrow windows. Dan knew that the main staircase was off to his right and that Gaetano had probably taken Jane up that way.

More gunshots. Closer. The rattle of automatic weapons. He could hear shouting now, heavy angry voices yelling back and forth.

They're not using tranquilizer darts, he knew. Gingerly pulling one of the automatic pistols from his belt, his palm and fingers raw from their scalding, he realized that he would be firing real bullets. And they'll be shooting to kill you, pal. Hope Nobo's team has night-vision gear. I'd hate to be shot by my own side.

He groped across the central hall toward the main

staircase, the pistol heavy in his hand. Slowly, carefully, like a blind man without a cane, he slid one foot in front of the other until finally he butted against the first step of the staircase.

He started up the steps. Uncertain of how high or deep they were, he nearly tripped on the first one. Cripes, he thought, if I fall down the gun in my belt might just shoot my *cojones* off. So he pulled the second pistol out with his left hand and proceeded slowly, gropingly, up the wide stone staircase, feeling slightly ridiculous, like a cowboy gunslinger in an old video with a gun in each hand.

He heard footsteps running against the stone floor up above. A voice, speaking low and swift in Italian. He froze on the steps. If I can't see them they can't see me, Dan told himself.

The thin beam of a flashlight lanced through the darkness, sweeping erratically along the staircase. Dan flattened himself against the steps. The flashlight beam swung toward him, hazy with dust motes.

"Eccolo! Fucile!"

Somebody at the top of the stairs sprayed a fusillade of automatic rifle fire at Dan. Bullets whined and cracked all around him. Stone chips flew from the steps and walls, slashing his back, his arms, his cheek. He remembered that the last time he had fired a pistol had been on a target range in Texas, nearly thirty years earlier. And he had been a rotten shot.

Big George had been down in the servants' quarters, as befits a chauffeur, when the lights went out.

The job Nobuhiko had given him was to make contact with Kate Williams and stay with her, wherever she went. Nobo's reasoning was that even if Dan and Malik failed to reach Jane, the only reason that Kate had left Alphonsus was to rendezvous with Gaetano. Therefore George was fitted out with a biochip earplug and told to be ready to move at an instant's notice.

Yamagata personnel tracked Kate from the Nueva

Venezuela space station to Milan's sprawling busy airport. She boarded a private plane. Satellite sensors picked up the plane as it cleared the airport while Yamagata agents pried its flight plan out of the airport computer. Kate was heading for Cagliari, on Sardinia.

Hasty plans were made. George and a pair of young Yamagata agents, a man and a woman, were picked up from the yacht by a chartered jet seaplane and flown at top speed to the airport at Cagliari. Breathlessly searching the small airport, they found the limousine waiting for Kate's arrival just a few minutes before Kate's own plane touched down. So swiftly and quietly that no one noticed, the two Japanese took the driver and security guard away at gunpoint.

That was how Big George, feeling silly in an ill-fitting chauffeur's uniform, drove Kate to the castle. The original chauffeur, together with Gaetano's security guard, remained at the airport under the watchful eyes of the two Yamagata people. He had thoughtfully taped the directions to the castle onto the limo's dashboard, saving himself an unpleasant interrogation by the Japanese, both of whom spoke Italian.

George did not, but he was counting on the hope that a mere chauffeur would be almost invisible to the people at the castle. He explained to Kate along the way who he was and what was happening at the castle. She said nothing, merely acknowledged his story with a nod that he saw in the rearview mirror.

Big George was hardly invisible. The minute he stopped the limo in the castle courtyard and trotted around to let Kate out, one of the narrow-eyed guards stepped up to the pair of them, one hand on the barrel of the shotgun he wore slung over his shoulder.

He said something in Italian, his voice suspicious.

"This is my driver," Kate replied. "I brought him with me. Good thing, too. Your people never showed up at the airport."

The guard said in hesitant English, "What do you mean?"

"You Latin types don't know how to meet an airplane at the time it's specified to land, that's what I mean," Kate said. "Your people are probably still at the airport bar, ogling the waitresses."

She strode off toward Gaetano and the others clustered around him, leaving George to fend for himself.

They clearly did not trust him, but George spoke to them loudly in his worst Aussie accent, cheerfully let them search him until he thought they might be falling in love with his body, and finally was grudgingly allowed to go down to the servants' quarters. He made a strange contrast to the dour, dark, swarthy, silent maids and valets, a massive shaggy red-haired giant who talked loud and nonstop to hide his anxiety at being alone among the enemy.

The food was good, at least. Lunch was large and tasty with pasta and actual veal and plenty of strong red wine to wash it all down. George avoided the wine almost altogether. He was shown to a narrow little room with a cot in it, and gratefully took an afternoon nap. Soon after he woke up the women were setting the table again for dinner.

The meal was almost finished when the lights went out. George knew immediately that the Yamagata assault team had arrived at last. He got up from the table amid the babble of the Italians' voices, and headed through the sudden darkness toward the courtyard.

Sure enough, the sky outside was fairly filled with shimmering black parasails gliding in, bearing armored helmeted figures beneath them, each of them bristling with weapons. There was firing from the windows and the invaders fired back while still soaring earthward, knocking chips of stone from the walls and parapets.

One of the first men to land and disencumber himself from his parasail ran up to George. In his armor and helmet and night-vision goggles he looked more like a robot than a human being. A small robot, George thought. The warrior barely came up to his shoulder.

"You are George." The warrior's voice was muffled by his visored helmet.

Thankful for the bioluminescent paint that had been smeared across his forehead, George said, "That's right, mate." The paint's luminescence was too faint to see with unaided eyes; only those wearing the low-light-level goggles could see it.

"Find a safe place and stay there," said the warrior. "We will take care of the rest."

George gave him a grunt that might have sounded like assent, but he had no intention of keeping out of this fight.

Guided by wavering pencil beams of flashlights, Gaetano's guards had rushed Kate and her sister up the main staircase and past the bedrooms on that level, and up a narrow winding staircase into a bare circular room at the top of one of the castle's turrets.

"You stay in there until we tell you it's safe to come out," one of them said. He slammed the door and shot the bolt home.

Kimberly clung to her sister. "What's happening?" she asked. "What's going on?"

They heard gunfire.

"Rafe is a crook, Kim," Kate said. "He's a murderer and he's kidnapped Jane Scanwell. Dan must have set up this rescue attempt."

"Attempt? What if it doesn't work? What if they set the place on fire? We're locked in here!"

"It'll be all right, Kim," said Kate with an assuredness she did not feel. She held her sister close and kept murmuring, "It'll be all right."

Blood was running down Dan's cheek from a stone chip that had nicked him. His back tingled from other cuts. But the firing had stopped and the flashlight gone out.

Total darkness and total silence. And he was still alive.

Whispered voice from the top of the stairs. A couple of footsteps. Dan started to slither down the stairs as quietly as he could, trying to get away from the two men up above. He heard muttering and the metallic sounds of an empty magazine being replaced by a full one.

The flashlight winked on again and caught him in its feeble glow. To Dan it seemed like the brightest spotlight in the history of the world.

Pfft. A yell and the flashlight beam went awry. Another *pfft;* somebody at the top of the stairs grunted as if he'd been hit in the gut. Then Dan heard the soft thudding sounds of a body falling, tumbling down the stairs. It came rolling toward him, arms flailing lifelessly like a rag doll thrown away by a thoughtless child.

The body hit Dan's flattened form and stopped, its sightless eyes staring at him. Before Dan could yell or move or catch his breath he felt hands pulling at him, helping him to stand up.

"Mr. Randolph-san?"

"Hai!" he said gratefully. Yes. He was facing a pair of figures all in black, barely discernible in the darkness even though they were hardly six inches away.

"We have control of the lower floors," the man told him in swift Japanese, "and the courtyard and outer walls. We have not yet found Mrs. Scanwell-san."

"They took her upstairs," Dan said.

"So." The armored figure handed something to Dan. "These will allow you to see in the dark."

Dan bent down and placed both his useless pistols on a step, then took the goggles and slipped them over his head. He wormed them into place, blinking. Night did not turn into day, but the scene before him now looked as if he were watching it on a computer display screen. The two figures that had been barely discernible in the darkness now showed a clear but sickly green against a flickering gray background. He saw that they wore helmets and armor, and had assault rifles in hand. The guns were muzzled by silencers.

More robotlike figures were scurrying across the floor of the central hall to join them on the staircase. Looking up, Dan saw the slumped figure of another man, his flashlight lying beside him.

The assault team leader motioned to his men and they swarmed up the stairs in swift deadly silence. Dan started after them, but the team leader put a gauntleted hand on his shoulder.

"We will handle this," he said in Japanese. "There is no need for you to risk yourself any further."

Dan shook the man's hand off his shoulder and started up the stairs. The team leader raced up beside him.

"I'm going with you," Dan said.

"Very well then. But no heroics."

"Me?" Dan grinned. "I'm no hero."

It was eerily silent at the top of the stairs. The dead man lay beside his flashlight, its beam splashing off the far wall of the long corridor. The night-vision goggles somehow automatically compensated for the light; it was not so bright that it drowned out everything else.

Jane's up here somewhere, Dan knew. Malik's with her. And Gaetano.

The first few rooms they looked into were empty. Then they reached the end of the corridor. One of the assault team members warily pushed the door open.

It must have been the master bedroom. It was large and deep, lit by a table full of fat candles off to one side, beneath a painting of the Virgin Mary and a small kneeling bench. Standing in front of the canopied bed was Jane, with Gaetano beside and partially behind her. He had a gun to her head.

"This nonsense has gone far enough. You will all drop your weapons and allow me to leave with Mrs. Scanwell."

Dan was behind the assault team leader. He saw the tableau over the smaller man's armored shoulder. Malik was in there too, a pair of gunmen flanking him. Another couple of thugs were on the other side of the room, covering the doorway with their short-barreled shotguns.

Dan took it all in with a single glance. Then his eyes locked on Jane and Gaetano and the pistol he held to her head.

"The shooting's stopped," Kate said to her sister.

They had been locked in the tower room for what had seemed like hours. The chamber's only window was wider than those down below, and unbarred. Kate quickly saw why. In the moonless night she could make out a straight drop down the tower and castle wall to the rocks hundreds of feet below.

The room was absolutely bare, nothing but a floor of warped wooden boards and heavy timber beams half-lost in the darkness of the high pitched ceiling.

Things fluttered and squeaked up there.

"Bats," said Kimberly.

Kate shuddered but Kim seemed unafraid of them.

"Is Rafe really a murderer?" she asked.

"He's a top member of the international crime syndicate," Kate said. "He gives the orders and other people do the killing."

"That's what I thought," Kim said. She leaned against the rough stone wall and slid down to a sitting position, arms wrapped around her knees.

Kate sat down on the floor beside her. "He's been using us, both of us."

"I know," said Kim. "He likes to hurt people, make them feel bad."

"He's been using you to control me."

Kim smiled sadly in the shadows. "And I let him do it."

"When we get out of here—"

"If," Kim corrected.

"I hope he's dead before the sun comes up again."

"Maybe we'll be the dead ones."

"What was that?" Kate asked.

"What?"

"I thought I heard something."

"More shooting?"

"No . . . listen."

Kim heard a grunting, puffing noise. Something scraping, slithering, like a dead body being pulled across stone.

"What is it?" Kim asked.

"It's your fooking chauffeur," Big George answered from the window. "Give us a hand, will ya?"

The two women ran to the window where George was trying to lift himself past the sill. They grabbed at his back and shoulders while he pulled with both hands on the edges of the window and finally heaved himself up onto the stone sill.

With more huffing and tugging George squeezed himself through the window—barely—and tumbled to the floor.

"Christ! I thought I was going to have a fooking heart attack. Been on the Moon too long to go climbing like that, that's the trouble."

"You're George Ambrose, aren't you? The one Dan calls Big George?" Kate asked.

"Friend of Dan's, right. Been trying to find a way into this bloody fortress that's not filled with blokes shooting at each other. Climbed up to the parapet and then spotted this window in the tower. None of the others looked wide enough for me."

"How did you climb it?" Kimberly asked, her voice hushed with awe. "It's a straight drop!"

Still puffing, George grinned weakly. "Looks straight to you. But I've climbed tougher cliffs in my day, believe me."

"We're locked in here," Kim said.

"Yes? Well, we'll see about that."

George heaved himself to his feet and marched to the door. He leaned against it. The heavy wood groaned slightly.

"Stand back a bit."

The two women backed away. George sucked in a deep breath, then kicked mightily at the door where the bolt was, on the other side. It sounded like an ox hitting a stout fence at high speed.

"Is it . . . ?"

"Not yet."

George thundered against the door again. And again. On the fourth try the latch holding the bolt against the doorjamb finally pulled loose with a shriek of ancient nails ripping out of the wood.

The door swung open. George, panting, bowed politely to the ladies and gestured for them to leave.

"Christ on a skateboard," he said as they started down the narrow winding stairway. "It's blacker than hell in here."

"Be careful," Kate said, "the steps are uneven."

They were almost at the bottom when they heard excited voices and hurried footsteps coming up toward them. They were speaking in Italian. Then George heard another sound: guns being reloaded and cocked.

FORTY-THREE

Go on ahead," George whispered to the two women.

"Don't leave us," Kimberly pleaded.

"I won't. You just go ahead a few steps."

"Please!"

"You can trust me."

Kate took her sister's hand. "Come on, Kim."

They started down the narrow spiral stairs again, just as hurried footsteps told them that the men they heard were coming up toward them. George saw the glow of a flashlight bouncing off the curving walls. He shrank back up the stairs until the two women were out of his sight.

"Hey!" a man's shouted. "How did you get out?"

"We tried the door and it opened," Kate answered.

"I bolted that door. It was locked."

"It opened when we tried it."

Kimberly said shakily, "We were afraid, all alone up there with all the shooting."

"I locked that door!"

"Never mind," came the other man's voice. "It doesn't matter."

"You saying I forgot to lock it?"

"It doesn't matter. You two get in front of us. You're gonna be our shields until we get out of here."

The other man chuckled. "Not bad-looking shields, eh?"

George saw the flashlight glow dwindle down the stairs and heard their footsteps going away from him. As silently as he could he tiptoed down after them, always staying around the curve of the wall so that they could not see him.

The women and the two gunmen reached the stone landing at the bottom of the spiral staircase.

"What do we do now? Those commandos are gonna be comin' up here any minute."

"Let 'em come. We got these two redheads to protect us. We go down to the courtyard, get in a car, and get the hell outta here."

George saw them standing there, one with the flashlight, the other with a shotgun in his hands. He was about a dozen steps above them, hidden in shadow.

"Come on," said the one with the flashlight. "We're not waitin' for those soldiers to find us."

No time left. George roared out a bellow that would freeze a buffalo herd and leaped at the guy with the shotgun. He hit him like a mammoth lineman blindsiding a quarterback. The man went down, the shotgun skittering across the stone floor. The one with the flashlight threw it at George and reached for the pistol in his shoulder holster as the two women clutched at each other and edged back toward the wall.

George rolled to his feet as the other man yanked the automatic out of its holster. With a single big ham-sized paw George grabbed the gunman's extended hand and squeezed. Hard. The man screeched with pain. George bent his arm back and he sank to his knees. With his other fist George smashed him in the jaw as hard as his massive weight allowed. The man's head spun almost completely around and he went limp in George's steel grip.

George spun to look down at the other one. He was sprawled on the stone floor, out cold or dead, it did not matter to him which.

"You didn't leave us," Kimberly said, almost breathless.

"Told you you could trust me," said George as he bent down to pick up the shotgun.

"You didn't leave us," Kim repeated, her eyes riveted on the big Australian.

Holding the shotgun in one huge hand, the pistol tucked into his waistband, George made another little bow to them.

"This way, ladies," he said.

"Thanks," said Kate.

Kimberly said nothing, but her eyes were sparkling.

"I mean it," Gaetano said. "Drop your weapons, all of you, or I'll kill her."

Dan knew that Gaetano and his thugs would shoot the assault team as soon as they had put their weapons down, the same way they had when they had abducted Jane in the first place. These guys are wearing body armor and helmets, he thought swiftly. But even if they don't get killed, that bastard will still be walking away with Jane.

Before anyone could reply to Gaetano's ultimatum, Dan yanked off his goggles and stepped out of the shadows of the corridor to the doorway, where Gaetano could see him clearly.

"Before you shoot her, you're going to have to shoot me, you sonofabitch."

"Dan, no!" Jane said.

But Dan walked slowly into the room, straight toward her. Gaetano's eyes were filled with fear, but his lips twisted into a nasty little smile.

"If you want to be shot I will be happy to accommo-
date you," he said.

Dan said nothing, just kept pacing into the big room,
closing the distance between himself and Jane. His weariness was gone. His legs felt strong and sure. He noticed every detail of the candlelit scene. Malik staring at
him with round eyes. The other gunmen shifting uneasily, knowing that if a firefight started they would be
quickly killed. Gaetano still smiling, moving his pistol
from Jane's head to point squarely at Dan's own chest.

Ten paces separated them. Nine. Eight.

Jane grabbed at Gaetano's crotch and squeezed. He
shrieked and doubled over. Dan dove into the two of
them, knocking them onto the bed and then over its
side to the floor as the room erupted in gunfire. Dan
grabbed Gaetano by the hair and pounded his head
against the stone floor. Again. Again. He bashed Gaetano's bloody head against the stone until someone
pried him off.

Jane was sitting on the floor beside Gaetano's inert
form, his pistol in her hand. The room was blazing with
light. Gaetano's dead face looked surprised, the back of
his head oozing a pool of blood.

"Are you all right?" Dan and Jane asked simultaneously. Then they burst into exhausted, relieved, almost hysterical laughter and fell into each other's arms.

Gentle hands pulled them apart and helped them to
their feet.

"That was a very brave thing you did," said the assault
team leader. "But very foolish." She had removed her
helmet, as had all the other Yamagata commandos. Dan
was surprised to see that she was a woman.

"You mean I'm a hero, after all?" he said, grinning
crookedly.

Then he saw that Malik was on a stretcher, his legs
soaked with blood, a plasma IV already inserted into his

forearm. All the gunmen were on the floor, dead.

"It's finished," Malik muttered as Dan went over to him. "It's all over."

Dan shook his head. "Nope. It's just beginning."

FORTY-FOUR

The room looked more like a conference center than a hospital suite. Malik had cranked his bed up to a half-sitting position, the best he could do while his legs were still in their casts. Jane and Kate Williams sat on comfortable leather chairs beside his bed; Dan, in white hospital pajamas, in a wheelchair between them. Nobuhiko's lean intense face filled the phone screen set at the foot of the bed.

The big TV screen on the far wall was still showing the devastation of New Orleans. Malik had muted the sound but none of them could take their eyes from the scenes of the flooding, the wreckage, the rescue workers searching in boats for survivors—and bodies.

"They're blaming us for the disaster," Jane said. "The public is confusing this tidal wave with the greenhouse effect."

"We can thank your pirate television broadcasts for that," Malik said to Dan.

Dan gave him a sardonic grin. "I guess you'll have to

explain the difference—and admit the truth of what I've been saying."

"All those people killed." Kate's voice sounded hollow, far away.

"Multiply it by a million," said Dan, his grin evaporating. "All the coastal areas on Earth will look like that if we let the greenhouse cliff happen."

"How can we stop it?" Malik asked. "We tried and look where it's brought us. We were merely arranging the world for the crooks to take it over."

Dan gave him an exaggerated frown. "Vasily, much as I hate to admit it, you had the right idea. Wrong implementation, but basically the right idea."

"What do you mean?" asked Jane.

"We've got to work together, the whole world has to work together, all of us, government, industry, the corporations, the GEC, everybody on Earth. The greenhouse cliff is a global problem and it can only be beaten by an all-out global effort."

"That's what I tried to do," said Malik.

"Not quite," Dan said. "You tried the old collectivist approach: take control of everything and make all decisions at the top. It didn't work in the old Soviet Union and it won't work now. It never works!"

"That's not entirely true," Jane said.

"And rain makes applesauce. Look, all of you, we need to have all the corporations work together with the GEC and all the individual national governments—but not all locked into some grand master plan that doesn't allow deviations or creativity or individual initiative. Free men and women can beat the greenhouse—and keep people like Gaetano from sinking their claws into everything."

"You believe so?" Malik asked.

"I know it," replied Dan fervently.

"Then what are you suggesting?" asked Jane.

"Run this battle against the greenhouse cliff the way a good general runs a campaign. Set out the goals that must be reached—reduce fossil fuel burning by so much each year, replace fossil-fueled electrical plants with fusion, build solar power satellites, make solar cells cheap enough so private homeowners can afford to cover the roofs with them, replace fossil-fueled cars with electric or hydrogen fuels . . ." He paused to take a breath.

Malik mused, "Greenwell of Detroit wants to produce hydrogen cars."

"Let him! Let a thousand flowers blossom, as an old Communist once said. As long as they're cutting down on fossil-fuel burning, let them work out the problem in their own way."

"It would be chaos," Malik said.

Dan shook his head. "It'll take a helluva lot of coordination from the GEC. Coordination, not control. But it can be done."

"Do you think so?" Jane asked.

"Yes."

"In ten years?" asked Kate.

"What choice do we have?" Dan countered. "If we do nothing half the world will look like New Orleans. If we try to *force* everybody into some master plan imposed by the GEC, it won't work—and bastards like Gaetano will be just itching to take it over for themselves. Let the people work out their own solutions, coordinated by the GEC. That's the way to win the battle."

Malik remembered something. "That old man that Gaetano took us to see, he's still there, you know. Neither Interpol nor the Italian authorities have any evidence that he's ever been involved in any crime."

"The rats are always hiding behind the walls, Vasily. That's part of human nature. You've always got to be on the lookout for them. But the more you centralize control the easier you make it for them to bend everything to their own uses."

"Yes," Malik admitted, "you're right. You've been right all along, I suppose."

"Then we can return Astro to Dan," said Jane.

Malik nodded.

"You've all forgotten one thing," Kate said. When they turned to her she went on, "You might be able to change over all the world's electrical power generation to solar and nuclear. You might even be able to replace all the transportation vehicles on Earth with ones that use electrical or hydrogen fuels. But what about the factories? What about manufacturing and metal smelting and all the heavy industries? They burn coal and oil and natural gas. How can you convert them to nuclear electricity?"

The others looked at each other. Then they all saw that Dan was grinning like a schoolkid who knew the answer.

"Well?" said Jane.

"You remember that asteroid we corralled ten years ago? We never even started to use its mineral resources, but it's still up there in a high Earth orbit."

"So?"

"We estimated it contained roughly four million tons of high-grade iron ore. Plus a few thousand tons of impurities like platinum and gold. And that was just a teeny asteroid, hardly bigger than a football field."

Malik groaned. "What you would do to the world market for precious metals by dumping a few thousand tons of gold."

"Screw the precious metals," Dan snapped. "There are thousands of asteroids out there. Millions of 'em! Some of them are miles wide! Enough metals and minerals to supply the whole world for a billion years. And we can smelt them in space, as well. Use sunlight for energy, focused sunlight for heat—"

"The capital costs would be tremendous," Malik pointed out.

Dan grinned again. "Well, if I can have Astro back in my hands again, I'll raise the capital. Don't worry about that."

Kate said, "I don't see how you or anybody else could replace the world's metals industry in ten years."

"We can't, Scarlett. But we can get started. We can go as hard and as fast as we possibly can. We'll have to get the leaders in the industry to go into this with us; we want cooperation, not competition. You'll have to sweet-talk a lot of those old farts on their boards of directors."

"Me?" Kate asked.

"Sure, you. Who else? I'm going to be too busy with the asteroid project to hold hands back here on Earth. You're going to be Astro's CEO."

She gasped. "You—you'd trust me?"

Dan laughed. "Your sister's fallen in love with Big George, hasn't she? That makes you practically a member of the family."

"You'd trust me," Kate said again, in a whisper.

Dan turned his wheelchair to face Jane. "And what about you, lady? Are you ready to step down from your lofty position in the GEC and marry a guy who's going to be spending most of his time in space?"

Jane raised a brow. "Such a romantic proposal, Dan. I'm swept off my feet."

"Good. Then that's settled."

"Now wait a minute—"

But he had already swung back toward Malik's bed. "Vasily, get well quickly. We're going to need you at the head of the GEC. And we'll do everything we can to support you."

"I never thought I'd hear such words from you, Mr. Capitalist."

"Strange times make strange alliances," said Dan. "We've got ten years to save the world."

"Do you think we can?"

Dan shrugged. "We'd better. If we can't, then who the hell can?"

That evening Dan and Jane had dinner together on the terrace outside his hospital room. The moon smiled lopsidedly down at them. The Mediterranean glittered in its silver radiance.

Dan was still in his hospital whites. Jane had changed to a peach-toned knit dress with a scalloped neckline.

"I'm serious," Dan said as he poured the wine. "I love you, Jane. I want to marry you."

"But you're going to be dashing off to the Moon again," she said.

"A lot farther than that, dear. The main asteroid belt is out beyond the orbit of Mars."

"You'll be gone for years at a time."

"I'd like you to come with me. The accommodations won't be plush, but we'll be together. Make a terrific honeymoon."

"And what will I do out there?" she asked, her voice low, trembling. "I'm not an engineer or an astronaut."

"You—well, you could be with me," Dan replied uneasily. "You could learn to help. You could start a new life."

She leaned across the little table and put her hand atop his. "Dan, I'm a politician. I'm very good at it. I can get people to work together. I've even gotten you and Vasily to work together, haven't I?"

"You . . . ?"

She smiled. "I'll take the credit for it. That's what politicians do."

"Okay by me," he said.

Her smile turned sad. "There won't be anything for me to do on your wonderful space missions, Dan. But there's an awful lot I can accomplish here."

"I don't want to be apart from you ever again."

"Me neither. But I'm *needed* here, Dan. Don't you see that? I can help! I can keep Vasily on track and help to keep things running smoothly here."

"But I want you!"

"Would you give up your asteroid project to be with me? Would you turn away from what you do best, for my sake?"

Dan looked away from her, out to the gleaming sea and up at the moon. It seemed to be laughing at him now.

"You won't marry me?" he said at last.

"I won't go out on your space mission, where I'll only be in the way," Jane said. "And you won't stay here on Earth when you've got so much to accomplish out there, will you?"

He saw that there were tears in her eyes. And he realized that his own eyes were misting over.

"You mean it'll never work out for us," he said, the words almost choking in his throat.

"You described it best when you said that what we're facing is a war. We *are* at war, against an impending disaster. You make sacrifices when you're fighting a war."

A million thoughts ran through Dan's mind but he could not find a single word to say.

"Dan . . . I'm sorry."

"Me too."

"Maybe when all this is over. Maybe then."

He looked into her eyes and saw his own pain mirrored. "Maybe then," he whispered.

Jane pulled her hand away and straightened up in her chair. Trying to sound more cheerful, she asked, "Do you think we'll really beat this greenhouse cliff?"

He shrugged.

"In just ten years?"

Dan pushed away from the table and got to his feet. "I don't know. Nobody knows. All we can do is try."

And he walked into his hospital room, went to the closet and began to pull out his working clothes.

TOR
BOOKS The Best in Science Fiction

LIEGE-KILLER • Christopher Hinz

"*Liege-Killer* is a genuine page-turner, beautifully written and exciting from start to finish....Don't miss it."—*Locus*

HARVEST OF STARS • Poul Anderson

"A true masterpiece. An important work—not just of science fiction but of contemporary literature. Visionary and beautifully written, elegaic and transcendent, *Harvest of Stars* is the brightest star in Poul Anderson's constellation."
—Keith Ferrell, editor, *Omni*

FIREDANCE • Steven Barnes

SF adventure in 21st century California—by the co-author of *Beowulf's Children*.

ASH OCK • Christopher Hinz

"A well-handled science fiction thriller."—*Kirkus Reviews*

CALDÉ OF THE LONG SUN • Gene Wolfe

The third volume in the critically-acclaimed Book of the Long Sun. "Dazzling."—*The New York Times*

OF TANGIBLE GHOSTS • L.E. Modesitt, Jr.

Ingenious alternate universe SF from the author of the *Recluce* fantasy series.

THE SHATTERED SPHERE • Roger MacBride Allen

The second book of the Hunted Earth continues the thrilling story that began in *The Ring of Charon*, a daringly original hard science fiction novel.

THE PRICE OF THE STARS • Debra Doyle and James D. Macdonald

Book One of the Mageworlds—the breakneck SF epic of the most brawling family in the human galaxy!